# THE FAMOUX

# THE
# FAMOUX

## KASSANDRA TATE

wattpad books **W**

**wattpad** books **W**

Content Warning: bullying, stalking, brief mention
of violence, brief mention of alcohol

*www.wattpad.com*

First Wattpad Books edition: January 2021

ISBN 978-1-98936-553-3 (Trade Paper original)
ISBN 978-1-98936-554-0 (eBook edition)

Library and Archives Canada Cataloguing in Publication
information is available upon request.

Printed and bound in Canada
1 3 5 7 9 10 8 6 4 2

Cover design by Ysabel Enverga
Images © Branko Starcevic via Stocksy, Hayden Williams via Stocksy,
Valerie Elash via Unsplash
Typesetting by Sarah Salomon

For Kalina, my best friend in every world,
even dystopian ones

# PART ONE

# FISSAREX

# PROLOGUE

When I was younger and more susceptible to liars, my mother let me in on a little secret that took me years to outgrow. If I really wanted something, she told me, all I had to do was think about it, and hope for it, and my requests would always be heard.

"Thoughts are powerful," she said. "Good or bad, they have their way of coming true."

Poor advice to give to a child, much less one as vulnerable as I was. I took her wisdom as fact and accepted no other opinions. As children do, I thought only of ways to make my singular life easier. I thought about acing my tests instead of studying for them. I thought about making good and lasting friends instead of being one in kind. I thought about standing up to Westin van Horne one day instead of ever becoming brave enough to actually do it.

But thoughts without action, as I'd later learn, are meaningless. My grades, my loneliness, and my torment persisted, because I didn't do a thing to change them. Yet, as I walked home, I kept my mother's promise in mind. I thought new thoughts of a better life, sure that these would be the ones to come true. And when I came home crying, she was there to wipe the tears from my eyes and feed me more honey-tasting lies. She'd tell me how my differences weren't flaws, and that I wasn't worth anything less than Westin or the other kids. She'd tell me I was beautiful, that unique was good, and a whole menagerie of other little myths long since proven untrue. I'm sure even then I knew they were lies, but oh, were they wonderful lies to live. I grew to depend on them—on knowing that no matter how bad the day was, my mother would always be there to comfort me with tall tales of a better future.

Which turned out to be yet another lie.

The morning in question wasn't inherently different than any before it. She insisted I wear her jacket to school, a blue corduroy thing lined with fleece, since mine was getting small in the arms. She told me as always to think positive thoughts that day while she fastened the buttons. I was fourteen at the time, so the sentiment was met with rolling eyes, a swat at her hands, and an assertion I could fasten a coat just fine on my own, thank you. At school, Westin and his group gave me their worst, and I fought tears the whole way home. It was the usual routine. It was expected. So when I creaked open the door and sulked inside with my usual, miserable flair, the last thing I expected was to find the house empty.

Sure, the furniture was still in place. The cabinets in the kitchen were still stocked. But the smell of peonies in her perfume was faint, as if she'd been out of the house all day. I didn't think much of it until I went to her closet to return the jacket and discovered her things were gone.

A thought tried to enter my head at that moment, but I

wouldn't let it. Thoughts had power, after all, and this was one I couldn't bear to let come true. But as I checked her empty drawers and noted the missing duffle bags in the hall closet, I realized it already had.

My mother was gone. She had run away.

I was the only one in the house for a long time that day. I tried calling all three of my other family members, but none answered. Too busy with their own things. My older brother was probably out stirring up trouble with his friends. My sister, the eldest of us three, was likely in the library, studying relentlessly in the hope of getting a good job after graduation—one over the ocean in Betnedoor, where things ran smoother and better than here in Eldae. My father was still at work, in that desk with the spinning chair I'd loved so much that day I got to visit. He'd been working overtime lately anticipating a promotion, so I knew he wouldn't be home until much later. None of them would.

But this was expected. My mother and I often had the afternoons to ourselves, and we'd spend them either talking on the patio or exploring the old-world ruins around the city. Eldae never cleaned up the rubble from the End, instead building cheap structures around it, which meant the neighborhood next to ours was full of ancient, decrepit houses that had somehow survived the bombs. Her favorite was this old yellow one with no roof, which I found to be quite frightening, but she loved it. I thought about checking it, to see if maybe she'd run there, but I knew there was no use. That house wasn't livable, and if she'd wanted to take her things and run, she wouldn't have moved practically next door. I stood by the phone, frozen, for hours and hours until the door clicking open prompted me to move.

It was Dalton. He wouldn't let me finish my sentence before he trailed off to his room, claiming I was being dramatic—that she was out running errands. Brandyce followed in a similar fashion, but I showed her the drawers and the missing duffle bags, and her denial grew louder and louder until she finally fell to her knees and shrieked. By the time our father came home, I was petrified to tell him.

But it turns out, he would do nothing. My father is a talkative man, the life of most dinner parties, but he had nothing to say as Brandyce and I presented the evidence. A blank stare deepened in the creases of his face, and slowly, he shrank at least three inches into himself, losing strength right before my eyes.

My parents once had a strong relationship, but years of bickering had frayed most of the cords that held them together. They tried not to argue when we were around, but thanks to my classmates who never included me, I knew well how to eavesdrop. I could hear their hushed voices down in the living room after we'd gone up to bed. They argued about me. Their most troublesome child, always coming home from school in tears. My father thought they should send me away to a school in Notness, where my differences wouldn't matter as much, and I'd have a fresh start. My mother found this insulting.

"You push things away when they get difficult," she told him. "You'd just love it if all of us left, wouldn't you?"

These arguments had to have been on his mind as he drove us to the local police station. Streaked with regret, my father told the authorities that his wife must've been kidnapped, because there was no way she'd leave us willingly. He insisted they file a missing person's report and send the search parties at once. But all they could do was apologize, because this didn't look like a kidnapping. Her belongings were gone, and it was well within her own free will to go if she pleased. Even if we knew where she was, we couldn't force her to come back.

On our way out of the station, one of the officers patted my father's shoulder and told him that the best thing we could do was think positively. Keep her in our thoughts. Maybe she'd turn up. It reminded me of what my mother used to tell me about thoughts having power. It felt like a sign. And so, for the whole first year of her disappearance, her return was all I thought about. It was a constant daydream in class, an ever-present prayer before bed. I thought about her so much, I barely slept a wink.

It was a long time before I realized my mother was lying about a thought holding weight in the world. After all, she had also once told me that no matter what, she'd be there for me, and I knew now just how untrue that was. Perhaps lying was well within her wheelhouse, more than I'd ever known.

It's been two years since then, and yet, things have barely changed. The scabs haven't healed yet; we have let them become scars. We keep picking at our wounds, willing them to bleed again and become scabs once more. It's never-ending.

We have vanished quite swiftly into a new routine. Our father, once a colossus we both feared and admired, lost his job at the civil service in the weeks following the disappearance after he'd had a breakdown in the office. The guilt became too much for him to properly function. He spends most of his days in his bedroom, staring at the ceiling and calling out for the wife that left him, as if she'll pick up the phone and answer. Without an income to support us and a will to pick up the pieces, it was Brandyce who was forced to forgo all her exceptional offers abroad and take care of Dalton and me, since we are still too young in Eldae's standards to fend for ourselves. Now, it's too late for her. Opportunities to leave Eldae for Betnedoor are few and far between, and if you don't seize one when it first arrives, another is seldom on the way. Brandyce resents us for this. Me, especially, as the youngest. She now works several simple jobs in town to make ends meet, and I do my best to stay out of her way.

Dalton is currently in his final year of schooling, and he will no doubt abandon us for better places the second he gets the chance. We don't blame him. When I'm out of school, Brandyce will do the same, finally free of the burden of taking care of me. She won't be able to go to Betnedoor like Dalton might, but she'll move far away to the other side of Eldae and never come back. And I will be left to take care of our father, the man who once thought of shipping me off and forgetting me. I'll do whatever small jobs downtown will take me, keep the house tidy, then lie on my bed just as he does, seeking the smell of her peony perfume and always coming up short.

We will dissolve this way. And since I know now that thinking won't change a thing, it is better not to think anything of it.

# CHAPTER ONE

My mother's favorite old-world house is haunted, I'm sure of it. When the sun hits it just right, the shadows of the ornate wooden banister look like a person reaching out for something, and the creak in the front door is like a voice, whispering a language at me that I can't understand. I've theorized ghosts before in the past, but on my daily visits to watch the sunrise, I have never actually seen one. But I've never felt quite alone either. I've felt comfort—the kind my mother used to give me. The kind I don't feel too often anymore except here.

There's no relief from the cold beneath the caved-in roof. I shiver as I navigate through the entryway, stepping over stray shingles. I'm nowhere near dressed for the weather, wearing only flannel pajamas and my mother's corduroy jacket. Tomorrow, I'll bring a blanket, although I know at some point soon, when the winter comes, I'll have to stop coming, at least until the temperatures rise again. It won't be this week, however. I'll muster through as long as I can. Watching the sunrise from my own bedroom window just isn't the same.

Once I get to the center of the room, I stop and lie down on my back, looking up and out at the sky. It's a perfect view. I never paid much attention to sunrises growing up. If I'm honest, I always missed them. Like most, I slept in, awakening to a sky already gray and a morning well under way. But after my mother left, a newfound restlessness took her place. Now, whether I like it or not, I watch dawn break every morning.

It's nothing sensational. A mixture of pale orange and lavender that appears brownish the poorer the air quality. I hear it's always this way in Notness, where they've stripped most of their land clean to build manufacturing plants. At least we in Eldae get the essence of colors, faint as they may be. Today's is the usual muted tangerine, getting more and more beige by the second. So pollution is bad today, I register. Good to know.

Few works of literature from the old world survived the End, but in one of them—a small poem found tucked within a cookbook with its byline ripped off—the sunrise is described to be vibrant. Vivid. With pinks and reds and indigo, streaked across the sky like a painting. Some mornings I look up through the roof at the brown and recite some lines of the poem in my head, and it baffles me how at one point, hundreds of years ago, the sunrise actually looked that way. But the world was different back then. We call it the *old* one for a reason.

We're taught the lesson of the End every year in school, to make sure we never forget. It began with a string of natural disasters—fires, earthquakes, and mass floods that rose high enough to engulf full countries. Quarrels as to who was to blame broke out between the remaining nations, which escalated into a full-scale nuclear war. Nearly everything and everyone was decimated.

But it was not a full apocalypse. Those who survived crawled out from the rubble, picked themselves up, and resolved to make good use of the last livable pieces of land left. They sought to create a new world—one more peaceful than that before it. Instead of breaking apart into separate nations like before, they formed a single country which they named Delicatum—a reminder of the delicate balance between us and this land. Delicatum has a single sovereign leader, to be elected every half decade as per the people's choice. This was all very important to our founders: the single country, the single leader, the unity in it. For if history has taught us anything, it is that the more countries and leaders and general separation, the more potential for conflict.

Delicatum is comprised of three united states, each serving its own purpose for the country. The largest state is Notness, which takes up most of what used to be the middle and western parts of North America. They specialize in manufacturing all of our commodities, with thousands of factories spanning the spacious land. And while many sovereigns have certainly attempted to push for more environmentally friendly means of production, the whole country lives under a near-constant shroud of smog.

My state, Eldae, is to the east of Notness, filling up the rest of what's left of America. Our southernmost region has enough fertile land to make us Delicatum's source for agriculture, but the northern region, where I live, is practically useless. With such close proximity to Notness, too, our skies are always gray. It's every kid's dream to one day get the chance to move away to someplace better—to Betnedoor.

Across the ocean in a small pocket of what used to be southern

Europe, Betnedoor is the most prosperous state in Delicatum. Their purpose is to produce new technologies, although not many of their advancements make it over to Eldae and Notness. Air travel is rare and expensive, reserved only for the wealthier elite, so it's a pipe dream to even consider visiting. Though we have plenty photos of it to prove otherwise, there is always a rumor amongst kids here that the streets in Betnedoor are paved with shiny gold.

We can try all we want to not make the same mistakes the old world did, but we can't control how their actions have affected us. The atomic bombs they dropped left chemicals that have conjured countless aftershocks, especially where the weather is concerned. Sometimes we have no rain for months. Our winters can be brutal.

And then there is the phenomenon we call Darkenings, where, every thirty days, with the moon cycle, thick chemical particles bunch into the air and cover up the sun. We live in complete darkness for two whole days.

In some areas, the effects of these particle buildups are so bad that the land is barely livable. Citizens of each state, regardless of radiation levels, get a mandatory immunity booster every year just to avoid any hugely adverse effects to exposure, like skin burns and diseases. That said, we've found ways to adapt the best we can, but sometimes it's distressing to think of the way the old world left us. Even now, as I look around the skeleton of this house, one of thousands like this one lying around Eldae, I am reminded that we live in the wake of something much, much bigger than us.

A hazy shade of gray settles over the sky, signaling daytime and my cue to come home. I cut through the front yard, stepping through weeds covered in frost. With a turn around the corner, the world changes from old to new. My home is a squat, concrete thing, the same as all the others down the street. These were quick and cheap to make in the beginning, much less expensive than trying to refurbish old houses. They might be terribly ugly, but they're some of the better living options in Eldae. In more crowded cities, like Colburn, these structures are stacked into big, grotesque apartment buildings. At least we have our own space, separate from our neighbors. And we're so close to the ruins, too, which is a plus. It isn't lovely, but we could do worse.

No one is awake yet when I creep in through the door. They never are. Father stays in his room all day anyway, and Brandyce and Dalton's alarms won't go off for another half hour. Mornings are always my time to breathe; the calm before the daily storms of judgment. In my room, I change into my school uniform: brown slacks, a button-down shirt, and a forest green sweater vest. The color varies based on which grade you're in, although most kids believe it's hardly necessary anymore. There are other ways to identify which class a student is in that you can't take on and off like a vest. Still, it's tradition. I tuck the wool into my trousers, then fasten it with a belt.

As I make breakfast I click on the television. My siblings hate it when I watch the news too early and wake them, so I keep the volume low. Normally I'd mute it and just piece the stories together based on headlines, but the red borders around footage of a podium bear the caption *Geddes to Make Statement on Upcoming Darkening* and I know I have to watch. This is important news. This is news about the Famoux.

There are plenty of celebrities in Delicatum, sure, and they do pretty well. But none quite hold a candle to the Famoux. They are an absolute force—the most beloved, most glamorous, and most entertaining clique in our world. Each member is gorgeous, the paragon of perfection in their own unique way. They're at the top of their fields, too, be it music, or acting, or sports, and so on. They rule over everything.

And then there are their broadcasts. The way their every step is documented and plastered on magazine covers, it's safe to say that the Famoux members already live their lives in constant spotlight. But their Darkening broadcast, called *The Fishbowl*, take this to its extreme. It airs for the entire two days of the blackout without stopping, giving viewers an uninterrupted glimpse into the way they live. It's watched by almost everyone. Even my family tunes in, though Brandyce thinks they're overrated.

As I settle onto the couch, the television screen dissolves into the view of a podium. There's no caption to specify where this footage is coming from, but I know from the sky that it's Waltmar, Betnedoor's capital city. All the way across the ocean from Notness's emissions, they are the least affected by smog, which means their sky is actually blue. Their sunrises have more color too. Not quite the vivid pinks from the old-world poem, but the photos I've seen show brighter oranges and bolder purples. It would be breathtaking to see a sunrise like that in person. Makes me wonder how many people over there sleep right through it, unaware of what they're missing.

Just beyond the podium, crowds of reporters and paparazzi stretch farther than the cameras can even catch, eager to hear the news. This is our second press conference this month from the Famoux's trusted manager, Norax Geddes, but they're usually a very rare occurrence. She only ever steps out to address scandals, debunk unavoidable rumors, or make big, status quo–changing announcements.

The statement earlier this month was one of the latter. The Famoux's status quo had certainly changed for the worse: one of their members had died.

We're lucky the cameras weren't on Bree Arch when it happened. Just before the accident we had been watching an argument between the others at dinner on the second night—some half-baked betrayal over Kaytee McKarrington's latest single. Bree had excused herself to go to the bathroom, uninterested in the drama, when the lights cut out. It wasn't until a backup generator restored the power that Kaytee found Bree lying by the foot of the crystalline stairs and screamed. One of Bree's limbs was twisted, a small pool of blood forming by her head. She'd tripped and fallen. She was dead.

Days after, I recall the blue Betnedoor sky feeling entirely too cheery during Norax's statement—insulting, even, given the way the Famoux was huddled together, crying by the podium. Norax tried her best to keep a brave face as she spoke, but even she faltered. She used that statement to assure the world that they would be taking the thirty days before the next Darkening to honor Bree with a memorial, make sense of what happened, and decide whether or not they'll be ready to broadcast *The Fishbowl* again with the next blackout. With the Darkening happening next week, the anticipation for this next statement has been high. Will *The Fishbowl* air, after what happened last time? Or will we have to sit through the darkness for the first time without them? The world has been speculating.

Today, Norax walks into view with her head held high. The five remaining Famoux members trail behind her, their eyes dry. They're doing better today, although they're all still wearing black, as I've seen in every paparazzi shot of them for weeks. As the cameras do a close-up on each of their faces, my breath catches in slight. They are impossibly beautiful, as always. Then the camera settles onto the other end of the podium, where an older man in a suit stands. Lennix Geddes, Norax's father. The founder and creator of the Famoux.

Lennix formed the idea over thirty years ago. He had a background in managing acts for the popular music label Buchan, and while there he saw the value in bands over solo artists. More members meant a greater audience reach. The first iteration of the Famoux had been a curation of the most popular celebrities in every industry. They became a team, supporting each other's work and creating great art together during the Darkening broadcasts. Ten years passed, and the members entered their later twenties, and the audience's interest dwindled. Lennix retired the group, picking out new stars he saw were gaining traction for the second iteration. He did this for a third time before declaring that, with the fourth iteration, two years ago, he would be passing over the reins to his daughter Norax.

The world had already been placing their bets as to which lucky celebrities would be asked to join next, but much to everyone's surprise, Norax decided to shake things up. After a long audition process, screening countless options, she plucked six new members we knew nothing about, and encouraged us to get to know them and their talents as they unfolded before us. It was a total success. The kids at school have loved spending the last two years figuring them out.

Since retiring, Lennix is rarely pictured at Famoux events. Having amassed quite some riches from the Famoux, he's been known for investing in tech advancements all over Betnedoor, becoming quite the influential figure. There are rumors that next year, when it comes time to vote in Delicatum's next sovereign, he'll run. If true, I am sure he would win. He has a level of maturity to him that our current sovereign, a forgettable man named James Atlas, so blatantly lacks. And I could only imagine how much Delicatum would change for the better if he ran it like he ran the Famoux.

He meets his daughter's gaze soberly and nods, perhaps permitting her to begin. She turns to the cameras and clears her throat.

Her voice is strong and clear. A true leader's voice like her father's. Perhaps she should run for sovereign some day too.

"We first thank you for granting us the time to collect ourselves before making a follow-up statement," Norax begins. She closes her eyes. For a moment I'm afraid she might break down like last time, but then she takes a breath, and her stoicism returns. "We know this has been a hard few weeks for our fans as well as our organization. Our Darkening show has always striven to be a source of entertainment and comfort for its viewers—a light to get them through the two days of darkness. But I am afraid that in our last broadcast, *The Fishbowl* was anything but a light. The horror we all had to witness, broadcasted across Delicatum, is something that I know will live with us for a long time. Nevertheless, I am so grateful for how we have all pulled through together in the last few weeks. We—"

"This is *pathetic!*"

I glance away from the television toward Brandyce, who's chuckling from behind the couch. Dalton stands beside her eating a bowl of cereal, a stain of milk visible on his navy blue uniform vest. I didn't hear them come in, and I'm surprised they haven't walked out yet. If we're not in the midst of the month-end

Darkening, with few options for entertainment other than *The Fishbowl,* usually the topic of Delicatum's favorite celebrity clique sends my siblings running in the other direction.

Not this morning. Brandyce snorts, joining in on the fun. "You can tell she's so done with having to talk about this. Look at her. No emotion."

On-screen, Norax's expression is stern, but there's a vulnerability to it. I admire her, but I wouldn't say that out loud; it'd be a step short of murder in this house to defend the Famoux. Dalton has friends who are fans, so his dislike plays mostly for jokes, but Brandyce really despises them. For years she's been rattling off how only mindless drones buy into their gimmicks. "It's the people too stupid to live their own lives," she'd say, "who want to sit and watch the Famoux live their lives the grandest."

A part of me wonders if maybe it's just an excuse for how little is going on for her nowadays. After all, it was only after Mom left that Brandyce started hating them with such fervor.

She isn't really wrong, though. For Eldae and Notness, where conditions are a far cry from grand, the Famoux is like a portal to another world. Beauty, riches, and opulence beyond belief. Their show might air only during Darkenings, but every day the magazines have new photos of them wearing the best clothes, eating at the best places, partying at the best clubs in Betnedoor. Even just the paparazzi pictures or grainy fan-filmed videos are thrilling to watch. There is a constant bustle with them—a sense of never-ending excitement for what'll come next. For most, following their lives is the only way to get that feeling. I know that's the case for me.

Dalton points at the screen, engrossed but hiding it. "And look at *them!*" he agrees. "They really don't care about someone who actually *died*, huh? It's so fake."

KASSANDRA TATE

As if on cue, the camera shifts, zooming in on the members. Specifically, Till Amaris, who appears to be having the hardest time staying dry-eyed today. I try to remember if Till was especially close with the girl who died, but it's hard to say. Their show churns out a new feud between the members each month, so it's not easy to tell who's on good terms. As we watch them, Norax's speech continues.

"The death of our beloved member, Bree Arch, was a tragic accident, and it is our job to make sure nothing like this happens again. Since my last statement, I have learned that the cause of this accident was a statewide power outage in Notness caused by the accidental activation of an abandoned manufacturing plant. For our next broadcast, at the week's end, which *will* be happening"—murmurs of excitement fill the crowd here—"we assure our viewers that new safety measures have been implemented and adequate backup power facilities are already in place."

"*New safety measures?* What are they going to do?" Dalton asks. "Childproof the place?"

"Well, the Famoux *are* children," says Brandyce. "At least, they sure act like it."

I can't help but notice how my sister pronounces *Famoux* so harshly. *Fame-ox.* Some of the aristocratic kind say *fame-oh* or *fame-ooh*, as if the *X* is silent. But when Norax Geddes says the name, the *X* is always included. She says it so smoothly: *fame-ecks.* Because sharing the word *famous* with every other notable person isn't enough, no; this group deserves a whole other adjective to describe their grandeur.

"With a special tribute gala to come soon," Norax continues, "we hope to properly honor Bree Arch's life and celebrate the good she did for Delicatum. We hope that you, the fans, stay with us as we navigate this unprecedented time, and much later, embark on the search for a suitable new member. Thank you."

With that, her speech is concluded. Dalton and Brandyce take turns critiquing each Famoux members' walk offscreen. Earlier this month, when the members were really mourning, they got a real kick out of watching them stumble through their tears. Even today, their harsh judgment makes me sick. If there's anyone who should know the feeling of unbalance after losing somebody, it's this family. But then I notice the way Dalton fidgets with his hands, and the way Brandyce's leg bounces in her seat. Nervous ticks. Maybe they're replaying the accident back in their heads, too, more affected than they're letting on.

I shudder as the image of Bree Arch at the bottom of the Fishbowl stairs fills my head. Horrific. For the last few weeks, it's been all the kids at school can talk about. And that image—it's still plastered on every magazine stand. I have to keep my head down when I pass storefronts.

"You know, maybe this girl isn't even dead," Brandyce says, as if she hadn't seen Bree's body too. She clicks the television off decisively. "What if she up and returns during this *Fishbowl* broadcast like nothing happened?"

"Oh, no," Dalton groans. "My friends would *never* stop talking about a Famoux member who eluded death."

"Doesn't it make you wish *you* were like Emilee?" she asks. "You know, so you wouldn't have any friends to listen to in the first place?"

Stinging singes through my chest, even though I expect this from her. Between Brandyce inside and Westin van Horne outside, I rarely get through an entire day without at least a few jabs on my behalf.

As if reading my mind, Dalton says, "Hey, come on, she already gets enough from the guys at school." Brandyce rolls her eyes but relents.

I'm thankful for it. Dalton might not defend my honor in front of people like Westin anymore, but he always does his best to keep the peace at home. It makes me shudder at the thought of how hard things will be when he leaves next year. The plans aren't set in stone yet, but I know he's already looking for opportunities in Waltmar, just like Brandyce had before our mother left. It's every kid in Eldae's dream to someday work in a lab in Betnedoor. And he's smart enough to get there too.

Dalton slings his backpack over his shoulder and gives our older sister a salute. "See you after school."

She groans. "I'll be here. As always."

I take my time grabbing my things. My brother needs the head start rather than me walking fiendishly slow to keep the distance between us. Dalton stopped walking with me to school when we were much younger, after his entire class shunned him for almost a whole year when they discovered we were related. It was hard work convincing everyone that he wasn't secretly a glitch like me. Luckily he's a year older, which corroborated his claims. Had he been younger, people would've assumed our parents realized their error and were trying to cover their tracks with colored contacts.

If only they'd done that in the first place with me—bought gray ones and forced me to wear them growing up. Dalton says our father once suggested it, but our mother refused. She didn't think anyone would care what color eyes I had. But she grew up in a version of Eldae much different than mine and my siblings'. Hers wasn't in the midst of a genetic phenomenon, where things as simple as eye color carry actual weight.

It's been this way for the last nineteen years. Since then, whenever a child in Eldae has been born, they are born with key identifying traits identical to every other child born within that year. The traits change every January, now known as Changing Month.

But they didn't know that at first, of course. Initially there were only outcries of confusion, of marital infidelity. Scientists weren't sure what to make of it. Known now as Gen 1, every infant born within the year had yellowish gold eyes. They kept the hair color, skin color, and so on passed down from family, but the eyes were all the same unreal color, like the children had been painted this way in an assembly line.

Brandyce was among these Gen 1 kids, much to my parent's surprise, as neither of them had an eye color close to that shimmery gold. Born in February, she was at the beginning of the wave too. Doctors ran tests on her and countless others—she has small scars all over her body to show for it—but they were inconclusive. Every gene chart somehow showed the same dominance for golden eyes, as if it was hereditary. They were ready to write it off as a fluke, but then the next January rolled around, and every baby born had plum purple eyes. Then came Gen 3—Dalton's generation—with emerald green.

These mutations were unique to Eldae—no similar phenomenon was occurring in Notness or Betnedoor. For a while, no one knew how to explain it, until a few scientists in Betnedoor theorized nuclear radiation. After all, radiation affects our weather patterns already, and Eldae's geographical location is said to have been a central point of conflict during the war. Notness to the west was hit badly, too, but nowhere near the devastation in Eldae. So if any of the three states in Delicatum were to feel delayed effects of radiation—the kind that could permanently mess with genetics—it doesn't take a qualified scientist with a measuring device to guess it would be Eldae.

And so it was accepted. For the first few years of the mutation, each Changing Month brought only new eye colors. After a decade, the mutation evolved, adding small, yet noticeable physical attributes. Some of these second-decade generations reach only five feet tall, while others are steadily growing, with pointed noses or clubbed thumbs or one arm shorter than the other. We're nearing the end of our nineteenth year, so there is much talk about what could be added next year as we enter the third decade of the mutations. Most guess hair color will be affected next. But what color first? Something natural like brown? Or something more interesting, like pink or green? I hear people in Betnedoor are already placing bets on it, like sports. To them, our mutation is a bit of a joke.

In any case, Changing Month is one of the biggest events Eldae has, with media coverage that rivals the kind of attention the Famoux gets. The more inventive the eye colors and attributes, the more coverage.

After three years of exciting eye colors, my Gen 4 was the first disappointment. The least exciting color of the first decade, eyes-only generations. Gray. Not even shimmery silver, like Gen 1's gold, but a flat pewter color with no flare or dimension. Unfortunately for me, being a part of the blandest generation makes my differences all the more blaring. I have my mother's eyes: icy blue, almost white. No generation has had anything close to this except Gen 17, with a shade of white-lilac. But they're two years old. Anyone who sees me knows right away that I'm an outlier.

But of course, my mother thought I was a miracle. When the mutations affected both Brandyce and Dalton, she rued the thought that none of her offspring would get her striking eyes. She had been the only one in her family to get them since her grandfather, since the color is so recessive and easily overtaken by newcomers with darker shades. My father has brown eyes, too, so even before mutations began she was worried none of her children would get them. So when I was born, she rejoiced. She never once tried to cover them up.

It's a shame. I would've been lucky to have needed only the contacts—not some kind of special surgery to change the length of my arms or anything like that. It would've been so simple to make me fall in line. But even when my father suggested the contacts, my mother was headstrong. She claimed there had to be others like me who hadn't gotten get the mutation. That flukes like this—no, *miracles*—happen often. She wanted me to be proud of myself. She didn't think there was a reason for me to hide.

Maybe she was right, and maybe there *are* others somewhere in Eldae who don't fit the mold. But they certainly don't go to my school. I am the only anomaly. When I was younger, the kids used to be so frightened of my eyes that they thought I was possessed— like I'd pass an evil spirit onto you if you met my gaze. A fun game they played was never looking me in the eye. It's still a game now, come to think of it. Most people at school pretend I don't exist, except Westin and his crew, although I wish they would.

× × ×

Turns out, Brandyce's joke earlier doesn't have much merit—even without actual friends, I'm still bombarded by talk of Bree Arch.

People have already been discussing her all month, but after Norax's statement this morning that *The Fishbowl* broadcast is in fact happening in a few days, I can't walk two steps in school without hearing her name from every direction.

It's sinister to admit, but days like this, when the Famoux has stirred up new drama for the kids at school to gossip about, are some of the best for me. After my mother left, leaning into this fantastic and flummoxing world became the best way to keep distracted. But I can't be a regular fan, like my classmates. I can't go out of my way to buy their albums or see their movies. Brandyce and Dalton would never let me live it down. My only way to hear about the happenings of the Famoux is by watching newscasts in the morning or eavesdropping on their most avid devotees.

Lucky for me, almost everyone at school is one.

"What do you think *Calsifer* is going to do in that house?" a girl asks her friends at the locker next to mine. "The memory of her . . ."

I'm fiddling with the combination on my lock, but in my peripheral view I catch one of them crossing her arms over her chest. "How many times do I have to tell you this?" she asks. "Bree wasn't dating Calsifer. She wasn't dating anyone."

"But they would've looked so beautiful together!"

I nod absentmindedly. They would've. Any combination of the members would. But the Famoux usually dates outside the clique, like Foster Farrand and his string of models, or Kaytee McKarrington and her long-standing boyfriend, Cartney Kirk. The two of them are musicians, and the duets I've overheard are sappy enough to make me feel like I know what love is.

A locker slams, and the girls head down the hall, out of my

earshot. It's no matter—all I have to do is step toward the water fountain to hear another group cooing over how handsome Chapter Stones looked this morning, in his all-black suit. They're right, of course. He seemed especially gutted today, which, according to these fans, means he looked especially good.

I catch more conversations like this on my way to class, and as the day progresses, I find that even those like my siblings who are too cynical to mourn Bree still have her name in their mouths, cooking up inventive theories as to how she died. Some believe it wasn't an accident—that someone must've pushed her. But the rest of the Famoux were in the main room at the time, so it doesn't make sense. Still, they insist it's true. Teachers try in vain to get attention in class, but even they know it's no use. The only topic worth any value today is Bree, and all lesson plans gravitate to her by the time everyone is in the room.

By the end of the day I'm so preoccupied with the mourning and the musings that I nearly let myself believe Westin van Horne will take a day off. As if he ever has. It isn't until a hand smacks down on my shoulder on the way to my final class that I realize just how conspicuously my guard had dropped.

"Hey Westin! I found Sticks!"

My flight instinct kicks in. I jerk my arm away, but I can't shake the grip. From the end of the hallway, a pack of about a dozen boys in green vests comes forth, their identical Gen 4 gray eyes eager. Westin van Horne's group. At some point they decided to call themselves the Greyhounds, as if a clique like the Famoux, although the Greyhounds aren't nearly as exclusive—there seem to be more and more of them every week. All you need to join are Gen 4 gray eyes, as per their namesake, and a hatred of me. Which means most of our grade, the way Westin has them wrapped around his finger. He leads the pack with a cruel smile.

"Look who it is!" Westin's voice brims with mock surprise. He pats my cheek. "*Sticks.* Lovely to see you, as always."

They've been calling me *Sticks* since we were young. They think it's funny, equating me to something so weak and breakable. As much as I hate it, I can't quite say it's inaccurate. The Greyhounds have been snapping me in half for longer than I can remember.

"Westin," I start. "Please—"

"What do you say, boys?" He turns to his friends. "What should we do today?"

In comes the choir of suggestions, most of which they've already done a hundred times over. Rip up my books, lock me in a room, tie me up to the school flagpole. A few of the boys carry notebooks, reading off a list of newer options, eager to be picked. These attacks are planned. A daily reminder that my very existence is a mistake. I don't know how many times I have to tell them they've convinced me already and can stop.

Felix, Westin's second-in-command and ever competitive to please him, speaks up above the others with wicked vigor. "I know. Why don't we throw Sticks into Clarus Creek? Haven't done that in months."

I grimace. The last time they threw me into the Clarus was horrible enough, and that was summertime. I could've sworn I saw frost on the surface on my way to school this morning.

"Oh, good call, man!" he says, pleased with the suggestion as the others ring in their agreements. He and Felix share a smile, and for a moment they look completely the same. Felix has a dedication to Westin that surpasses mere admiration. He moved to our city, Trulivent, only a few years ago, just around when my mother left, but he quickly cemented himself at his leader's right hand. They both have brown hair, and Felix cuts and styles his hair the same way, and even buys the same belts and shoes. Anything to look more like Westin.

It was hard enough growing up with one Westin—now I have to deal with two.

Four of the Greyhound boys grab hold of my arms, dragging me down the hall like a doll. I plant my feet firmly into the ground, but I'm no match for this many of them. My shoes leave marks on the linoleum floor as we go. I push and pull and protest all I can but decide there's no use. I've never been able to shake them, not once. Why would today be different? There have been much worse days than this, anyway. And I've survived it all so far.

Through the loudspeakers, the late bell for my last class rings. I guess I'll be missing Eldae History today. It's no surprise; I usually do. More often than not I fail whatever class falls last on my schedule, since Westin loves to drag me out of it. But Westin's parents are wealthy, perhaps one of the wealthiest in Trulivent, so they pay the school good money to assure he never fails, even if he misses all his tests. Maybe he promises the same to the Greyhound members, as extra incentive to join. Although they hardly need any.

Once outside, a brisk gust of air greets the back of my neck, and I perish the thought of how much colder the water will be when they throw me in.

Clarus Creek is a narrow strip of water that snakes through Trulivent, all the way to my neighborhood at the edge of the city. It serves as my main pathway to and from school. Until Westin decided the river was a great place to torment me, it had been a safe haven of sorts. Even after the worst of days, reaching the Clarus meant I was on my way home—that no one could hurt me anymore. All I'd have to do was follow the streams of colorful fish. Then Westin realized its value around the time we turned twelve, after he started following me home. The Greyhounds have been throwing me in at least once a year ever since.

Our school rests on one of the creek's banks, so it's only a few steps before they let me go, tossing me brusquely to the marshy grass. On my knees I get a good look at the water, at the clean sheet of ice on its surface. I shudder, which makes Felix laugh.

"Nervous, Sticks?" he sneers.

I swallow hard, trying to be clear and grounded, like how I saw Norax be this morning. She spoke with such confidence, even when it was clear she was breaking. If she managed to show strength in her own trying time, it could be worth a shot.

"This isn't necessary," I say, voice struggling to keep level. "I'm the worst. You don't have to prove it."

"Oh, but we *like* proving it," insists Felix. "If we're not consistent, you might forget."

"Please, I swear—"

He digs one of his long, dirty nails into the back of my neck, right where the skin is exposed. My wince is long and involuntary, which the rest of the Greyhound seems to enjoy.

"No, Sticks," he hisses. "It's *quite* necessary."

Beyond us, Westin brings a hand up. Felix stops what he's doing, alert and attentive. His leader gestures to the water. He is the one clear and grounded like Norax as he asks me, "Are you going to do it yourself, or are you going to make us?"

I hesitate.

A mistake. Westin takes this second to give his group a small, yet godlike nod. Before I can so much as open my mouth to say I'll jump, Felix is pushing me in.

First, I hear the crackle of the ice as I break through it. Then, I feel it. The chill slices through me like a knife. I involuntarily gasp, water filling my mouth, and I gag, which only makes it worse. Clarus's water is a murky green that's impossible to see through, but I manage to get my feet on the edge of the bank and push, propelling me farther to the center. That's crucial if I want to surface and breathe. The first time the Greyhounds did this, I came up immediately, and Westin was already crouched on the ground waiting to grab my head and hold it underwater.

When I tear through more thin ice several feet from the edge, they're booing. "Come on, Sticks," taunts Felix. "We promise we won't bite."

It's hard to focus on anything other than the agony of the cold. A numbness is already stretching over my legs, making it harder to tread water. I muster a small bit of strength and resubmerge, hoping they'll be gone the next time I come up. The last few times, this has worked, but it was warmer and easier to stay under then.

I surface again, too quickly. They're still here.

"Sticks," Westin warns. "Don't make me come in there—"

But I'm already going under again before he can finish. I've known Westin long enough to recognize when his threats are just bluffs. There is so much dirt and algae in the Clarus, I'm positive he wouldn't risk ruining an expensive school uniform for this. He never has in the past. Plus, he sees the ice I smashed through coming in the water. No one in their right mind would willingly join me.

I force myself to stay put, holding my breath until my lungs burn. I count thirty seconds. A minute. Maybe it's my imagination mixed with the numbness, but I feel myself sinking, as if there won't be enough time for me to get back to the surface before I absolutely need to breathe.

When something breaks the surface beside me, I writhe, jerking sideways. Did Westin actually jump in? I push myself as far away as I can get until my head hits the other end of the creek with a *thud,* and I come up.

To my relief, it's just my backpack. My work for the semester is ruined, but not beyond repair. My mother taught me how to clip the papers up on a string and air dry them in the sun after the first time they threw me in. When I come back to the surface, Westin and the Greyhounds are gone, running back toward the school to catch the rest of class. Another few minutes and they're through the doors, and I'm safe. I clamor out, my skin burning with what I hope doesn't turn into frostbite. I've lost a boot in the mud, but I don't care. I run the whole mile-long distance alongside Clarus back to my house without stopping once, shivering and shaking with the cold.

Long gone is the comfort I once got as a child, returning home to my mother. I'm sopping wet and still gasping for breath when I open the front door and rush inside, but Brandyce doesn't bat an eye. She only regards me with annoyance.

"Em, come on," she says. "What are you doing?"

"I—Westin—"

"Don't ruin the floors."

# CHAPTER TWO

In the beginning years of Delicatum, people thought the first-ever Darkening was a sign of the end of the world. It's not hard to see why. A few days before one occurs, small black particles begin to pepper the sky, growing thicker with each morning. And then, when there isn't any more sky left for them to block—darkness. Two whole days of it.

But these first survivors in Delicatum didn't know it would only be two days, then. For all they knew, it could've been forever.

They panicked. These were people who had survived mass floods and atomic bombs to get through the End. But this? This didn't have the same kind of easy scientific explanation. It felt divine, like a punishment for the way the world had ended up. The two days of that first Darkening were filled with absolute chaos. One of the reasons Betnedoor is the most prosperous state today, with high-tech buildings and freshly paved streets, is because its citizens set fire to nearly all of their ruins then, desperately trying to create their own sunlight. They had to build from the ground up when the sun returned.

Nevertheless, the sun *did* return. The world rejoiced. They'd survived. They were apprehensive when the particles returned weeks later, but they survived it again. They began to piece it together. This wasn't an unpredictable attack, but a reliable weather pattern. There was nothing to fear at all.

Today, Darkenings are a calm affair. A welcome one, even. The last two days of every month are considered holidays now, for everyone to stay home and decompress after a long month of working. Some people use the time to rest, to read, to start something new. Nowadays, however, most people spend it watching the Famoux.

Over the week, the sky has slowly gotten grayer than our usual smog coverage in anticipation of this month's blackout. I've endured a whole array of torment from the Greyhounds, as they try to inflict as much pain as they can before they have to take two days off. It's not favorable, but the promise of a break at the end of the week, filled with only the Famoux, makes me grit my teeth and bear it.

Today is the day before the Darkening, and the streets of Trulivent are bustling. The news about the Fishbowl coming to town was all anyone could talk about at school. Usually I run right home after class to avoid Westin sniffing me out around town, but I can't help myself from following the hordes of students rushing to the main square to catch a peek.

Even in the soot-covered sunlight, it glitters. Three times larger than my own house, this one is made entirely of glass. The aptly named Fishbowl, where *The Fishbowl* broadcast will happen. The Famoux will roam about this house like rare, alluring fish for our Darkening entertainment. Since Eldae and Notness don't get to see the Famoux roam their streets every day like Betnedoor does, the Fishbowl house moves to different cities over here every blackout, giving fans *all* over Delicatum their fair chance to see it in person. This is a high honor for us to get the Fishbowl for a Darkening that promises to be eventful. The first one without Bree Arch.

There is an incredible number of tents pitched up around the glass house, with fans milling about to find a good viewing spot. Though there's technically a country-wide curfew during the Darkenings to reduce any potential crime, the Fishbowl comes here so infrequently that when it does, authorities don't get too mad about people camping out in the square. It becomes somewhat of a festival, even. My family doesn't join in on this, of course. We opt for watching inside, usually muted so Brandyce and Dalton can dub ridiculous conversations over whatever is happening on-screen.

On nights before the Darkening, our house may as well be as muted as our television set. When I arrive home, stillness has already set in the air, thick and impenetrable. My family eats dinner, the clink of silverware serving as sporadic background music. Every so often I'll meet Dalton's gaze, but then he turns away to our father, for whom Darkenings are impossible reminders. The day after my mother disappeared we entered into one, and he kept pacing the floors and murmuring about how wherever she was, she likely couldn't find her way home without any light. Even when the sun came up two days later, it may as well have never surfaced again for him. He picks at his food and even thanks Brandyce for making it, and she lets the comment hang. Silence pervades over us all, a gash gone untreated for years.

Full from the meal, my father retires to his bedroom, while my siblings and I migrate to the living room area a few feet beyond us to catch the opening of the broadcast. With a click of the remote, our ancient television sputters to life. Dalton takes it to channel eight—the Famoux's special channel—and their logo appears big, black, and bolded on-screen. The waiting screen.

"Here we go again," Brandyce complains.

Staring at the logo, a strange elation stirs in me. When I was younger, watching the third iteration of the Famoux with which I grew up, I used to wonder how it was possible that six lives could be stuffed within the confines of this television. They seemed unreal.

I barely remember any of their names, though. All past eras of the Famoux pale in comparison to this one. The older *Fishbowl* broadcasts were a much more literal interpretation of the show's idea, with the world getting a glimpse into their *actual* every-day lives, mundane as they might be in the confinements of a house. But this current era brings all kinds of story lines to the Darkenings—drama over what's been going on in the month leading up aired out in front of our eyes. Most of the fights seem almost scripted, but the fans don't mind. They love the never-ending threads of narratives being spun. I do too.

The bolded logo fades out into a crisp and clear fly-on-the-wall view of a room I've seen so many times, it's practically engraved in my mind. We all settle on the couch as bolded text comes over this view:

WE USE THIS DARKENING TO
REMEMBER THE LIFE OF BREE ARCH.
MAY SHE REST IN PEACE

"Until she shows up again," Brandyce murmurs.

Several cameras zoom in on objects within the room. I take in the sights—the scatter of velvet and leather couches, the spotless marble flooring, the huge ivory grand piano in the corner. Somehow, they transport all of this to different cities every month for our viewing. It is the stuff of dreams. At least, the fantasies I had as a kid.

Suddenly, a girl saunters into the frame on massive high heels. She wears a powder blue dress, her dark hair twisted tight into an elegant knot. Kaytee McKarrington. I can almost feel the whole of Delicatum lean toward their screens, eager. She is one of their favorites. They'd love for her boyfriend Cartney to be here, surely. If they could, they'd make him an honorary member.

Right on Kaytee's heels, the lovely Till Amaris practically dances through the door. As they laugh together over something, the final three members enter: Foster Farrand, Calsifer Race, and Chapter Stones, all conversing calmly, as if no one is peering in on them.

The cameras zoom in on Chapter, as he opens his mouth to say something.

Then the screen goes black.

I sit up straight. Is something going on? Another power outage?

"What happened?" I ask.

But then I notice Dalton setting the remote down and yawning. "This isn't interesting," he says. "I'm going to bed."

"What, you miss them?" Brandyce asks me, amused.

"I—no," I say. "I was just wondering."

As my siblings rise to leave, I sneak a longing glance at the screen. The first night of the first Darkening without Bree is *definitely* interesting. We haven't even gotten to see them approach the stairs where the incident happened. The tension will certainly be unmatched. But I couldn't insist we turn the television back on—Brandyce would never let me live it down.

✕ ✕ ✕

I wake up early as usual on the first day, but with no sunrise to catch, there's no use sneaking off to the ruins. This hour is typically my only opportunity to watch *The Fishbowl* with the volume up, but since they're in our time zone, the Famoux are all asleep, save for Chapter, who sips a cup of coffee and stares into space. By the time my siblings stir and emerge from their rooms, the action is just beginning, much to my dismay.

Throughout the day, the Famoux members seem to have a thousand different arguments, which Brandyce and Dalton talk right over. They decide that this current one at the dinner table is stemming from the fact that Foster accidentally took Till's spoon.

"I can't believe you'd do this!" Brandyce mocks for Till. On-screen, Till is crying, pointing her finger at him.

Dalton plays Foster, who's got his arms up, as if surrendering. "Look! We have fourteen different pieces of silverware! You had at least five other spoons to choose from!"

While they get a kick out of this, I try to read the members' mouths. They're talking with such passion and conviction, it's difficult to decipher. It must be something about Bree—it's the only word I can make out, although it could be *free* or maybe *breathe*. I'll have to catch up on it later, through my eavesdrops at school.

"I don't want those spoons!" Brandyce insists. "They're too small!"

"Well, too bad! I need two this size!"

At some point the argument subsides, and dinner is over. We're given various shots of them retiring to their sitting area, then one of a door on the ground floor opening, an array of maids coming in and scurrying to the dining room to clear the dishes.

"The silverware thing really *is* ridiculous," comments Brandyce. She shakes her head at the screen as Famoux employees pick up full plates of food, now cold. "And their tables are always full of food they barely touch, do you ever notice that? Why do they need all of it? The excess is sort of disgusting."

"But that's just Betnedoor," says Dalton. "Everything's like that there."

"No it isn't," says Brandyce.

"Oh, so you've visited?"

His words were said with a teasing tone, but the moment draws stale immediately. Any lingering amusement in Brandyce's face is flattened down as her lips purse into a fine line. She shifts her weight on the cushion, her hesitation filling the air.

Poor Dalton doesn't notice yet. He's gesturing to the screen, at a close-up of crystal glasses being set in front of each chair. "I can't wait until I have at least six knives in my table setting," he declares. "I'll give them all names."

Brandyce rises from the couch, moving to the kitchen area. Dalton watches her go, surprised by her abruptness.

"What?" he asks.

She distracts herself by opening the cupboard doors, looking for nothing and finding only a growing frustration. When she slams the last one shut, which holds our ceramic plates, I hear them rattle.

Dalton's caught on now. His nose scrunches up. "Brandyce . . ."

"Do you even know how few jobs Betnedoor companies give to people out of state?" she spits out. "How much of an honor it was to be chosen?"

"Of course I do," he says quickly. Dalton splays his arms out, reminding me of the Famoux argument they just mocked, now real and their own. "Look, I was just making a joke. All my friends and I joke about Betnedoor, so I—"

"Do you forget that *you're* the reason why I had to turn my offers down? Do you really think I would like those jokes?"

"It was stupid, I—"

"You just want to rub it in my face how *you* get a life and I don't!" She paces the floor, a hand on her forehead. "I worked so hard, studied so much for nothing! I should be in Betnedoor right now, working at a lab. Not making dinner for you ungrateful . . ."

It fades as she lets out a shriek I'm sure she's been holding back for two years. Brandyce has always thrown jabs at us about having to stay in Eldae, but she's kept considerably calm. Beside me, Dalton sinks into his seat, helpless. Dalton is a peacekeeper. I think of all the times he's come to my defense with her, and a moment of stupid bravery overcomes me. I stand.

"It's not Dalton's fault," I peep up.

I'm about to point out that it's our mother's, for choosing to leave, but when Brandyce turns her heated gaze on me, my well of words dries up.

She lets out something like a cackle. "That is *rich* coming from you, Emilee. You know what? You're right. It's not his fault. It's yours!"

"I—"

"She wasn't tired of anyone but you, you *glitch*! Because you make everything so difficult! Every single day you have some new problem to come home crying about. Nothing is ever just *fine*." She storms back into the living room, getting in my face. It takes everything in me not to cower back down to the couch. "The more I have to take care of you, the more I understand why she'd run!"

For a moment my face stings, and I think she might've slapped me, but her hands are at her sides balled up in fists. It's her words that have hit.

"That's not fair," Dalton says. "Emilee isn't—"

But Brandyce cuts him off. All she can focus on is me, her stare cold and unrelenting.

"If it had just been Dalton and me, she would still be here. And all of our lives would be better."

"You don't mean that," says Dalton.

"I *do*," she says. "I should've said it a long time ago."

In my vision, the world doesn't blur. I don't feel dizzy or faint. Instead, the room looks clearer, and I feel unnervingly solid. The incredible conviction in her words has frozen me in place, my legs like rocks anchoring me to the ground. I'm not sure I have the strength to even open my mouth. I may never move—this moment may never end.

For the first time in my life I truly feel as stuck as Brandyce probably does.

I find it in me to move, but only my eyes. I look back to the screen, to the Famoux. Till and Foster, who had been yelling at one another all day, are sharing a laugh as they return to their rooms. The rift between them had only been a small fissure, easily mended with a smile and an apology. But I know the one between Brandyce and me is far more cavernous. As we walk toward our own rooms, there is no laughter shared.

Lying on my bed, sleep is an impossible feat. For hours I toss and turn, my mind playing over Brandyce's words until they burn a hole in me. I've always known that she resented me. I've always assumed alongside her that our mother left because of me. There is nothing I can do to take back what I've caused, so why does she keep reopening the wound? What does she expect me to do about it? I can't apologize for existing in any way that would make Brandyce less upset that I do.

Suddenly the room has no air. I wish my ceiling would crack open, like the roof of my mother's favorite house. I sit up, gasping for breath, but there's no relief. I need to get out, if only just for a minute. I rise from the bed and don a pair of shoes. My hands reach for the corduroy jacket, but I hesitate, my stomach twisting up.

My mother gave me this on the day she left us. When she fastened the buttons, she was smiling. I can't help but wonder if, in that moment, she had already decided she would be leaving. Did her smile mean she knew this would be her last time ever comforting me—a smile of *relief*? She should have told me I was exhausting. If I had realized how much of a burden I was, I could have changed, finally stood up to the Greyhounds. Everything could be different. But it's not.

I let the jacket drop to the floor and run.

Stepping outside with only my sweater feels like jumping back into Clarus Creek. My cheeks sting instantly, but I ignore it, starting toward the ruined houses. But then I falter. Do I even want to be there right now? Somehow I know the solace I've always felt will be gone today. It might even be gone forever.

Where am I supposed to go? The only two places that ever offered me comfort no longer feel like home.

Somewhere in my haze of my emotion, my feet start moving on their own. Not toward the ruins. Not to my house. I walk right into the forest in the direction of Clarus Creek, as if I was going to school. It's so dark I can barely see what's in front of me, but I've taken this path so many times I could do it blindfolded. When I reach my school, I keep going. The destination is clear now.

I'm going to the Fishbowl. Maybe they can give me the sense of belonging I so desperately crave. Brandyce would think I am acting ridiculous. I don't even know the Famoux members, she'd say. But I am drawn toward the glow of the Fishbowl like a moth to a flame. And in all this darkness, I could use some light.

Even in early morning, the town square is lively. People in tents mill around in clusters, talking and singing. A dozen fires lay scattered, providing heat and delicious scents. A thick crowd of fans gathers around the perimeter of the massive Fishbowl in the center of it all, their faces pushed up to the glass that reveals the dining area. Prime seating for potential arguments, since most of the conflicts happen during meals. The Famoux isn't seated yet, but breakfast could begin at any minute.

I head straight toward the glass and weave through the people, searching for a member—any member. It's not a difficult feat. I round a curve, and there is Foster Farrand, wiping sleep from his eyes as he gets out of bed. He can't see out of the glass, since it only goes one way, but he looks over in our direction and winks just the same. The fans around me grab onto each other and screech, and he smiles big. Foster doesn't have to see them or hear them to know the effect he's having.

Foster Farrand is the friendliest, most playful of the members, always with a witty remark up his sleeve. And he is gorgeous, too, with his deep brown eyes and olive skin. They're all models in their own right, but that world is Foster's specialty. He is in every runway show, every magazine, on the side of every building advertising clothes and products. His photos are ubiquitous—that smile, that wink. Seeing it in person makes me dizzy. I wish I could walk through that glass and talk to him. Something tells me he would know how to make me feel better.

When Foster exits, a large chunk of the crowd migrates with him. I follow the flow of the crowd, now outside Calsifer Race's room. He's just looking through tie options, but crowds are loving it, hooting encouragingly though Calsifer can't hear it. Quite notably, the interior glass walls in his room are covered in paintings. All his own. He's the artist of the group, and his works are lauded as some of the freshest concepts in the last few years. He's soft-spoken and humble, too, providing juxtaposition to Foster's high-spirited energy.

As Calsifer fiddles unsuccessfully with a blue necktie, Kaytee McKarrington struts in. I watch her mouth move in the motion of a laugh, and she helps him knot it correctly. All of Kaytee's motions are fluid, as if her limbs are made of silk. She dances as well as sings in her performances, and it's hypnotic to behold.

She tightens the tie to his neck, and I read Calsifer's lips: *Thanks, Kay.*

The two of them leave together, and the crowd migrates again to watch Till twirl in myriad dresses. She changes in the bathroom, the only portion of the glass house that's opaque, for privacy. Each time she surfaces, she shows off the fabric and sparkles to the window, a makeshift fashion show.

The dresses look gorgeous on her; she has a much more muscular figure than Kaytee's, as a result of all her tournaments and championships. Till is a sports star, excellent in a variety of them—individual ones like tennis and golf, and even snowboarding in winter. Just recently she's ventured into film, starring in a series of superhero movies called *Riot!* that put many of her athletic skills on display.

Though her productions have seen plenty of success, the film industry, as I've heard far and wide, belongs to Chapter Stones. He's the group's movie star. There isn't a scenario he hasn't played out at least once before. I've never seen these films fully, but I've looked over shoulders at classmates' devices as they've played clips of them in class. In some he's a spy, or a doctor, or creature from another world. Always a hero.

He isn't in his bedroom, but when I make it around the Fishbowl, I see him seated at the dining table as the rest of the Famoux mills in. The other boys are formal enough in dress shirts and ties, but Chapter wears a full gray suit, fiddling with a pair of silver cufflinks. Maybe it's just because the fans at school talk about him the most, or because I typically see him sipping coffee in the morning, but I've always been partial to Chapter. I guess I'm sort of jealous, too, that he gets to live so many different lives while I only have the one, and mine is nothing special.

Foster says something that makes them all laugh, and though we can't hear it out here, I laugh too. Whatever it is, I know it's funny, if Foster has said it. I realize in this moment that I might know more about the Famoux members than my own family. I couldn't say what Dalton's favorite subject in school is these days or what Brandyce dreams about at night, but I know each and every Famoux member as if I shared a house with them instead. Most people around Delicatum see the Darkenings as welcome breaks from their normal lives, but for me, they might be the only time I actually *feel* normal anymore.

"What do you think they'll do about *Key*?" a kid asks their friend near me, interrupting my thoughts. "Cancel it?"

Oh, right, *Key*. Till isn't the only one of them who's made a recent jump to film. This was going to be Bree's first role. Now, her last. People were buzzing about it ever since photos of her and Chapter on set leaked. Bree was no stranger to smaller screens—as her Famoux career, she hosted a variety show that aired weekly on *The Fishbowl* broadcast channel—but fans were thrilled to see her branching out. And alongside Chapter too. It's the first time two members have been in a film together.

"They won't cancel it," says the other kid. "They'll release it. In her memory."

What a grand occasion that will be. I'm sure it'll break all the records.

In the dining room, the members regard one another with what looks to be kind formalities. The three men sit on one side, the two women on the other. And then, at the end of that row, next to Kaytee, an empty chair.

Now that they're all seated, servers and maids scurry about, setting the table with a whole spread of breakfast foods. Usually, this is the time when I have to press mute on the broadcast before Dalton or Brandyce enter. I wonder if they even notice that I'm not at home.

But then two rough hands seize my shoulders and pull me back with a gleeful refrain:

"*Sticks!*"

I yelp, but it's drowned out by a cheer from the crowd. The Famoux must be doing something exciting. Westin turns me around, shoving me tersely.

"I can't believe we've run into you during a *Darkening!*" he exclaims. "What a fine time for us!"

Next to him, three other Greyhounds chuckle. I writhe as he grabs hold of my wrists and nods to the others to grab me too.

"Why don't we take her somewhere less public?" asks Westin.

A team effort, they each take one side of my body, dragging me toward the darker, emptier streets of town. I assess the situation. It's just the four of them, not the entire Greyhound group. No Felix either. My chances have never been higher to break free and make a run for it.

As I'm planning my escape, they plot what to do with me.

"How about the creek?" asks one.

"We just did that," another says.

"I've got it," Westin states. "Felix's mom has a storefront on Eighth Street. We could lock her in the cellar, come back after the Darkening."

This gets encouraging hoots from the group. They yank me toward Eighth Street, and I screech. It's no use; no one hears me. We're far enough away from the Fishbowl now that the lights are a faint yellow glow at the corner of the street. Once we turn, there will be no more glow. Just darkness.

"Westin," I beg, "you can't—"

"We can and will," Westin says.

"But I can't—"

I'm cut off by a foreign voice. It's like a clatter of spare change—melodic without any sort of melody.

"Excuse me, dears?"

The other Greyhounds tense up, thinking they've been caught, but Westin simply loosens his grip on my arm, his face transformed into a well-practiced look of innocence. Beside him, the others can't help but gasp. I get it—something like an electric shock is sending currents down my spine. Considering the thought that she might be an apparition, I blink.

Her long black trench coat and gray cap tell me she must be purposefully disguising herself. With her head down, she could be anybody.

But this isn't just anybody.

It's Norax Geddes.

"I—*what*?" one of the Greyhounds stutters, dazed. Norax might not be a member herself, but there's something about her— some ephemeral glow that makes anyone starstruck. I blink a few times. She's still there. She's here. How is this happening?

Norax smirks at our reaction. It's the most perfect smirk I've ever seen, but it quickly evaporates into a stern, almost disappointed look when she settles on Westin. "I was taking a stroll," she says casually, "and I saw this little scene."

She was taking a stroll? Shouldn't she be somewhere behind the scenes, controlling the broadcast? Beside me, the Greyhounds look like they could faint. The kind of trouble someone of Norax's stature and power could get them in, I can only imagine.

When it's clear no one is going to say anything, Westin speaks up. "What . . . do you want?"

"You see, I saw this young lady you boys are fighting over." When Norax looks at me, the sharpness in her face softens. "I was wondering, could I steal her for a moment? Or is this a bad time?"

"You want to *what*?" one of the Greyhounds scoffs.

"I wish to speak with her," Norax say, firmly.

She wants to talk to *me*? I step back in disbelief and accidentally lean into Westin. He shoves me away.

"Fine, take her," he barks. "We were done with her anyway."

Westin suddenly lacks his usual bravado. His eyes are glued to the ground. She grabs his chin and brings it up, willing him to look at her. "Thank you, honey," she says. That term is one of endearment, but her voice is devoid of any. "And don't shove her," she adds. "She could bruise."

Norax wraps her arm around my shoulder. She radiates this unbelievable warmth, even in the midst of the cold weather. I don't know how it's possible. She starts walking us into the darkness without another word to the Greyhounds, in a hurry to get me away from them. This direction seemed dismal a few seconds ago, but her glow makes the journey feel like daytime. I sneak a glance over my shoulder at them, but they're already gone, ducked down the corner toward the Fishbowl.

Norax leads me down the street. Every piece of me seems numb, like I'm in the middle of a dream I could wake up from any moment. She carefully looks around us, and when she's sure the street is vacant, she stops, settles her eyes on me, and smiles.

"I'm sorry about pulling you away," she says in a much lighter tone than she was using on Westin. "I didn't like the way they were treating you."

"It's okay." My own tone is excruciatingly meek. Talking to Norax Geddes feels like I'm talking to some kind of higher power. It feels wrong to say too much too loudly.

"The way they were shoving you along, like you weren't even a person . . ." She furrows her brow, then straightens it out again, taking a breath. I watch in awe as she gathers her composure like I saw her do just days ago on TV during the press conference. "What's your name, dear?" she asks, like she's just remembering that I'm a stranger.

"Emilee."

"Just Emilee?"

"Laurence."

"Emilee Laurence," Norax parrots. "Hmm." She surveys me again, then asks the obvious question. "How old are you, Emilee Laurence?"

"Sixteen," I say.

"Now, correct me if I'm wrong, but these are not the eyes a sixteen-year-old from Eldae is supposed to have, correct?"

I hesitate. "They are not," I admit.

A part of me expects her to turn up her nose in disgust. But she doesn't. "Do you know why you look like this, and not like the others?"

"No one does."

"How utterly remarkable," she murmurs to herself. "Just like them."

"Them?"

Her perfect smirk returns again. Just then, a big black car pulls up on the curb in front of us. I get the urge to duck away from it, but Norax tugs me toward the door, giving my shoulder a few fast squeezes. "Quick, come in," she whispers. "Before those boys return and I have to be less kind."

There's not much I can do but follow her lead. I assume she'll be driving me back toward civilization, but the car goes right past the main square—past the view of the Fishbowl and the surrounding tents—without slowing a second. My stomach instinctively flips.

The car lights cut through the darkness, and the sight of her face makes me fuzzy all over again. I grip the leather of the chair beneath me, hoping for stability.

"Do you need anything?" she asks. "I'm sure we have some water somewhere in here."

I tell her I'm fine. One of the bodyguards sitting in the front seat passes back a glass bottle anyway. As I fiddle with the cork, my hands shake.

"Is that water all right for you?" she asks, watchful. "I'm sure we have sparkling water, if you'd prefer it."

"Really," I say. "I'm fine."

But she motions to the front, and another bottle comes my way. Now I have two. One still, one fizzing through the glass. I probably identify most with the latter at the moment.

Out the window, I don't recognize the buildings anymore. We're far from the familiar sectors of Trulivent, now nearing the outskirts. In the flare of the headlights I can see large brick buildings come into view. Old factories, most abandoned, from the old world.

"Where are we going?" I ask.

"Someplace a little more private," Norax says innocently.

"Why?"

The way Norax looks at me somehow dissolves all my concerns about the safety of getting in this car. Her look gives me warmth. The comfort I was craving.

"I want to get to know you."

# CHAPTER THREE

The car pulls up in front of a large brick factory and parks. When I ask Norax what this place is, she flicks her wrist, like it's obvious.

"One of our many control centers, of course," she tells me.

"But you guys live in Betnedoor," I say.

She smiles. "This one is for Eldae specifically."

I'm not sure what she means, but two surly bodyguards usher us inside before I can inquire further. The inside of the place is surprisingly modern. Not what I expected at all from the almost old-world exterior. The lobby floor is made of a sleek black marble, and in the center of it all is a long ebony reception desk where a woman greets us with a bow of her head.

Norax nudges me toward her. "Zoya, I have somebody for you to meet. This is Em."

*Em.* The word is thermal enough to settle my nerves instantly. Any nickname I've ever had has always been at my expense. Not this one.

The woman, Zoya, repeats the nickname a couple times, as if to test it out. "Pretty," she decides. "Wherever did you find her?"

"Around the Fishbowl, being tormented by fleas."

Zoya studies me carefully. "Would you look at those *eyes*. Spectacular. Shall I keep them?"

"*Keep them*?" I ask.

Norax blushes like she's been caught in the middle of something. She tells Zoya, "I've just brought Emilee out here to have a talk, that's all."

"You brought her *here* to talk?" Zoya shakes her head. "Take the sitting room. I'll be drafting up a few models."

Before I can ask what she means, I'm being pulled into a small room off the main lobby that houses a table and a bright white couch. No normal person could so much as breathe near this room without the fear of making some kind of stain, but Norax sits us down on the cushions like it's nothing.

"Can I get either of you anything?" Zoya asks.

I'm granted not even a moment to decline before I'm being served five different selections of hot tea from employees in nondescript uniforms. They set down cream and various condiments, a tray of sandwiches, then a massive array of pastries—far too many for just the two of us. It reminds me of what Brandyce said last night about the Famoux's excess.

*Brandyce.* Have she and Dalton woken up yet? Are they wondering where I am? I try to picture myself turning up at our concrete house in an hour or so with this tale of how Norax Geddes picked me up and gave me tea. They'll never believe it.

"Try the lemon first," Norax insists, stirring me from my thoughts. As I pour myself a cup, she offers a pot of what looks to be honey. "With a hint of the nectar too. It's all the rage in Betnedoor."

I've never once tasted a thing like this, but some foreign nostalgia creeps up anyway as I take my first sip. The concoction tastes like home, somehow. I look at Norax, who smiles like she's just shared a secret with me, and I feel eerily peaceful.

"Do you like it?" she asks.

"I love it."

She's satisfied with this answer. As she pours herself a black tea, she launches off into her questions. "Now, tell me. Do those gnats do it often?"

"Who?" I ask. "And what?"

"The boys back there. Do they pick on you a lot?"

It feels somewhat embarrassing to be admitting my grave unpopularity to one of the most popular people in the world, but I do. "Yes."

Norax gives me an apologetic, knowing look. "They can't even *begin* to fathom your beauty, can they?"

This almost makes me laugh. "No, it's not . . . I'm not . . ." I try to let it fade off, hoping she'll understand, but she doesn't seem to.

"You don't think you're beautiful?" she asks.

"Well, no," I say.

Her face is suddenly filled with genuine surprise. Her surprise surprises *me*. "How can you not think that?" Norax exclaims. "Have you ever looked at yourself?"

My blush is immediate. "I just . . ."

"You know that's why they do what they do, right? They're jealous."

"Jealous?" *She's really on a roll now.* "No, they're not."

"They are. They were all a part of the fourth generation, no? Blandest eye color of the lot of them. But yours . . . Jealousy makes people do things that don't make sense, dear. Things that aren't justified," she tells me. "They wish they *were* you, so they punish you."

I sip my tea, unsure of what to say. She has it all wrong. The Greyhounds call themselves that for a reason. They're *proud* of their Gen 4 eyes—not envious of mine. But Norax is so sure of herself that I know there's no use explaining this. I say, "Maybe."

"Trust me," she says. "You *are* beautiful, Em. Beautiful enough to be a part of all this."

A gasp escapes me. "Of what?"

Norax breaks our eye contact to examine her perfectly crafted nails, a grin splaying on her face. Then she glances back at me, eager. "Tell me. Are you a fan of the Famoux?"

"Of course," I say, my pulse racing.

"You must then be aware of our current predicament," she says. "We're in need of a new addition to our group."

"I guess, sure."

"And you know what I think, Em? I think that person should be you."

"*What*?" I ask. The word comes out of my mouth involuntarily, before I can even register the weight of what Norax has just said. As my eyes stare into the golden Betnedoor nectar for stability, the whole world sways, and the teacup I'm holding is suddenly far too hot, and I have to set it down.

*She just asked me if I wanted to join the Famoux.*

Norax lets out a little laugh. "You heard me correctly, dear. I was thinking it over on the drive, and I'm certain now that I want you to join us."

"I don't understand," I say. We know she plucked the newest era of the Famoux's members out of obscurity, sure, but it wasn't random. They have actual, established talent. She doesn't know a thing about whether or not I can act, or sing, or paint, or swing a tennis racket, or *anything* the Famoux seems to do so easily. "Isn't there an audition process?"

"Oh, that was just an excuse, dear," she tells me. "To make people think it was fair. On the contrary, I perused smaller towns in Eldae until I found each of them. Handpicked."

"*Eldae*? I thought the members were from Betnedoor." Every article about them said so. I remember at school, when the new era was first announced, how some of the kids who'd auditioned really wailed over how unfair it was that the new members all hailed from the golden state already. *It had to be rigged*, they said. I guess they were right, but not in the ways they thought.

Norax's grin returns. "That's also an excuse. A little lie we tell so no one wonders about their looks. Can you guess why?"

The members are all close to my age, each one a year or two older. I go through images of them in my head. If they are really from Eldae, none of them have the right eyes for their generations. It all comes together.

"They don't fit the mutations," I say.

"Yes, dear," confirms Norax. "They are all anomalies like yourself."

My head tries to wrap around this concept, but it feels impossible. They're *like me*. The Famoux members are *like me*. My mother always used to tell me there were others, and I didn't believe her. I thought it to be another one of her many lies.

"But of course, as you may have gathered now, their true hometowns don't know who they are," Norax says, "and that is because the members have had to shed their old selves to become a part of this. If you choose to join us, Em, you will have to do the same."

"Wait, what do you mean?" I ask. "Their *old selves*?"

She reaches out and touches my hair, wistful. "When my father Lennix ran the Famoux, it was merely a group comprised of the best of the best. Celebrities used to work for *years* in hopes that Lennix would consider them for the next era. In the end, it turned into a clique of people so high up at the top, that joining the Famoux was a mere next step. They barely even realized how blessed they were to have been given that opportunity." Norax shakes her head. "I always knew that when I inherited the Famoux institution, I would give that chance to people who deserved it. People who are never given any reason to believe they are worthy of the world's love. People like *you*. But every member has a group of boys in their past just like yours. It breaks my heart. So we change your name, conceal your past . . . it's the only way. By joining the Famoux, you would be giving yourself a new life. A new chance in the world. This building is here in Eldae for that reason—I wouldn't whisk any of you off across the ocean until I was absolutely sure you were going to accept that new chance. If you go to Betnedoor with us, you go as one of us."

Now my head is spinning. Suddenly, the taste of nectar in my mouth makes me nauseated. "But how will my family . . ."

Then I see the sad look on her face, and I know exactly what she's going to say before she even says it.

"They can't know. No one here can. This is a secret that only the other members, myself, and special staff like Zoya can be privy to."

Just then, Zoya emerges at the door. "Did she say yes yet?"

"She's deliberating."

As they watch me carefully, the reality of the offer sets in. Joining Norax means leaving forever. Slipping out of the house without a word, just like my mother.

*What would they say?*

Roaringly overwhelmed, tears perk up in my eyes before I can stop them. Norax consoles me with a hand on my cheek.

"Oh, dear," she says. "Have I misread the situation? I presumed, from the boys, that you would want out of your life. But if your family . . . If you already feel the love I am seeking to give you, Em, by all means we will drive you back home."

My sister's words from last night flash through my brain. *If it had just been Dalton and me, our mother would still be here. And all of our lives would be better.*

*Do* I feel that love Norax is offering from them?

I force myself to think rationally. If I were to leave right now, Brandyce would be free of taking care of me for my final year of schooling. She would be able to leave as soon as Dalton graduates. They could head off to Betnedoor *together*, too, if he gets a job there. They could bring our father. All he would need is a room to himself, and they'd never see him, like now.

It could work for them. It could be even better than it is today. But what would they say? Would they look for me?

Beyond us, Zoya notes that, technically, I know too much already about the Famoux to back out now. Staying this long in itself is tantamount to saying yes.

This should trouble me, but it doesn't. With Norax's gentle arms wrapped around me, the overwhelming feelings subside. Even with a dull ache in the shape of my family thrumming in my chest, there is a stronger ache everywhere else that feels a lot like relief.

Sickening, freeing relief.

"Okay," I say, and the sound of acceptance in my voice surprises me. This is the way it has to be. This is what saves my family. This is what saves *me*. "I'll join."

✕ ✕ ✕

Upon my acceptance, Norax declares that we need not waste any time, and I am swiftly whisked into another room and told to change into a white gown. As Norax leaves me to make a few calls regarding my new-member status, I am taken by Zoya to a sterile room in the back to a machine she refers to as the Fissarex.

Maybe it's the dark chrome finish or the intimidatingly thin width, but my palms get sweaty just at the sight of this thing. It's like a trap Westin and Felix would've loved to lock me in. I look to the door, a wave of strategies to escape flushing over my mind like they had earlier outside the Fishbowl. I wish Norax hadn't left me alone in here with only Zoya.

"How does it work?" I ask.

Zoya presses a finger onto the silver surface, causing a keypad to appear, its buttons beeping red. She hits a few, and a hidden door swings open slowly. She then pulls a slender onyx stick from her belt and points it directly at me. "Your figure is going to be projected on the Fissarex screen out here, and I will use *this* to make my edits. Whatever I paint onto you will appear; whatever I erase will disappear. Erasing your skin might hurt a little, but it'll only last a few seconds, I promise."

I gulp. "Will I need a lot of erasing?"

"Let's see." She touches my hair. "Hmm. It's just so dark."

"Is that bad?"

"I was thinking about making you blond. But I'll need to pull it all out and restitch new strands."

The idea makes me light-headed.

The sound of Norax's heels clacking toward us eases my nerves. "Zoya is going to make your beauty shine even more, the way only the Famoux do," Norax assures me. "Every member had to go through this. We enhance the features they already have. Find the perfection within and bring it out. And you've seen them now . . ."

I have. They *are* perfect. All different kinds of perfect too. Between hair, eyes, and complexions, no two members look fully the same. I always thought Norax must've sifted through thousands of options to find people on this level of perfection. But in reality, no one is on that level. Zoya has made them this way. And now she will do the same to me.

"They were good sports about the whole thing too," Zoya adds. "Stood as still as they could. The less you fidget, the quicker I can get my job done."

"And the sooner it's all over," Norax completes.

I have no more time to hesitate or protest as Zoya gestures me into the foreboding machine. The interior walls of the Fissarex are black—as dark as the Darkening outside. With the swift press of a button, Zoya makes the door slip down, entrapping me within the onyx void. Although I know the machine is only wide enough to barely fit my figure, it feels like the dark ahead of me is endless.

Taking a deep breath, I go to smooth out my paper gown, but I can't feel my arms anymore. I try next to touch my face, and it's like I don't have a hand or a face to me at all—as if my body doesn't exist. My mouth opens to scream, but some kind of unearthly force compresses down on it before anything can come out.

"We're all warmed up now." Zoya's voice comes in from a speaker somewhere in the vast blackness. "Stay calm, stand still, and we'll be golden."

"Try to distract yourself!" Norax calls out. "Think good thoughts!"

I squeeze my eyes shut, heart rattling in my ribcage so hard I can hear the clamors. Taking Norax's advice, I start thinking. This is a distraction tactic I employ often, whenever I can't fall asleep. I state as many facts I know about a topic until I'm too tired to think any longer.

It feels fitting that the topic today be the Famoux.

*The Famoux was founded*, I think to myself, *thirty years ago, by a man named Lennix Geddes.*

Suddenly, the feeling comes back to my waist, and I quickly wish I was numb again. The pain all over my sides is unlike anything I've ever known. It's like someone is carving remorselessly at my skin with a blade.

*Lennix had experience in management and wanted to use his expertise to—*

The end of that sentence can wait. The pain slowly slips down my legs, searing off flesh as it goes down. Immeasurable. Unbearable.

In the agony, I forget what I was thinking of. I need a new fact.

*There have been only four eras of the Famoux so far.*

Pain all over my stomach.

*The Famoux switched to their current cast two years ago.*

Pain all over my arms.

*With the switch, Lennix put his daughter in charge. Norax, who—*

Pain in my chest, punching my ribcage.

*These new members are—*

Sweltering, white-hot pain all over my scalp. All thoughts break off completely. There is no room in the world for anything besides this pain.

"We're almost done, I promise!" It's Norax, from outside. "This is the worst part, but you're doing so well!"

I can barely hear the end of it; the pain is all over my head now—hitting my cheeks, my nose, my jaw. It's impossible to distract myself from this level of pain. It pounds at my skull, as if trying to drill into my brain.

And perhaps it does. In a swell of agony, I lose all consciousness.

× × ×

When I come to, the door of the Fissarex opens for me, white light pouring onto my face. I welcome it graciously. No more darkness. I'm through with darkness.

My balance falters as I step out. It's like I've never used my legs before. "Careful!" shouts Zoya. She brushes dust off my gown. "Don't wreck the beautiful new body I've made!"

It clicks. *New body.* I glance around the room for a mirror, but there are none in sight.

"How do you feel?" she asks.

"I don't know. Different."

Just standing here feels foreign, like my posture has changed. I feel several inches taller too. I wonder if I am.

Norax is wiping tears from her eyes. "Oh, Em," she breathes out. "You're absolutely *remarkable*."

"Of course she is!" Zoya twitches the paintbrush at us. "I create only remarkable things."

Norax leads me out of the reformation room to a new one with a mirror that stretches the length of a wall. I try not to predict anything, but my mind can't help but wander to thoughts of the current Famoux members, how perfect they seem to be.

When I step into the room my eyes meet themselves first. *Same eyes*, I notice. Same eyes, but a completely different person.

My face is that of a stranger's. New cheekbones, sharp and defined. New eyebrows, dark and plucked to perfection. New, full lips, tinted a permanent rosy pink. My complexion has no spots, no blemishes. Flawless.

The gown they've dressed me in is boxy, but even with it on I can tell my waist is lean, my stomach flat, my legs thin and muscular. No longer are my arms weak, but toned, as if I've exercised for years to make them this way.

And then there is my hair. The biggest change of all. Like a pale sort of gold, cascading down the papery gown and framing my face in layers. When I reach out to touch it, it's soft and glossy, a thousand threads of silk.

"Bree's entire structure was different," Zoya says, referring to data on a clipboard. "She had that dark hair. A rounder face too. Less angular. You need not worry about people comparing you on this level."

"How could they ever compare her?" Norax says, touching my new, perfect cheek. "She's got this whole different essence to her. Rebirth, adventure, *youth*." To Zoya, she notes, "She's younger than the rest, you know. Sixteen."

The others aren't much older—most are around eighteen or so. But Zoya jots this fact in her clipboard. "Youth will be a welcome change."

The way Norax gazes at me through the mirror is unreal. I have never been looked at in such a way in my entire life. "You're a lumerpa."

"A what?"

"A pretty little bird from myths of the world before us," Norax says. "I love old-world things, don't you?"

My mouth drops open. The Famoux is so modern, I wouldn't guess it. "I do."

"A lumerpa's one and only purpose in life is to *illuminate*. Legend says it shines so brightly it soaks up everything dark, even its own shadow. Darkness cannot dare extinguish it," she tells me. "When I first saw you in the crowds, you and those eyes, I knew right then. A beautiful lumerpa. And now, here you are."

I look back at myself, the way I glow. She's right. The gold of this hair, the sheen on my skin, even in the bright and unforgiving lights. A lumerpa. That's it.

"I'm telling you, Zoya, the entire world is going to absolutely fall in love with this girl," Norax declares, proud. "With . . . *Emeray*."

"Emeray?" Zoya asks.

"That's the name. Emeray Essence."

Zoya scribbles this down. Just like that, it is set in stone. *Emeray Essence*. It sounds so new, so sophisticated. A name no one's ever used to taunt me.

Norax squeezes my shoulders. "Emeray!" she squeals. "Emeray Essence, member of the Famoux!" The room is buzzing with so much joy and excitement that the floor seems to be shaking. Maybe it's just standing on my new legs. *New legs*.

Even as Norax is thanking Zoya and whisking me away again into a car, I can't say much of anything—all I can think about is my new reflection, my new identity. My eyes can't resist the urge to scan my arms and hands for details. Even in the darkness of the car, my skin still glows like it's made of a thin sheet of shimmer. Then I notice finer details. Gone are my pores, gone is the freckle on my wrist, gone is the scar from when I turned around too fast in the kitchen and Brandyce accidentally swiped my arm with a kitchen knife . . .

*Brandyce*.

My eyes dart up and I notice that our car is passing the

Fishbowl. Then we're passing the forest where Clarus Creek is. Then we're passing streets and streets of concrete houses, and I know one of them is mine.

The very hand I was just examining presses instinctively against the window, as if I could reach for my family. The car is moving so fast that I can't pick out my house. But they all look the same. This one with the porch light on may as well be mine.

They must realize I'm gone by now. What are they thinking? Will Brandyce smile at the chance I've given her, or will she regret what she said, and how it pushed me out?

*No.* It won't be the latter. This decision helps them as much as it helps me. I'm freeing them of the burden. They will thank me for this. I have to believe it.

Norax picks up on my turmoil. She asks me what's the matter. When I tell her I don't want to talk about it, my voice catching in an attempt not to let out a sob, she doesn't pry further. Instead she slides over a little closer to me in her seat, puts her arm around me, and starts telling me about the fun little facts and features about the private plane we're about to take to Betnedoor. The reason the furniture inside is all powder blue, the meanings of all the hand-painted designs on the walls, how the plane's engine is the most advanced in the world and cuts standard travel times in half—apparently we'll get all the way across the ocean to Betnedoor in three hours, as opposed to the eight or so it used to take.

I lean into the warmth of her arm. I wonder if she, too, uses facts to calm herself down, or if she just somehow knew exactly what to do to console me.

# CHAPTER FOUR

When we get on the private jet, Norax insists that I get some rest after the long day we've had. The Fissarex took a toll on me, so falling asleep is no trouble at all. I've completely passed out under a blue cashmere blanket before the plane leaves the ground.

The flight is shorter than I'd anticipated, so Norax has to stir me awake before the plane lands. Outside the window, the next morning's sunrise is just beginning to break through the darkness. Even at this early hour it's the brightest, cleanest shade of orange I've ever seen.

A Betnedoor sunrise.

The view is far more encompassing up in the air than on the floor of my mother's favorite house. From this height, it's like I'm living inside it—like I could scoop out the color and hold it in my hands. As the minutes pass, the color only deepens. My heart swells up. Now that I'm Emeray Essence, a *Famoux member*, this will be my everyday sunrise. Someday I'll even grow used to it.

"Good morning, lumerpa!" Norax's voice draws my attention

away from the sky. She stands next to my chair holding two mugs, the scent of lemon and nectar wafting with the steam. When I take the mug, she looks almost triumphant. "Enjoy the last couple minutes of relaxing, because we have an *even bigger* day ahead of us than yesterday. But first we need to stop at the hideaway so I can take care of some managerial business," she declares. As she has me change from my Fissarex gown into a pair of nondescript black pants and a white shirt, Norax tells me all about how much the members relish the return to their *little hideaway* on the edge of the city when the Darkenings are over.

I've seen it in pictures, so I know it will be a large house, but I'm not fully prepared for just how massive it is.

Using the word *hideaway* to categorize it seems a bit of an oxymoron. A mansion like this couldn't possibly hide, not even deep within the woods. It sits upon a huge sweep of land at the top of a hill, a skyscraper in its own right. As we go up its winding driveway, I feel glad that the Darkening is over, and that I can glimpse this oxymoron and all its fine details in the light of day.

Not the typical Betnedoor-modern in the slightest, it must be an imitation of some grand, old-world palace in which kings and deities once lived, with towers and columns and tall gates of golden metal. Thick vines snake up the exterior of the first few floors, breaking away to reveal a stunning expanse of stone and mortar. The very top of the house is painted a shade of ebony, like dark candle wax pouring over the parapets. I get an intrusive thought of what it would be like to see the wax-like details on fire, but I shake it away, moving on to the grounds.

Flanking every end of the mansion are miles upon miles of snow-capped acreage, spanning the whole stretch of the hill. The scene is somewhat ghostly with all the white from winter, but I have little doubt that spring sings a different tune of grassy fields and flowers in abundance.

"A lot to take in, isn't it?" Norax asks.

"It's . . ." I wrack my brain for the proper word to describe it before settling on *magnificent*. But even that seems too simple.

"You'll get the grandest tour of it all once the day is done," she assures me.

The Famoux mansion is but a small pit stop on our larger itinerary for today. In fact, we're in such a rush to get to the city that Norax has me wait in the car while she retrieves a few forms and files. She thinks I'm disappointed that I can't go in yet, but secretly I'm thankful. The Famoux members usually leave the Fishbowl and board their jets the second the sun rises after the Darkening, so it's unclear if they've returned yet from Eldae to decompress after the Darkening, and I wouldn't want to take my chances and run into one of them. Norax aside, I've never actually met a celebrity before. Even just seeing the members through the glass was enough to make my whole body feel like static buzzing. I'm not quite sure how I'd react if the crowds and the glass between us were gone.

Norax emerges from the entrance with a young man by her side. He wears the same dark, nondescript garb as the people stationed on their side of the doors. A guard.

"This is Gerald!" she exclaims when they enter the car. "He'll be your personal bodyguard while you learn the ropes of being a celebrity."

"I get a personal one?"

"He'll be escorting you everywhere!" she says. Then, her voice drops low. She presses a button and the partition between us and the driver goes up. "As your personal guard, he knows about your . . . transformation. He's aware of how big this change is for you, and it's his job to help make things run as smoothly as possible. But not every staff member is privy to such info. You understand, it's quite a secret to keep."

"Oh," I say. *Right.*

I get a good look at him. He's even younger up close—probably only a few years older than me. His hair is jet black, and it pokes out from under a uniform cap. He looks stern, ready for anything. If his eyes were gray, and not chestnut brown, he could've fit in with the Greyhounds.

"Hi," I say, somewhat intimidated. "I'm Emeray."

Gerald's mouth twitches up into a smile, dissolving my fears. "I do know that already."

Our car continues right into the heart of Waltmar, the capital city. Everything about Betnedoor strikes this aura of refinement for me. Eldae is still covered in ruins, and Notness is shrouded in pollution, but every road here in Waltmar is clean and precise, and the sky is a pure, magnificent blue. It's a marvel to look at—almost as impressive to me as the mansion.

"It's so refreshing to return here after a Darkening in Eldae," Norax says. "All those shades of the same drab color give me a headache after a day or two."

Much to my surprise, the car stops in a dark alleyway. The kind of area I imagine Norax would avoid, not willingly bring me into.

"Are we in the right place?" I ask her.

"This is the back entrance." Upon my still-confused face, she says, "We certainly can't take *front* entrances with you just yet. Do you want to be seen?"

I don't, of course. But the next thing I know, I *am* being seen, fully seen by five pairs of eyes all crammed in one small room.

Norax and three guards by the door watch as Swanson, the head Famoux seamstress, helps me strip down for the measurements she's about to take of my body. They claim I have nothing to be bashful about, but my cheeks are a permanent shade of magenta the whole time.

Swanson is a stern, precise woman. Like Gerald, she must be in her twenties but has an air about her that tells me she's lived a thousand lives, and her mouth seems permanently curved into a prescowl. It's this exact expression she wears as Norax explains how many gowns we'll need for me. I'm not going to be revealed until after the gala, but once I am, I'll be going *everywhere*. I'll need a whole special-event wardrobe to match.

"Don't worry about time constraints," Norax adds. "We aren't going to be revealing Em for another month or so. We still need to hold our *audition process* for the new member."

The seamstress only laughs. "How many gowns would you like?"

"It's your call." Norax motions to me. "*She's* the muse. How many dresses can you make for a face like that?"

Many, it appears. As Swanson takes her ruler to every inch of my skin, she also makes a few sketches in a tattered notebook. Not a few. A dozen, at least. Even just in a scribble of pencil, I can already somehow see the shimmer and the color.

To Swanson's credit, she does her best to make me as comfortable as she can throughout this whole measuring process. She distracts me with lengthy stories about her time at fashion school—most specifically, about the time Norax strode into her class one fine morning and plucked her right from her seat, no explanation, and named her Head Seamstress. Her story really resonates with me. There's a comfort in similar origins.

Once she's gathered everything she needs, and has sketched enough to fill a picture book, I'm given back my clothes, which I toss on as quickly as I can possibly muster. In no time, the guards are escorting Norax and me out of the mirrored room, and we're on to the next stop.

"Now, that wasn't so bad, was it?" Norax asks me in the car.

"It was odd," I say.

"You ought to get used to being watched and admired now," she tells me. "Soon enough, it's going to become your norm."

The Emilee part of me finds this hard to believe, but I don't doubt her. I've seen the way the Famoux are gazed at—the way there's a new photo of them every time they step outside, their every movement a painting to be framed. Even I admit I've admired them with great detail.

"How long did it take for the other members to get used to it all?" I ask Norax.

"It varied for each of them," Norax admits. "Kaytee loved stepping out for the paparazzi from the first moment she did. It took Race the longest . . ."

"Race?"

"Oh, Calsifer," she says. "We all call him by his surname back at the house."

My mind files this away: *Calsifer Race is just Race.* Despite how well versed the kids at school made me, this is a fact I didn't know. Makes me wonder how many other things I don't know about them.

Our next destination is the headquarters of *The X*, the only trustworthy news source for all things Famoux. By now, everyone knows to rely only on *The X* for the real news, but their issues aren't published as frequently as other publications. They release a new issue every month, whereas gossip tabloids drop rumors every day. The purpose of our visit is to begin what I'm told will be my debut cover spread, which will be put out into the world just before the next Darkening.

"It will be your formal introduction," Norax tells me. "They will have a whole magazine of facts and photos to get to know you. No sudden drops of information. No pulling the rug out from under them."

*Them*, I suppose, is the entire world. I think about the glossy copies of *The X* people from school would pass around. The thought of *me* on one of those covers makes me almost giddy as we pull up to the sleek headquarters.

Gerald and the other guards that lead us through to the headquarters' hallways are so tall, I can't see past them at all until we make it to a door. Norax inputs an elaborate code on a keypad, and it swings open, revealing a room that feels like an optical illusion. On the left side, we might as well have walked straight into the past: vintage trunks for tables, patterned sofas, distressed hardwood floors. The other side, in contrast, is what I've grown to expect from the Famoux: large silver screens, machines with blinking lights, and dark metal tables.

"Oh! Hello!"

My eyes fall on the young girl sitting cross-legged on the paisley couch. She, like Swanson, is young and beautiful, with her hair pinned up in a bun.

"Miss Abby Booker," Norax greets.

But Abby barely even sees her—she's too busy gaping at me. "Oh my gosh. Is this Emeray? She is . . . well, she's indescribable!"

"I've been telling her all day."

"As you should! A face like hers deserves constant reminders!"

My eyes shift to the floor, a smile creeping up on my face. Compliments have always been like rare gems to Emilee Laurence, but it looks like Emeray Essence is irrevocably adorned in jewels. It's going to take some getting used to.

"Why is the room like this?" I ask, in a somewhat forced attempt at steering the conversation away from myself.

"I'm indecisive," Abby says, and nothing more.

"You better have made some decisions, at least, about the spread," Norax teases. "How is it going?"

"Please, take a seat!"

On the couch in the vintage section, Abby hands us what she's worked on. Though she's only had a day to prepare, Abby has already made a magazine template, with blank, labeled spaces for where writing and photos will go. It's long, perhaps a hundred pages, and it's baffling. Will there really be this many photos of me? Is someone really going to want to look at this?

Norax points to a few pages with nothing on them besides the other members' names. "What are these?"

"Oh, I want them to write about her," Abby tells her. "I think it would be very effective if the members told their fans what they love about Emeray in their own words."

The names are suddenly like sirens, blaring out at me from the paper. *Kaytee McKarrington, Till Amaris, Foster Farrand, Calsifer Race, Chapter Stones.* The idea that they would have things to say about me at all, much less things they *love* about me, feels impossible. That static buzzing begins to rise up my fingertips.

One of the later pages near the end of the spread is labeled *CAREER.* "We'll put her upcoming projects here, so fans know what to be eager about," Abby says. "Do we have any plans for what she's going to do yet?"

"What would you like to do, lumerpa?" Norax asks me.

This is a big question.

"I don't even know what I *can* do," I admit.

"She could absolutely be a model," says Abby. "I mean—Emeray, stand."

I expect to hobble to my feet, but I rise with a fluidity I've never felt before, causing me to pause and gape with wonder at my new body. *Even the way I move is new?* Every muscle feels like it'd been dipped in gold, if dipping something in gold makes every piece of it more smooth and refined and lovely.

Abby grabs an old-looking camera, one I've seen only in textbooks. She squeezes the button before I even have the chance to smile.

"I wasn't ready," I say. "Can you take another?"

"Nonsense," she says.

"Have you ever seen a bad photo of the Famoux?" Norax asks. "They don't exist. Zoya took care of that."

A slip of thick paper spits slowly from the camera. In a matter of minutes, it's ready. Even I have to gasp. Somehow, my startled, unprepared stare has translated into determination, focused nonchalance. I've always hated having my picture taken—not that the occasion presented itself all that often. But looking at this instant photo, I want to sit for a thousand more pictures and look through them over and over. The sudden burst of vanity would usually embarrass me, but wanting to look at pictures of this new face doesn't feel superficial—it just seems right.

"I think I'll make a copy of that immediately," says Abby. "That could be the cover."

"How did that even happen?" I stammer. "I didn't even pose."

"Looks like you've no idea what you're capable of, Emeray Essence," Norax says.

*I guess not.*

"She could definitely model, all right," Abby says. "I can't stop looking at this!"

"Do you think modeling is something you'd like to do?" asks Norax. "Anything you want. The options are endless for you."

Endless options. And to think, just two days ago I thought my life was set in stone.

"I want to do everything," I admit. "Anything I possibly can."

"Perhaps not talk shows," says Abby.

She's right. That was Bree's.

"I don't think I'd want to do that anyway," I say quickly, almost defensively. But it's true. The idea of sitting down and making small talk with a million different people every week sounds like my own personal nightmare.

"So not *everything*, then," Norax teases.

For the next couple hours, we go through a few sample interview questions and photoshoot ideas, and I hear a dozen stories about Abby and her husband, a TV host named Sam. Between her and Swanson, so far it seems as though everyone who meets Emeray Essence feels compelled to tell her all the ins and outs of their lives. I love it. It's so different from the way people used to ignore me at school—how I could last a whole day without speaking to anyone. What a welcome change this is.

Before we leave, Abby gives me the instant photo to keep. Norax and I admire it as we walk out. Norax tells me she likes how soft, yet severe I look in it. It reminds her of her favorite book, she says. "It's in the hideaway's library," she tells me.

"We have a library?" I ask.

"Of course," she says. "We've got all the books you could ever want."

They have more than all the books I could ever want, they have *everything* I could ever want. On the car ride to our next destination, Norax tells me all about the other rooms within the house. Viewing rooms, tasting rooms, recording studios, ones covered wall to wall in the group's ever-growing accolades.

Abby made copies of the photo she took but has given me the first one to take home with me. Staring down at my face, my chills are nonstop. "None of this feels real," I admit. "I don't understand how I'm here."

"I saw something in you," Norax reminds me.

"Right," I say. "I looked different."

"It was more than that." Norax gazes out the window. The sun is almost fully set now, casting her face in orange and gold. "You looked so broken out there, Emeray. And those boys . . . I knew your life couldn't have been easy."

I think about my mother, my father. She doesn't know the half of it.

"All the members had that same look to them. That broken look. It just . . . It feels so much more righteous for it to be people like you who the world should admire so deeply. Not just any old person dreaming of fame—someone who needs it. Someone who *deserves* it."

Norax's eyes are swimming in some emotion I can't place. "Lennix didn't love the idea of choosing people like you for the Famoux. He liked the way he ran things. He was the one who insisted we had to make the Fissarex in the first place, if I really wanted this." Norax touches my golden hair. "Believe me, I wish you didn't have to go through all this to live this life, lumerpa. But now, you get to live it however you want."

The car slows down at our next stop. It's dark out now, so I can barely make out the shape of an alleyway through the window.

"Where are we now?" I ask.

"It's—"

Her sentence is cut off when I open my door. In an instant, every shred of softness we were just sharing is halted by a stampede of light and noise.

Not so secret an entrance, I guess.

"*There they are!*"

The sound of cameras popping is sporadic. I can't find a rhythm. All there is in front of me is pure and utter chaos. I try to see the ground below me, but I can't make out anything except light and the voices. All yelling. So much yelling.

Yelling my name.

"*Emeray Essence!*"

It is a careening chant among blinking lenses, clipped quick and sending my whole system reeling. I recoil into Norax as Gerald in the front seat leans to the back of the car and slams the door shut.

"Back in!" he yells, flustered.

Just like that, our car is flooring it down the street, taking us far away from all the commotion. But even when we're past it all, it's still ringing in my ears. I don't even register where I am for a few moments.

*What just happened?*

When my vision is no longer dotted with camera flashes, I see Norax beside me, barking orders into her phone. Panicked.

"What was that?" I ask. Perhaps I shout it—I've lost my gauge on volume.

"Paparazzi," she says.

"They were saying my name."

"I know," she says. Then she swears, murmuring to herself, "It's barely been a *day*. One day, and—"

"Norax, do they . . . ?"

"They know," she confirms. "I don't know how they know, but your secret is out. Well, the secret of *you* is out."

The aftershock of all that noise and uproar is an evasive drum in my ears, beating on my skull. I close my eyes, the reality of what's just happened to me setting in. They know.

They know I'm here. No more waiting for the gala anymore.

# CHAPTER FIVE

We're zooming through streets and intersections with reckless abandon, but I can barely see it over the splotches of light still streaking my vision.

They've found us. *They've found us.* Three days ago I was watching fans at school, crying together. Crying over Bree. Saying a whole year would be too soon to replace her.

What are we going to do?

I can't get the crying faces out of my head as the car comes to a halt in front of the mansion. The grounds are guarded, so there's no one waiting when we step out. Even so, I'm whisked inside at lightning speed. There isn't a spare moment for me to take in the splendor of the foyer for the first time before I'm shoved down the hallway, being herded to my next destination.

"Your tour can come later," Norax asserts. "Right now, we need to get to the Analytix."

"The Analytix?"

She yanks me down the hall past doors painted a bright white.

We don't stop our scurrying pace until we reach one labeled *888*. Norax exhales, punching in codes on the keypad with trembling fingers. When the code comes up as incorrect, and she lets out a mangled cry. I grab her hand and squeeze it.

"Everything's okay," I tell her. But even as I say it, I don't believe it. *Is* everything okay? I have no idea. I haven't yet seen Norax this distressed. The sight of it sends shrill bursts of frenzy through me.

She inputs the code once more with slower concentration. It blinks green. We scamper inside.

The majority of this room is sectioned off by a wall of glass. Beyond it is a closed-off space with a single chair. No towering object like the Fissarex. Just a glass wall and a silver stool.

"Where is the Analytix?" I ask.

"Right there. Take a seat."

The logical, problem-solving Norax from the press conference is back, which calms me. I'm still confused, but I oblige. The chair is cold on my legs, which makes them shake even harder than they were before.

"What now?" I ask.

"You listen."

A few seconds pass in silence.

"There's nothing—"

"It's starting up." Her voice is muffled from the other side. "They'll be coming any moment."

I sit so still that I can feel how unsteady my heartbeat is. Just as I begin to think that nothing will happen, suddenly—

A *voice*.

It slices through the quiet, almost startling me off the stool. The voice is strong and assured, with odd, dramatic newscast music playing faintly behind it. It doesn't talk to me, but *about* me, like it doesn't know I'm there.

"*. . . So far there's no word on whether or not Emeray Essence is in fact the real deal. No official response from the Famoux headquarters. Our question remains: Who is she?*"

The music swells before coming to its end. I inspect the ceiling, the far corners, but there is nobody else in this room except Norax and me.

"Norax?" I call out. "I think there's—"

But a new voice cuts in, cuts me off. Someone talking to a friend.

"*Did you hear about the new member? Do you think it's fake?*"

"*I kinda hope it's real!*"

"*I really like her name. Emeray!*"

My heart leaps. I want to stick with them, hear more of this, but their conversation fizzles into a rough and bustling meeting. Someone with a particularly brutish voice seems stressed.

"*We need pictures now! Were any of our connections there today? Do we have any employees from* The X *willing to be a source?*"

"*We're developing some shots of her stepping out. They're blurry, is that okay?*"

"*As long as we have a cover for tomorrow, I'll take anything. We'll forge an inside source. We just . . .*"

His sentence dissolves, and in comes another newscast, its intro music filling the air around me. A reporter declares, "*While it's too soon to say, Emeray Essence seems quite fit to be Bree Arch's replacement. We have a correspondent on the scene to investigate further.*"

A horn jingle and a swishing noise are followed by fuzzy

audio. *"We're on the scene where Emeray was spotted attempting to exit a Famoux vehicle. We can deduce from the following candid shots captured out here that she is indeed a member. Look at her outfit. Nothing we haven't seen before on Bree Arch, right? We most definitely have a replacement."*

The clothes were the ones Norax handed me on the plane this morning: black pants, white shirt. Incredibly regular clothing. Is this really something *noticeably* Bree Arch? But I can't dwell on it for long. Next interrupts a group of chuckling friends.

*"I think she's pretty hot."*

*"Yeah, yeah!"*

*"You guys are gross. She looks young."*

*"Old enough."*

More laughter. Heat rushes to my cheeks. They're quickly intersected by a new set of voices—these ones, in the middle of an argument.

*"How the hell did they replace her so fast? She hasn't even been dead for a month!"*

*"It doesn't mean they planned it!"*

*"They'll probably kill this one, too, just to spice things up!"*

And in comes another group, bearing complaints instead of compliments.

*"This is a nightmare! She is a nightmare!"*

*"Where did she even come from?"*

*"And, like, Emeray Essence? What kind of a stupid name is that?"*

*"I can't believe they want us to accept this cheap knockoff of Bree. The nerve!"*

Pulled back by my own mortification, I jump off the stool. The voices cut out all at once, like I've pressed pause on some sinister recording.

"Have you had enough, lumerpa?" Norax asks.

"Yes," I pant. I've probably had enough for my entire lifetime.

As she emerges from the other side of the glass, I put my fingers on my temples, rubbing the divots. "What *was* that?" I ask.

"Our little Famoux secret," she says. As if they don't have many, *many* Famoux secrets. "We've got special magnets and minerals embedded into the walls here." Norax gestures to the stool. "When you sit, you're in the exact right configurations to hear what anyone in the world is saying about you."

"All the time?"

"As long as there's somebody talking."

"Oh," I say. "Wow."

Norax pulls up a tablet device with a screen coated in dots, graphs, and percentages. "This is how we make sense of what you heard."

In one corner of the screen, there are paparazzi shots of me surfacing from the car, eyes wide with surprise. In another, there's a sea of articles already bearing my name, big and bold in the title. There are also clippings of videos from different news stations, registers of all the "sources" claiming they know me and my story, and a bursting list of comments updating so fast, I can barely read a word before they're gone, replaced by new ones.

Above it all is a blazing headline:

EMERAY ESSENCE

"You're doing fair, considering the circumstances." Norax slides her fingers across the screen, zooming in on charts and graphs. "We can work with this."

I nod along, feeling relief. Good. She knows what to do. But of course she does—she's Norax.

Norax clicks on a title labeled *Consensus.* Two options pop up. *Positive* and *Negative.* She chooses the former first, revealing a small list of words in a shade of mint green.

"*Pretty,*" I read off. "*Mysterious.*"

"These are great reasons for you to be liked," Norax says. "Useful reasons."

I'm distracted by that bright-red second title, the negative end, like it's a raucous signal. "And what do *they* think?"

"I typically like to check this part alone. It's so early, I'm not sure if you . . ."

"Please," I say.

Norax sighs, then reluctantly taps on this section. The words, red against a white background, become like thorns, pricking me one by one:

*Fake.*

*Unwanted.*

*Replacement.*

"Don't take any of this to heart. This is fine," Norax assures me. She pats my back encouragingly. "Had we been able to wait for your reveal after the gala, as intended, they *still* would've tried comparing you."

But the words have already nicked me. I look down at my hands, half expecting to see them bleeding. It hits me for the millionth time where I am and what I've done.

*Right.* I have just taken the spot of the girl who died on international television a month ago.

Norax doubles down on the reassurance. "Lumerpa, we'll do our damage control as best we can." She clicks the tablet off, placing it in her bag. "The Analytix is a useful tool. The main thing you have to remember is that no matter what it tells you, it's on your side. It *wants* to help."

"How often do I go in?" I ask.

"Usually once a day," she says. "Sometimes more. In your case, it will be more."

The Analytix and its silver stool now appear just as menacing as the Fissarex. All I can hear in my head is the roll of thick accents calling me a *nightmare* on a daily basis.

"Come," Norax says. "That's enough for today. Let's get you to your room."

× × ×

*Replacement.* That's the main word on my mind as Norax leads me to my living quarters. Replacement for Bree. No matter how many times Norax has insisted I'm anything but, and that I look nothing like her, it's getting harder to believe it. It's what *they're* all thinking out there, after all. A whole different look isn't enough to separate us.

Makes me wonder what sort of horrible things those people might say if they ever knew what room Norax has chosen for me.

Bree Arch's bedroom feels something like a crypt. Norax is as cheery as she can be while she shows me around, but my stomach is in knots. The expanse is far too enormous to be homey. There's a large living room–like area with sleek leather couches, onyx chandeliers, and a wall-sized vanity with a mirror almost double my size. The color scheme of it all is harsh, stark—black and white, nothing more. And it's neat. Painstakingly so. Every cushion on the king-sized bed is tucked perfectly, and every surface is spotless, as if dusted thrice a day at least. Had I not been informed it was once Bree's room, I would've assumed this was the guest quarters.

Or maybe I wouldn't. There's the feeling that someone's lived here, definitely. Norax guarantees the sheets have been washed twice over, and the floors have vacuumed up every step she's ever taken, but it is impossible to mop up the chill in the air I feel the moment I step inside. It's there. Or maybe I'm paranoid.

"Get some rest," Norax tells me. "It's going to be a big day tomorrow."

"Again?" I sigh, and this makes her laugh softly. "Am I going more places?"

"Oh, absolutely not. Tomorrow, we'll be debriefing the members."

"They're back?"

"They're set to arrive at the mansion later tonight," she says. "And I am going to be *quite* diligent about keeping them from the Analytix before they meet you. We'll be able to tell them the news on our time."

The thought of meeting the Famoux members twists my juxtaposing emotions. One half of me is fearful. Are they going to hate me? Are they going to think the same things as those voices in the Analytix? But the other half of me can't picture their faces without getting giddy. *I'm going to meet the Famoux!*

The giddiness subsides fairly quickly when Norax leaves. Suddenly, the air is deadly still, and the coal-colored bed frame grows more coffin-esque by the second. This might've been a fan's feverish dream a few months ago—getting to stay in the Famoux mansion, in one of their rooms—but standing in here by myself feels a lot more like a nightmare.

*Calm down*, I tell myself. This is just a bedroom. This is *my* bedroom. With morbid curiosity, I inspect the place closer. But as I look through vanity drawers and find half-used makeup containers, and I check the closet and find rows of satins and silks I could picture her wearing, I can't fight tears from forming in my eyes. This doesn't feel like *my* bedroom. I feel like an intruder. And that presence of *something* in the air is so overwhelmingly prominent now, I can't stand it.

There's only one colorful piece in the wardrobe, and even then, it's barely a shade past white. A pale yellow thing made of satin. It almost knocks me right to the floor. This is the color of my mother's favorite house. The one in which I watched the sunrise.

The bathroom is a curious combination of dark marble and steel, and the shower has even more buttons than one of Norax's Analytix devices, but I barely inspect these things. I dart right over to the crystal faucet, running warm water on my hands to get some feeling back into them. I hadn't realized until just now that it was so cold in this room, they'd gone numb.

I need to calm down. I need to distract myself, like I did in the Fissarex. Letting the water get scorching hot on my palms, I wrack my brain for more historical facts about the Famoux to recite. But Bree is an invasive thought.

*The Famoux was founded by—*

And there's her face filled with horror and shock on my television screen, just shot down.

*—by a man named Lennix Geddes—*

And there's a chorus of people calling me a *cheap replacement* over and over and over again.

*No.* I can't think about this. I need something else. I turn the faucet off and look up, meeting my mother's blue eyes in the face of a stranger's. Who even is this? Who even am I?

I run my hands along my arms. They're far more muscular than Emilee's ever were. And my face, so sharp and exact. I don't think there's a single inch on my body that hasn't been changed by the Fissarex, besides my eyes. If my family has looked at all at the news and have seen the photos of this *Emeray Essence* girl, they'd never be able to feasibly guess it's me.

Shivering in the ghostly cold of Bree Arch's bedroom, I sink down to the floor and let myself cry. What is my family doing right now in my absence? Have they gone to the authorities like they did when our mother left? Have they told anyone I'm missing? Do they think I've been kidnapped in the midst of the Darkening, and that they could someday find me? Or do they suspect the truth: That I am our mother's daughter, selfish enough to leave our house without a word or warning?

Suddenly the dreamier ideas of their future fall away. I can see Dalton having to forgo getting a good job, just like Brandyce did, to care for our father. I can see none of them getting out of Trulivent, getting to Betnedoor. I can see them spitting on the floor of my bedroom for ruining their lives one last time. The guilt is like a second aura all its own, swirling around me now like fog before a Darkening. It makes me feel faint.

*This is just a thought. The better one can still exist*, I tell myself. But when I close my eyes to block it out, I see the word *unwanted* from my Analytix review, bright red and bloody again. Right. I might've just ruined my entire family's life, just so I could hear the same thing Westin has been telling me for years. *Unwanted*. If I died tomorrow, I doubt any fans of the Famoux would cry the way I saw people crying for Bree. Some might even call it poetic justice.

Imagining their jeers, like Westin's multiplied by a million, makes me ache with fear. How do I even *expect* myself to win people over now? All I've ever managed to do is repel and draw people away from me—even my own mother. The Fissarex hasn't changed the way I think or act. That's still Emilee.

I manage to calm myself down by thinking about Norax. I am not alone. She's on my side, at the very least.

Rising from the floor and willing myself back into the main bedroom, I think about what she said on the car ride from *The X*. I looked broken when she found me. I was broken then. And through my reflection in the vanity as I crawl to the bed, Emeray Essence looks impossibly whole. Scared and crying and unsure, but whole.

I *am* different. I'm not a breakable stick. I am a diamond. A diamond doesn't break when it falls, so I won't either.

And I'm not powerless. Not with the Famoux behind me. I'm sure I could easily ask Norax to at least check up on my family— make sure they're coping. With the number of bodyguards I've seen flanking the mansion, I might even be able to get an actual search party to find my mother. I don't know if any of this is even possible, or allowed, but it feels as though it ought to be. The idea of asking this of Norax is the only thing that's able to lull me into a semisound sleep for at least a few hours.

But like a child afraid of the dark, I curl up under the covers, unable to shake the feeling that Bree Arch is somehow still in this room—maybe standing right over me right now, staring, trying to figure me out.

*Replacement*, she seems to whisper, just like the rest of them.

I'm out of the room before dawn.

# CHAPTER SIX

Without a clear plan of where I'm going, I venture deep into the throngs of the Famoux mansion, getting more lost and more relieved with equal measure. I don't want to be anywhere near Bree's bedroom if I can help it.

This place really ought to have maps. The hallways are like optical illusions, deceptively long and winding. I walk for what feels like half an hour, and suddenly the doors are crimson. I must've entered a new wing.

This wing has carpeted floors and plenty of artwork. As I stare into the two gigantic blue eyes of a painting down the hall, I wonder to myself just how many parts and sections a place this big might have, and if they even go explored. If I wandered too far, how long would it take for someone to find me?

"Are you lost, love?"

The sound of another person's voice makes me jump, like I'm in the Analytix all over again. The panic doesn't exactly subside, either, when I whirl around and see the voice's source. In fact, I have to lean against the wall for stability, for fear I might keel over.

Chapter Stones is the only other member with blue eyes, but his are not as stark and whiteish as mine. His are as blue as the painting in the hallway. Even bluer. He rubs the grogginess from them, blinking at me with pure confusion.

"Who are you?" he asks.

Suddenly it's as if I've never learned to talk. Of course it's Chapter who I run into. *Of course.* Maybe I'd stand a chance with one of the others, but he's so elegant, so tall, so intimidating that suddenly, all my thoughts of Bree and home and *everything* are wiped away into oblivion. He's asked me who I am, and I can barely remember my name now. I stand there like a fool, mouth agape, for what feels like a full minute before I come to my senses.

"Um. I'm Emilee," I say. And then I realize. "Wait, no. *Emeray.* I mean, um—"

Chapter seems amused by my sputtering. I'm sure he gets this reaction from everyone. "You got your own name wrong?" he asks.

"Well—" I hesitate, searching for some brilliant excuse.

My mind is going haywire trying to decide, but then Chapter laughs and says, "It's all right. I get it."

"What?" I ask.

"It's a new name. You're getting used to it." Upon my hesitation, he adds, "Well, you *are* the new member, aren't you?"

"Norax said she wasn't letting you go to the Analytix yet."

"Didn't need to," Chapter says. "I mean, we heard the crowds shouting outside the car pretty clearly."

"I just want to—"

He gestures toward the end of the hall. "Would you like to get some coffee, Emeray?"

My jaw drops again. Now *this* can't be real. How many times have I seen Chapter Stones drink coffee during early mornings in *The Fishbowl* broadcasts?

"You—you're always doing that," I stammer.

"I'm always having coffee?"

"I mean . . ." I'm kicking myself for saying anything in the first place. "Well, yeah."

"Did you watch us a lot? Before?"

"No, I didn't," I answer quickly. He thinks I'm a rabid fan. I'm certainly *acting* like one. I feel the sudden urge to double down on proving I'm not. "My family didn't even really watch the broadcasts," I say. "When we did, we watched them muted."

"Why did you do that?"

"Well, my siblings . . ." I falter, now wishing I hadn't doubled down, ". . . they'd make up stupid things you guys were saying."

Oh, wonderful. Insulting him. That's even better now. I'm just about ready to dissolve right into this carpet when I hear Chapter laughing.

"That's incredible," he breathes out. He turns to go down the hall, nodding to me. "Come, I need to hear more about this."

The kitchen Chapter takes me to is enormous. From the entrance, I can't take in the whole thing and have to turn to capture all the massive slabs of granite and steel. The appliances are so polished, I can see my own reflection in them. While I take it in, Chapter moves around the space casually. This is a normal room to him, somehow. He prepares black liquid in a clear carafe.

"If your family never really watched the broadcasts, how did you come to this little conclusion that I always drink coffee?" Chapter asks.

He smiles, light, and it reminds me of the photo Abby took of me. Somehow, he looks just like a poster on a fan's locker, every new motion a perfect pose. But the posters usually have him in costume or in a sleek suit. This morning, however, he's still wearing what he slept in: pants of a soft material, a dark gray T-shirt. It occurs to me that this is a rare sight not many are privy to. And then it occurs to me, I'm staring at his clothes, and he's asked me a question.

"I mean, you always were drinking coffee when I'd see you," I say. "I used to wake up early."

"You still do now," he says.

He asks me what I put in my coffee, and I have to admit I've never actually had it before. He prepares both cups the same. As we settle into two stools by the counter, I taste it. A bit too strong for me, but I'm glad to have it. It makes me feel warm.

"Were you from Eldae too?" he asks.

"I was."

"So you were . . ."

I recall what Norax said about the other members. *They were all anomalies like yourself.* I nod, confirming his suspicion. "A glitch, yeah."

He furrows his brow at the word *glitch*. It's not intense, but enough to make me blush and wonder what I've said wrong. "Which generation?"

"Four."

"Ah, the boring group," he says. "Mine was the one with the purple."

Gen 2, I gather, two years above mine. I try to picture Chapter's eyes purple instead of blue, but then I remember that he must've looked *entirely* different then. The thought is a little baffling. I take another sip of the coffee, and it does well to center me.

"How did Norax find you?" Chapter asks.

"She walked up to me."

"That's it?"

"Was it different for you?"

"I mean, I guess not. But she watched me get kicked out of my house first. Asked if I wanted to stay with her instead." He motions with his burgundy mug to the kitchen around us. "Obviously, I did."

"Did you say good-bye to your family?" I ask.

"I wouldn't have wanted to."

He says this so simply, I can't tell if he feels remorse. His tone doesn't carry much in it. My first instinct is to inquire further, but I decide instead to admit the details of my own experience with Norax—how she pulled me away from Westin and Felix when she found me.

He seems surprised by this last bit. "They saw Norax too?"

"They were shocked."

"I bet they were," he says. "They sound terrible." Chapter notices the way I've bristled just talking about them, so lifts his mug to me. "And now they're just memories."

In my peripheral, his hair is catching light, almost golden in the glow. I'm wondering how this moment is actually real when suddenly, it's over—the telltale sound of clacking heels makes us both turn to the kitchen entrance.

"What are you doing here?" Norax asks, gaping. "What is this?"

"It's coffee," Chapter says.

"But you're not supposed to . . ." Her gaze falls on me. "Did he coax you into a confession?"

"We heard all about it on the drive over, Norax," Chapter says. "Couldn't have been a surprise even if you wanted it to be."

"The horrible paparazzi," she mutters. "Tell me, did the others seem keen on meeting her?"

His hesitation before he says something about how they're all *curious* is just long enough for me to want to curl up under the table. He's sugarcoating it, and we know that. Curiosity may as well be another word for outrage.

"Come," Norax tells me. "We have a few hours until our tea party with the members. It's time to give you the tour."

"Okay," I say. "Thank you for the coffee," I tell Chapter.

He smiles and winks. "If you ever want more, you know who to come to."

There are several wings within this massive hideaway mansion, and each has its own colored doors. Behind a pair of green ones, our first stop is a huge indoor gym, with a tennis court on one side and a whole slew of equipment on the other.

"Till practices here," Norax explains.

I'm at first confused, because Till's been photographed at several gyms and courts. But it occurs to me that those visits must be more performative than anything else. *Here*, in the mansion, is where Till can actually practice with no prying eyes.

Next, on the second floor, is a teal door for Race's artist's studio, with rows upon rows of canvases, either blank or completed or half done. It's these last ones that make me excited—no one in the world but him has probably seen these. Not yet, anyway. But somehow I'm here, getting to take my time in examining them, even daring to touch the brushstrokes.

The only painting in his grand collection that's hung on the wall is a surprisingly small one, barely the size of a book, of a woman at a desk. With her cascading dark hair, I wonder if Kaytee posed for it. She isn't facing us, but rather has her attention on something she's writing. It's in his usual style, realistic with an abstract flair, so it's hard to tell what it is. Perhaps one of her songs.

We then move on to another wing, to a room the guards call the viewing room, where the walls are covered ceiling to floor in a massive screen that shows Chapter's movies. Then, the room next door, the *audio* room, with perfect acoustics for listening to music. We're served lunch here as Norax has me listen to a few of Kaytee's albums top to bottom.

"Her voice is just beautiful, isn't it?" she asks.

"It really is," I say.

"Yours is too."

I peg this as an empty compliment until she insists I try singing a few lines of the current song's chorus. Before I know it, the maids serving us are in tears. I don't believe them, so they record it on one of the many devices in the room and play it back for me.

Listening to a singing voice so perfect, it doesn't sound real, I'm forced to recall the white-hot pain I felt on my neck inside the Fissarex. I thought Zoya was only changing the shape of it, but it turns out, she was also hitting my vocal cords—changing my *voice*. When the singing ends and I say, "Is that enough?" I sound absolutely nothing like Emilee Laurence.

"Unreal," a maid whispers.

"You're more than a lumerpa, it seems," says Norax. "You're a songbird!"

When we wander the halls next, I keep putting a hand to my throat and singing, just to hear the vibrations. Had I even *tried* singing when I was Emilee? I might've had a good voice then, too, without even knowing.

The final room she takes me to is one with a mock runway. For

Foster, she explains, to test out his new lines of clothes and see how they'd look in one of his shows.

"All of the Famoux members have rooms special for the light they bring into this world," she tells me. She grabs my hand. "And soon, *you* will too."

As she walks me back to the room to get ready for the tea party, it strikes me how few people in Delicatum had the opportunity to see the private workstations of the Famoux. They are perhaps the most public people in the world, but what I have seen is something special. Something reserved for just them.

Because I'm one of them, I remember. *I'm one of them.*

The preparation for what Norax has been referring to as a *lovely little tea party* is neither little nor lovely. It takes an army of maids to scrub every inch of me in the bathroom, cover me in lotion, and dry and style my hair to perfection. As they work, Norax explains to me how none of this is *necessary*, per se, thanks to the Fissarex, but, "It's just so fun to be pampered, isn't it?"

Fun isn't the word I'd use, but hate isn't either. I'm still not used to people invading my personal space like this, so the right word might be embarrassing. Even so, their excitement is slowly but surely infectious. I find myself smiling along as the whole room cheers over yet another perfectly curled piece of golden hair, as if it wouldn't have curled perfectly every time.

When I emerge from the bathroom, I discover a garment bag hanging proudly by the vanity. Apparently, I've already become a style muse in less than a day. Norax informs me that Swanson stayed up all night making a dress for me. She unzips the bag, revealing soft pink satin.

It is a gorgeous dress. Fitted, but not tight. Somehow just the right shade of pink. Any brighter or paler, and it wouldn't quite work. Emilee would never wear this shade, I'm sure of it. The color would make Brandyce scoff. If I'd seen it in a store, I wouldn't have picked it up.

This reminds me of the plans that lulled me to sleep last night. "Norax?"

"Yes?"

It felt much more reasonable in my head, but much more impractical out loud. "I was wondering . . . Can I check up on my family?"

"Famoux members aren't allowed to interact with their past lives. I told you this."

"I know," I say. "I don't want to interact with them. I just . . . I need to know they're okay."

"Were they in danger when you left?"

"Nothing like that," I insist. "But I want to know what they're doing. How they're coping."

"Lumerpa . . ."

"It's important to me."

Norax considers this. "It's not something we'd want to get into a pattern of doing. Having Famoux guards weeding around your hometown could draw curiosity. But I could send a few under-cover to look. Just once. But I can't guarantee anything. They'd be watching them from afar—not knocking on the front door."

"That's absolutely fine," I say. "That's more than enough."

She has me write the address on her clipboard, then insists we go.

The Fissarex has made it virtually impossible for me to sweat, but I can't stop wiping my hands on the satin as Norax takes me to a new area of the mansion for our tea party. It was a nervous habit I had as Emilee that I suppose has transferred over, even in its futility. I'm glad Swanson isn't here to see it—she'd probably scold me for wrinkling the fabric.

The doors in this new wing are all painted a soft, pretty orange. The color is cheerful enough, but does nothing to calm my nerves, which seem to grow bigger by the second. Maybe it would've been better all around to run into each member separately, like I did Chapter. The other four at once is all too much.

"You've no reason to worry," Norax reminds me. "You're not a fan waiting for a meet and greet today. You're on *their* level."

I don't know if I'll remember this, though, when I see them. I surely couldn't when I saw Chapter.

My stomach does a flip as she turns and opens one of the orange doors, and I half expect all the Famoux members to be standing right there.

Not quite. The first thing I see when we step out is an older, narrow-looking man in a crisp salmon suit.

"*Father*?" Norax gapes.

"Norax," Lennix Geddes greets. "Always a pleasure to see my . . . favorite daughter."

Norax is flustered. She looks every which way, perhaps looking for whoever brought him in. "What are you . . ."

"*This* must be Miss Essence, who I've been hearing so much about?" he asks.

"This is Emeray," she says.

He clicks his tongue. Lennix's cadence is cool and even, unnervingly so. Not a single waver. "I was surprised to see her face in the papers this morning," he says. "Very bold choice to announce a new member barely a month after your last one died on *live television*."

My stomach drops. Norax steps in front of me, putting herself between us. "Do you have a reason for being here?"

"Are you honestly *daft*?" he asks. "Couldn't you have waited a moment before plucking her out of thin air? You're making the Famoux look like a factory, pumping out new members like they're interchangeable! Give a few months before you—"

"Don't tell me how to run my institution," Norax interjects.

"*Your* institution?" Lennix scoffs. "*Sure*. I have a campaign I'm about to announce! I can't have you making the—"

"*Enough*," says Norax. Since she's in front of me, I don't see her face, but I imagine it's terse as she says, "If you want to have a private meeting with me, you can schedule it. You know how."

Before Lennix can say more, Norax leads me through another door into a dark and empty room. For a moment it's deadly silent, and I wonder if I should say something. Then Norax exhales, perturbed, and I know to keep quiet.

"We're fine," she whispers, maybe just to herself. "Right on track."

A control pad materializes, commanding identification to enter the adjoining room. Norax places a palm down on it, then has me do the same. I half expect it to not recognize me, but it does. With a touch, the screen illuminates brightly with my name. Larger locks from within this door unbolt, and before I can even brace myself, it opens.

Bright light from within pours onto us. I have to squint my eyes. Adjusting to the light, objects of exorbitant pomp come into vision: the rosewood floors, the glistening gold chandelier, the ornate table with a vase of white lilies.

Mourning flowers.

Chatter wafts from the room to the left, and my breath catches.

Despite my urge to step back through the metal door and run, Norax moves us forward.

"We've been trying to reach you all morning," one of them tells Norax. I can't tell which one. The tone isn't as gentle as I would've liked. There's a distinct edge to it, just sharp enough to hurt somebody.

"I was helping Emeray get ready," Norax says.

The tone gets even sharper, if that's possible. "Yeah, in *Bree's* bedroom?"

I peer up, and there they are.

In one unit like this, they are absolutely *unreal*. Chiseled, prodded, and perfected by way of the Fissarex. Their outfits, though different styles and colors, somehow match together impeccably. Even though their faces are riddled with worry, my mind instantly tells me to smile, idiotically, and nothing else.

All at once I understand the term *starstruck*.

This last remark about Bree appears to have come from Till Amaris. She's the one staring the biggest daggers at Norax. When she directs her gaze over to me, it feels like I'm being set on fire.

"There are a million rooms in this place," she says. "Why does she have to stay in *Bree's*?"

Although I'm just about ready to disappear into thin air, Norax inhales, remaining leveled. I'm sure the conversation she's just had with Lennix contributes to her brusqueness as she snaps, "Till, *all* of your rooms belonged to the members from the era before you. They're not *yours*. They're made for Famoux members."

"They *retired*!" Till says, unrelenting. "It was different!"

Foster Farrand, who's picking at the pastries on the table, speaks up. "You know, Till, this really doesn't need to be the hill you die on."

She gasps. "*How* can you talk about death so flippantly? After everything that just happened?"

His face puckers up, realizing it.

Just then, a guard steps in from the same door we just came from, whispering something into Norax's ear. I only catch *Lennix*, and she instantly pales.

"I need to step out," she tells us. "Start without me. *Please*, be civil."

Suddenly, such a request seems impossible.

All eyes are on me again, now standing alone. But I get barely a moment to panic before Kaytee McKarrington strides up and hugs me tight. With her arms around me, I see words written all over her dark skin in pink marker. Lyrics for songs. This is something she does often. I recall fans at school always squinting their eyes at her paparazzi pictures, trying to read them and get a hint at her next hit single.

"Sit with me," she says when she pulls back.

"Really?"

"Of *course*." Then, "Your eyes are the prettiest blue I've ever seen in my life!"

Kaytee's acceptance cuts the tension in the room, albeit just a small amount. I end up at the edge of the table, between her and the empty spot at the head where Norax should be. Directly across from my seat is Chapter, who pours tea into my cup and offers a knowing smile.

"Cream or sugar?" he asks.

"However you like it," I say.

He prepares the tea, and I wonder if he's mentioned to anyone how we've already run into each other this morning. It doesn't seem like it.

At first, conversation is sparse and limited to comments on the food. I don't want to so much as glance over at the other end of the table where Till is, fearful of what she'll say next. We carry on like this for a good while until Foster takes an especially loud sip of his tea, drawing all eyes over to him.

"Now this," he laughs, "is *hands down* one of the best teatimes I've ever been a part of."

"Don't be foolish," Till murmurs.

Foster rolls his eyes. "Why are you being so weird about this? You didn't even *like* Bree!"

"How dare you!"

"I'm not saying I'm a saint! I didn't either!" he admits. "I mean, the only one of us who actually tolerated the girl was Chapter."

Surprised, I look to Chapter for confirmation, but his head is down now, his blue eyes looking deep into the swirling contents of his teacup.

"I'm just saying," Foster continues. "Bree was going to make her film debut with Chapter, right? That was about to be a bigger hit than *Riot!*? Why are we pretending Till wouldn't want her dead?"

"Foster!" Till shouts. "Bree and I were competitive, of course. But I wouldn't—I'd never wish—" She puts a hand to her mouth, tears springing up in her eyes.

"Oh, great," murmurs Race from the other side of Kaytee. He takes a sip of his tea and shakes his head, like this is their regular routine. "You've made Till cry. Again."

"I was just stating facts," Foster says.

"You can state them delicately," he says. "There are no cameras around, man. Who are you trying to impress?"

Watching them quarrel like this really *does* feel like the cameras are around, and I'm seeing them on my television. Granted, most of the time I couldn't hear what they were shouting about on my screen at home, but this is hardly the first time I've seen Foster angered or Till crying.

And for the topic of discussion to be *me*?

Kaytee reaches out to Till, sympathetic. "Honey, we don't think you wanted Bree dead." She looks to Foster. "*None* of us does, right?"

"Fine," Foster says. "I just don't get why she's so bent out of shape about . . ." He looks to me, suddenly lost. "What is your name again?"

"It's obviously too soon!" Till exclaims. She looks to Chapter. "How are you so silent about this? Don't you have anything to say about your girlfriend's *replacement*?"

"Till," Chapter starts, "Bree didn't—"

"It's okay if you think it's too soon," Till tells him. "You don't have to be stoic about it."

Chapter falters, raking a hand through his hair to compose himself. Meanwhile, I'm searching my memory for any time where Bree Arch and Chapter Stones were ever rumored to be dating. But there's nothing. Last I recalled, Chapter was never tied down to anybody.

"I doubt Norax wanted the world to find out about this so fast," Chapter says, voice leveled. "But they found out. There's no use complaining about it now."

It occurs to me that he might *want* to complain. If Bree was his girlfriend, he certainly must. I feel a sudden wave of embarrassment over earlier this morning. How horrible it must have been for him to make me coffee and entertain my stories, when all the while . . .

I finally meet his gaze, but it's unreadable. He looks down at his cup.

"She obviously joined this group for a reason," Foster says. "Same reason as us. To get away from the bad stuff. Too early or not, cut her some slack, Till."

Till is still crying. I don't know what I've done to provoke this. Beside me, Kaytee lowers her voice to address only her, but she's no match for my years of listening in on other people's conversations. "I know you feel guilty, but it's over. We *know* it's over. The least we can do is welcome Emeray in, right?"

Till wipes her tears and manages a nod. Without another word she rises and exits the room. Teatime is over. This is how my grand meeting with the Famoux has gone.

I can't help but wonder how much better it could've been if it had happened a month or so from now, like Lennix mentioned before we entered.

On the way out of the room, I want to catch up with Chapter, maybe say something about Bree, but Kaytee wraps her arm around me and pulls me away. "Hey. Don't worry too much about Till, okay? She's competitive. And you're just *so* beautiful."

Before I can utter a thank-you, Foster Farrand is on my other side. "She's right. You have the best face I've ever seen," he decides. "I want to do a photoshoot with you."

If they're trying to make me forget how rough that tea party was, they're succeeding. As they lead me through the maze of hallways toward my room, they keep me distracted with lofty future plans of magazine covers and runway shows. Foster uses wild, redundant hand gestures to prove his points.

"Picture it. The two of us on the side of the biggest building in Betnedoor, wearing absolute killer leather jackets. Don't you see it?"

Just the mere thought of a photo of Foster and me being pasted to the side of a building, like all the ones I've seen before, nearly sends me reeling.

"What a bright future for style," Kaytee chuckles.

"Oh, no. It's a *dark* future for style. Did you even hear a thing I just said?"

Foster's fun nature fills me with a sense of ease. Famoux fans think of him as candid and playful, which is exactly how he's shown himself to be so far. It's magnificent to see that most of their personalities have rung true, even without the cameras. I was a tad nervous they'd turn out to be something other than what the public thinks they are. But so far, they have it down pretty well: Foster, *playful*. Kaytee, *sweet*. Till, *headstrong*. Race, *earnest*. Chapter, *mysterious*.

*And what am I?* I wonder.

It's too soon to say. I guess I'll have to find out with the rest of the world.

# CHAPTER SEVEN

"You're at an after-party for a movie premiere. Crowded club with an open bar—you know, the whole thing. Now, some hotshot singer you happen to recognize walks up to you. Say it's . . . What singer do you *really* like?"

I blanch. "I don't know."

"Too many favorites?"

"I don't . . . listen to anyone."

Lennix Geddes pinches the bridge of his nose. It's not the first time he's done this today, and likely won't be the last. He rises from his chair and paces the room, defeated.

"Norax, sweetheart, there's not much we can do here," he calls out. "She barely passes as a regular member of society, much less a *notable* one."

The sting of his remark burns my cheeks. We've been in this sterile sitting room next door to the Analytix—the Control Room, they call it—all day, practicing etiquette. These lessons are going to be, as Lennix says, the first of many steps in doing damage control on me.

From the end of the table, buried in a heap of magazines plastered with my face, Norax glances up, annoyed. "I already *told* you she didn't follow other celebrities before joining," she says to her father. "You're just asking her that to make her feel bad."

"She should be doing her homework," Lennix insists. "From now on, she studies celebrities."

When Norax was pulled out of the teatime by Lennix, I am told they discussed how he will be working closely with us for a few days to mend this rocky start. Normally, he doesn't meddle with Norax's Famoux, but he is only a month or so away from announcing his campaign for Delicatum's sovereign, and if his life's work looks as dysfunctional as it is now—a dead member, a new one leaked too soon—voters might speculate that he won't run our country well. It is imperative to him that the Famoux is still seen as a well-managed, cohesive unit. It seems irrational to me, since he isn't the manager anymore, but I wouldn't admit it. When he explained it all to me this morning, I nodded, obedient.

This is only our first day of lessons, but as far as I've gathered, Lennix Geddes is a man who *looks* proper, but speaks with a vulgar cynicism only a man who has spent years studying popular culture could have. He has a penchant for peppermint tea, and has had five cups of it already before noon. He's paid me no compliments on anything but my appearance, which he credits to the Fissarex, his creation. Besides my newfound beauty, I'm certain he hates me. Despises me, really. As Norax told me before, he didn't like the idea of making mutation glitches like me Famoux members, which leads me to believe he doesn't share her belief that I'm a *miracle*. No, as far as Lennix is concerned, I am a mistake, especially now that he's discovering just how socially inept I am. To Lennix, I'm ruining his chances of becoming sovereign.

For our first lesson, Lennix wants to skip the basics and get an overview of what he's dealing with. He's drilling me on scenarios I might find myself in and judging my gut reactions. It's clear by the way he phrases them that he doesn't want me to answer correctly.

"Okay. It doesn't *matter* what singer," Lennix says. He stirs his tea, the sixth cup now. "Picture any non-Famoux celebrity walking up. They start flirting. What do you do?"

Just the idea makes me flush. "Are they complimenting me?"

"Sure." He leans in close. "They're telling you how *gorgeous* you are. Especially those eyes . . ."

"You're baiting her," Norax calls out.

"Will they *not* be baiting her?" he asks. When he sees her roll her eyes, he adds, "If I don't go through these scenarios with Miss No-Human-Interaction over here, she'll fall in love with the first loser who tells her she's pretty. And *then* she'll tell him all our secrets and burn this show down, would you like that?"

"You're paranoid," Norax says.

"You should be."

It's hard to believe they're even related, the way they process things so differently. While Norax has always approached me with such patience and kindness, Lennix opts for the opposite. It's a wonder that his eras of the Famoux were known to be friendlier and more united than Norax's. It doesn't seem plausible.

"Tell me, what do you do?" Lennix asks me again.

"Well, I guess I'd thank them?"

"Don't ask me, tell me."

"I'd thank them," I say, firmer. I wrack my brain for the right option. What would *Lennix* think is the right answer? "And then I would walk away, so they don't think I'm overly interested."

"You'd walk away, just like that?" he asks. "No good-bye?"

"No, I'd—"

Lennix's eyes narrow, challengingly. "Oh, my bad. I forgot that you don't know *how* to say good-bye. You just up and left your family without a word—that must feel natural to you, right?"

"That's *enough*," Norax snaps.

I have to grip the edge of my chair to stop the tears from forming in my eyes. Still, a few spill out.

"There we go," Lennix says. He points to my tears, satisfied with his work. "Norax, she can't control her emotions. What'll she do when someone calls her ugly on the red carpet?"

But Lennix doesn't know the abuse thrown at me on a daily basis back in Eldae. Jabs about my appearance, I can mostly tune out. It's the only part of me where I have a somewhat thick skin. But the comment about my family was too far. Anything that deals with the past is a fresh, tender bruise and no person on the red carpet would know to say something about it—that, I'm sure of. And even if they did, it's not like they'd throw me in the creek afterward.

When Lennix brings the lesson to its conclusion, I can't get back to Bree's bedroom fast enough. It's a testament to his teaching style that I find myself longing to return here, though the fear in the air has all but diminished. I burrow my face into a pillow, thinking I might scream. But I don't. I keep crying. Lennix isn't throwing me into rivers, sure, but he's playing Westin's game all the same. Trying to make me feel small, inadequate. Only this time, it's not on account of my eyes. It's everything else.

At some point in my crying, Norax wanders in and sits at my

bedside. She says nothing but *sorry* and *don't listen to him* while she plays with my hair, and it makes me feel like I'm eight years old again, being comforted after a long, hard day with Westin.

And here I thought being in the Famoux would mark the end of that.

The next day, I resolve to be better. Control my emotions. Lennix is one man, whereas Westin had a whole band of people behind him. And with Norax on my side, not his, the scale is already tipped in my favor. But breakfast throws me off when I run into Till and Foster. He's kind and cordial to me as usual, showing me how to make his favorite oatmeal, but Till pointedly ignores me, only vaguely acknowledging my pink coffee mug: "Bree used that one. Hmm." It takes a single small comment from Lennix on how I'll never live up to Bree Arch to make me tear up. And then he leans back and grins. Another victory for him.

Later that afternoon, we practice walking and posture. I'm a natural at the latter, thanks to the Fissarex. Whereas Emilee used to slouch into herself and hide, it's as if my new shoulders couldn't turn in that way if they wanted to. It's the walking I struggle with. Too fast, and I'll seem unfriendly. Too slow, and I'm awkward. Under Lennix's gaze, of course, I never find the right balance.

"You look like you're running from something," he critiques. To Norax, "Is that how she looked? When she ran away from her family?"

I grit my teeth and slow my pace.

The next morning we focus on fan interactions. Making celebrity friends, Lennix claims, is easy. As far as he's observed, no one actually likes one another, but pretends to for the sake of looking good. It's the fans who will be the most genuine relationships I'll have.

"Any celebrity who's lasted more than a month are the ones

who made friends with their fans," he tells me. "Musicians, actors, they're a dime a dozen. Fans find new ones. But if they *like* you, they stay." He looks me up and down with distaste. "And now, we have the task of making you likable."

It'd feel more like an insult if I didn't fully agree that this will be difficult. I've never made a friend in my life. Kaytee, Foster, and Chapter were all friendly, but I didn't do anything to warrant their friendliness. I don't know how it goes—how you approach someone and hold small talk and leave feeling enriched by it. As we go through scenarios like my first lesson, I'm lost.

"You're on your way into an interview that starts in five minutes, but a fan outside the studio yells for you to come back. You didn't give her a hug," Lennix starts. "Do you go back?"

Does the Famoux stop for everyone? I swear I remember seeing videos where they breezed right past the crowds. But did I only see those videos because their fans were angry about it?

"Yes," I decide. "I'd go back."

"Okay. And now, thirty more fans are saying the same thing. They're forming a line. Are you going to hug them all? You're already running late."

"I— Is that going to happen?"

Lennix looks at his wristwatch. "Oh, the interview is starting. You'll never be booked for this show again."

"But won't they be mad—" I start.

"You're exiting the same way," he says, like it's obvious. "Your fans already know that if they wait, they'll see you again."

"Oh."

"They're not your little siblings, Emeray," Lennix sneers. "They're not going to sit around and wonder why you've abandoned them."

"I don't have little siblings," I say.

"Well, that explains a lot. Maybe if you did, you'd know how to take care of something."

"Father," Norax warns. "Enough. Don't you have a flight to catch?"

He does. Lucky for me, today is the last of our lessons for a while. Lennix will be leaving the mansion for sometime on business in Notness—sorting out deals with company owners for endorsements on his sovereign campaign. After this one-on-one time with him I am less certain I would ever want him to run Delicatum one day, but if this trip means he's gone for a while, I'll happily take it.

"I expect these lessons to continue in my absence," Lennix tells his daughter. "Unless you want to throw an actress in your little box and make her look like this. Save us a load of time . . ."

This last comment sends me off to my room fuming. I pass Till on the way there, who addresses me coldly. I don't understand her problem with me. She doesn't need to remind me that I'm here too early—the entire world is already doing that for her. I've been checking the Analytix every day, and it's only getting worse.

Norax brings lunch up to my room. I wish she'd leave it by the door and walk away, but she stays, settling down on my bed beside me, ready to comfort me again. Embarrassment burns in me like a fire. Perhaps I start crying in hopes it'll snuff it out, but it only makes me more embarrassed. All I've shown Norax this week is that I don't know how to carry myself in social situations and can cry at the drop of a hat. If she didn't believe Lennix in the beginning when he said I was a bad choice, she almost certainly does now. As she pats my head, I know she must be regretting this. Like my mother, she must be planning an escape.

"Lumerpa," she says. "I'm so sorry. He's only being harsh on you to punish me."

But I know Lennix wouldn't be this harsh if I excelled in his training. If I had the easy kindness I saw in Kaytee at the tea party, or Till's iron resolve, or the magnetism Chapter seems to command on instinct. If I was witty and fun to be around like Foster, or quiet in a brooding, important way like Race. Then, Lennix would be chastising Norax only for the fact that my name leaked early. *That* would be the mistake, not *me*.

But I am awkward and unsure of myself. I don't have what comes to them so easily.

"Did you watch Lennix's eras of the Famoux?" Norax asks.

"Not closely," I admit.

"They were members who always said and did the right things. Who got along perfectly. Flawless." She shakes her head. "He claims he retired them because they were getting older, but the truth is, the world kept getting bored of flawless. They *want* flaws."

"But Famoux members are perfect," I say.

"They're perfect in their own, *unique* ways," Norax says. "Not the same boring shade. And you will be perfect in your way too."

But how?

As Norax plays with my hair, she explains how she thinks *newness* could be my defining quality. "You were brought onto the scene so suddenly, it should be natural that you don't know how to handle yourself in every situation. You might slip up sometimes. You're not perfect. People will like that. They'll see themselves in you as you figure it out. And when you're not new anymore, you'll still have your youth. Your naivety, as the youngest."

"I'm only two years younger," I say.

"A couple of years can make a difference."

I have to admit, I like her idea. If there was a Famoux member like the one Norax thinks I can be, I'm sure that member would be my favorite. Someone empathetic. Approachable within the unapproachable Famoux way.

I tell her this, and she agrees. "Of course, my father won't listen," she says. "He's so backward in his methods."

"Who is?" asks a soft, familiar voice.

I sit up straight. There's Kaytee McKarrington, skipping toward me in a bright, blue dress. And while I'm still sort of crying. Great.

"I haven't seen you in ages!" she exclaims. "Are those tears? Here, come here." When she reaches us, she hugs me, and just like at the tea party I see a line of lyrics scrawled across one of her forearms. Something for one of her love songs. "This has to be so stressful for you. I heard what they've been saying in the tabloids." She notices me wince at this and changes course with ease, gesturing to the room around us. I can almost see Lennix applauding her expertise in my head. "Have you been cooped up in here every day?"

I sputter through a poor explanation of my last three days of etiquette classes, which I'm sure only further proves their necessity. All the while, Kaytee listens, visibly engrossed. Did *she* ever need lessons to be this way? It slightly frustrates me just watching her.

"That sounds dreadful," Kaytee says. "Norax, do you think she could take a break? Grab a coffee at Wes Tegg's with me?" She notices the tray Norax has set on my nightstand. "Or maybe another time?"

I know Wes Tegg's. Everyone does. The Famoux's favorite

place to stop by on their walks around Waltmar. When classmates used to muse about weekend trips to Betnedoor, half the plans involved camping out there. A sure way to see them.

"Kaytee, Emeray really shouldn't—" but then Norax stops herself. I see the wheels turning in her head. Lennix isn't here anymore; his car was waiting for him before we left the Control Room, and for all we know, he could be already in the air on the way to Notness. If there was ever a time to prove this *new, youthful* angle, it would be now. "You know what? Yes."

"Are you sure?" I ask.

"Don't talk to paparazzi. Don't leave Kaytee's side. Be in and out quickly. It should work."

I'm reminded of the chaos I encountered when I stepped out of the car last time. All the lights and screaming . . .

Kaytee nudges my arm. "It's not nearly as scary with a friend by your side. You'll love it, I promise."

They leave me in my room to get ready. At first I'm stressed, thinking about the lights and the cameras, but after a while of searching through racks and racks, my stress transforms into excitement. I'm picking out an outfit to wear to go to coffee with Kaytee McKarrington. Somehow this is a realistic situation in my life.

It is unmistakably Emeray Essence who smiles back at me in the tight black pants and burgundy sweater I've fished from a drawer of cashmere things. Emeray's body, but Emilee's brain. Somehow, this combination is going to work.

It has to.

As I'm picking out a pair of umber boots, which have the lowest heel of my whole selection, I'm interrupted by a low voice. Chapter's voice.

"Are you going somewhere?"

I look up from the laces. He's leaning against the door frame, clad in black slacks and a dark gray coat, like he's just been out. Everything I heard at the tea party about him and Bree comes back to me. A million apologies brim up on my tongue, but all that comes out is, "I—um—is it cold out there?"

"A bit," Chapter says. He looks down at his hand, where a black winter hat looks to be dusted in snow. "I mean, quite a bit, actually."

I try to concentrate on my shoes, but it's hard to, with Chapter across the room. He has an air about him that makes it impossible not to look. I suppose it's why they put him on the big screen.

"Where are you headed?" he asks.

"Wes Tegg's," I say. "With Kaytee."

"You're getting coffee?" Chapter can't help but grin. "You're always having that."

I hope he can't see my blush from all the way over here. Do Famoux members even visibly blush? I can imagine that kind of telling emotional trait might be erased by the Fissarex. At least, I can hope so.

When I'm done with my shoes, I see that Chapter is looking at a vase of flowers on one of the many onyx dressers. "There used to photos here," he observes.

Right. This was *Bree's* room. The ache creeping up on his face makes me want to disappear.

"I'm sorry," I say.

"Why are *you* sorry?"

"I know it's uncomfortable. I had no idea you and Bree were . . . If I knew, I would've—"

"We weren't dating," Chapter says.

"But the members—"

"I was her only friend here," he says. Chapter inspects the vanity now, with its bone-white wood and massive mirror. He meets my gaze through it. "Bree was hard to get to know, but I already knew her."

"Already?"

"We were neighbors. Before the Famoux."

My eyes widen. "How is that possible?"

"Norax found Bree first. Bree told her about me," he says. "We don't talk much about past lives in the Famoux, but Bree and I already knew each other's, so we kept together. The others assumed that meant something. I loved her, of course, but it wasn't like that."

I can't read Chapter's expression fully, but I can tell he's thinking of a memory, replaying a moment as he looks at the vase where photos used to be. There's an ache there that makes the scabs of my own past feel like they're being picked at.

"It's hard to lose someone who knows you," I say. "Who *really* knows you."

"Been through it too?" Chapter asks.

"My mother. She ran away."

My candor surprises me. I didn't expect to say it, but Chapter has the kind of face you want to reveal secrets to. Maybe that makes him trustworthy, or maybe it makes him treacherous. Either way, my heart jolts at the mention of my mom, and I have to look away from him.

From the hallway beyond us, I can hear "*Emeray!*" being called out by Kaytee, whose footfall grows louder as she reaches the door.

"Ready to go?" Kaytee asks.

"I think so," I say. The nerves of what I'm about to do kick in again as I grab the first coat I see in my closet and shrug it on. It's a bit too big, but that's fine. My corduroy jacket from back home used to be a little too big for me too. It's almost a comfort.

On the way out, Chapter stops me. Even through my coat and the sweater, the contact of his hand on my arm sends a spark through me.

"Bring this," he says, holding out his snow-covered cap for me to take.

"But it's yours," I say.

He shrugs. "Maybe you'll need it."

# CHAPTER EIGHT

The lights are going wild. We haven't even set foot outside the car yet, but through the blackout windows they persist, making the glitter on Kaytee's skirt twinkle.

"Wow," my bodyguard Gerald breathes out from the front seat. The crowds are as foreign to him as they are to me. "Look at all those *lights*."

No one had to tell the paparazzi we were coming; they knew. The moment a car leaves the Famoux hideaway, hidden photographers like vultures seem to descend on it, following it ceaselessly to whatever its destination. This is why, Norax believes, my identity was leaked to the public so quickly. Even though our vehicle took several unnecessary loops and exits and tunnels on our way into Waltmar to prevent it, her small visit to the mansion put them on the scent.

I fiddle with the knitted pattern on the hat Chapter gave me, trying to ignore the fact that my hands are trembling uncontrollably. The lights are surely frightening, but it's the roaring commotion, above all else, that has me the most scared. It had been the worst part about getting caught in the alleyway—all the screaming and shouting. Granted, their presence had been a surprise then. I wasn't expecting it. But I'm surely expecting it today.

Before we left, Norax gave me a few pointers for my smile, which has to be just right—what with all the magazine covers it'll be on. "Make it as bashful as you can," she told me. "The world needs to believe it. *Lennix* needs to believe it."

Kaytee has helped me practice this smile a few times in her compact mirror on the way over. I'm not sure if I have it down, but I guess I'll have to. The car is slowing to a stop in front of the café right now. As it reaches the curb, she lets out a squeal.

"I *love* making history on a regular afternoon," she says. "Don't you?"

"I . . . never have."

*But I guess I'm about to.*

Bold and unfazed, Kaytee surfaces from the car first. Gerald and I exchange alarmed glances as the volume outside increases tenfold. For whatever overwhelming mile we are about to brace when we step out of the car, we're already floundering in an inch of it.

I put on Chapter's hat. There's no more time to waste. It's our turn to join the circus.

"Are you ready?" Gerald asks me.

"I hope so," I say.

He exits first, coming around to my door to escort me out. I take a long deep breath, then the plunge.

All at once, the roar for Kaytee turns into something bigger. My name ripples across the mass like a resounding chorus, only everyone is singing it brash and off-key. Camera clicks ring out, rapid-fire, and shouts build into screams so loud I can barely hear anything anymore. I can't tell if they're happy, or mad, or anything, and it's so bright that I can't see their faces. It's hard to know what the response is at all.

"She's here!"

"She's with Kaytee! She's got to be—"

"Emeray Essence, over here!"

*Over where?* Trying my best to follow Norax's advice, I look around, and the lights meet me everywhere. Black splotches dance across my vision. I can't make out a single thing, but I smile at them anyway. All of them. The muscles in my face ache almost instantly.

Gerald is stunned by the whole ordeal too, and another Famoux guard grabs my arm, pushing me to walk right through the pandemonium. He hollers at the photographers until there's a sudden clearing, and without any care for my balance I am shoved through it, straight into the café's doors.

Like a flash, it's over. The café is playing soft music, the chaos now a murmur through the walls. I'm left wondering if I smiled enough, or too much. Norax will let me know in due time.

"You made it!" Kaytee exclaims. "That wasn't so bad, right?"

Gerald is beside himself. "Not so bad? How do you *ever* get used to that?"

At first I believed this café had to be empty, but the awed silence of the entire room is but an occupational hazard for a Famoux member. Nearly every table is filled, and every eye at them is on us as Kaytee leads me toward the corner of the room. I keep my head ducked down, hoping to hide, but it's no use. They're all staring. Maybe I actually prefer the chaotic anonymity of the crowds outside to something as intimate as this. I feel like

I'm Emilee Laurence again, walking down the hall on the way to class. I'm too busy thinking about this to even realize that Kaytee's sitting me down at a table.

"Wait, aren't we just ordering at the counter and leaving?" I ask.

Kaytee shifts on her feet. "Well . . ."

"*Is that my girl?*"

Just then, a young man wraps his arms around Kaytee, twirling her around in the space between our table and a group of young school kids. The kids look like they're about to faint, and I don't blame them: this is Cartney Kirk—Kaytee's megafamous musician boyfriend.

I've only ever seen them together in photographs. In person, they're like a perfect painting. He pulls her into a tender kiss, and I find myself wondering if I'd ever seen my own parents treat one another with such affection.

"You must be the girl of the hour, huh? I like the hat." Cartney extends a hand out to me, taking a seat.

I gape at him. I've already done *far* more talking than I was supposed to on this trip. Now, I'm expected to sit down in this crowded café and hold a conversation?

I look to Kaytee, desperate, but she's sitting down too. "I thought it'd be nice if you two met," she says. "Can't we stay for just a few minutes?"

I want to explain to her my grave unpreparedness for this kind of social interaction, but there are so many eyes on us, evaluating our every move, I know I can't. I paste on the smile I've been practicing and sit. In a flash, a waitress is there to take our order. This isn't even a café with table service, but I suppose such a thing exists everywhere for the Famoux.

The *just a few minutes* turns out to be several. Far more than I'd prefer. Considering how much I genuinely like Kaytee, and how much I genuinely felt their love when Cartney Kirk first entered, I'm stunned by how little a liking I take to him. It's clear that the proximity to the Famoux has gone to his head: he oozes a sense of superiority over almost everyone, going on long monologues about himself and his life journey. I guess I'm lucky that he's so talkative, though. It means less opportunity for me to embarrass myself. I get a lot of practice keeping quiet and grinning until my cheeks hurt.

"So." Cartney takes a long sip of his drink. It's a vanilla latte. His favorite, I've been told. "We're going to be recording a little something with you soon, right?"

"What?"

"Cartney!" Kaytee whispers, but loud enough so the room can hear. "What are you talking about?"

"That's why we're all here, isn't it? To talk about a song?" he asks. "I heard Norax on the phone with Buchan about it."

"Whatever it is, it's not set in stone yet." Kaytee punches his arm playfully. "Keep your voice down!"

"Nah, let it leak. The other musicians better know about the threat now," he says. "A song with all three of us would probably *demolish* the charts."

I laugh along with them, but my eyes are on the door, where Gerald and the other guards are waiting. I'm sure Norax is wondering why we haven't left yet. Her instructions were so clear. In and out. Minimal talking . . .

"Does this mean you're going to be a musician from now on, *Ray*?" Cartney asks, using an odd nickname for me he has decided will stick.

"I don't know," I say. "I want to try everything right now."

"If I were you, do you know what I'd do?"

"What?" I ask.

"*Nothing.*"

"You're already doing that," murmurs Kaytee. "You haven't made a new album in over a year."

Cartney's grip on his cup tightens. He plays it cool for onlookers, but I can tell a new tension has surfaced between them. "I'm letting the inspiration take me wherever it wants, *dear.*"

Waiters come around with free pastries to give us, and Cartney declines, his face suddenly sour. I'd assume this would mark the end of our meeting, but no such luck. The moment the waiters leave, Cartney launches into a long soliloquy about his meteoric rise to fame.

It started three years ago, when he was just a new artist at his record label, Buchan. This was around the time the Famoux started their new era, so he and Kaytee got together at the start of their careers. They've been topping the charts together ever since. It's a story I've heard a million times before in the hallways at school, but I couldn't tell him that. As I've been warned by Lennix, the world needs to think I've been homeschooled, since Emeray Essence has never existed on a real class roster.

As he tells the story, Kaytee chimes in a few times to make corrections. "It was actually your solo album," she says after he's told me about a project called, of all things, *Kaytee.* "I was featured on some songs, but it's yours."

"Technicalities," he murmurs. "When *will* we be doing that duo album, then?"

"Soon," she promises.

Though trying to conceal it, the tables around us twitter with excitement.

As he goes in depth about his fourth studio album, called, of all things, *McKarrington*, it occurs to me that if I can't escape through the front door, I can certainly make a break for the bathroom. I excuse myself.

On my way back, I run into two girls who don't look to be much younger than me. Maybe I don't run into them, though. Judging by the magazines and pens they're both holding, it looks like they planned this encounter.

"Are you Emeray Essence?" one asks.

For a moment I forget to speak. Being approached in a public area has always meant bad news for me. One of Westin's friends finding me in the wild. But then I remember who I am, and I nod.

"Yes," I say. "That's my name."

Just like that, any calmness they were managing cracks, erupting into a choir of yelps. "Could we please get a photo?" the other asks.

Just like that, I forget who I am again. "With *me*?"

"Yes!" She holds out a silver device. "We love you, like, *so* much!"

They *do*? How? Staggered, all I can think to do is says, "I—I love you too!"

This gets a whole extra round of squeals. I doubt I'm being composed enough for Lennix's liking, but I don't think these fans notice or care. Gerald, who made his way back when he saw people approach me, playfully grabs the girl's device, and he takes the calmest series of photos I've experienced all day.

As they gush to me about how exciting this is, I notice a small line of people has now gathered, waiting their turn. The scenario Lennix proposed earlier jumps into my mind. Do I stop for them all? One look at their faces, so light and happy to see *me*, and I decide, yes. I'll take every photo until the line's finished and try to enjoy it.

I barely even have to speak—they walk up, we pose, and then they hug me, thank me, and leave. They seem to know this drill, like they do it every day with celebrities. For me, it all feels something like a strange, impossible dream. It wasn't long ago at all that I was being thrown straight into rivers. And *now*?

"Emeray, we're going," Kaytee calls out to me. The line of people waiting wail at this, but Kaytee has the answer. She has Gerald take a group photo of all of us, including her and Cartney, much to everyone's delight. As we leave the café, it hits me just how good she is at appeasing masses.

Out in the commotion of paparazzi flashes, Cartney bids us good-bye. He pulls Kaytee into a rigid hug and a long kiss that makes the cameras go crazy. As she ducks into the car, he moves on to me, plucking my hand from my side and giving it its own kiss. This is a whole bigger performance for him, I realize. Everyone's eating it up.

"It was *lovely* to meet you, Ray," he says.

I narrow my eyes. "Why Ray?"

"We're friends," he insists. "Friends give each other nicknames, don't they?"

The whole ride home, Kaytee can't stop apologizing about her boyfriend's behavior. "He never knows how to act around Famoux members," she tells me. "He's far too proud to feel comfortable in a room where he isn't the most important person, so he overdoes it."

"What about when he's just with you?"

"What do you mean?" she asks innocently.

"You're a Famoux member too. Does he act differently when it's just you?"

She doesn't seem to understand the query. She shakes it away, sharing ideas for the song we'll split between the three of us. She thinks perhaps I can learn to play the piano for it. She'll provide the guitar. The people, she says, will love it.

The first person Kaytee and I see when we enter through the foyer is Foster, emerging from the kitchen, eating grapes. He regards us with wide cobalt eyes. "Well *that* was a pretty long coffee run," he says.

Kaytee lets out an exasperated sigh. "If we could've gotten out of there sooner, we would've."

"Yikes," says Foster. "Was the coffee that bad?"

"No, I always love Wes Tegg's."

Foster nods. "Ah. Right. It was *Emeray*."

Just beyond us, Race emerges from another hallway. He has barely enough time to speak, much less open his arms before Kaytee barrels straight into them like they haven't seen each other in years. She buries her face into the side of his neck, kisses him, and he lifts her up in their embrace so that her feet dangle above the ground.

I'm wholly stunned. But Foster doesn't seem surprised at all. He continues eating his grapes, like it's nothing. When Kaytee and Race finally pull apart from their embrace, she tells him, "Cartney's gotten worse, if it's even possible."

"Did he check himself out in his silverware?"

"Constantly."

Beside me, Foster murmurs in my ear, "Must be pretty nice to come home to somebody like that, am I right?"

"Wait. They're together?"

"Oh, you didn't know? It started back in the beginning," Foster says. "Before I even got here, actually. They liked each other immediately."

"But what about Cartney?"

Foster hesitates. "Well, she's not really *with* Cartney. It's the contract."

A dating contract, it appears. Foster explains that she signed it under the assurance from Norax that it was a good career move. Solidified an ally in Buchan, the record company.

"But now the contract's always getting renewed, and she and Cartney are far too popular as a unit," he says. "People would lose it if they ever broke up."

"Will they have to keep renewing it forever?" I ask.

"Certainly appears that way."

As Kaytee talks to Race, her hand absently traces his, and I realize she didn't hold Cartney's at Wes Tegg's at all. In fact, the moment they sat down, their act deteriorated in front of my eyes. Their strange behavior from this afternoon now makes sense. I can't help but think about the painting on Race's studio wall. The girl with the dark hair, writing something. It *has* to be Kaytee. Perhaps she was signing the contract.

"It's nice they have the hideaway," Foster says with a low whistle. "Some of us aren't as lucky."

When I ask him what he means, he grows bashful, the most I've seen him be so far. As it appears, he's got somebody back home he writes letters to.

"Norax lets you talk to somebody from your old life?" I ask.

"Technically, she doesn't know I'm writing these letters," he says. Then winks. "I've got a good deal with our mail person."

For a moment I think about sending a letter to my family, explaining everything, but then Foster reveals his love, a man named Finley, doesn't know where he is now. "As far as he knows, *Scott* has run away from our town and will never return. Which makes sense. People didn't like me too much."

I couldn't send them a letter. Not just to tell them I ran. They'd never forgive me. They wouldn't even forgive me if I told them the truth.

"Is it hard to lie to Finley?" I ask.

He shrugs. "It'd be harder not to write."

For a group so highly publicized—not to mention *constantly* scrutinized when inside the Fishbowl—it's interesting to see that so many of them have great, inconceivable secrets.

I want to hear more about Foster and Finley, and how their dynamic works, but then Norax enters the foyer and grabs my arm. "*There* you are," she says, exasperated. "We need to get you to the Analytix! People are talking."

My breath catches. "Does Lennix . . ."

"I haven't heard anything from him yet," she says. "But I'm sure we will soon."

Kaytee joins our trip to the Analytix, announcing how she'd like to see *how much they all love me now.* I hope she's right. We all cram into the room together—them on one side of the glass, me on the other.

Even though I know it's coming this time, the voices startle me again when they pop out of the silence. The first is from a news station, the anchor reporting to viewers that, according to the evidence, I certainly must be a confirmed Famoux member.

"*It's either that or she's got very, very prominent friends!*"

Next he brings up how charming it was that I smiled at the cameras. Apparently, most Famoux members throw on a smolder and walk right past them.

"*Bree, especially,*" he says. "*Does everyone remember the glares she'd give us?*"

My heart surges with victory. Norax was right! My smile was

spot on. That's something, albeit something small, that sets me apart from Bree.

As the man's voice fades out to bring in new ones, a curious numbered list pixelates out of thin air and right in front of my eyes. It is constructed of specks of shimmering copper dust. I reach out to touch it, but my hand goes right through it.

Comprising this list are seven names, printed neatly, in one straight column:

1 – Roman
2 – Quinn
3 – Odette
4 – Scott
5 – Holden
6 – Emilee
7 – ~~Tiffany~~

My eyes widen at the sight of *Emilee*. And Foster just told me his name used to be Scott.

The old names of the Famoux members?

As the Analytix continues its report, the list order fluctuates, *Emilee* dropping up and down depending on the conversation's consensus. A group of friends deliberating over the photographs together brings my name up to the fifth spot. But then, a few broadcast hosts commenting on my reaction to the paparazzi seeming fake brings it down to spot six again. Then, there's a whole long gaggle of Kaytee's fans making a stir about the photos I took with the fans in the café, which brings me back up to the fifth spot again. All the while, the other names in front of mine are going crazy, dethroning and rethroning one another at the top spots for reasons I don't hear. It occurs to me that this ranking system must be determined by what people are saying about us as they say it, in real time.

It's certainly an impressive technical feat, although I'm not sure what purpose it serves for us to see it. All it does is make me tense, waiting to see where my name goes. As more and more people wail *Too soon!* the sight of my name in that sixth-place spot makes me feel even worse. When Norax calls for me to come out, I can't stop staring at my name as I rise from the stool.

"Good reception?" Norax asks.

"It was fine." At least they weren't *only* comparing Bree and me.

"It's more than fine," says Kaytee, with one of the tablet devices in her hands. "They're intrigued!" She clicks on the positives list for the descriptors. "They think you're a potential musician! They like it!"

My negatives are still the same, but Norax assures me we can work through that, especially given the way things went today. As they pat my back and cheer, I try my best to join in. But in the back of my head, I keep seeing *Emilee* in sixth place.

"Hey, what was that list all about?" I ask Norax.

She furrows her brow. "What list?"

"Wait. Hold on." Kaytee shoves the tablet in front of Norax's face, pulling her attention away. "You need to see this. Immediately."

"It's . . . a list of fake song titles for the single," Norax observes. "It's nothing, doll."

But Kaytee is undeniably rattled. "I . . . I was *just* thinking about writing a song called 'Seashore'! Do you think it got leaked somehow? With all these leaks going around our mansion?"

Norax doesn't believe it's that serious, but Kaytee makes a big enough fuss about it that she relents, agreeing to investigate further.

"*Please*, get to the bottom of this," Kaytee insists. She gestures to me, visibly shaking. "I don't want *more* of our things to get revealed before they're ready, you know?"

"Of course, dear," she says.

Our manager leaves to make a few calls for her. I go to follow Norax's lead off to the main wing, but Kaytee *yanks* me back to face her, eyes wild.

"Okay, she's gone," she says, suddenly frantic. "You have to tell me. *What* was on the list?"

"What?"

"You said there was a list?"

She's got this talon-like grip around my wrist, nails seriously digging into my skin. I pull away from her with a wince. "There was a list. Yes."

"Did it have our names on it?" she asks.

"Not . . . I don't know."

"Holden? Odette?"

"Those were some of them."

Kaytee releases me, stumbling back toward the Analytix's glass doors. "*No*." She says the word over and over again, pacing toward the door like a ghost.

"What's wrong?" I ask.

Kaytee lets out a sudden, wretched sob. She bolts right out of the room, tears streaming down her face. I chase her down several hallways, into a wing where all the doors are a soft powder blue. She pushes right into the one that's slightly ajar.

I stand cautiously in the doorway, within the room without

intruding. This is Race's bedroom, with big navy carpets and warm orange wood in all the furniture. Cozier as this seems against Bree's, the chill I feel in there is still unavoidably present in here.

As Kaytee collapses into his arms, Race meets my eyes, worry splashed across his face. He asks me what's happened, and I don't have an answer.

"She was just—I don't know—"

"It's happening again," Kaytee manages. "They're doing it again, Race."

He pales. "You don't mean . . ."

"DEFED is doing it again."

She weeps into his chest. I watch as his shoulders slowly slump, some realization washing over him. Seeing them this distressed makes me anxious.

"What is DEFED?" I ask.

"Not a *what,*" he says. "A *who.*"

"Who are they?"

Race takes a deep breath. "The people who killed Bree Arch."

PART TWO

# VOLX

# CHAPTER NINE

The other Famoux members have made it into Race's bedroom for a secret emergency meeting. Secret, in the sense that neither Norax nor Lennix are present. I'm not sure why.

We sit cautiously around a circular coffee table, the air both still and wavering at once. Chapter is the first to speak, at the head. In Norax's absence, he's a makeshift leader. "We didn't really take the Volx as seriously as we should've," he tells me. His face dims. "But then, of course, the Darkening happened."

The Volx, I'm explained, is the name of that list I saw in the Analytix. It sprang up for the Famoux months ago alongside a ransom note in Chapter's room. He still has it now, which he's brought to show me. The paper is golden, the type jet black and bold.

> **We are your biggest fans. You must hear this a lot,**
> **but we assure you, it is true. We pride ourselves in**
> **knowing more about you than anyone else.**

Before you, our lives were dull. A perpetual Darkening. Then, you arrived and brought light into our world. You gave us entertainment. You gave us purpose.

But your light is losing its luster. With existences as perfect as yours, it must be so easy to get complacent. For the past few months, we haven't found you quite as compelling as we know you can be. And the darkness is starting to creep back in.

We can't have that. You understand, we have to do something.

We feel as though you are lacking motivation, so we decided to give you some.

By now you have probably seen our lovely little list, which we call the Volx. Whoever is at the bottom of it by the next Darkening will die. We know this sounds scary, but this is what you need.

We ask that you do not share our Volx with anyone. If you tell anyone, you will die before the Darkening can even arrive. And what a shame that would be! No fun for us.

Sending you good luck,
DEFED.

They don't know who DEFED is, nor what their name stands for. They sent them their list, and then their note, and then nothing else.

"Wait, so they're *fans*?" I ask. "That doesn't make sense. Why would they try to kill you if they loved you?"

"They don't love *us*," says Chapter. He points at a few words on the note. "They love the *entertainment*."

"They've got nothing going on with their lives, so they think they can play with ours," says Till bitterly.

I'm struck with how similar this is to Brandyce's old complaints about Famoux fans. How they're *too stupid to live their own lives*. Even I can see myself in DEFED's beginning sentiments. A dull life. A perpetual Darkening. I depended on the Famoux just as much as this group. Something about it fills me with dread.

"But—but I thought Bree's death was an accident," I say. "She wasn't killed. She fell down the stairs."

"Meals are the only time when outsiders are allowed in the Fishbowl," says Foster. "The place was crawling with servers and maids before the power outage."

"So she was pushed when the lights were out?"

This seems implausible. The power surge had affected all of Notness. If someone had planned to kill Bree in that exact moment, they also would have had to cause the surge.

"The whole Fishbowl went black, anybody could have done it," Foster says.

"I remember the stairs were all wet when I found her," Kaytee stares off, wracked by the memory. "They were glistening. She either slipped, or someone wanted it to look like an accident."

"A mole in the staff is our best guess," Chapter tells me. "It would also explain why they were able to figure out our past names for the Volx. You'd have to be on the inside to get those."

"And I'm sure they weaseled their way into *that* room of documents," says Foster. He shakes his head. "Either that, or they could've blackmailed a guard into telling them. They're obviously more than willing to make a threat."

My mind fights to process all this information. I glance over at the ornate walls. So many secrets are being held in this mansion—more than I ever would've thought. Kaytee and Race. Foster and Finley. The Fissarex and the members' pasts. And now this. The persistent threat of being killed off.

They share their old names to give me context for the list, and I share the placements I saw. In first place is Chapter, *Roman*.

Till is in second, *Quinn*.

Kaytee, *Odette*, is third.

Foster, as I knew, is ranked fourth, *Scott*.

Which makes Race *Holden*. He is ahead of me in fifth, which put me at a tentative sixth. I say tentative, because mine and the other names were wavering so much, there's no telling where they might be now. Even so, being in sixth place doesn't even make me at the bottom of this Volx list. There is still the name *Tiffany* at the bottom, with a dark, bolded line crossing it out.

Bree.

When I share with the rankings, Kaytee addresses her boyfriend with gravity. "Race . . ."

"You're in a great spot," he tells her, deflecting. "You'll be all right."

"Do you think we should tell Norax?" I ask. But judging by the ransom note in my hands, I know it's a stupid question.

"If you want to tell her and die, be my guest," says Till. Upon everyone's shocked faces, she shrugs. "What? That's what would happen."

All this information coming at me is bewildering. I can't even wrap my head around how much weight they've been carrying. Is that what Kaytee meant when she told Till not to feel guilty about Bree at my tea party? Was her name, Quinn, at the bottom of the Volx before they entered the Fishbowl, sure she'd be the one to go?

"But why is this happening again?" Kaytee cries. "We had a whole other Darkening, and no one died then! Why would they come back *now*?"

All eyes fall over in my direction, and it's clear I'm to blame. A flare of shame streaks through me. "Wait," I say. "If I had known—"

Chapter grabs my hand. "It's not your fault."

"It *could* be her fault," Kaytee whispers to herself. She doesn't mean for me to hear, but of course I catch it, and it festers in my brain all the same.

I stammer. "I don't want—I wouldn't—"

The words are hard to find. I've only just officially met these people, but I feel as though I know them. How could I not, after these last two years getting to know them in the spotlight? I don't want to see them dead any more than I wanted to see Bree die.

"Maybe we should help each other out," Chapter announces. "Instead of getting competitive."

This gets an eye roll from Till. "That's easy for you to say, most-popular."

"You're just behind him," Foster mentions.

"And you're just behind me!"

"And *this* is the kind of behavior they want from us," Race says. "Comparing each other. Getting in our heads about it." He regards Chapter. "Maybe we *should* work together. Try to be equally popular? That could work."

"Oh, like that's possible!" Till snorts. "No matter what we do, one of us is going to die."

"But there has to be a way to stop them," Race says. "I mean, there *has* to, right?"

For a moment, no one responds. *Is* there a way to stop DEFED? One name on the Volx is already crossed out . . .

"I guess I'm gonna check the Analytix for myself," Foster finally says.

Till hops up from her seat. "Me too."

Leaving Race's room feels like moving through a crowded street—heads lowered, arms turned in, no acknowledging anyone. Following Kaytee down the hallway, I feel helpless. "Do you want to do another coffee run tomorrow?" I ask. "With Cartney? Wes Tegg's?"

She goes to say something, but stops herself, her face changing. I can't read the expression. "Sure," she says. "That sounds lovely."

Kaytee assures me she'll come up with a time and place for us to meet, and we part ways. But then, the next morning, she's already out of the house when I wake, and I don't see her at all for the rest of the day.

I see her picture later, though, in paparazzi shots at a nice new restaurant downtown with Cartney. Right next to them, on the other side of their booth, is Race and a girl I don't recognize, but whom the tabloids call an emerging figure in the art world. A fake double date like this must've been excruciating for them, but they don't show it on their faces at all. They clink their champagne glasses together and beam.

And when I check the Volx, both of their names are several spots higher.

× × ×

The next couple of days see a titanic rise in Famoux member productivity. Everyone seems to be undercutting the other with big announcements and reveals.

Kaytee's high ranking on the Volx takes a dip when, the same afternoon that she heads out for coffee, Foster announces a new line of clothing he'll help design and model in Bree Arch's honor. To get back at him *and* raise her boyfriend's ranking, Kaytee has Race announce he'll be painting a portrait of Bree to be the cover art of her new single, *For Bree*. Using nostalgia to get a better ranking seems to be the key: the three of them spar for second and third spots on the Volx like a death match.

Since all this infighting pushes Till to fifth place just above me, she gets desperate to return to a higher rank. She's spotted at numerous tennis courts, which takes her fans by delightful surprise, as her jaunt into filmmaking with *Riot!* was supposed to mark a hiatus from sports. Her Volx ranking skyrockets, and the name *Quinn* circles up comfortably near the top again.

Chapter hasn't gone as frenzied about the whole thing as the others, but even he's busier than usual—on a small media blitz for *Key*, which is getting more and more momentum as we near the premiere date. He doesn't need to worry about overflowing his schedule like the others. No matter what they do, Chapter always remains somewhere within the top two spots on the Volx. He seems to have the largest subsection of fans. Or at the very least, the most dedicated.

Since no one can admit to Norax what's going on, she perceives this sudden burst of activity to be the members' first steps at moving on and returning to normal in a world post-Bree. She's thrilled, since Lennix had suggested to her that she have the group lie low and mourn longer. For the members to be doing the opposite and succeeding at it is a personal victory on her end.

But not everything has been quite as victorious for her. When Lennix was in Notness and caught word of my trip to Wes Tegg's she got an earful about it. The entire time the Famoux was out making publicity appearances, Norax was fielding more angry phone calls from her father—he was livid.

He had ample reason to be. As made perfectly clear to me in the way my name persists at the bottom of the Volx, me going out and getting coffee was a bit of a slap in the face to some of Bree's biggest fans. How could I be parading around Waltmar in the midst of their mourning? And I didn't even wear black.

So as far as Lennix is concerned, he's right. It's far too soon. When he returns, three days after my outing to Wes Tegg's, he insists that we cease all future outings for me until we make a proper game plan for my image. He refuses Norax's idea for the new and naive angle, too, asserting it gets old quick. "Think Daisy Dolores," he said.

"Who's Daisy Dolores?" I asked.

"*Exactly.*"

Lennix wants to take extra time preparing me for the public before I step outside again, but how am I supposed to tell him that I don't have that time to wait anymore? I've been part of the Famoux for ten days already—which means there are only twenty more until the next Darkening.

This is the thing on my mind as I check the Volx this morning. Time is uncertain, which means time is everything. Ever since my coffee outing, all the talk I've been hearing is back to being about Bree, and how I don't stack up.

"*Do you think she's going to be there today*?" someone asks their friend.

"*I doubt it.*"

"*She'd* better *not show her face.*"

They're right: I won't be. Because the event in question is Bree Arch's memorial service. They already had a private funeral for her last month that the paparazzi managed to snag photos of, but this is the big, public event. Hundreds of Betnedoor's finest celebrities will be in attendance, not to mention all the newscast coverage. A part of me feels like I should be there, paying my respects, showing the world I care, but Lennix disagrees. He thinks it would be in bad taste, especially since there are rumors I killed her.

While everyone is gone, I am to memorize a booklet of celebrity names and faces—Lennix's orders. Unlike Norax, he still insists I should be someone who knows everything and everyone at a glance. I get through a few, but the faces all blend together after a while. No one can possibly stand out quite like the Famoux.

After an hour, I head back toward the Analytix. I already checked it today, but my curiosity is too strong not to visit. At this point the memorial service has certainly begun, and I want to hear what people think of my absence.

"*Oh, of course the killer doesn't show.*"

"*No Emeray, hmm.*"

"*She had enough time to get a coffee, but couldn't make it to this?*"

Their words make me restless. Lennix was wrong. I *should* be there. I know it, but he wouldn't listen.

As expected, my name is still at the bottom of the Volx. A part of me expects Bree's name, *Tiffany,* to rise above me on a day like this, but I think her name is dormant now. Just there to psych us out.

1 - Roman

2 - Odette

3 - Scott

4 - Quinn

5 - Holden

6 - Emilee

7 - ~~Tiffany~~

There's one lone, "*I hope that Emeray girl doesn't feel too much pressure*," that gives me a shred of relief. I decide to end here and rise from the stool.

Rounding the corner away from the Analytix room, I notice my whole body is shaking. A few days ago, the world seemed to be full of only ease and excitement. Dress fittings and café trips. But now, when I think back on Wes Tegg's, and the fans I met there, the lightness in my chest is now a heavy weight. I already know the next time I encounter fans, I'll be examining every smile and squeal carefully, wondering if my name is rising on the Volx. While attention was once a free perk to this new life of mine, it has now become a vital currency.

And the other members are striking it rich. *It's not fair*. I've barely even seen them these past few days—they're all gone before I wake and still out when I've gone to bed. The image of the Volx flashes across my mind again, and my knuckles clench. For the first time I feel *anger*, and the anger stays fresh in my mind when I return to my bedroom. I get another wave of fear like my first night—like Bree is here, somewhere, wishing to scare me. No amount of deep breaths will curb the paranoia.

I crouch down to look underneath the bed. Nothing. I check in the closet. Nobody hiding. There's no one lurking in the shower. No one squeezed behind the doors. Every plausible spot, I search, feeling both ridiculous and practical at once, and it all turns up as nothing. But no matter how many times I remind myself that Bree Arch is not a ghost, I can't shake the fear. Because she is one, in a way. As long as people keep saying her name when they're saying mine, she will continue to haunt me. All I can do right now is hope someday I escape it.

It's either that, or I join her, and it's my funeral next.

*What am I even doing here?* Norax promised me glamour and endless possibilities and adoring fans, and all I've seem to get so far is negative backlash, no matter what move I make. She's letting Lennix keep me tucked away inside the Famoux fortress. And that could get me killed. I'm not in control. The world starts blurring. *I am not in control.* On my feet again, pacing, I glance in the mirror at my perfect reflection and surprise myself when I let out a frustrated screech.

She promised me glamor, but she also promised me *family*. Family, kinship, solidarity in the Famoux—not these strangers. Not rivals. This thought tips my anger into sadness and releases discomfited tears. I thought I did, but I don't really know the Famoux members. I don't feel like one of them.

Norax's Famoux *does* boast competitiveness, and less unity and camaraderie than in those before them, but I don't want that. I want the Kaytee who offered to go to coffee with me, the Foster who drafted photoshoot concepts with me, the Chapter who gave me his hat—not these cutthroat, silent rivals. I want to be able to stand next to them and comfort them at the memorial service of their loved one, and not be accused by anyone of doing it for show.

And suddenly my head feels clear, and my body knows exactly what to do next as I rise from the floor to the closet and pick out a black dress.

Gerald, who I find playing solitaire in the guards' quarters, looks very surprised to see me.

"Are we going somewhere?" he asks nervously, as though he was supposed to know and forgot. With one frantic swipe of his hand across the table, he gathers all the playing cards in one and stands up.

Luckily for me, Lennix didn't seem to tell Gerald I was forbidden to leave, and if he did, Gerald is too nervous to tell me no. Quicker than even I thought possible, we're in the car en route to the service. Any nerves that try to rise up within me, I deny outright. *I've made my choice, and it feels like the right choice, and that is that,* I tell myself. This becomes a mantra as we pull up to the cemetery.

I don't think I've ever seen so many people in one place. This completely surpasses the crowd around the Fishbowl in Eldae. People must've traveled from all over Delicatum to be here, And even with all these people gathered, I'm sure this broadcast will still be the most viewed non-Darkening broadcast of all time.

"All right, we're a little late, but I'll get the crowd to break up so there's a path to the other members. Then I'll escort you through. You stay here," Gerald says factually, as though trying to convince himself this is the right plan. He's as flustered by the volume as me. He leaves to go talk to the security.

Suddenly I am dizzy. I'm going to have to walk *through* the crowd. There's no other way. The part of the broadcast I saw had the Famoux members centered in the cemetery, circled by press and fans. Making a scene is the only way.

Before I can even think about finding Gerald and telling him to stop and have us turn around, he is already back. Out the window I see security guards herding people around and I lose the ability to exhale.

Gerald reaches out his hand, maybe in sympathy, maybe just to prompt me to move, and I have no choice but to take it and get out of the car.

The last time I stepped out like this, it was to a flurry of shouts and camera shutters. Today, it is so silent I can hear my shoes crunching the icy grass. It's a true winter day, but the eyes of everyone on me makes me feel like I'm on fire.

*I am a member of the Famoux and I deserve to be here*, I tell myself.

I look up and see mouths agape and people leaning in to share whispers.

*I am a member of the Famoux and I deserve to be here.*

I finally make it to the center and the seven of them are stunned. Norax looks nervous, Race and Kaytee confused, Foster intrigued, and Till almost disgusted. Chapter doesn't seem to be wearing a lot of emotion on his sleeve today but he is definitely surprised. And Lennix just looks angry, like an explanation is due immediately. I should say something, justify myself.

When I open my mouth, the world leans in, and I realize that in explaining myself, I'm going to have to give an impromptu speech.

"I . . . I know how much she meant to you," I utter, my voice wavering. "And how much she meant to me, as someone whose Darkenings were made brighter by her."

My voice catches because I realize, as ridiculous as that just sounded, it *is* true. While the encounters were brief, Bree *was* a part of my life for two years, part of the phenomenon that allowed me to escape. Kaytee must see this realization play out across my face because she reaches out and grabs my hand.

I try to channel Norax and her composure as I address the members. "I'm aware that I didn't know her like you did, but I felt like I needed to be here. I needed to pay Bree the respect she deserves."

This is all I can manage. As I bow my head to pay respect, Gerald scrambles over with an extra fold-up chair in his hands, and I quickly sit down in it, head spinning. Kaytee gives my hand a squeeze, and for a moment, it's like we're outside Wes Tegg's again.

I guess my entrance interrupted the Famoux members' own speeches, and they resume with Race rising toward the podium. Even as the other members take the spotlight, the feeling of eyes on me never lessens, never subsides. But it doesn't matter, because it means I'm here. I brought myself here. I'm in control.

# CHAPTER TEN

The service is long. It isn't until late afternoon that the speeches end, the condolences wrap up, and the feverish camera clicks finally rest.

I expect some sort of fire and brimstone rage from Lennix, but what I get instead is even more unsettling. The walk back to the cars is silent and I'm thankful that Gerald and I get to ride back to the hideaway alone, but I know it is just delaying an inevitable blowup.

And yet when I walk through the door, there are no explosions. The other Famoux members seem to have disappeared to their rooms, and I find Lennix in one of the lounge areas,

Instead of running, I stand in the doorway, almost like I *want* to be yelled at, or at least have what I did be acknowledged. Behind me, Norax appears.

"Emeray, come with me, we need to check the Analytix *immediately.*" Her tone is not stern per se, but certainly angrier than she's ever been at me. I look at her, then back at Lennix, as if to give him a chance to say something before I go.

Norax grows restless. "Come *on*, lumerpa, we have to—"

"Do you know who she is?" says Lennix suddenly.

Both Norax and I are bewildered as he gestures to the photo of a young girl with brown hair and wispy bangs.

"She was at the service today," he adds. Then with more force than the first time, he repeats, "Do you know who she is?"

I hesitate, then offer, "A . . . golfer?" I offer.

"What is her *name*?"

He stares me down for an uncomfortable amount of time as I stand, answerless. Norax's nervous energy isn't helping either. I finally break. "I don't know," I say. "Who is it?"

"Her name is Ritter Hare," he says. "And she's not a golfer. Come on. Only one of the biggest up-and-coming actresses."

"I haven't seen any movies," I sheepishly admit.

"Of course you haven't."

Another silence falls over us. I make a bold decision to step into the room fully. As I open my mouth to say something, I'm not even sure what, Lennix beats me to it.

"You were not welcome today." He looks up from the booklet for the first time, directly into my eyes.

"I—"

"You were *not* welcome today," he repeats sharply.

I think back to Wes Tegg's—the long line they formed. For some reason I can't help but bring it up. "But Kaytee's fans liked me at the café," I point out, instantly feeling silly. "They took photos with me."

"People also take photos of natural disasters," Lennix asserts, not quite a roar but definitely louder. "It doesn't mean they liked you, and it certainly doesn't make them your fans. What have you done to make anybody *your* fan?"

*Nothing!* I think. *Because you haven't let me do anything!* I wish I was the kind of person who fights back to get what they want, who could just lash out and say what I think . . . but I'm not. The power I felt when I decided to go to the memorial service has shriveled up. My strongest urge right now is to get up and run out of the room. If there's one thing I know, it's that Emilee Laurence always fancied flight.

"Norax!" It's Kaytee's voice, trailing down the hall. "Swanson hasn't brought me my dress yet!" She peers into the room and blushes, realizing that she's interrupted something.

Norax turns to us. "You two continue without me."

"No," Lennix asserts. To Kaytee, he prods, "What's going on?"

"Race has an art show tonight," Kaytee says quietly, a forced attempt at her usual cheeriness. "It's . . . a small thing for Bree."

"Can I come?" I hear myself ask.

Lennix cackles. "Absolutely *not.*"

Norax tries to take this moment to flee with Kaytee, but is not quick enough. All Lennix has to do is put his hand up and she stops right in her tracks. It's strange to see her like this, just as she was when my name got leaked to the public. So frantic, timid, *human.* And to think she seemed anything but when I first met her.

Lennix is swift in his verdict.

"Norax," he starts, stern as ever. "You can't control your Famoux. As this is my creation, I refuse to let you soil its reputation any longer. I will be comanaging Emeray Essence's career. Actually, no. I will be managing her completely. *You* will report to *me.* She won't move a single muscle without my approval. Do you understand?"

All she says is, "Okay."

It does and doesn't surprise me that she puts up no fight.

"Now," Lennix directs his icy attention to me. "You. You're no exception. You will do nothing and go nowhere unless I authorize it, okay?"

The intensity in his eyes makes me know he means it too. No more stunts like the one I just pulled. Or else. The reality of unknown consequences strikes a spark of fear in me reminiscent of the DEFED message. This is serious.

Just like Norax, I say, "Okay."

He surveys us both, as though he is looking for a trace of a bluff. Finally he declares, "Okay. Good. You both may go."

As we scurry away, Norax grabs my forearm and gives it a quick squeeze in comfort but doesn't say a word before disappearing down a different hallway.

I know Lennix is probably right. I can't go to the art show. I've shown my face enough today. And yet I still feel irritation rise in me. I took a stand today and what did it get me? I'm even more trapped than before. On my way to one of the staircases I see the other members in the kitchen, dressed up, waiting for the car to arrive. It makes me want to scream.

As I climb the stairs I bite my lip so hard, I'm scared it'll bleed. I can't stand Lennix. Like Westin, going out of his way to make me feel inadequate every day. And after the memorial service mistake, I know he's not even the genius he claims to be. Why is my life in *his* hands? Once I think I'm all alone in a long hallway I let out a frustrated yelp.

My yelling has startled a guard, who turns the corner at the wrong time. She's got a pager in her hand, which she points to with a slender, glove-clad finger.

"Miss Essence, they want you formally dressed and downstairs as soon as possible. The car is leaving soon," she says.

"They *what*?" I ask. "Who said this?"

"The members, Miss."

I blink, not sure if I've heard her correctly. The *members* got Lennix to budge? So quickly? I try to ask her what they said, how it happened, but she tells me she only knows her orders, then leaves.

Back in my room, I scour through my closet, trying to piece this together. The only person who saw me show interest in going tonight was Kaytee, which means she had to have been the one who requested I come. I know she has a way with people, but to convince Lennix to let me out right after he declared my detention? Is she really that good?

It's hard to remember what the members were wearing when I passed them. I barely looked in my anger. I find a dark gray, tea-length frock that I think is understated enough. And close enough to black to show I'm mourning still. But yet again, *should* I be dressing more outrageously, as per Norax's *naive* angle? Certainly not on a night like this, right?

When I surface in the kitchen, the members are all looking at me, eyes gaping. I instinctively look down at my outfit.

"You're going to need to change," says Foster.

My brow furrows. "Why?"

"You have to wear . . ." He looks down at a slip of paper in his hands, which I notice are shaking. In fact, almost everyone standing there is shaking, in some way. Their faces are paler than I've ever seen them.

"What's wrong?" I ask.

Foster holds out the paper. I take it, leery.

"They just . . ." He can't finish.

The slip is made of golden paper. Sentences of jet-black ink are pressed on with precision.

And as I read the words, I realize I was stupid to think before that my life was in Lennix's hands, or even Norax's. Maybe it was once, but it isn't anymore.

None of ours is.

**We loved our new girl's unexpected entrance today.**
**That's more like it.**
**Make sure she's there tonight. Tell her to wear the**
**yellow dress too.**
**We know it will remind her of home.**
**DEFED**

✕ ✕ ✕

There's what I'm told is a modest red carpet spread out at the entrance of the art gallery. Modest, because it is only about a quarter the length of one for a typical movie premiere. But like how Norax called the mansion a little hideaway, I have a feeling this carpet is going to be far larger than anything I could've pictured.

Roaring fans on one side, roaring paparazzi on the other. They have us flanked, snapping photos and shouting with identical ferocity. It would be an exciting, thrilling evening if my heart was beating fast only from nerves. All I can think is, which side of the room will DEFED be on? Are they the devotees with pens and posters, or the voyeurs with long-necked lenses? It seems as though the way they love and watch us closely, they are a mixture of both.

All I know is that they'll be in attendance. They want to see me *in person.*

No one has spoken a word about the note for the whole drive. No one has spoken a word about anything, actually. Scanning their hardened gazes, it's difficult to deduce what they might be thinking—if they perceive the note as a threat to me, or to them. After all, DEFED *did* get me out here tonight. They've done what Lennix is unwilling to do, and they've put me in the ring once more, competing for a higher Volx ranking with the rest of them.

Unless Lennix is right, and this outing is seen as egregiously disrespectful. Then, DEFED will have been doing them a favor, cementing me at rock bottom.

Do they want me to have a fair chance, or do they want to start digging my grave?

I should be more worried about Lennix, and whether or not this will blow up in my face. He just gave me explicit orders and I have betrayed them. I should be anticipating the way he'll blame Norax and call for my removal again. But it's the last thing on my mind. As all eyes stare at the fabric of that yellow dress from Bree's closet, all I can think about is whether or not DEFED is here. They need to be here, and to see me. Because they know my old name. They know the color of my mother's house. *Her* hideaway. And my mind is spiraling, thinking about everything else they could know.

When someone taps my shoulder I nearly jump in my seat. I whip my head around and it's Chapter's hand recoiling back.

"I just wanted to tell you that it was really cool of you to . . . come out there today," he says, with the ghost of his usual intensity. I can tell he's still a little off—he buried his childhood friend today, after all.

His eyes shift down to his hands and I feel a sadness twinge in my heart. He's always so stoic, and I can tell he's trying. "Bree would've liked you."

Out of the corner of my eye I see the others focus in on us. I don't break eye contact with Chapter, though, even though looking at him kind of feels like staring into the sun.

Another hand on my shoulder. I look down and it's Foster's. "Yeah, Em," he adds. "She would've."

I brave a glance around the car. Race smiles weakly, Kaytee rests her head peacefully on his shoulder, her eyes closed. Till looks out the window.

As the car stops by the curb and the members start piling out, my heart patters quick and nervous in my chest like it could burst out of it. This is Emilee's heart. This skin might have never lain back on the shingle-coated floors of that yellow house, but this heart did.

As Gerald extends a hand out to me, he wishes me luck. He must think I'm nervous only that this is my first red carpet.

I wish that were the case.

Out on the carpet, the members disperse around the perimeter like they're stationing for battle. A few of them take the first post in front of the paparazzi, and the others scatter about to the fans. The visible normalcy of their actions is a wonder to me. They know now's not the time to show fear. They wipe their faces clean of any emotions they carried in the car, offering up only picture-perfect expressions now. I'm so in awe that I don't remember I, too, am in eyeshot, until—

"Emeray Essence, over *here!*"

"No, over *here!*"

Where do I start? *The fans*, I decide. They should be my first priority, if I hope to win them over and make something useful of this situation. I hurry over to the barricade holding them back, a flurry of camera shuffles capturing my every step. Screams engulf me as I close the distance between me and an almond-eyed girl in a T-shirt with Race's face on it. Watching her nearly crumble with excitement to see me is effervescent. For a moment I forget everything else.

"No *way*!" The girl grabs my arm like I'll fly away, hands sweaty and trembling. "I can't believe you're *here*!"

"I'm so happy to be here!" I tell her, cheerful as can be.

She pulls out a device, extending out to me. "Can we take a picture?"

Lucky for me, all of the fans I encounter are kind, despite what I've been hearing in the Analytix. I only get a few weird looks, which last a second before giving way to delight. I'm yanked in all directions if I stand in one place too long, so interactions are short, like in Wes Tegg's. Even if they don't speak to me at all, they're dying to get a photo, jutting their devices out for me to use. In the back of my mind I can hear Lennix's comment about natural disasters, but I push it back, hoping every picture I take is one with a newly made fan.

There's so much about this moment that's twisted up. One part of me feels like I could burst out of fear, and the other, exhilaration. People shout my name and clamor for attention. And it's all in a good way, as far as I can see.

I'm blasted with brusque photographers like cold air when I cross to the other end of the carpet. They yell my name so loudly, their commands become inaudible. *Pose here! Over here! No, here!*

Mimicking Kaytee and Till's actions farther down the carpet, I put my hands on my hips, tilt my shoulders, pivot. I can't figure out what to do with my face other than smile, since pouting or feigning being unamused feels ridiculous. For a few snapping photos I even laugh when I try.

I'm overstimulated by the time I reach the end. Luckily, I'm not the first one there. Race is standing by the gallery doors, inspecting the glint of his leather dress shoe.

"Why aren't you still out there?" I ask. "This is your show."

Race shrugs. "I'm not much of a red-carpet guy. Don't really like posing. Or being shouted at. Not my thing."

I nod. Even without DEFED, the long walk down the carpet was a lot to take. I can see how the thrill of it could wear off after a few hundred jaunts.

On the last portion of the carpet I spot Kaytee and Cartney standing together, his arm around her waist, her hand on his chest. Photographers are loving it. I wince, thinking about the portrait in Race's studio. But when they're finished, they separate unceremoniously. Kaytee does everything she can not to run over to Race. He keeps his face casual, but I can tell he's glad she's with him now. "That looked superfun," he tells her, sardonic. "Glad you brought him tonight."

"If it gets more press for your art, it's worth it," she says.

Kaytee sees me, then averts her gaze. Race notices. Mercifully, he brings me into their conversation. "This is a good event for Em too. It'll be nice to see her approval go up."

Kaytee makes a face. "No, it won't."

My chest gets tight.

"*Lumerpa?*"

Oh, no. On the edge of the carpet, Norax is rushing toward us. Her cheeks are bright red from the chill in the air, but the more I look at her, the more I think they might also be red from anger too. The audience is still watching us, so she feigns nonchalance, pulling me into a hug—the picture of a proud manager greeting her newest member.

"Why are you *here*?" she practically yells in my ear.

Most of the other members are finishing their walks now and all eyes are on me, wondering what I'll say. I'm wondering too. During the silence of the car ride, I should've been thinking of some brilliant excuse.

"I . . . wanted to go," I manage.

She strains. "You can't—Lennix will never—" As she sputters, I realize she's not actually angry at me, she's scared of her father. After his outburst earlier about her not being able to manage her members, this was the single worst thing I could do.

"Norax," I start. "I'm sorry, I—"

But a sudden outburst of cheering and shouting turns everyone's attention back to the carpet. At first, all I can see is the paparazzi leaning toward something, their bulbs going off at lightning speed. And then it's so bright that I see nothing.

Just beyond me, I hear Kaytee—who's already as far from Cartney as she can be—groan. "Oh, that *jerk*."

They're well adjusted to camera flashes, but my vision's still spotted. I squint. "What's going on?"

Race shakes his head, like this happens all the time. "Oh, Chapter's just one-upping us, that's all."

There's a clearing in the light for me to finally see the scene ahead. Sure enough, there's Chapter, leaning over the barrier where the fans are, his face hyperfocused on one of them. It's hard to see who exactly, since the whole group surges toward him like a stampede. I'm fearful for a second that he might get trampled.

The whole carpet has their attention on him now, watching intently as Chapter takes the hand of a sobbing girl with dark brown hair. A bodyguard lifts her up over the barrier and onto the carpet beside him. Once she's on the other side, they hug.

"What is he doing?" I ask.

Chapter takes the girl's hand, leading her out into the middle of the carpet.

"Making her his date, it would appear," says Race.

"And at *your* event." Kaytee's eyes roll like marbles. She murmurs, lower, "Always available to date his damn fans. It's shameless."

Hands jut out at Chapter with animalistic force, some faces even angry now. Chapter takes a moment to run back and say something that softens the whole group in a second. Just like that, they're back to smiles and encouraging cheers.

"Bet he just promised to do this for all of them one day," says Till, monotone. "Like that's even possible."

"I don't get it," I say. "He's already . . ." I don't complete the sentence in Norax's presence, but they all know what I'm getting at. Chapter's already in great standing on the Volx.

"Yeah, and that's what sucks," Till says. "He doesn't even *think* about us."

For whatever reason, this bothers me. As Chapter walks his date over to where we're standing, I think about the knit hat he once gave me, and how he didn't panic and start filling his schedule like everyone else when the Volx came up. Somehow it made me think he was different than the others. But maybe Chapter was planning this bigger move all along.

"This is Lex," he tells us when he reaches us. "She's very important."

The name brings a wave of familiarity. My mother's name was Alexandra, and every so often my father called her Lex. Only teasingly, though, because he knew it bothered her. She favored her full name far more.

One by one, the members give their best and most captivating greetings. Kaytee tells her she has the prettiest eyes she's ever seen in her life. Exactly what she told me when she met me. My anger is swelling like a broken bone until it's my turn, and I finally get a good look at her—this girl named Lex.

Suddenly, I could faint.

Her name felt familiar, but her face is something else. It's like looking in a mirror and seeing some strange, altered version of my old self. Her hair is the same shade of brown mine used to be, and though her blue eyes aren't quite as light, they're close. I see a thousand bad memories of the Greyhounds flicker in them, and it takes everything in me to just smile at her, instead of scream. I must not have sold it convincingly, because she looks away from me fast, tucking a hair behind her ear.

Lex lives in Betnedoor, so I know she doesn't have to worry about judgment like I did, with no mutations. Those eyes aren't considered a glitch; they're just beautiful here. But even so, I can somehow tell it's been hard for her, just from how she's holding herself so inwardly. Or maybe I'm projecting my past self onto her.

Either way, it's difficult to get her face out of my head during the show. Race's work is almost dreamlike in its abstractions, so I encounter Lex's eyes in blue sky, her hair in dark shadows. Somewhere along the way the visions become less Lex, more Emilee. Somewhere further, they blend.

It's Norax's voice that shakes me from my trance. "What do you think we should tell Lennix?"

"I don't know," I admit.

After a pause, she says, "Well, you're a *Famoux member*. You deserve to be at these events as much as the rest of them. He should know that."

I ruminate on this, but my attention holds on Norax for only so long. Like a magnet, my eyes flicker back to Chapter and Lex across the room. She's giggling over something he's said. My mind can't make sense of it. There's no way Chapter knows what I used to look like, so this can't be on purpose. And even if he knew, why would he do it? All I know is that it's baffling to see him with her. It's like he's laughing with me. Hugging *me*.

My thoughts are interrupted again, this time by a young man tapping my shoulder. He's tall, with a sharp jaw. "Marlon," he introduces. Then, as if realizing I might not know him, "York."

I actually do recognize him from Lennix's quizzing. He's another musician from Buchan—Cartney's label.

"Hi," I say. Norax nudges my shoulder: *Be friendlier*. I stiffen my posture and try again, this time more animated. "How are you doing?"

"How are *you* doing?" he asks. "How has this whole adjustment to celebrity life been? Good so far?"

I nod. Another nudge from Norax. "*Yes*," I exclaim. "The other members have been so . . . wonderful and welcoming."

"That's good," he says.

He goes on to say the word *good* in just about every sentence that follows. He's nervous. I don't blame him—just beyond us, everyone in this gallery is staring relentlessly at Marlon, the lone man brave enough to approach me. This obviously messes with his presentation.

"Well, I should get back to my . . ." His sentence fades off as he starts backing away awkwardly. "But maybe we could get together sometime. Play some music?"

He must've heard the rumor Cartney planted at the café. Maybe Buchan told him about it and had him approach me.

Regardless, I tell him sure, and he's so delighted, he actually skips away.

"That's a *great* idea, lumerpa," Norax says when he's gone. "We'll get his fans on your side!" She pushes me toward the center of the room. "Go, make more friends."

It appears my talking to Marlon has been perceived as an open invitation to now approach me. Members of Betnedoor's elite line up just like the fans did in West Tegg's, taking their turns introducing themselves and complimenting me. Even when I struggle through the conversation, or don't offer much when they ask me personal questions, they still persist in talking, bringing up new topics until the next person boots them out. It occurs to me in the middle of this meet and greet of sorts that DEFED said they were going to be here. I might have already spoken to them without even realizing it. I wouldn't know. Everyone is perfectly cordial and happy to see me—not a single shred of ill will. Somehow, that makes the wondering even worse.

When the show is over, Chapter sends Lex home with one of our drivers. Before they part outside the gallery doors, he whispers something in her ear. I eavesdrop my hardest, but I make out nothing.

I'm so busy watching the exchange, trying to figure this out, that I don't realize the others have already gotten into our car. I have to miss the end of their good-byes to duck into the final row.

The whole drive home I stare at my hands, a dozen emotions running through me. I'm overwhelmed, delighted, confused, scared, but above all, and most curiously, glad. I'm glad when I think about how DEFED didn't do anything else tonight besides send that note. I'm glad that, despite the crowd of fans seeming like a huge mass, it was actually on the smaller side, according to the others. I'm glad knowing that every Famoux member encounters hundreds to thousands of different people every day. Because this means that, realistically, there's little chance I'll ever see someone who looks like Lex—like *Emilee*—again.

# CHAPTER ELEVEN

Lennix made a point of refusing to see Norax and me when we returned home from the art show, instead having a guard relay a message: *We'll speak in the morning at the Analytix.*

I shiver at the thought of weathering more of his quiet disdain and find myself hoping his wing of the mansion is far enough away that his resting anger doesn't permeate into my room. I broke his one rule tonight.

As I toss and turn in my bed, I play over a hundred potential outbursts. Since I've disobeyed him, he'll surely have to be angrier, opting for behemoth yelling over quiet fury, but then again, maybe he'll favor passive aggression. I'm just determined not to cry again in his presence. The only times Westin made me truly cry was when he'd find new ways to show his hatred. There will be no methods for Lennix that I haven't already encountered—not a single one. He won't surprise me.

But then, of course, he does.

I am not greeted with shouting when I walk into the Analytix.

No slamming his fists on the table. None of it. His crisp white button-down may as well be a white flag, and he waves his cup of tea at me with such vigor, I'm scared he'll stain a sleeve.

"Congratulations, Emeray," he greets. There's nothing threatening about his grin, but even so, I'm swallowed up in fear.

"Why?" I dare ask.

"You've proven yourself again to be too foolish to be managed." He takes a celebratory sip from his cup, as if it's champagne. Then again, maybe it is—I can't actually see the liquid. He sees I'm confused and decides to stoke the fire. "I really do admire you."

None of my dozens of scenarios last night unfolded anything like this. What is this? "What?"

"You're making her pay for this decision," he hums. "All this trouble . . . And over *you* . . . It's a delight to watch, my dear. A delight."

He must be drunk. I scan his cup for a teabag as he adds, "You know she was my second choice? For my heir?"

"What?"

Lennix takes another smug sip. As he tilts it back, the teabag string slips over. Not drunk. Just oddly honest. "Poor thing had to grovel for the job. Said she'd do it perfectly. And now she gets too zealous, and she picks you, and you're everything you are. And yet, she can't control you. It's poetic."

Norax being a second-choice heir is news to me, and I choose to focus on that part of what he said. "Who was the first heir?"

"Someone I used to know," he says. "They were far better suited for the job, I'll tell you that. Actual experience."

This conversation comes to a close as Norax enters, a stack of new tabloids in her hands. "Good morning," she says. She clears her throat the same way she does before delivering a prepared speech. It's obvious that she was up late last night planning our defense. "As you can see, Father, Emeray and I have—"

"I loved it," he says.

Her eyes nearly pop out of her head. "You what?"

"Ambitious. Unexpected. Let's keep this train rolling, just with me on board this time," he says. "Say to hell with the people who can't get over Bree. Where can we place Em *next*?"

"Your sarcasm is not appreciated here, Father." Norax frowns.

When we check the Analytix, it's evident that people don't quite know what to make of me. I show up late to the memorial service and give an impassioned but somewhat trite speech, then show up to an art show honoring Bree later that night. Some find it all to be insensitive, while others actually call it the smart move. They think I showed respect with my speech by recognizing her impact, instead of simply crying in silence. "*Is Emeray Essence actually outsmarting all of us?*" asks a gossip reporter. "*We'd like to know.*"

Thoughts like these get peppered with compliments on my look. People liked the way the yellow looked on me, as well as the fact that I wasn't wearing any makeup. "*Very youthful,*" says a fashion expert.

Norax will be glad to hear it.

It's overall a mixed consensus that keeps me in sixth place on the Volx. As I get up from the stool, however, I take extra note of that seventh name, Tiffany. For Bree to have died in the Darkening, she had to have been the least popular member. Which means most of these fans mourning her are probably performative ones, just shocked by what they saw live on TV. Maybe they're having a surge of regret that they didn't love her enough when she was alive. But if she was low enough to be DEFED's target, I really shouldn't have to worry about competing with her forever. *Not necessarily.*

Lennix has decided he can't hold me down any longer and thinks we should press on with his guidance. To Norax, his approval is both a blessing and a curse. On the one hand, we've gotten our wish that I make more appearances. On the other, he's still in control. She didn't get to give a rousing speech, or defy him, or prove herself. It is *his* call, not hers. It's *his* choice that we're talking about my career now. What Lennix told me before she entered the room—that and the shocking fact that he's not angry at me—are two things tossing in my head as Norax glares at him flipping through tabloids, reading out rumors.

"Are we really doing the singer thing?" he asks, holding up another headline claiming they've leaked a song that doesn't exist. So far, every magazine has been buzzing about the song Cartney hinted at in Wes Tegg's in some way or another. "Seems like a dumb choice. We already have a singer."

"*I* already have a singer," corrects Norax, terse. "And it wouldn't be permanent." My talk with Marlon York last night appears to have spurred a good idea, because she adds, "Getting preexisting fans on board with Emeray is a good move. We should be doing more of this."

"Having her leech off everyone? Come on."

"It would *help* her," she says. "A duet with Kaytee. A photo-shoot with Foster. A role in one of Chapter's films . . ."

"She could make a fool of herself playing tennis with that Till girl too," says Lennix with an eye roll.

"Don't try to tell me that's not a good plan," Norax says. "Half her spread in *The X* is going to be the members' letters telling their fans to love her anyway."

"Fine, sure, it'll work," he says. "But at the end of the day, those are *their* things. When that's all over, what's *Emeray's* thing?" He looks over to me, expectant. "What can you offer us?"

This stumps me. I think back to my tour of the mansion. Till's court. Race's studio. Kaytee's audio room. Places built for them, for their talents. Because they all bring something to the table. Acting, sports, music, fashion, and art fans—*all* fans of the Famoux, because of them.

This could be the decision that defines whether I live or die. One activity to define me, to define my fanbase, to define everything.

"I don't know," I say.

"Somehow I thought you'd say that."

Lennix pulls out a folder of potential options he's come up with, rifling through them one by one. The other members seem to have chosen the best ones, though, because none of these seem quite as alluring. He offers up becoming a chef and doing a restaurant and a cooking show. In response, I tell a story of the time I tried to make dinner instead of Brandyce, and almost burned our house down. Then he suggests politics, which Norax dismisses instantly as too polarizing. Further down the list, he laughs out loud. "I wrote comedian," he says. "We can go cross that out."

By the end, we've gone through the whole list and have come up with nothing.

"Emeray doesn't *need* to know what she's doing yet," defends Norax. "Not if we fill her schedule with more events with the members. Once she's through with those, we'll have a better grasp of where she fits."

"She can't ride on the coattails of everyone else forever," Lennix says. "If she's aimless, I'm sorry, they're going lose interest. People are going to want something from her."

She shoves the tabloids toward his side of the table, her voice escalating. Today, with Lennix, her fuse is considerably short. Not enough to explode. Not yet. "Well, can *you* discern what they want?" she asks.

"What if I just asked them?" I blurt.

They turn to me like I've said something ridiculous. I try my best to not shrink any further into my shoulders than I already am.

"Pardon?" asks Lennix.

"I know we have the Analytix and the tabloids saying what they think," I say, "but what if I . . . asked them directly what they want?"

Norax is getting it. "Like doing a broadcast? An interview?"

The thought of that sort of thing puts a lump in my throat, but I nod. "Do you think that would work?"

"You'd almost certainly bomb an interview at this point in your development," Lennix says. But I can tell he's thinking it over in his head. "If we gave you a foolproof backstory, though, a whole script to follow, perhaps you'd manage enough to charm them with your . . . pleasantly awkward demeanor."

I can see Norax brighten a shade or two in my peripheral. They're choice words for the *young and new* angle she's concocted, but an acknowledgment all the same. "You could be a member *for* the people," she muses. "Interactive with them. Perceptive. Not just the music girl, or the sports girl—"

"The *world's* girl," completes Lennix.

That kind of a title sends a roar of adrenaline through my body.

Lennix raises his eyebrows at me. "And you'd want to ask the public directly what they want? You know that means you'll have to go with the popular vote, whatever it is, right? If they actually say comedian, and you have to become funny very quickly. They say die, and well . . ."

Normally, I think this is when I'd back out, tell Norax and Lennix that they know best, and let them choose some occupation for me. Let me be a chef and make painfully simple dishes for the rest of my life, so long as it guarantees me a life at all. I know I'd have to get used to cameras by the time a Darkening rolled by, but right now, the idea of an interview broadcasted to millions sounds like a whole other dimension of Westin's torture.

But that view of *Emilee* sitting at sixth place on the Volx, even after two outings, gets bolder with every blink. There's really no choice but to trust the public. I need them to like me if I want to survive.

No. I need them to *love* me if I want to survive.

"Yes," I say. "I'll do anything."

× × ×

They get to work at finding me the best interviewer. Naturally, every host from every station is dying to land my first television appearance, but the best person to do it, they decide, is none other than Sam Booker. His talk show, *Sam on 18,* has dismal ratings, and he's never had any huge (or small) guests on air. Seeing the ratings on Norax's tablet, he's one step away from cancelation.

But Norax seems to really like this. "Your first real interview will also be *his* first real interview," she says. "People will like that."

A few calls are made, and it's swiftly set into motion. For the next two days, vague commercials for the interview are being broadcasted on every channel. On the day of the interview itself, posters are plastered over every inch of Delicatum. The ads offer little to no explanation as to what the night might entail, much less who it's with, so as to create intrigue. The poster is a deep black backdrop with a golden message:

GRAB A COFFEE AND CATCH UP WITH YOUR NEWEST FRIEND. SAM ON 18. TONIGHT AT 6.

Norax claims everyone will know it's me by the mention of coffee, somehow, as my trip to Wes Tegg's with Kaytee and Cartney has become a bit of a . . . thing. "Getting coffee is your signature!" she tells me. She says she's already meeting with different brewing companies about maybe getting my face on a brand.

Since the interview is scheduled for tonight, I've spent most of the morning hours at *The X*'s headquarters with Norax, Lennix, and Abby. Sam is Abby's husband, so she already has a long list of questions he'll ask, and Norax supplies an adjoining list of perfect replies. It is *imperative* that I have an airtight alibi for who Emeray Essence is, where she's from, and where she's headed. My backstory must be the right amount of tragic and the right amount of favorable—a delicate balancing act to make it so the most on-the-fence viewer could take a liking to me. Not a full sob story, not a full cakewalk. Somewhere in an indiscernible middle.

No matter how much we practice, I can't help but worry I'll mess up. Forget a detail. Explain something wrong. My life quite literally depends on getting this interview right, which makes memorizing facts about a life I've never lived all the more stressful. If the world doesn't like me more after this, I'll stand next to no chance in getting my ranking higher on the Volx. The pressure makes me wish we'd scheduled this for next week. But as we drive home from *The X*, I see a dozen of the cryptic posters, reminding me there's no turning back. Ready or not, it's happening tonight.

Naturally, Swanson has prepared a dress for the occasion. Only, it's not much of a dress at all, but a bright magenta top and a matching skirt. Norax stops by my room while I model it, and she sings her praises. Apparently, the casualness of a two-piece just *screams* youth to her.

"It's about the naivety," she tells me. "We want *that* to be your signature too."

But it might be more conceivable for us to make being intensely nervous my signature. The uproar outside of Sam's studio makes me hide my face in Gerald's jacket. Kaytee said I'd get used to all of it, but I'm not sure if I will. Either way, the paparazzi doesn't respond well to my hiding. I am escorted into the studio by a refrain of disapproving jeers.

The leather couches in the studio of *Sam on 18* are a homesick-color yellow, like my dress from the art show. They're so bright and happy, I could suffocate. This must be written all over my face, because Norax asks, "Are you doing all right?"

"Of course," I say. "Nerves."

"You'll do amazing, lumerpa."

Beside her, Lennix adds, with a shred of irony, "Just be *yourself*."

Right. As long as I stick to my fake backstory while sitting here in a body that isn't mine. No problem.

From an intercom, there's an announcement that we have only five minutes until showtime. Suddenly, I can't stand still. I'm lucky Sam's show doesn't have a studio audience, or I fear I wouldn't be able to go through with this at all. But it's just going to be the three of us: Sam, me, and the camera.

As I struggle to remember how I was raised as an orphan (no parents to hunt down) in a small house in Betnedoor (nondescript), I watch as Sam Booker strides onto the set and takes a seat on a yellow couch. He's just about everything I expected Abby's husband to be, with a boisterous laugh and caramel hair mussed up over his head. He's like a son trying on his father's clothes in a blue suit two sizes too big. I wonder if that's the whole point—the whole angle. Lennix's cynicism seems to be getting to me.

"We've got royalty joining us tonight, brothers!" he shouts to the crew. "The first-ever interview of Emeray Essence! Who's ready?"

His crew gives encouraging cheers.

A deeper voice. "Are you nervous?"

The backstory I've been practicing wipes away when I see him. Chapter Stones is standing beside me, sipping a coffee from the stand I saw in a back room. I used to think of Bree when I saw him, but that's all been replaced by Lex now.

"What are you doing here?" I ask.

He points to an exit door. "I was filming an interview for *Key* at another soundstage. Saw all the commotion over here. Thought I'd check it out."

"And they just let you in?" But of course they would. He's Chapter Stones.

"I liked the posters they set up for this," Chapter says jokingly. "You're always getting coffee, you know that?"

"It was Norax's idea."

"It's cute," he says. He nods at my pink outfit. "Is that what they're going for with you?"

I really hope the audience likes a youthful blush, because now it seems permanent. I look to the floor, changing the subject. "I *am* nervous, to answer your question."

"Why?"

"I've never talked to this many people before."

"You've never talked to millions of people at once?"

The number nearly knocks me to the ground. I knew it would be a lot, but I hadn't thought of the actual number. I'm sure even my siblings will tune into this. They never could resist Famoux drama, even if they claimed to hate it. Will they watch it muted, coming up with obscene remarks I could be saying? How many other households will refuse to hear me out tonight?

"This is a lot of pressure," I say. "What if they all don't like me?"

"They already like you," Chapter insists.

"I'm in sixth place," I say.

"But you have their intrigue."

"Being intrigued with something is different than liking it." People were intrigued with Emilee too. I think about Lennix's words: *People also take photos of natural disasters.*

Chapter eyes me from over his cup. "Don't assume people will hate you by default tonight, Emeray. I know that might seem like the gut reaction, but for better or worse, you're not who you used to be. Whenever you can, use that to your advantage."

*To my advantage.* Like how he uses his fans to keep his ranking up. I think about Lex again, and my stomach twists into knots.

"You've got this, Em." He smiles, backing away into the dark.

The crew members are counting down the final few minutes now. I mutter what I can remember of Emeray Essence's fake origins like a prayer. When it comes down to the last minute, my pulse is racing. I barely have the chance to take a deep breath before a voice on an intercom announces that we're going live . . .

*Now.*

A television implanted into the wall beside me sparks to life, broadcasting the words *Sam on 18* in gold letters. I watch, shaking and trying so hard to keep Chapter's words in mind. I'm not who I used to be. I don't have to be who I used to be. At this point, it absolutely needs to be an advantage.

Sam's voice comes from hidden speakers all over, like an omnipresence. "Good evening, Delicatum."

The gold on the screen dissolves out into a wide view of the set. All the mystery and seriousness of the moment disbands as a grin splays across his face. "My name is Sam Booker," he continues, "and you're watching *Sam on 18*. Of course, I don't expect you're here just for my good looks and killer sense of humor. You were probably lured in by the very cryptic signs plastered around the world."

He gestures to the air beside him, where an image of the poster pops up. Animatedly, he recites, "*Grab a coffee and catch up with your newest friend. Tonight at 6.* Tell me, Delicatum, do you have your coffee ready?"

He waits, like he'll be able to hear the response right through the camera. His grin widens. "I can tell you that *we* certainly do." Sam points past the camera's view. "Rick, is it all brewed? Can you bring two cups up here for my guest and me?"

Rick, clad in a black shirt proclaiming *Staff*, scurries onto the stage with two matte black mugs. Another crew member follows with cream, sugar, and a thin vase bearing a bustle of white oleander flowers. These are all things that should've been set up earlier, but I see this is part of the charm of Sam's show. Not quite all put together, not quite all professional.

Once the coffee's been set up, Sam addresses the camera again. "Delicatum, I'm not sure if you've noticed, but the past month has had its ups and downs."

He's silent for a moment. A tribute to Bree.

"*But.* If there is anything that has shone like a light in all this darkness, it is certainly our special guest." Sam gestures to the side of the stage, toward where I'm standing. "People of Delicatum, you've seen her at the coffee shop, and you've seen her on the carpet, but now, I believe, it is time for you to *officially* meet Emeray Essence."

Music swells. I walk so fast onto the main set that the spotlights struggle to keep steady on me. When I reach Sam, I look out at the camera, but I see nothing. The lights they have on me are so bright that everything past our stage is black.

"Emeray." Sam extends a hand out to me. "It's an absolute pleasure."

I shake daintily, light-headed. I better not faint up here. "Thank you for having me."

"*Having you*? Thank you for choosing us! Now sit. How do you take your coffee?"

I tell him he can prepare it any way, so he passes a cup to me with cream and sugar. I thank him kindly.

"To be honest, I'm glad it was just coffee," he says, putting a hand to his chest. "Imagine if all you did was visit historical parks. I would've had to commission an entire monument to get you in here."

I giggle, then instantly wonder if it comes off as annoying. Did I use to get annoyed back at school when people giggled? Surely, the Fissarex must've made mine pleasant—the kind that makes you want to join in. Sam joins, which calms me considerably.

"Coffee aside, we'd like to learn a thing or two about you," he says. "Can I ask some questions?"

"Of course," I say.

"First, where are you from?"

And so the script and the lies begin. "I was born right here in Betnedoor, actually."

"How lovely! How many years ago was that?"

"Sixteen."

Sam's jaw drops. "Sixteen, *really*? I suppose you do seem quite young. Still, I assumed this was just that Famoux glow."

"I'll be seventeen in a few months," I say, "in March."

"I can't wait to see the party they'll throw for you!" he declares. "Now. Tell me more about your childhood."

My vague, but specific-enough life story follows. Sam is attentive, absorbing everything. He offers extra questions that I don't need to panic about before answering, and after a while it feels like an actual, private conversation. I almost forget about the cameras entirely, aside from the times when Sam brings Delicatum back into the discussion, turning directly to them every so often to offer a rhetorical question.

Sensing this personal touch works in his favor, I try doing the same. When he asks about my career aspirations, instead of looking down bashfully, I say to the camera directly. "I'd love the people of Delicatum to tell *me* that, actually," like planned, I ask the camera directly.

"You want Delicatum to *choose*?" He shakes his head, like it's absurd. "Too much power and jurisdiction in the world's hands!"

"I'd love the input, honestly," I say, back to bashful. The script is too comfortable to deviate for long.

"You know what? Why don't we get some input right now!"

Sam glances past the set. "Rick, do you have a fan chosen yet for Emeray's video question?"

"Video question?" I ask.

Sam turns to the camera, chipper. "We here at *Sam on 18* have been searching *all* night for a lucky fan to take part in Emeray's first live interview. We've actually been wanting to do this bit for months, except no one watches the show. So, you know, there were no questions." He gestures to me, delighted. "But now, with *Emeray . . .*"

"All good to go," calls Rick from offstage.

"Incredible! Let's meet our lucky pick!"

Sam points to the screen next to a camera, where an image of a young boy sitting cross-legged on his bed is sputtering to life. The image is grainy, so I have to squint.

And then, in a twitch of white-hot panic so sudden, it takes everything within me to not get up and run.

*No.*

"Hello there!" Sam chirps, unfazed. "Welcome to *Sam on 18!* Could you tell us your name?"

The boy's voice is cool and collected.

Just like I remember it.

"Felix."

Westin's second-in-command.

"Congratulations on being chosen!" Sam says. "My stats tell me over four million fans entered to win this opportunity!"

"I'm honored," says Felix.

Digging my nails into my palms, I force myself to maintain my outward composure, but I can barely focus. I've never once heard Felix say he likes the Famoux, but I haven't heard him say much besides insults against me. He could be a huge fan, for all I know. But my skin feels like it's being pricked by needles as Sam continues, "Now, Felix, you are the lucky person to get to tell Miss Essence what you think her career path should be. You speak for the people here, so make it count!"

He doesn't hesitate. "She can do whatever she wants. I just want to know: Are you happy with this life you've got, Emeray?"

This was not a question we prepared for earlier today. There is no reply that we planned and studied to make sure I'd answer with finesse. There was no warning that Felix would be here, eyes wicked as ever through the camera in his house, reaching me hundreds of miles away in another state and another body.

I inhale deeply, willing myself to look at him, not willing to believe he recognizes Emilee beneath all of this. "Yes," I say, finally. "I am."

Beside me, Sam clears his throat. This obviously wasn't the kind of fun question and answer segment he was anticipating from the video call. "Do you have anything else to say? Any hobbies you like that you might want to see her try?"

"No," Felix says. "That's all."

And the screen goes dark.

I am speechless, trying to steady my expressions, trying to look happy, confused, blank—anything other than scared. I look to Sam, who lets one more awkward second of silence pass before exclaiming, "Well! You really picked a thinker there, didn't you, Rick?"

I let out a small phantom laugh along with him. As he comically muses about if *he* is happy with his life, I lose focus, the dissonant cadence of Felix's voice multiplying in my ears like an out-of-tune chorus. I thought I'd seen the last of him, Westin, and the Greyhounds. But the sight of Lex at the art show should've been a clear reminder—the world is not large enough to separate me from my past. Even with millions tuning in, the one face I see might be one of theirs.

Suddenly afraid I've missed something, I snap back into the moment as Sam says, ". . . I'm curious to hear more about these music rumors?"

*Music rumors?* My mind goes blank, and then I exclaim, "With Kaytee! And Cartney . . ." I try to sound enthusiastically vague. "You never know. Maybe!"

"Oh, a woman of mystery!" He looks to the camera, his lips frowning but his eyes still smiling. "I guess we'll have to wait and see! That's all the time we have tonight! Thank you so much for tuning in, and thank *you*, Emeray, for joining us."

I smile, still feeling far from grounded. "Thank you for having me!" My eyes dart quickly to the camera. "Thank you!" I offer meekly.

"I hope you enjoyed your six p.m. coffee, and your subsequent inevitably sleepless night! My name's Sam, and you just watched *Sam on 18!*"

The little red dot that blinked all the while during the interview dies, and I let out a breath I didn't know I was holding.

Sam offers me a quick and gracious thanks before rising from his chair to speak to Norax and Lennix. I, however, stay glued to mine, taking in the bustle of the crew, trying to remind myself of the distance between Betnedoor and Eldae. But all attempts are futile—it still feels like the spirit of Westin van Horne is in the room.

"Well that—" a voice starts, but I cut it off with a sharp gasp.

I look over my shoulder and Chapter is sitting on the leather armrest where Sam used to be, his hands up in defense, one still holding his cup.

"Didn't mean to startle you there."

"I—I'm sorry." I flush, leaning forward to rest my head in my hands.

He chuckles a little. "I was *saying*, that went well."

"You think so?"

He shrugs and takes a sip of coffee, which I imagine is cold now. "I thought it was charming. Even with that randomly existential question."

"Thank you," I begin. I'm not sure what else I would've said next because Lennix is suddenly standing in front of me.

He purses his lips. "Well. That was . . . a start."

"A good one?" Chapter offers.

Lennix doesn't seem to feel the typical Chapter effect, because his demeanor remains stern and focused. "It was fine. Like I said, a start." To me, "We'll discuss this later."

I hold onto what he's said. A start. A start in the right direction. A start toward distancing myself from Felix, Westin, the Greyhounds . . . all of it.

That is, if they don't come up again.

When Lennix walks away, Chapter raises his cup. "To a fine start, I suppose."

# CHAPTER TWELVE

Following the interview, Norax and Lennix stay up all night reviewing the footage and analyzing it minute to minute, frame by frame. They share the notes with me the next morning.

"You just mentioned a birthday," Lennix said, pressing pause. "Is *Emilee* turning seventeen in March too?"

I hadn't thought about it. "Yes, but—"

"It's good you didn't give an actual date, at least," Norax offered. "This will just have to be a coincidence."

"It just felt natural for the conversation," I explained. "I didn't mean to—"

"You got too comfortable with Sam," Lennix said. "Never get comfortable in front of a camera. With secrets like the ones you keep, it's *dangerous*."

I'm both relieved and a little surprised when they glaze over Felix's question. Perhaps I did a better job at keeping my calm than I'd thought.

Then they have me step into the Analytix, and the Volx results surprise me. Turns out, I presented myself well enough to place me between fourth and fifth place on the Volx. As the reporters and fans sing their praises, I even venture up to third place for a brief moment. Third place! It's a random spike that I come back down from immediately, but the high lasts long after I leave the Analytix room. The idea of being a fixture in the top three, if I keep it up, makes me feel like I might actually stand a chance of living past the Darkening.

The general public consensus about what my career path should be is unclear. The video question had meant to give us this clarity. The media, however, did seem unanimously jazzed about the idea of a collaboration with Kaytee and Cartney, so Norax assures me she'll schedule a time to record it. I need to move on all these projects and features with the other members. Norax also plans to have me attend one of Foster's fashion shows, drafts up some shoot dates for a potential role in Chapter's next film, and muses about a very public painting lesson with Race. The first thing she's able to secure is a spot for me on the guest list for a tennis match as Till's plus one for the afternoon.

Naturally, Till in particular hasn't loved the idea of this forced inclusion. She gives my car the wrong location for the court, then tells all the reporters there that I'd ditched her. Instead of rushing me to the match Lennix insists we just check the Analytix, and luckily, people don't seem too bothered by Till's comments. I think her fans must've taken one look at my clumsy walk up to Sam and decided I wasn't going to offer much in the sports department anyway. But even so, my ranking on the Volx drops back down to fifth. There's no room right now to be anything but pleasant, and Till made me seem rude.

Till's betrayal hurts, sure, but it isn't unexpected. She hasn't really liked me since the moment she met me. The others are pretty indifferent so far. But it's Kaytee's silent treatment, above all, that's been hurting me most. She had been so excited and willing to bring me to Wes Tegg's with her before she knew DEFED was back. *She* was the one who thought it would bring my likability up. I'm not DEFED. I didn't even know they existed before I got to the hideaway, and I have as big a target on my back as the rest of them. So much for being all in this together, I suppose. Another performative aspect for the cameras, the show. If only Brandyce knew how right she actually was about all of them.

It's becoming clearer why someone like Bree wouldn't have many friends here.

"No more tennis matches," Norax decides when I surface from the Analytix.

"I think we gathered this much," says Lennix.

They have Gerald escort me back to my room, where I'm told to pick something sparkly out for tonight. Alongside the now-canceled tennis matches, Norax has packed this week's schedule full of appearances. Coffee shop visits, club nights, and so on. Apparently, this is the name of the game when it comes to keeping momentum up. If I'm seen getting my photo taken in all the hottest places around all the hottest people, then I'll always make the tabloids the next morning. People will get used to always seeing me around. Even more, they might grow to love it.

Tonight is my first club appearance, which makes me nervous. I'm not great with crowds to begin with, much less intoxicated, dancing ones. Still, I am to show up at one called Ace, and I am encouraged to rub shoulders with as many celebrities as I can. Kaytee is supposed to come with me, but I doubt she will show.

With a wide selection of glittery things in my closet, getting dressed is easy. It's the makeup part that causes the most trouble. I've been told that when going to clubs, a fresh face is the wrong move. But I've never done my makeup before, and sitting down at the vanity, I feel a little helpless. Kaytee and Till seem to put it on with such *ease* when in the Fishbowl. I wish I could ask them how, but the thought of wandering into one of their rooms to do so feels ridiculous.

I pull the cap off an eyeliner pen and poise it, prepared to make an error. The moment the ink hits my skin, however, it glides. It practically moves my hand for me, knowing where it needs to go without guidance. After the same results with eyeshadow and blush, I theorize this makeup must be responsive to me, some-how. It knows my face.

Examining the finished product, I'm surprised by my choices. Emilee Laurence would not choose this dress. The red sequins running up my torso would be far too attention grabbing. And what event would I have worn it to? No such events existed for me. No, if I were still Emilee Laurence, I would be lying on my bed tonight, staring at the ceiling and doing nothing.

But here I am, twirling for myself in a sequined red dress. And I do look beautiful. Westin and Felix and the Greyhounds couldn't call me *Sticks* at all, with legs and arms like these.

There's no way Felix could've known that was me he was talking to on the screen a few days ago. There's just no way. He wasn't even with Westin and the others when Norax found me. I remind myself this over and over until it's too much to bear, and I shove the thought of Felix from my mind. I can't think about this. I'll go crazy if I consider it for too long. I grab a pair of modest-looking heels and rush out the door.

I'm right to assume Kaytee won't be escorting me to Ace

tonight. At the last minute she insists she has unavoidable plans with Cartney. Norax has to corral Foster in from the hallway to take her place.

It's weird to be with him in the back of the car. The last time I *really* spoke to Foster was after my trip to Wes Tegg's, when he told me about Finley. All of that still baffles me.

Lucky for me, Foster is still friendly, like he was the first time he met me. It's a relief that not everyone's acting like Kaytee.

"So," he starts. "How have you been?"

I don't know how to answer that.

"Pretty hectic lately, huh?"

"Is everyone usually this busy?" I ask.

"No," Foster admits. "These are just . . . quite unusual circumstances."

An understatement. We watch the streets from the window as one of Cartney Kirk's songs plays in the speakers next to us. I think about our order on the Volx—Chapter, Kaytee, Foster, Till, me, and Race. Foster should be feeling good about his. Third and higher is a great place. A *safe* place. My position at fifth isn't preferable, but it's obviously better than sixth. It's a step between life and death. While I'm busy picturing the gauge in my mind, I almost don't hear Foster speak.

"I'm sorry, Em."

"What?"

"I would've hated coming into it like this," he says. "Death threats? That would've felt like a cheap trick."

I look down at my red sequined dress. If I wasn't here, I'd be lying in my room and feeling dead already. No real threat of it, but was that *living?*

"It's okay," I say.

"I swear it's better than this," Foster says. "Calmer. There's still a lot of fool's gold, sure, but there are also a few diamonds."

For a moment I'm silent, thinking of what the fans used to say about him. The funniest, the most welcoming. He was certainly so when I arrived—going head to head with Till to defend *me*, a person he barely knew, a person he barely even knows now. But that's also who he is. Everyone's friend the moment he meets them.

I can't help but wonder how much of it is wish fulfillment; how much he wanted that kind of person in his life back when he was Scott.

He contemplates me carefully. "I won't undercut you, okay?"

"What?"

"Those other brats are fair game," Foster says, "but you should make it. So you can actually live."

I don't know what to say. Had he been planning to undercut me tonight? Or later in the future? I guess it's futile to ask.

When the car pulls up and we step out, Foster turns his charm on like a light switch. He's several strides ahead of me, waving and winking at everyone. I try to mimic this as Gerald weaves us through a wall of light and sound.

The ruckus doesn't stop when we get inside—in fact, it gets *louder*. Drums are pulsing, techno melodies twisting and bursting. All I can make out of my new surroundings are silhouettes jumping, pumping their fists in the air, gyrating together on a dance floor of neon colors. There's a hint of smoke all over the place too—from what, I have no interest in investigating.

"Let's go to the second floor," Foster tells me. "All the *importants* are there. Keep your head up."

A bouncer ushers us toward a silver staircase. With my head

held high on Foster's request, people notice me, and their faces twist up in surprise. Now that the interview with Sam has aired, I am no longer only contained within a few quick camera shudders. They have now seen me talk, and laugh, and share my story with great vulnerability.

And, most importantly, they *liked* it. Maybe not *loved*, but we're getting there. Fans reach out toward me as we go, hoping to get a touch of my hair, or my skin, anything. We have to pick up speed when they almost pull me into the throng.

Ace's second floor is significantly more subdued than the downstairs romp. Here, there are leather couches and brightly illuminated tabletops; long-stemmed glasses and people wearing jewels larger than my fist. Toward the bar in the corner stands Betnedoor's elite flock, reaching out for colorful liquids, then spilling them all over the floor with carefree countenance. It's a lot to take in.

They notice Foster and me immediately. These celebrities have an air about them that's different from the fans downstairs, and I'm about to squirm thinking about all the ways they're scrutinizing me until I realize they're not doing that at all. Their glares aren't *glares*—I'm just still not used to people staring at me being a good thing.

The first person who dares to approach turns out to be Marlon York. "From Race's art show," he reminds me.

"I remember you," I assure him.

He reddens, a blush. If my own blushes are that telling, I'm in trouble. "It's really nice to see you again," he says. "We should still get together sometime. I'd love to talk music."

When he leaves, Foster is grinning at me.

"What?" I ask.

"This Marlon guy wants to go on a date with the new girl, huh?"

"That's not what it is."

"That's *exactly* what it is."

"No, he just wants to be a friend." Although I can't be sure, it feels genuinely absurd that someone would want to go on a date with me. But then I catch my reflection in the wall of mirrored material, and I'm reminded again—I'm not who I used to be. This is a face that has the potential to be desired. It makes my heart race.

Like at the art show, Marlon has opened the floodgates for the others. In come the crowds of celebrities hoping to speak to us, to get new insight into who I am. Insisting it'll help me be more sociable, Foster gets us two glasses filled with a crystal-blue liquid. I don't drink mine, but once he's got a few in his system, he's practically a caricature of himself.

He tells long jokes to everyone around us, garnering laughs and even a little applause. They tell him he should be a comedian. He flicks his wrist and insists he couldn't possibly. Perhaps only because he's a hint inebriated, he leans in close and doesn't even whisper when he tells me, "Finley always used to say the same thing."

I've been wondering about Finley—the star-crossed lover from his past life. Where does he think Scott went? Where does he think the letters are coming from? I can't ask these questions, though, nor can I let Foster keep talking about him here, in front of everyone. I look to the corner of the room where luckily, Gerald's already walking over. We're able to communicate somewhat wordlessly: I nod to Foster and say, "He should . . ." and Gerald nods back and puts his arm under Foster's to support him, escorting him to the stairs.

"You're right," Foster says as we go. "I need to get home and write a letter." He eyes me, mischievous. "You should too."

"To Finley?" I entertain.

"No, of course not," he says. "To . . . I don't know. That Marlon guy? Maybe Chapter?"

I almost stop walking completely. My face must have some tell to it, because Foster bursts into laughter, which only gets bigger when he spots somebody beyond us and points.

And of course, there he is. Walking slowly, looking thoughtfully at the dance floor, perhaps creating some complex opinion about it in his head. It's Foster's laughing that makes him notice us.

Chapter's eyes widen. "Emeray?"

I'm instantly flustered, thanks to Foster. "Hi."

"You had an appearance here too?" he asks.

"I—yeah. Foster and I were—"

But Foster and Gerald aren't beside me anymore, instead down near the entrance. As I watch them go, about a dozen people try to make eye contact with me, already walking up to introduce themselves.

Chapter signals to a corner of the room. "Do you maybe want to get some air? I know all the secret hiding places in these clubs."

"I . . ." I look back to the entrance. Gerald and Foster are gone now, already out. And the crowds are coming. If I try to meet up with them, I'll be stopped for a whole hour. "Yes," I say.

Then Chapter grabs my hand, and we go.

✕ ✕ ✕

The hidden outside patio of Ace is completely empty and completely stunning. The perimeter is flanked by dark wooden beams and maroon canopies. Blooming in the bushes is a multitude of flowers—vicarias, fresh gloriosas, and cherry red rosebuds covered in moss. Ace isn't modest about their collection; as I walk past, I observe a dozen signs proclaiming the flowers' names, prices, and in even smaller print, their ancient symbolism.

"Bree loved sitting out here," Chapter mindlessly notes. He realizes what he's said and shivers. "I mean, who wouldn't like it, right?"

"It's beautiful," I manage.

The mention of her name hangs in the air as we settle into one of the couches set around massive fire pits. Now the commotion from inside the club is a distant refrain in the midst of our silence, and the flames beyond us flicker, illuminating his face in orange and red. I can't tell what he's thinking right now. I never can. The other members are so straightforward with their leanings. Every glare from Till, every joke from Foster. I know where they stand. But Chapter is a mystery. Not even the other members seem to have him down. To them he's dating Bree, but he's not. To them his kindness is calculated, which cements himself in first place on the Volx. But I'm still not sure.

"What is it?" Chapter asks.

I decide to bring up something else. "The DEFED note," I say, "from the art show. Do you think they're going to send another?"

"It's hard to say," Chapter says. "Maybe, if they think it'll be useful."

"What do you think DEFED stands for?"

"No idea."

With that, my buffer conversation has started and ended, and we drift into another silence. Chapter isn't anything like the celebrities at the show or in Ace tonight either—he doesn't fill this moment with needless talk. He seems comfortable, propping a foot up on the edge of the fire pit.

Chapter sits up straighter, maybe self-conscious. "What?"

"I . . . nothing," I say.

"I don't know if you know this," he smirks, "but your stare is quite intimidating."

"I've heard," I say, ignoring the waves of my heart fluttering and dropping. Is that why he picked Lex at the art show? Her eyes?

"They're really yours, though," he says. "Not created by the Fissarex."

"How did you know?"

"Asked Norax," he says simply. "She was telling me about your role in the movie."

"So you asked her about my eyes?" I ask.

"Well, since you're always staring at me."

My gaze drops from his instantly, as if it'll prove my point. "I'm not always," I say.

"You are," Chapter insists, his smirk widening. "It always feels like you know something I don't."

I could say the same to him.

I try to imagine Chapter Stones asking Norax this. About my eyes. Did he really ask her, point blank, if they're mine? If Zoya concocted them? It's weird to imagine him talking about me at all.

Another lull stretches over us. The third tonight. I wonder to myself in odd anticipation who will first break it.

Then I realize Chapter is looking at me, challengingly, the way I supposedly look at him. I meet his eyes, and we stay there. Me staring at him, and him staring right back at me.

But Chapter's the first to break it, with an exasperated laugh. "It's too much," he insists. "Believe me, I wish I could be the one person who can look at you for longer than a minute, but it's very clear I'm not." He continues, "What are you thinking about now? What do you know that I don't?"

I anticipate my answer to be a question about the movie, what my role is, but I say something else entirely. I need to figure him out, even just a little.

"Why did you pick her?" I ask.

"Who?"

"Lex," I say. "At the art show."

Chapter thinks on this, then shrugs. "She told me she'd had a rough year. Almost didn't make it. I wanted to make it better. That's the best way I can."

"It wasn't because of the Volx?" I ask.

"Do you really think that?" Chapter shakes his head. "I was concerned about her," he says. "I wanted to help."

"Concerned?" I ask.

"It's my way of saying I care," he says. "Concern is a good thing. At least, I think so. When you're concerned about someone else, it's not about you. It's selfless. You'll do things for them that you get nothing out of, because you have to. You're concerned."

"But picking Lex made you look good," I say. "You got something out of it."

"Doing anything publicly seems like a calculated act, sure. But I did have genuine concern. I've checked up on her since. And if she wants to inform the world I've done that, she can. It's out of my hands whether or not the members will think it's deliberate."

"You checked up on her?" I ask.

"She has a lovely home."

I picture my own house. The boring, concrete walls. Lex lives in Waltmar, so she couldn't have one like that. She'd have a nicely built, attractive thing, with dark red bricks. Betnedoor's standard. Her life *is* different than mine.

"Concern is good," Chapter says. "I think it's got more to it than love."

I think about this. My family never seemed too concerned about Emilee Laurence. I'm certain—if only slightly—that they must've loved me, but being *concerned*? That was what my mother did. My siblings rolled their eyes at my tears coming home from class, but she would spend the whole afternoon trying to make me feel better. She was always concerned, she said, about me going to sleep still upset. That was how she'd say it: "*I'm concerned about you going to sleep upset.*"

He's looking at me again. I've created a pattern. Maybe my eyes are piercing, but I could say a similar thing about his entire face. While I hold it for as long as I can muster, I wonder if my own face is as unreadable as his always seems to be, or if I'm an open book.

It appears the latter. "Who was the boy in the video question?"

My blood goes cold. I'm the first to break the eye contact this time, glancing straight into the bonfire beside us. "Who?"

"From your interview," Chapter says.

Just the thought of Westin threatens tears in my eyes, so I lean in closer to the fire, hoping maybe the heat will stop it.

It's been nice to have no one bring Felix up in the Analytix, and for Norax and Lennix to glaze right past him, unaware of that slight flicker of fear in my eyes when he came up on-screen. It's allowed me to push him back as far as I can—pretend it didn't happen. But I guess it did.

"You knew him," Chapter says. "You were scared to see him."

And I'm also scared to even *think* about him right now, even in the safety of this patio. Some dormant flight instinct believes him to be lurking down a dark corner, his sidekick Felix and the other Greyhounds ready to drown me for good.

"I did," I say. A tear escapes. Of course. I wipe it hurriedly, only for a dozen more to spill. I guess these are overdue. Even when I came home from the interview, I didn't cry over Felix. I was still shocked. "Do you think he knew it was me?" I ask.

"He'd have to know about the Fissarex," Chapter points out. "Which he couldn't."

Chapter's right. But the fear has taken its toll now, and I'm crying freely at the thought of it. It's maddening. Somehow, Westin van Horne is managing to make me feel helpless again, even in this new life. Making me uncertain, unsure of myself. He should be a memory. But he's not.

"I'm sorry about what he did to you," Chapter says. "For whatever he called you."

"It's not your fault," I say, like he once told me about Bree.

Chapter reaches out, wiping a tear off my face. Maybe he knows my mind will wipe clear upon the contact, and he's trying to help me. Distract me. "I saw my siblings in the crowd of a premiere once."

"You did?"

He keeps the hand on my face, but looks off into the fire, nose scrunching up at the memory. But he persists in telling it. "They were so happy to meet me. Like they never had before."

"Did you tell Norax?" I ask.

"I didn't tell anyone."

We have this kind of trade-off, I realize. I told him about

my mother, whom I haven't even told Norax about, because of him and Bree. And now he's told me this, which he's kept secret, because of Westin.

He mentioned once how his family was kicking him out when Norax found him. My own didn't exactly love me, but Brandyce never threw me out on the streets. On the day I left, I ran out on my own. I chose to leave. It's hard to imagine what led up to his situation.

But I won't ask. There's something about the gravity in this moment, grounding me in this seat, reminding me we're *here, now*, in Betnedoor and not Eldae. We don't have to be there right now, not even in our heads.

"Chapter," I say.

He looks back to me. His face is so close to mine now. Close enough to make every nerve ending in me go haywire. Maybe it's all the honesty swirling in the air, or the memory of a life much harder, or the still quiet just beyond a roaring club that makes his face inch forward. Or maybe mine does. Or maybe they both do.

And the patio door swings open.

We draw back swiftly. The music from within Ace bubbles louder before muting again as the door clicks shut. Cartney Kirk stumbles toward us, a glass of amber liquid in his hands. I can smell the liquor on him before he's even down the stairs.

And he is positively *thrilled* to see me. "Ray! My dearest ray of sunshine!"

He's drunk, I register. And it doesn't look like he saw anything. My heart is racing as Cartney pulls me into a hug that outstays its welcome tenfold. I squirm out of it, hastily touching my face to make sure my tears are gone. "Where's Kaytee?" I ask.

"Who's Kaytee?" he replies, coy.

Chapter jumps into action and takes the glass from Cartney, who doesn't even notice—he's already over at the flower display, reading off the meanings.

"Look at this," Cartney says. "Vicarias mean *dance with me*." He extends a hand out in my direction. "Shall we, Ray?"

"I think we should be getting you back to Kaytee," Chapter says. "Where is she?"

"Why are you two going off about Kaytee? She's not here!"

"You had plans tonight," I say.

"If the plans are having no plans, then sure, Kaytee and I had a *lot* of plans tonight." Cartney slumps down onto one of the couches, suddenly grief-stricken. "Where did I put my glass?"

We're unable to get him through the club without drawing attention. Two Famoux members and a Famoux member's boyfriend—we paint an odd enough picture that we may as well be part of an exhibit, the way people gape as we go. The cameras out in front go absolutely mad for it, and all I can think about are what the headlines might make of this tomorrow.

"Chapter! Over here!"

"Emeray, give us a smile?"

"Over here, all of you!"

Bodyguards help us get Cartney into the backseat. Once the door shuts, he flails out, resting his head on my lap. "You are so much kinder than her," Cartney slurs, closing his eyes. "Kaytee would've pushed me away the second we got in the car."

As Cartney drifts off to sleep, we take in this turn of the night. I'm not sure where I expected it to go, but any vision I had certainly didn't end like this. I didn't expect any of this.

I can barely look at Chapter now, I'm so muddled. He may never have to worry about me staring again. I can't think straight about it, about anything. Take a moment to think, and everything drops like a terrific avalanche.

"It was *Sticks*," I say, suddenly.

"What was?" Chapter asks.

"You said you were sorry about whatever he used to call me," I say. "Well. That's it."

I'm not sure why I want Chapter to know this, but I do. Someone ought to.

"Sticks," he repeats, testing it out. "*Sticks.*"

The way Chapter says it is nothing like the way Westin and Felix used to. They'd always spit it out, like a swear. But the word becomes delicate now. A whole new thing entirely. It honestly feels sort of like a fever dream to hear that ancient word in his careful cadence.

Cartney opens an eye, alarmed. He pokes at my cheek. "Somebody calls you *Sticks*?"

I hesitate. "Well—"

But he's already past this, poking Chapter's leg. "And you're Chapter *Stones*?" He shakes his head, closing his eyes again. "Sticks and Stones. It's just mystifying."

*Sticks and stones.* I remember my mother saying that. She loved more about the old world than the ruined structures left behind— she also loved stories of it, passed down from the survivors. When my siblings and I were young, she'd teach us all their old stories and all their old sayings. This was one of her favorites to recite to me about Westin, in the midst of all her other little lies: *Sticks and stones may break my bones, but words will never hurt me.*

It didn't feel true. Westin used sticks, stones, words—whatever weapon he could find—and it hurt me every time. I never found much value in the sentiment.

"Sticks and Stones. How fantastic," Chapter says. He nods to me, something in his eyes I can't pick up. "It's like they knew you'd need me one day."

The car drops Chapter and me off first. Two guards assure us they'll get Cartney into his apartment even if they have to wrangle him inside, and then they're off.

There's an unusual awkwardness in the air between Chapter and me on our walk to our wings of the mansion. The bashfulness is usually just on my end, but even he is giving off a nervous energy. I start to feel stupid all of a sudden for revealing so much. He didn't ask what Westin used to call me. Why did I think he cared to hear about it? But just as I'm getting in my head, Chapter says, "I think I'll call you Sticks now, if you don't mind. Not in public, of course. But in the hideaway."

"Why would you want to?" I ask.

He smiles. "So it's no longer a bad memory."

# CHAPTER THIRTEEN

When I check the Analytix the next morning, my name has taken a dramatic fall in the Volx. At least, as dramatic a fall from fourth place can be, for me.

All the way back down to the bottom.

"*I heard she ignored a lot of people at Ace,*" says a gossip reporter. "*It's like—just because you're in the Famoux doesn't mean you get to be a brat!*"

"*That's an awful outfit,*" somebody tells their friend, scrutinizing paparazzi shots. "*Who wears that?*"

"*She's absolutely irritating,*" says someone else. "*Who does she think she is?*"

Almost every conversation I listen in on is a variation of this. Compliments and kind words come and go, but my brain can't filter them in. All I can do is listen in horror as a stronger, louder few take special note of my *every* action, singling out my slight turns or small faces as if they were life-defining personality traits.

And all I can think is, *what happened?*

It takes everything in me not to burst into tears as Norax clicks into the *Consensus* charts. It appears my positives are still the same as they were the last time we checked—*beautiful, interesting, refreshing.*

But there is one new thing in the list of negatives, and it may as well be in all caps.

"*Chapter Stones,*" Norax reads out.

"What?" I ask.

I expect her to be just as confused as me, but Norax seems to get it. Her lips are tightened into a thin line. "Of course," she says, setting the tablet down. "I should've known when I saw the photos."

"Known what?"

"They thought you and Chapter were on a date last night."

My mouth drops open. Oh, no. Someone must've seen the patio. Was it Cartney? I reel back, panicked.

"It wasn't a date," I insist.

"You two have been seen together multiple times now," Norax says, piecing it together. "He was even at your interview with Sam."

"He just stopped by," I say.

"None of the others did."

The Analytix room's door clicks open, and Lennix enters, calm as ever. He holds a peppermint tea in one hand, a stack of tabloids in the other. "So," he says, slowly. "Can anyone tell me what happened last night?"

I dare to flip through the stack. Each headline is more outrageous than the next. One claims I've ensnared Chapter in "a web of lies," whatever that means, and another insists I killed Bree in order to become a member and get to him. I scan the pages, and there's no mention of the patio. No pictures. Good. That makes me exhale.

Norax glances at the headlines and sighs. She stares off at the stool behind the glass. "They love him best when he's alone," she whispers. "That way, they don't have any threats."

"Who's *they*?" I ask.

But I already know. His fans. His massive, unfathomably dedicated fans. My memories of home can confirm this. Any rumor of Chapter and some costar or model was always wailed about upon inception and celebrated upon closure. What Kaytee said at the art show about him and Lex comes back to mind. Always available to date them. Being available, as it seems, is a massive part of Chapter's charm. So long as he is romantically unattached, then *anyone* in the world has the potential to someday be his. If someone was to stand beside him for too long, or to be seen in too many places with him . . .

The headlines are all the same. *She's tricked him. She's trapped him.* I am the villain, and he is the innocent victim. They don't need any proof. They're not looking for any. It makes me feel ill.

But Lennix starts laughing.

"*Wait*," he riles. He puts a hand to his chest. "Let me get this perfectly straight. You're telling me that you have a Famoux member who completely *annihilates* the popularity of any girl he's with, and you just let him waltz around the same club as the girl?"

Norax rubs her temples, clearly frustrated. "I didn't know Chapter was going to be at Ace," she says.

"Do you or do you not have control over your employees?" He's really laughing now. "Don't they work *for* you, Norax? Or is it just the other way around?"

Norax is visibly embarrassed by his elation. I strain. "It wasn't a date," I say again, pushing the magazines as far away from me as I can.

But I should've kept them to myself. Lennix grabs one, leafing for a specific page that cracks him up. "Look at this. They say they have footage of you two going into a back room. Didn't peg you for that, Emeray!"

"No," I stammer. "It's not—"

"This one says you were wearing his *hat* earlier? Now what's that all about?"

I pale. "Really, it's not—"

But just as quickly as it came, Lennix's laughter dries up like a desert. He slams the magazine down on the table with a loud *thud,* and the whole mood of the room shifts. "Norax," he says, stern. "I *told* you she was going to do something like this. Mess everything up just because she's got some crush. Didn't I tell you?"

"She didn't mean to," Norax says.

"Didn't mean to? Hold her accountable!" he shouts. "Actually, you know what? You decided this girl was worth it. Hold *yourself* accountable."

"This is just a bit of bad press!" Norax says. "You act like she's dismantling our entire institution!"

"And I wouldn't be surprised if that was your goal all along," he spits, venomous. "Some kind of sick way of ruining my campaign to get vengeance."

Norax glares. "Father, you have been free to leave the whole time. I am not asking you to stay. Emeray isn't asking you to stay."

"We both know that's not an option," says Lennix. He leans back into his chair, as if now bored of the subject. With his usual cruel calm, he moves right along. "Well, we all know the sure-fire way to fight this, don't we?"

"What is it?" I ask.

Lennix grabs a tablet from the tabletop, pressing the screen a few times. When he turns it toward us, there's a blown-up photo of Marlon York's face. "People also saw you talking to him last night." He sees I don't understand. He sighs. "Why don't you date him?"

"What?"

"Oh, don't play shy now," he says. "He's no Chapter, sure, but pretty handsome, right?"

"He asked her to play music sometime too," adds Norax. "At the art show."

Lennix shakes the tablet, triumphant. "Then he needs no convincing! Why don't we draft it up?"

"Draft what up?" I ask.

"A contract, of course."

I freeze. Cartney and Kaytee flash before my eyes. The strained embraces, the lingering bitterness under every sentence.

"No," I assert. "Can't it just be one date?"

"Contracts are only a safety precaution," Norax explains. "It prohibits non-Famoux members from saying anything bad about you or our institution."

"*All* my members had contracts," Lennix adds. "And let me tell you, they never had problems like the one you're in!"

"I don't want to do it," I say.

"You don't get to choose."

"I don't want to!"

"We need to do *something*," he shouts. "Your approval is in the gutter! Unless you want us to just kill you or something, so we can start all over again!"

Instantly, the tears fall, even though I swore I'd try to not cry anymore around him. It's embarrassing and doing me absolutely no favors or sympathy. Lennix just laughs bitterly. It frightens me to my core to know that if we can't salvage this, if I can't bring my spot up on the Volx, maybe he'll get his wish.

Norax grabs my hand. "Lumerpa, a dating contract is not the only answer. If you really don't want to, we can find other ways to get your approval up."

"Norax," Lennix says. "It's the smart move."

"She's a *Famoux member*, Father. Not a prisoner," she says. "We're not going to force her into this."

He exhales. "Do it your own way, then."

When I emerge from the Analytix room, Kaytee, Foster, and Race are both loitering in the hallway, waiting for their turns. Foster whistles low. "What *happened* after I left? Till said you're back at the bottom? What, did you throw drinks at everybody?"

"It's nothing," I say.

"Doesn't sound like nothing."

Beside him, there's a ghost of a grin on Race's face, and it makes me sick. I want to scream at him and Kaytee for being so cold to me, but I know I can't. Not with Norax and Lennix on the other side of the door.

But then he speaks. "It's odd you're having so much trouble," he says, "since you've got Norax *and* Lennix paying attention to you and everything."

"Excuse me?" I ask.

"Norax is barely even *looking* at the rest of us lately," Kaytee says bitterly. "And now you have Lennix too? I don't get why you get special treatment!"

"Hey." Foster comes to my defense. "Guys, it's just because she's new."

But they are unrelenting. Race shoves Foster aside, eyes locked on me. "You know they all think you killed Bree to get here, right? Does that make *you* DEFED?"

Kaytee perks up, and I realize they've thought of this together. "They didn't show up again until you came. If you hadn't showed . . ."

"What's going on over here?"

As if this couldn't get any worse, there Chapter is, coming down the hall to us. Just seeing him makes a dozen headlines flash before my eyes. I step away from Kaytee and Race, which means slamming my back against the wall.

"*Great* work yesterday," Kaytee tells him.

"What?" he asks.

"You derailed another career."

Chapter notices my crying face and realizes. "Wait—" He reaches out for me, but I sidestep, running away to my bedroom.

But is it even *my* bedroom, really? I would've never chosen the dark black bed frame, or the bright white vanity. I would've never chosen such stark colors in my life. Looking around the place, I get another wave of fear, only this time it's not Bree's presence I feel, it's her *absence*. This is her room. This is a set someone else has made for me, and I have been playing the part all wrong. A horrible impostor. I need to play this role better. And I really need to stop crying, letting them see my weaknesses. Pretend Kaytee's just another version of Westin. Be numb.

Chapter's hat is resting by the flowers, and my mind goes wild trying to piece things together. He had to have known the paparazzi were going to trace that back to him! He'd worn it earlier in the day! How can I be so—

"Sticks?"

Hearing the nickname stirs an odd feeling in my chest. It's

nothing like the jeers I used to get. In Chapter's voice, the word becomes so delicate, so disarming.

But it's not the voice I want to hear right now.

"I'm busy," I say.

"Can we talk?"

Chapter is at the door, adjusting his cufflinks nervously. Always the suit. Always the cufflinks. Even if he has nowhere to go. It's what his fans love, I grasp, so it is what he does. It's why he's always at the top of the Volx.

"*What*?" I snap.

He's surprised by my curtness. He takes a step back. "Sticks, if I knew any of—"

"Don't call me that," I say.

He frowns, but even an expression that somber on Chapter Stones makes me dizzy. The Emilee side of me can't even begin to grasp that I could be seen as an option in his orbit, much less a viable threat to his fans. Chapter is one of the most handsome men in the world. Sure, I'm Fissarex-perfect now, but how could *anybody* be a contender? They should glaze right past me in the photos without a moment's worry.

"I'm sorry," he says.

"It's fine," I say. I'd like him to leave. "It doesn't matter."

"It *does* matter," Chapter says. "I didn't—I wouldn't . . ." I've never seen him so tongue-tied. Usually, he's the one who knows exactly what to say and exactly how to say it. No wavering, no faltering. "I don't want you to think I did this on purpose," he finally says.

"So you *didn't*?"

"Of course not. I wanted to be there for you. Really, Sti— Emeray. That's all."

"Well. I guess it's just a few complaints in the Analytix," I say, bitter. "*Sticks and stones*, right?"

He frowns. "Emeray, I'm sorry."

As he leaves, the headlines flash through my head, an endless slideshow. *She's tricked him. She's trapped him.* They're just words, I remind myself. Just words.

And words, apparently, aren't supposed to hurt me.

✕ ✕ ✕

In the next few days, I make plenty of appearances, but I do them pointedly without Chapter Stones. Norax has decided our best bet now, if we're forgoing a contract, is to have me be seen with nearly every celebrity I've ever spoken to. That way, what might've seemed like a date once to the paparazzi now appears to be the first of many friendly trips with a whole revolving cast.

"You're getting to know your new *friends!*" she tells me, emphasizing the last word as if willing the media to start incorporating it into their headlines.

This angle is supposed to do more than just damage control on the Chapter situation—it's also working to further separate me from Bree. She not only had few friends within the Famoux, but also few outside of it. Sure, her television show had numerous guests, but she met them on the air. She was never seen partying with them, or zipping in and out of their houses. She kept to herself. If I can be the opposite of that, all the better for me.

The night after my career-killing club appearance with Chapter, Foster is kind enough to take me to one of his runway shows. Since he's onstage the whole time, I don't get to talk with him much, but it serves both of us just fine: I'm seen supporting a different Famoux man, and his show gets an extra surge of attention with my arrival.

"I was keen to take you to *this* show," Foster tells me on the car ride back to the mansion. He brings the collar of his leather jacket up—a piece from the collection. "Thought it'd be wise to plant those seeds for that little photoshoot we were planning, right?"

Norax wants my next Famoux outing to be one of the tennis matches with Till, but Till actually snorts right in Norax's face about that. They end up negotiating that I go to the court with her for a morning practice, which puts me out in the cold, getting tennis balls hurled at my face. This new body of mine is dexterous, sure, but I have no idea how to use it. I'm ducking for cover most of the time.

At a water break, however, Till actually apologizes for how curt she's been. "It's nothing against you," she declares. "You're just not going to be the reason I die. That's all."

I can at least respect her frankness.

Later that night I have dinner with a non-Famoux actress named Ritter, whom Lennix has mentioned. She's perfectly kind, and from what I've heard, immensely talented. But I've never seen her films, so we run out of things to talk about quickly.

Much to my surprise—and to Kaytee's disappointment—Race is willing to be my next public jaunt. Norax had us scheduled to make another appearance at Ace, but he turned his nose to that. Like Bree, he hates clubs. We grab lunch instead, at a place Lennix insists is casual enough to eliminate the wonder as to whether or not *this* is a date too.

It's hard to get to know Race, since he's such a closed book. At nineteen, he is the oldest of the members, Brandyce's age, which gives him the exact opposite air Norax wants me to be putting out. If there's one thing I do learn about him over the course of this lunch, it's that he's actually uncomfortable with a lot of the charms of this Famoux lifestyle. While waiters dote on us, presenting us free appetizers, he shakes his head and firmly insists we pay. When fans come up he's welcoming, but always a hint tired, too, like he wishes we could just go home.

At first, there's nothing to talk about. Even a topic like the weather is too fearful—*see any Darkening particles in the sky lately?* But after a while, Kaytee comes up, and the whole ordeal from outside the Control Room. When he's sure no waiters will come in and overhear, he tries to justify their terseness.

"We're very haunted by what happened to Bree," he says. "Kaytee especially. They weren't the best of friends by any means, but she was there. The first one to see . . ."

I know what he's talking about. In the Fishbowl on that fateful night, Kaytee had been the one who found Bree first. She put her hands all over the blood, her scream almost audible, even through our muted television.

"Kaytee really wanted to be your friend in the beginning," he tells me. "If I'm honest, I was fine with us just being acquaintances. But Kaytee . . . if she couldn't be close to Bree, she wanted to be close to you."

But that seems to have gone out the window now, with DEFED back. It's not worth getting to know me now, if I'm just going to die in the Fishbowl. I guess he and Kaytee assumed I'd stay at the bottom of the Volx for the whole month, because my spikes have been cause for worry. "Tensions are high," he says. "But we shouldn't have been so harsh to you."

On the drive back to the mansion, I can't help but wonder, if I were the next victim in the Fishbowl, would Kaytee cradle me, scream for *me*?

From the sounds of it, she'd just sigh with relief.

It's clear that Kaytee isn't pleased by this lunch when we arrive home. She clanks pots and pans loudly in the kitchen while she makes her own lunch, maybe hoping Race will notice she's just making hers now, while he'd been out eating with me. It oddly strikes me as something Cartney Kirk would do. Perhaps they are more alike than I initially thought.

Thanks to these outings, my low likability is budging. On the Volx, my name is fluctuating back into fifth place again. Not high enough for me to feel safe, but I wasn't there to begin with. And it's coming up again, now that Chapter's fans have started to calm their raging fires. That's a relief.

There's only one more chance for me to bring my ranking up tonight. The Famoux is scheduled to attend the premiere for Till's final *Riot!* film. This is my first premiere, so most of the talk about me in the Analytix is light and excited, thankfully. Everyone seems to be buzzing only about *what I might wear*!

Since the films are action driven, Swanson has provided juxtaposition in the form of a dainty, bright red ballgown. The red, her note attached says, is on theme with the film. The endless tulle and sparkle, however, is on theme with my own naivety. That's the buzzword. And with all the damage control we're doing after the Chapter incident, we could use all the sympathy we can get for a sweet, bright-eyed girl.

I'm advised to wear absolutely none of the eyeliner and mascara I was trying out at Ace. That way, I'm a different person than the girl in those photos with Chapter. Looking at my fresh, makeupless face in the vanity mirror, surrounded by a sea of bright red skirt, I look like a child playing dress up. But Norax loves it. "Bree was always so done up too," she tells me. "No one will draw any comparisons tonight."

I've been so distracted that it's yet to really hit me how this is my first movie premiere. The carpet at Race's show was only a small fraction of what I'll face tonight. As I brush through my hair, Norax briefs me on which reporters to stop at, and which to avoid, and what poses for the cameras get the best feedback. Lennix certainly would want to be with her, probably contradicting everything she says, but he's off on campaign business again—this time, in Eldae.

"Speaking of Eldae," Norax says. "I was just given some news. We've heard back from the guards I sent to Trulivent."

I stop what I'm doing, the hairbrush freezing in the middle of a gold lock. I look at her through the vanity. "You did?"

"They're doing fine," Norax tells me. "The guards saw your siblings out together at a market last week. We only saw your brother and sister, though. They couldn't seem to find your father."

"Oh no, that's okay," I assure her. "He doesn't leave the house."

Norax pats my shoulder. "Then they're all fine, lumerpa. Safe."

My stomach churns a little, although this is good. They're doing okay. They're moving on. But somehow I'm surprised that I was right. I *was* the problem all along. Their lives truly *are* better without me.

She's about to turn to leave the room, but I call her back.

"Wait," I say. "There's something else."

"What is it?"

It's a long shot to ask for this. But if they can't have me, they should have her. "My mother . . . She went missing two years ago."

It feels odd that I've never shared this with Norax. Somehow I've told Chapter this, and not her.

"I'm so sorry," Norax says.

"I was just wondering if it was possible for the guards to maybe look for her too?" I say. "Her name is Alexandra Laurence."

Norax frowns. "Emeray, two years? That's a lot to ask of me."

"I know," I say. "But I was just thinking—"

"There's no telling if your mother is even in Eldae anymore," she says. "If she's been gone for that long . . . I don't know where we could start."

The air in the room gets thick. Suddenly I regret asking. She did a nice thing for me, checking on my family, and I asked for more. I apologize, tell her to forget it.

"No, I *want* to help," she insists. "I just don't think we could do anything here. I'm sorry, lumerpa."

I swallow hard, returning to my brushing. Right apace with me, Norax launches back into giving me little tips on how to act at the premiere. Then she tells me about the calls she's had with Abby about *The X*. It feels like it's been ages since I last saw Abby Booker—since I last stood in her curious vintage-modern office. Norax tells me that they're ramping up the release date.

"When is it supposed to come out now?" I ask.

"Nothing set in stone yet. But certainly before the next Darkening."

Muscles I didn't even know were tense relax. Good. The sooner we can get it out there in the world, the better. Let Abby's work in the spread show everybody a million more reasons to love me.

Down in the foyer, the rest of the members are waiting. Seeing them all dolled up like this makes me a little starstruck all over again. Till has on a patterned dress, her bobbed hair in textured curls. Kaytee, in her usual fashion, is in a bright blue number. She looks me up and down when I walk in, then says, "Pretty."

I'm surprised by her attention. "And you look amazing," I say.

But the moment is over. She's turned to Race, whispering something in his ear as Norax bids us good-bye and takes the first car. She arrives at our events before us to assure security teams are amply prepared for our arrival. There have apparently been quite a few instances of catastrophic unpreparedness in the past.

"Here we go. Your last film," Chapter says to Till. Just hearing his voice makes me want to run far away. "How do you feel?"

"So, *so* happy," she tells him. "I hated these movies with a passion."

"No more acting?"

"You can keep that job."

They laugh. For a moment, his eyes flick over to me. Like Kaytee has done to me so many times before, I look away. No more staring at him, like I apparently do.

Gerald comes in to inform us the car is ready, then retreats to the garage. As we grab our coats to head out, a shrill cry and a clatter of dress shoes from another room startle us.

"*Wait!*"

It turns out to be Foster, who darts into the foyer with wild eyes, shaking a thin golden box. "We can't go!" he shouts. "Not yet!"

"What is it?" Chapter asks.

Foster holds up the box, panting. "We're supposed to open these before we leave."

"Who told you this?"

"The mailing guy. I was just sending a letter, you know, but then . . ." He rakes a hand through his hair, distressed. "We all have one. *DEFED.*"

Instantly, any calmness we might've had cracks like a thin

layer of ice. I feel like I'm sinking underwater as I follow the others into a sitting room with pink velvet couches. The color shouts for lightness, but everything's so heavy. On the coffee table: six boxes, all different sizes. Each with a brilliant gold tag. And one letter addressed to all of us.

> **What fun hearing about our young one's fake past**
> **the other day!**
> **It excites us so much to see the stories you craft,**
> **as we are in on the real secret.**
> **Speaking of, we have sent a few tokens from our**
> **prized collection.**
> **Please wear them tonight. Or else.**
> **DEFED**

Till gets worked up. "Why would they do this before *my* premiere?"

"Because we're all going," Race guesses. "They wanted to give us these all at once."

We stare at the boxes in a line, no one daring to make a move. Finally, it's Chapter who goes first. Ever the leader. He grabs the box with his name on it—one of the smaller ones. He reads the note attached carefully.

"To Chapter," he says. "These belonged to Bree."

He takes off the lid, and everybody holds their breath. Chapter's brows furrow as he examines the contents, but once he's gotten a good look, his face wipes completely blank.

"They're cufflinks," Chapter says, simply.

"Bree owned cufflinks?" Foster asks.

"No."

Chapter raises one up for us to see. They're white, but not perfectly white. A little cloudy. They've been cut haphazardly— one edge is jagged, another smooth, the centers haphazard and bumpy. I can't figure out what's wrong with them until all of a sudden, it clicks.

Kaytee puts a hand to her mouth. "Are they . . ." She closes her eyes, letting her question fade off.

But we all know exactly what she was going to say. And she's right. They are.

The cufflinks are made of *bone*.

# CHAPTER FOURTEEN

Movie premieres are like a game of falconry. The Famoux members are the falcons, ornamented in silk gowns and suits like little hoods and bells strapped to our heads. Norax is the falconer who dons the long leather gloves, letting us perch three to an arm at the start of the red carpet. Once the night is over, and we've done our hunting for attention and photographs, we will retreat right back to her. That is, if we're not hunted first.

Norax is all happy exclamations when we surface from our car. "Stunning!" She grabs my cheek, examining my face. "Did you get here all right?"

"Fine." I don't know what else to say.

If she sees how shaken I am, she must be writing it off as nerves, because all she says is, "You'll do amazing. You're a lumerpa." She glances over to the others. "You're *all* lumerpas, my dears."

A bird so bright, it absorbs its own shadows. I wonder if any of the other members are also thinking about how untrue this feels. We have not been able to absorb *any* shadows as of late.

I don't know how Chapter is wearing these cufflinks tonight. His hardened expression marks his discomfort. He's careful to keep his hands behind his back as Norax dotes on us.

The other gifts were their own form of unpleasant, although none quite as sinister as Chapter's cufflinks. All pieces of their past. DEFED's way of showing us just how dedicated their devotees are.

Kaytee was given a red silk headband her mother made her. "She put these little stitches on the back so I'd always know it was mine," she told us, frantic. The headband clashes in every way with the color of her dress, but there's no option except to wear it. When Norax asks about her accessories, she offers a curt shrug. "Swanson picked it out," she lies. "Obviously, it's a trend."

Beside her, Race's gift fits well enough with his own black suit. He was given a white leather bracelet and positively refused to explain its meaning. It has to have evoked some kind of horrible memory, though, because he got as white as the material when he saw it.

The same look struck Foster when he opened his gift: a long chain with a locket pendant. "I gave this to Finley," he told us. "Said he'd never take it off."

And yet, there it was, right in front of Foster.

It's the intrusiveness of these gifts that makes them so frightening. These objects aren't as foreboding as the bones, but just like their note to us before the art show indicated, it is clear that DEFED has access to our past lives, our past homes, our past people . . .

"I have no idea if Finley's safe," he told me, staring down at the blankness inside the locket. No photo, although he swears there used to be one.

"You're doing everything you can," I said.

He shook his head. "I'm letting them win."

"There's no winning," Race asserted from the backseat, grave. "This is a game to them. They think they can play with us like dolls to make their lives interesting."

Of the six of us wrapped up in this game he mentions, Till is the only one unwilling to play tonight. She opened her own small square box quickly, as if she already knew what was inside.

"Of course," she said, holding up a dainty silver ring with a brilliant diamond. The very sight and size took my breath away.

"That was *yours*?" Kaytee asked, surprised.

Till nodded, letting the ring drop back into the box. "And I won't wear it."

"You have to," Foster said.

"This is *my* premiere. I won't."

At the edge of the carpet, I wonder if she wishes she'd slipped it on before we left the mansion. After all, if Chapter can brave the masses with his cufflinks on, surely she could've worn a ring. Of course, rumors would've spread like wildfire if she had, speculating on who the lucky fiancé could be.

Norax draws us into a reluctant huddle. "All right, kids. This is our first official premiere *without* Bree, and our first official premiere *with* Emeray. Let's make the most of this."

At the mention of my name, I shrink. The other members are frustrated by my gift, no doubt. I don't blame them. Because the contents of my box were not from my house they know the color of, nor from my school I'm sure they're aware I attended, nor from any part of my past. Just a pair of ruby earrings.

"What do they mean?" Foster asked in the foyer, bracing to hear the worst.

"Nothing," I said.

The truth is, I've never seen these earrings before tonight. My mother didn't own any like this. Neither did Brandyce. I'm not sure if I've even seen a ruby up close before opening the box.

The other members' tags were simply labels. They didn't come with explanations like Chapter's did, revealing the origin of the bones. They didn't need to—the members knew what their objects were. But DEFED must've known I'd be confused, because mine had a note attached as well.

**These will look so pretty on you.**
**Have a lovely night, darling.**
**Much love.**

It's that final bit, the *much love,* that has stirred the most unrest from the others. They got horrid reminders, and I got a gift? And *love*?

"You have *got* to be kidding me." Kaytee exhaled sharply, tossing her headband to the floor. She whispered to Race, "They can't *seriously* favor her too!"

She's still fuming on the red carpet, refusing to meet my eyes. Most of them are.

The earrings *do* look pretty on me. DEFED was right. The red matches my dress so perfectly, it's frightening. When Norax sees them, she makes a special note of their sparkle. "Did Swanson give you those?"

"Sure," I say.

"They're perfect."

After more encouraging words, Norax releases us from our huddle—from her leather glove, sending us off into the glitzy woods to hunt. The falconry begins.

Like last time, I begin at the barrier for fans. Everyone I speak to brings up different parts of the fake past I shared on Sam's show with shaking, pseudocasual tones. They give condolences for my fake parents, query about what my fake homeschooling was like, and beg to know more about all my fake hobbies. I smile brightly and answer as vaguely as possible.

Unlike Race's art show, this premiere has an extra element to its red carpet: reporters. From what I've heard, they can be quite relentless in their pursuit of new gossip. Norax gave me a whole list of nicer ones to gravitate toward, but even they get too terse for my liking.

"Tell me about *Chapter*," one says, shoving her microphone in my face. "What was it like to go on a date with the world's most eligible bachelor?"

"I didn't," I say. "I went to Ace with Foster."

"Are you saying you were on a date with Foster?"

"No—we're friends."

The reporters on this carpet are not like Sam on his show. They all appear to be great at spinning the story, right before my eyes. I watch what I say like a hawk. I can't be a rabbit here, falling into their traps.

"What about Marlon York?" a different one prods. "I've heard around the rumor mill that you might be going on a date soon?"

The contract Lennix proposed runs through my head. I play dumb, like Norax suggested. "What are you talking about?"

"He said himself that he talked to you. Are you denying his claim?"

I hesitate too long. A million camera flashes capture me caught in a lie. "Oh, I think he mentioned playing music once," I relent. "But that was a while ago. I forgot."

"Does this mean you're officially a musician?"

"I'm just trying things out," I say earnestly. The viewers need to know this next part. "I'm open to doing *whatever* people want to see from me."

Somehow, I make it out of the reporter trenches and into the main part of the carpet. The paparazzi, with their sporadic yelling, actually soothes me after all of that. I give them my best poses, getting nothing but praise in reply. This is by far the easiest of exchanges to be made on the red carpet. I stand, they shoot, and we're both happy.

Someone comes up close to me, talking into my ear as I adjust my arms on my sides. "Do you mind if I stand near you while you take photos?"

Cameras go off eagerly as I notice Marlon York smiling beside me. I step away. "I'm not supposed to be posing with any people tonight," I lie.

"Come on," he insists. "Just a few photos?"

Now I'm getting mad at him. Does he *want* to be corralled into a dating contract? Maybe he does. It would certainly only benefit him to be aligned with the Famoux. Maybe his label's been putting him up to it all along. It makes me fume.

The two of us standing near each other is causing quite a commotion. I tell Marlon I have to go, then dash away, joining Foster, Kaytee, and Race by the theater doors. It's too late, though. The damage is done.

"Nice show," Kaytee remarks. "Didn't know you knew Marlon."

"He walked up to me," I say. "I didn't—"

"Are you trying to copy me?" she asks me. "Get a contract? Release albums with him?"

"Of course not."

"DEFED already likes you. Just lay off *my* life, okay?"

I touch one of my earrings, feeling self-conscious, as Foster reminds Kaytee that I've been at the bottom of the Volx plenty of times, while she still hasn't yet.

"So them sending her *much love* doesn't make you think maybe they like her?" she asks.

"It was honestly ominous," Race admits, which only riles her more. "If they ended *your* note with that, you'd think it was a threat."

It looks as though she may be considering this, but she says nothing. She adjusts her homemade headband, bored. "Whatever."

In a matter of minutes, Till finishes her walk and meets up with us, letting out a tired sigh. "I'm not going to miss this," she says. "Where's Chapter?"

"Choosing his newest date, I'm sure," says Kaytee.

He very well could be. He's at the barrier, laughing with the fans I'm sure have raked my name through the mud this last week. As he poses for photos with them, he keeps fidgeting with the cufflinks, attempting to hide them. I can't imagine what he'd say if anyone brought them up.

When he leaves the barrier, he leaves empty-handed. No date tonight. The reporters are curious about it. Some of them are close enough to where we stand for me to listen in.

"I see you're not doing a repeat of your last appearance," says a reporter called Thomas Hotch. In the time I spoke to him, he tried to convince me that I was actually in a secret tryst with Ritter, the actress from my week of outings.

Chapter waves a hand casually, as if to dismiss this, then quickly covers his sleeve. "Oh, I'm not going to make a habit of it."

"But your fans loved it! I think half of them here tonight wore formal wear just in case!"

"Better to keep it special," he says. "Or else it would lose its meaning."

"Well, speaking of *dates*," Hotch presses on, getting to the meat. "Could you possibly tell us anything about the one you went on last week?"

Chapter crinkles his nose. "What date?"

"Surely you've heard the rumors about you and Emeray . . ."

"Oh, that wasn't a date," Chapter insists.

"It wasn't?"

"Emeray and I, *dating*?" Chapter shakes his head at this, like such a thing would be impossible. "We ran into each other at Ace, that's all. We're friends."

"You're close friends?"

"Of course, the Famoux is a family," he says. "But that's it." He looks to the camera, voice turning playful, albeit exasperated, as he adds, "Everyone out there can stop harassing her now, all right? She doesn't deserve that."

My shoulders, initially stiff in anticipation that he might throw me under the bus, soften. Their conversation changes course with ease, and he laughs brilliantly at one of Hotch's jokes. Just beneath the cameraman's eyeshot, he twists at the cufflinks, unable to let them go untouched for more than a minute.

While Hotch began this interview with a hungry face, ready to rip into a scandal, he's pleased as he turns away from Chapter. It is something else to behold. Absolutely nothing like the way things went down with my interviews. I'm not sure how Chapter has such an effect over fans, reporters, *everyone*, but I'm glad. If they've all listened to him tonight, I'm in the clear.

As we make our way into the theater, I catch up with him and whisper, "Thank you . . . Stones."

He smiles. "Least I could do, Sticks."

Till's final *Riot!* film is a blurry haze of explosions and fight scenes. To the audience, it's crystal clear, in the highest definition possible, but it won't focus in my line of vision. I'm thinking about Chapter's message to his fans. A part of me wants to get up and run to check the Analytix right now—hear what the people are saying about his statement.

It'll have to wait until we leave the after-party, though, which is being held at Ace. The place has transformed completely for the event, made to look like one of the sets in the film. The dance floor is bedecked in movie paraphernalia, with gadgets encased in glass and dummy props strewn on the floor, like confetti.

"Do you think we can take these stupid things off now?" Race asks, pointing to his bracelet. Music from the band in the corner is thumping now, so it's hard to hear him. "The premiere is technically over, right?

"I wouldn't count on it," Foster says. "If there was going to be any place they might be lurking to check, it'd be here."

He's not wrong—the place is packed. Subtracting the lucky plus ones and sweepstakes winners, the bulk social stratum is a sleek shade of celebrity. I see some faces I've encountered during my outings—a long list of names I can barely recall when they walk up to me and shout *Hello!* and *Remember me?* I do my absolute best to pretend that *yes, of course I do!*

The after-party operates like the red carpet, another game of falconry. We go off on our own, forging different paths with different packs. The other members do this easily—anywhere I look I find one conversing, barely needing a beat to breathe. This past week, socializing every night has been exhausting. I've never had to talk to so many people so often in my life. How long will it take before this kind of activity doesn't tire me? How long until I arrive someplace and *expect* everyone's eyes on my movements, everyone's ears on my words?

Feeling egregiously antisocial, I migrate toward the bar, though I have no intention of drinking. Still, multiple glasses are passed my way, their holders hopeful for acknowledgment. Only one of them gets my attention . . . in the form of an eye roll.

"You like gin, right, Ray?" Cartney Kirk pushes a clear glass toward me. I push it back. "Oh, come on. I know you'll like it."

"I'm fine," I say.

He places the glass in front of me, decisively, but I hand it to the bartender. Cartney shakes his head. He drums the bar top, impatient to converse. "Have you noticed Kaytee being weird lately?"

"What do you mean?"

"It's like every single date of ours *needs* to be public nowadays."

"Aren't they all public?"

Cartney gives me a look. "Ray, she's my girlfriend."

"But not really," I say. "I mean, she has . . ."

It fades off when his face contorts, even more confused now. He must not know about Race. Of course. Why would Kaytee let him in on that, if it means more potential loose lips?

And now I'm backed into a corner. My mind reels, backtracking. "I mean, don't you just do all that for the media?"

"I play music for the media," Cartney says, "but that doesn't mean I'm not allowed to play my guitar a little when no one's around, does it?"

I shift, uncomfortable.

Cartney sets his own glass down in front of me. "Loosen up a little, Ray."

He walks away. I give the bartender the glass, and he gets me water.

My attention is piqued by a woman moving through the club. She's older than perhaps everyone here—around Norax's age, maybe—so she sticks out even as she weaves through the dance floor. I get the urge to follow her lead, pushing past groups with arms extended out for me to grab.

When she reaches the door, she looks over her shoulder, locking eyes with me.

And I stop dead in my tracks.

This person looks like my *mother*.

It can't be. Her hair is gray. My mother is not that old. But the same sensation I got when I saw Lex at the art show waves over me, making me feel light-headed. Of course it's right now that another person tries to approach.

"Emeray!"

I've never seen this man before, but he acts like I have. Primped hair, blue suit, and a face that's so animated, it's nearly a mask. He grabs my shoulder and digs deep, simulating camaraderie. Anyone around us would think he knows me.

I'm about to tell him to please leave me be, but then he says, brightly, "I'll go for the *E*. For your name."

And then everything goes into complete hyperspeed. He slips his hand down from my forearm to my palm, holding it out in front of me. Before I can squirm, he's pushing something silver against the skin below my thumb with white-hot proficiency.

I let out a shriek, recoiling my arms into my chest. My skin is *searing*—a glowing red curve on the edge of my wrist. Using every piece of strength the Fissarex has given me, I shove him off just as Gerald grabs hold of me. Before Gerald can catch the man, he disappears into the crowd. Gerald herds me to the exit.

"Stay calm," Gerald says. "People will stare."

"What happened?" I ask.

"Stay calm."

They must think I'm drunk and whining as he weaves me through the crowds. Meanwhile, I can barely function, the pain is so sharp and so searing. And that woman, my mother's looka-like, I can barely remember her face over all this pain. Everything that's just happened is too much to process.

We leave Ace through a back door to the car waiting in an alley. Lucky for me, this isn't a repeat of the day my name was leaked to the public. The bustle from the front of the club is a distant cry. The expanse between the door and the car is empty.

As frantic as I feel in this moment, I can't help but notice this is the calmest walk outdoors I've had in a long, long while.

× × ×

There were five of them stationed around the perimeter of Ace, waiting. They wore party-appropriate attire, blending into the mix with ease. When their job was done, they left no trail, not even the slightest indication of their existence. We know next to nothing—we don't even know for sure if there were just five of them, or if there might've been more lingering elsewhere. All we know for sure is what they did.

"They branded you," Zoya tells us through the screen of Norax's tablet device the next morning. I haven't seen her at all since the Fissarex, but as Head of Reformation, she's the expert on our bodies. Still, it's odd to see her, even in this digital format. It's like she's a part of my old life.

"Branded us?" Kaytee looks at her wrist, where an off-centered letter *D* blisters red. "Why?"

When we all place our wrists together, they almost spell *DEFED*. Almost, had I not pushed my own person back. What was supposed to be a curved *E* is incomplete, just a curve. Chapter got the other *E*, though, and he assures us the pain of his burn was formidable.

But DEFED only has five letters, and there are six members. The only person not to be branded at all is Till, and she's been a mess about it.

"People were around you all night," Foster tells her. "It was your after-party. Nobody would've been able to just come up to you."

"But the word is *complete*," she cries.

"They could've added a—"

"It's a message, Foster!" Her voice raises with a crack. "I should've just . . ." She stops herself before revealing any more. "I'm so *stupid*!"

"I don't know why you're all so adamant that the word they were trying to spell is *DEFED*," Zoya says, clueless. "It's not even a word."

"Whatever it is, I don't like it," Norax says firmly. I can tell she's glad Lennix isn't here, and she can deal with this alone. Gerald and the other guards were good about getting us out of the club before anyone noticed. I doubt this branding will make the news at all, meaning it might go unmentioned to her father. "I don't know what these punks want, but I don't like that they think they can get away with this."

But she doesn't even know the half of what they've gotten away with.

Zoya has explained to us that branding was an old-world

practice, mostly used in farming. When done purposely, it is meant to be permanent. To mark territory. "Even though I have designed your skin to never scar, not even you Famoux members can escape that level of extreme heat," she says. "There will be a mark left if we don't treat it."

"*Really*?" asks Foster. He stares at his letter, the only *F*, with wonder.

"A branding burn typically takes six months to finally scar white," Zoya explains. "But Fissarex creations heal faster than the average person. Your scars are going to become white in no time at all. I'd give it a day."

". . . But we'll be getting rid of them today," Norax asserts. Before Lennix comes back, I gather. "You're all scheduled to go back to the Fissarex so Zoya can use her little eraser. We'll be leaving in an hour." With this, she exits, leaving the members and me to stare at our blisters, stunned.

"DEFED is going to kill me," Till says. "This is a message, just like any of their notes. They're really going to kill me because I didn't wear a *ring*."

"You don't know that," says Chapter.

She huffs. "You don't even *know* what it's like to struggle on the Volx, you—"

"Till," Foster warns. "Let's not argue this early." It's odd coming from him, remembering how he addressed her at my tea party. All the sharp accusations. But he's really become somewhat of a peacemaker lately. It must have something to do with his constant spot in third place. Comfortable enough to not be afraid, but not high enough to be a perceived threat.

Till takes a deep breath and stands. "I'm checking the Analytix," she announces, then exits.

A stillness settles between the rest of us. What a night. The gifts. The branding . . .

"Why would they do it?" whispers Kaytee.

That's what I'm wondering. Are they messing with us? Trying to get in our heads? There was no reason to send Chapter cufflinks made from the bones of his best friend. There was no reason to press white-hot pokers to our wrists.

"It's like they said in their first note," Chapter says. "*We're lacking motivation.*"

"I'm pretty damn motivated by the threat of dying," says Race. "Why do they think we need *more* motivation?"

I look down at my blistering arm. An old-world practice to mark territory. Race's thought about DEFED thinking we're their dolls comes back to mind. They want to play with us. As far as they're concerned, they own us.

"Are we really going to have to go back into the *Fissarex* too?" Foster asks, shuddering. "I hate going back to Eldae."

That hadn't occurred to me. I look down at the curved blister on my wrist, suddenly nauseated. The pain of the Fissarex is bad enough, but it's no match for the dread that hits me at the thought of being in Eldae. It would mark the first time back since that night at the Fishbowl—since everything up to now was set into swirling motion.

"I don't want to go," I whisper.

"Then don't," Chapter says.

"You heard Norax."

"Are you guys not going to go?" asks Foster. "Because I'll join that." He shows us the *F* again. "When you really think about it, it could stand for Finley." Just the mention of the name makes him tense up and look at his locket again. "I guess DEFED knows I need a lot of reminders. Keeping it could help."

Chapter glances down at his own letter on his wrist, the curved *E*. He considers this. "It's sort of interesting to have something that stays." He asks me, "Do you remember what scars you used to have?"

Observing my flawless skin, I can barely name one. I know there used to be a scar on my arm from an accident in the kitchen with Brandyce, but I don't recall how long the cut was. Maybe at some point I'll forget it entirely.

Chapter, Foster, and I end up not going to the Fissarex for scar removal. Norax looks like she could faint when we tell her, but we're unyielding enough that she finally relents. She's not going to force us like Lennix would. Of course, Kaytee and Race have no use for the two *D*'s branded on them, so they don't back out. Norax is absolutely aghast at leaving four of us at home without her, but eventually, their car pulls away from the mansion.

My first order of business when they're gone is to check the Analytix. My name stays put in fourth place on the Volx as I hear a whole assortment of Chapter's fans accepting his statement and dismissing me as no longer a threat. I swear I hear a few voices I recognize, people from back at school, but maybe I'm just paranoid.

1 – Roman
2 – Odette
3 – Quinn
4 – Emilee
5 – Scott
6 – Holden

When I exit, Chapter's in the hallway, examining his mark. It's in the scab phase, red and embossed.

"Are you going in?" I ask.

He looks to the Analytix, as if just remembering it exists. "I was waiting for you," he says.

"Why?"

"Well, it's already morning again," he says, suddenly wry. "Eventful night. Did you want to have some coffee?"

The carafe is already chugging away in the kitchen when we get there. As he prepares the cups, I can't stop noticing every single thing he does, as if strung out in slow motion. He fills a mug with coffee, and I notice the vein in his arm when twisting to pour. He takes a breath, and I count the seconds until he exhales. When he holds out the cup, all of my senses ebb and flow. I don't know why.

"So you're looking at me again," Chapter says. "I missed it."

"I'm sorry for how I overreacted—" I start.

"You didn't overreact," Chapter says. "The fans did. They mean well, always, but I'll be the first to admit they're sometimes over-zealous." He takes his own mug in his hands, shifting in his seat. "But now they know not to worry. Since we both confirmed it was nothing."

"Right," I say.

Maybe it's just me, but the air gets awkward. As I take a sip, I notice my hands have started lightly shaking, the pink curve of my scar blurring with the movement. It was undoubtedly an eventful night, but the shaking is a new development. It takes until he speaks next for my heart to suddenly jolt, and for me to realize it's because of him.

"You're doing better on the Volx," he says. "All those outings really undid my damage, huh?"

Have his eyes always been this blue? How did the girls at school ever gaze at photos of him in their lockers like they used to? I can barely look at him anymore without feeling like I'm on fire.

"It was nice to be around the others," I manage. "I had a good lunch with Race."

"Getting to know our costar," he says.

"Our costar?"

"Norax told me he's joining in on the movie. *Algus & Alondra*, it's called," he says. "They're making the announcement soon."

Now Till, Race, and I will have invaded his career path, not counting Bree with *Key* before the Darkening. That's over half the Famoux. It's hard to tell if Chapter's bothered by this, so I decide to ask.

"Not really," he tells me. "I mean, I get it."

That we'd all want to encroach on his unrelenting success. Get a shred of what comes too easily to him. He doesn't have to say it in those plain terms, but I'm sure it's on his mind.

"Better set for me, anyway," Chapter says. "The *Key* set with Bree was great. Easy. I'm sure you're aware of how celebrities tend to act a little like fans when they're around us."

I think of Marlon—the way he's always sputtering on his words and blushing. But half my interactions with Chapter have been a version of that. Maybe the glint in his eyes suggests he knows this.

"That makes sense," I say anyway.

I find Foster later in the library, flipping through the mystery section, still wearing his locket from Finley. He's still considerably wracked by the gift.

"He hasn't sent a new letter in weeks," Foster tells me. "I just thought he was busy, but now I'm thinking . . ."

"He could be busy," I say.

"Or they could *have* him somewhere."

"They'd tell you if they did," I guess. But we can't be sure.

Foster insists he doesn't want to think about any of this any longer, but then tells me more about Finley anyway. Distracts himself with the origin story. Apparently, his name isn't even Finley—it's Lee Finnegan. He liked coming up with variations of his name every so often, as if creating new identities for himself. I'm told of the time Finley asked their whole school to refer to him only as *Finn*, and another time when he wrote *Leonardo* on all his papers for an entire semester. When choosing an alias for him and Foster to use in their written communication, he decided *Finley* was a substantial enough variation that, if anybody were to happen upon a letter by chance, they'd never even guess that it was him. So it seems their love was secret, even before the Famoux got involved.

But DEFED certainly knows about it.

Finley works at a grocery store in their hometown, a small one in east Eldae called Gateswood. Most of the letters he sends are mundane, full of complaints about the customers and his troubles making ends meet. Foster tells me how he wishes he could send money—for apparently, we do deal with such currencies, even though most things are given to us freely—but Norax is in charge of our finances. He can't request this without her finding out about them. Just writing the letters is a big enough risk.

Thanks to the short flight times on the Famoux jet, Kaytee and Race manage to get back to Betnedoor by the evening, with freshly repainted arms that almost seem to glow with a strange newness. Race tells me about the pain, how it's worse than I even remember. A few hours later, I watch him use that new Fissarex

hand to sign his contracts at the *Algus & Alondra* announcement, thus unveiling his role as Peter, the best friend character to
Chapter's titular Algus. Apparently his character is an artist, just
like Race. They take photos of me signing my contract, too, as I
will be Alondra.

Lennix returns, complaining about the weather in Eldae,
which is a dozen times colder than here. He doesn't seem to know
that Norax and a few of the members were also in Eldae at some
point during his trip. Neither does he notice my scar, it's so small
and indistinct. I keep my hand on it anyway, just in case. As he
launches into my tentative schedule moving forward, Norax and I
exchange knowing glances. Neither of us will tell what happened
at the after-party.

In the Analytix that evening, I am relieved when Chapter's
fans barely bat an eye over the announcement that I'll be in the
film alongside him. They trust his statement at the *Riot!* premiere,
and they're indifferent to me now. That's good. Indifference is far,
far better than hatred.

Walking back toward my room I hear muffled, almost argu-
mentative tones down the hall. I can't resist following the voices
into one of the sitting rooms. There I find the other Famoux
members.

"I was just about to go find you," Chapter offers.

I'm about to ask why when I see a golden letter in Till's hand.
She looks angry, but more than just angry at getting another
DEFED letter—angry at *me* in particular.

When I reach out to take it from her, she nearly throws it at
me.

We simply had to <u>mark</u> the occasion, hoping you don't mind.

Our young star is already shining so brightly. Her unpredictability excites.

From the rest of you, much excitement, much activity, yet we still feel the darkness coming back.

But new members are bright. Perhaps we'll need more than one next time.

Anxiously awaiting your next moves,
DEFED.

# CHAPTER FIFTEEN

We are thrown into reckless overdrive. With the new threat in mind, and the Volx ever changing, absolutely nothing is off-limits anymore.

It starts with Foster. That night, after reading DEFED's message, he leaves the mansion. Doesn't tell anyone, just takes a car and goes. The next morning the tabloids have already found him. They've photographed him a thousand times over entering the apartment of a fellow model named Marilyn.

Foster's fans and Marilyn's fans have been rooting for them to get together for years. They've done more photoshoots together than can be accepted as friendship. And Foster's fans aren't territorial like Chapter's—they've wanted to see them as a couple more than they've wanted anything else. Of course, he always held off, out of loyalty and love for Finley.

Not anymore.

For the whole day, their romantic excursion is heavily documented. They're seen going out to breakfast, then to lunch, then coffee, then dinner. They're seen holding hands and laying their heads on each other's shoulders and laughing at jokes we can't hear. The fans eat it right up, and Foster's name peaks higher than we've ever seen it. He's usually in third place, but he spikes up to number one.

"I had a moment of panic," he later tells me. We're in the kitchen, his bags on the ground beside him, just arrived home. "I mean . . . I just—I had to do *something*. For Finley. I have to be alive to write to him."

Thanks to Foster's rendezvous, Kaytee and Race are now lingering lower than usual, in the fourth- and fifth-place spots, propelling me back to the coveted third-place spot, where I stay for a little longer than last time.

1 – Roman

2 – Foster

3 – Emilee

4 – Odette

5 – Holden

6 – Quinn

In retaliation, the next day Kaytee drops three separate bombs of news at once.

First, she announces that she and Cartney Kirk will *finally* come out with the duet album the fans have been begging for— the one I heard them hinting about back at Wes Tegg's. Second, to give them a sneak peek, Kaytee says they will be releasing a single early as a part of the soundtrack to—of all things—*Algus & Alondra*. Even more, it's not just *any* single that's going to be on this soundtrack. It'll be "Seashore"—a name I hear about in the news. And finally, apparently I'm a part of it.

I thought for sure the trio idea had been scrapped. But Kaytee gushes to a gossip reporter immediately following the news that we're *such* good friends, and how she can't wait to share my talents with the world, and I almost believe it. She must've noticed the intrigue that's been following everything I do as the newcomer. She wants as many ears on this song as possible.

In addition, Race reveals a new painting of his *Algus & Alondra* character Peter, reiterating the fact that he'll be starring in a film soon. Both their attempts work, taking one afternoon for the two of them to shoot back up to better places.

1 – Roman
2 – Odette
3 – Holden
4 – Foster
5 – Emilee
6 – Quinn

Race's entrance on the higher rankings is a threat all its own. So far, he's been almost consistently around the bottom. Being in third is displacing everything. Foster gets that, and makes it clear he does. Dinner that night is trench warfare.

Foster begins the ordeal. Ammo, cocked back with an inhale. "I heard about the album."

"You did?" Kaytee asks.

"Who didn't?" Foster says, sour. "When's the first song coming out?"

Then Kaytee's voice gets smaller. She knows what he's getting at. She distracts herself with the buttons on her shirt collar. "With a movie."

"A movie?" Foster acts surprised. "What movie?"

"I don't know what it's called," she says. She looks to Chapter and Race. Pointedly not to me. "You're both in it. What is it?"

"*Algus & Alondra*," Race answers, cautious.

"I think I've heard of that," Foster says. He puts a finger to his chin. "Didn't you just paint something for that? What, did you stay up all night to get that out? I don't think that movie even has a finished screenplay. Why do all this *now*?"

Kaytee hesitates. "Cartney wanted people to know about the song."

"Did he really? You discussed it?"

"We—"

Then Foster lashes out. "You two are so selfish!" he shouts. "You *know* I'm lower on the Volx!"

"You've been behind me this whole time!" Kaytee cries. "You have *never* been on the bottom like Race has!"

"He's allowed to fight for his spot. You never have to fight for your spot! Because everyone still feels bad for you! You kept going to the spot where you found Bree and crying last Darkening! Exploiting her death for sympathy!"

"And what, your new line of black clothes isn't the same thing?" she asks. "You hypocrite!"

Foster scoffs. "I'll *happily* make a line of black clothes for you next."

Till stands up. "Okay, let's cool down." She reminds them they should feel lucky. They aren't at the bottom like she is. That shuts them up, and right before Norax can enter too. Our manager mills around the kitchen, happy to see us all in the same place at once. Unaware of the fight that just transpired.

As it turns out, Till knew even when she broke the fight up

that she didn't need to worry about her placement on the Volx for long. The next morning, she announces with fake excitement so realistic, she could win an award, that she will be signing on to star in another line of movies within the world of her *Riot!* series. Even though she was celebrating her freedom from the franchise not a week ago after the premiere, she's already back in it. Desperate times call for desperate measures.

And the announcement surely measures up. Her film fans go ballistic, and she rises like a phoenix from the ashes, knocking Kaytee and Race down toward the bottom. After the news comes out, I see Kaytee leaving the Analytix in tears.

1 – Roman

2 – Quinn

3 – Scott

4 – Emilee

5 – Odette

6 – Holden

Now, inching closer to the next Darkening each day, Kaytee is bent on getting back on track. I'm plucked from my bedroom that afternoon and sent straight to Cartney's studio—a sprawling expanse filled with more instruments than I knew existed. The only thing on our agenda today is to record our song and release it as soon as possible.

"That's a *banjo*," Cartney tells me, pointing to one of twenty hanging on a wall. I can't tell if the indication is meant to be thoughtful or pretentious. Pretentious, it seems. "If you've never seen one in the flesh, that's it."

"Interesting," I say.

"*Have* you ever seen a banjo?"

"Cartney, come on. She didn't live under a rock before the Famoux," says Kaytee.

The truth is, I *hadn't* seen one before, but I don't admit it. That would mean breaking this thin layer of camaraderie between us. As it turns out, when I'm in a room with only her and Cartney, I become her much-preferred option to talk to. She's looking at me again, and now, even defending me. Only to make him angrier, sure, but I'll take it.

Right now, Kaytee is in the recording area, blocked off by glass. This reminds me of the Analytix, only instead of bringing sounds in, this place is meant to bring sounds out. Namely, the guitar in her hands.

"Do your job," Cartney tells her. "I'll talk to Ray out here all I like."

She sighs but obliges.

There is a noticeable, fiercer strain between them today. It's about their contract. On the car ride over, Norax informed Kaytee about how the renewal was coming up. "We're nearing a year," she told her.

"Already?" Kaytee asked, absent. "How many has it been now?"

Two years—as long as this era of Famoux has been around. Although I'm sure their fans would claim they've never really known a life without the epic love story.

When we got out of the car, Kaytee leaned in and whispered, "Whatever you do, don't *ever* meet up with that Marlon York."

"I wasn't going to," I said.

"Good. Because you can't do *anything* with a Buchan artist without getting forced into a contract."

With the renewal hanging thick in the air, everything Kaytee and Cartney say to one another today is an insult—direct, back-handed, it doesn't matter. They flow freely.

"You sang off-key at the end," Kaytee tells him when he's in the booth.

He glowers. "You always do, *dear*. No one says anything because you're footing the bill."

It's horrible to be in the middle of it. I feel like I'm watching my parents bicker. But most of *their* fights were only about me. What is happening here today is bigger than me. Kaytee wants to end it and be with Race, but Cartney doesn't know that. To him, there's no real reason to leave the relationship they've made so perfect together.

The song is set to drop after the Darkening, despite Kaytee's insistence we release it earlier to boost our likabilities beforehand. But as Foster brought up, *Algus & Alondra* is barely a finished script. Why release a song for it now?

"We'll get them around to the idea," Kaytee insists in the car. "If not, this song will just have to leak."

In the Analytix I learn that the photos of Kaytee and me entering Cartney's studio have created a stir. My positive descriptors are a long list of praise. Norax beams. "You are positively shining, my lumerpa!"

Not enough, though. The only place on the Volx where you can feel even a little safe is the top three, which I've only ever been in briefly. It isn't lost on me, either, that every time the other members have made a jump to this part of the Volx, it's been a time when they've catered to their audience. Given them some-thing they've been asking for. But I don't have a group like that to hold onto yet. I don't have my own set career path. And with so little time left before the Darkening, it's unrealistic to think that we'll figure it out before I enter the Fishbowl. It looks like I'll be coming into that glass house with the tentative support of everyone else's diehard fans.

At least it seems like DEFED likes me—in their own twisted way. If I can keep them interested, I can keep myself alive. They're the most diehard fans we have, after all.

That night I arrive in my room to find a few duffle bags packed by the door and Lennix standing beside them.

"What's this?" I ask.

"We're going on a small trip for your film's preparation," he says. "Since you're such an actor all of a sudden."

"Where's Norax?"

"She's otherwise occupied." When I just stare at him, he shrugs. "Look, she's not coming."

Leaving me in Lennix's care for a trip, even a one-day trip like this, feels like a cruel punishment, and I wonder what I've done to deserve it. Race and Chapter join us in the car, which is taking us to the airplane, but Lennix tests only *my* acting skills, drilling me on speeches from movies I've never watched. I decide this would definitely be the worst penance, if Norax ever was mad at me.

It isn't until the car pulls up to an airplane that I realize where we're going. Lennix stretches out his arms and yawns. "Just got back from here, and now I'm returning."

My chills reach the bone. He went to Notness for his first trip, but the last one . . .

By the way Chapter looks at me I can tell he's realizing what's happening too. We thought we'd evaded it by not going to the Fissarex to get our scars removed, but sure enough, we're coming back to Eldae.

Back *home*.

# CHAPTER SIXTEEN

Eldae is a big country. That's what I keep reminding myself on the plane ride over. There are hundreds of towns, with thousands of people, and the majority of them have never seen Emilee Laurence in their life. In fact, I'm sure I could go live in a city just a few miles away from my old one and never once run into someone I used to know.

So why is it that, the moment we step out and greet the crowds waiting for us, I'm struck with the fear that they see right through me—that they've seen these eyes before, and they've hated them?

"Smile," Lennix commands, nudging my shoulder. "They waited for hours."

I paste one on as best I can. The time difference makes me feel foggy. I would likely be sleeping right now in Betnedoor, but the sun has only just begun to set in Eldae. The cameras shutter with approval as Race, Chapter, and I approach the fans, who are blocked off by a barrier. As a consequence of Eldae's genetic mutations, I can tell all of their ages just by looking at them.

A girl gives me her camera to take a photo, and I know she's around fourteen depending on the month she was born, Gen 6, from the dark reddish eyes and pink-streaked hair through her screen. A cluster of friends with hair like copper and strong angled features toss me a pen and some tabloids to sign, and I don't have to ask to confirm they're all about eleven, Gen 9. I know a boy is Gen 4, like me, and I know it before I know even his name. To my relief, he's not Westin. Not Felix. It's Sam, he says. Just another sixteen-year-old from Eldae. He probably didn't even know Emilee. But he could've.

Just breathing in the air out here feels like breathing in sixteen years of the past. When I reach the end of the line, I lean on Gerald for support.

"It's a lot, huh?" he asks.

My bodyguard doesn't know anything about what I went through as Emilee in Eldae. He must think I'm nervous about being an actress.

"It is," I agree anyway.

He pats my shoulder, and I wonder how trivial he thinks my problems must be.

On the drive to an evening costume test—because, as Lennix puts it, *why waste any time?*—Lennix gives the three of us our itinerary for this day trip. It's nothing particularly exciting, just the costume fitting tonight and a table read tomorrow. There's not much else yet at this point in development, besides the costume ideas and the script, which they are so delighted to show us. With the big announcement of my song—thanks to Kaytee and Cartney stirring excitement from the masses—the overall development process for this project has sped up considerably. We still won't shoot until after the Darkening, but this is better than nothing. It'll give the paparazzi more than enough chance to take pictures and get people interested.

"Hope this speeding up doesn't affect the quality of the film," Race says, a bit upset.

Chapter is amused by this. "Don't want to make *Riot!* films like Till?"

"I'd quit," he declares.

As they quip, I'm busy looking outside. We're in the city of Colburn, nowhere near Trulivent, so the streets look foreign through the tinted windows. Even so, my eyes fly about, meeting every face on the sidewalk. It's almost like I'm trying to create a record of how many people I can see in Eldae whom I've never seen before. Or maybe I *am* looking for people I've seen—fishing for my past like the streets are Clarus Creek.

The car hits a bump, and my focus momentarily shifts. Since Chapter is in the middle seat, next to me, his leg has been hitting mine every time the car makes a movement. So far it's been the only thing pulling me from my thoughts about home.

"Sticks," Chapter says, close to my ear. "Are you doing all right?"

"I'm okay," I say.

"I know how Eldae can be."

Race pulls Chapter's attention away from me with a new note about the script, which they've been reading dramatically out loud. As Chapter laughs along at some ridiculous line he's supposed to deliver with the utmost seriousness, he reaches over and almost mindlessly intertwines our hands, just below everyone in the car's line of vision.

Maybe he knows this is going to be all I think about for the rest of the drive, and he's done it to distract me from looking out the window. If so, it works.

There's a fairly large gaggle of photographers around the entrance, so Lennix has us exit one at a time to avoid arousing any suspicion based on how closely any of us walks next to each other. It seems like a ridiculous thing to be worried about, but he insists even the *slightest* few inches of proximity could be scrutinized. Ever since the Chapter incident, Lennix has abhorred the idea of me starring in this film, or being anywhere near Chapter. So did Norax, for a while. It took Race being a buffer to make them bend a little and agree this could help my career much more than it could harm it.

"You first," he tells Chapter.

Our hands unclasp, unceremoniously, and Chapter doesn't even look at me before getting out of the car.

We're whisked to a room filled with clothes. *Algus & Alondra* is a dramatic film—one they anticipate will be swept with critical praise. It is a tall order for my first film ever, but everyone in the room seems to think I'm some kind of seasoned pro. It's then when I remember that my fake backstory to Sam Booker mentioned some acting lessons.

"You'll look *incredible* in this," our director Maly tells me, pushing a wad of faux leather my way. Maly is easy to talk to, and I find myself agreeing, even though I'm fairly sure leather is not my thing. It reminds me of that photoshoot Foster keeps insisting we'll have. From the looks of how ridiculous I appear once I've put it on, that photoshoot might become obsolete.

Once the costume designers have got hold of me, I barely recognize myself. Jeans ripped to obscurity, and a T-shirt chopped and bleached to look like it survived the old world's apocalypse and was found in an abandoned drawer. My eyes stand out so much more against the bright pink wig they've put me in, I have to look away, suddenly a bit more understanding of what every-one's been talking about when they call them intimidating.

As I adjust, Race steps out of his dressing room. He is usually one to have his hair primped and handled before he gets down-stairs for the day, but today it's been mussed up, tangled, and posed sky-high atop his head. "Different," he says to the mirror.

Chapter emerges next, and I gasp before I can help it. Meticulous focus must've been put into painting the gray scale tattoos snaking up and down his arms. His rolled-up flannel for-bids me from seeing them all, but I notice *X*'s and dotted lines, various cursive words and symbols.

"My eyes are up here, *Alondra*," he teases.

We get our photos taken in the getups, then try on several more and repeat the process. I sample pink wigs in more styles than I thought existed.

Then we're whisked off to the hotel, and Lennix reminds us we have an early start tomorrow, and we should all get our rest. The moment I step foot into my room, however, I know I can't. The walls are painted that pale yellow, the same as the couches in Sam's studio. The same as my old home. I recoil back into the hallway instantly.

"What's wrong?" asks Chapter. He's standing in the doorway of his own room across the way. It reminds me of the first time I saw him. For some reason, I get the same starstruck feeling.

"I don't like my room." As if that's an adequate answer to his question.

"What's the matter with it?" he asks.

"The walls are yellow."

He doesn't know what I mean, but he nods like he does. "Do you want to come in here?" he asks. "My walls are painted blue."

In the room's kitchenette, the coffee machine churns, a stream of jet-black liquid filling a red carafe. "You're making coffee?" I ask. "Right now?"

"I'm always doing that," he jokes.

We sit at two chairs next to the massive, floor-length window at the end of the room. This isn't my city, but it is Eldae, all right. Unmistakably. While the skyline in Betnedoor is a sleek shade of silver, Eldae has browns and coppers, old ruins all over. Both Betnedoor and Notness got rid of every shred of the past when they rebuilt. They wanted to start new. Eldae didn't.

It's impossible, I guess, to be rid of the past here.

"It's odd," Chapter says. "No matter how many times we come back and I think it'll be different, it never is."

"How often have you been back?"

"Just a few. Usually for *The Fishbowl*." He pauses. "It's always the worst when they put it here, in Colburn."

"Where did you live before?" I ask.

"Well, Colburn."

My eyes widen. "You lived *here*?"

"Until Norax picked me up, yeah," Chapter says. He takes another sip of his coffee, his voice lacking its usual conviction. "And every time I'm back, I'm fifteen again."

I think to his name on the top of the Volx. *Roman.* At one point he walked these sidewalks with that name. At one point he lived a whole life as someone else entirely—someone I don't even know.

Chapter points at some part of the skyline. "I lived right around there."

There is so much to take in, I'm sure we're not centered in on the same thing. Still, I nod. "I wish I could see it," I say, and I'm not sure why.

"Why couldn't you?" he asks.

"What?"

"See it? We're here, aren't we?"

As Chapter stands, I grip my mug. "What are you talking about?" I ask.

"If there was a time to see the past, it'd be now," he says. "Do you want to?"

"We couldn't," I say. "We're . . ."

I can't find the right word besides *Famoux*. Colburn is as busy as daytime out there. How could we take a single step out of this hotel without a horde of cameras and shouts following our every move? Not to mention what Lennix would do if he found out.

Chapter knows what I'm getting at. "When you think about it, sneaking out *is* a very young and naive thing for someone to do. Fits Norax's angle like a glove."

Sneaking out alone, sure. But sneaking out with Chapter Stones? I can't imagine what people would say. It occurs to me right then that Chapter has this unique luxury of taking chances with his name so frequently at the top of the Volx. And if our last time being photographed together has taught me anything, I don't share that luxury. Not at all.

But there is a waver in his mischievous look that I've never seen before. When he peers out at the skyline again, he falters with a pang of memory, of curiosity. He *wants* to see his old home. Just as I asked Norax to check on my family, he wants to check up on his. To know what they're doing, how they're managing without their son and brother Roman. And when he looks at me again, I know he doesn't want to do this alone. He needs a Famoux member there to remind him he isn't who he used to be. He's Chapter, now. *Not* Roman.

In spite of the risk it puts me in, and the way my name could plummet on the Volx in a mere second if we're caught, I rise from my seat. At the door, Chapter holds out an extra coat of his for me, and I take it.

× × ×

There are no cameras waiting for us when we step outside. Like muscle memory, I brace myself anyway, pulling the collar of the large black coat over half my face. Chapter sees this and laughs.

"Paranoid?" he asks.

"How are you not?"

"I am," he says. "I just don't show it."

The wind is even stronger than it was earlier. People across the street move with purpose, their heads cast down at the ground to fight the chill. No one is looking up to look at us, I realize. We've never been more in the clear.

Chapter knows this city enough to know the less-populated sidewalks, and he takes us through them as if he still does this every day. There's the faint sound of chatter from adjoining streets, but it's subdued over here. I'm reminded of the quiet corners Norax walked me through before asking me to join the Famoux. Surely, the slight flutter of anticipation I felt in my heart then is felt here. His strides are so long, I have to jog to keep up.

"Have you ever gone back?" I ask.

"Like this?" He shakes his head. "I've never been stupid enough to do this."

"Why now?"

"You're here," he says. He nods to me, confirming my suspicions in his hotel room. "I'd rather go with someone."

His eyes, an unreal shade of blue, make me think of the hottest part of a flame. I'm filled with a similar heat just for a second. But he turns away again to lead us down a new street, and the chill of the night returns.

The streets are already so much simpler after a minute or two of walking. While the hotel and the office buildings we've visited thus far on this trip paint a picture of pure opulence, from the looks of it, Chapter didn't come from any place like it.

A lingering worry is nagging me the farther we go. What if Lennix decided, randomly, to check our hotel rooms? There could be a search party scouring the streets for us right now. And when they caught up to us, what would he think, finding me wandering Eldae with the one Famoux member they've deemed off-limits?

We walk past a street sign that reads *Red*. Chapter bristles but keeps up his pace. "We're close," he tells me. He gestures to a storefront on our left as we go. "Sometimes I went there after school."

It's a small market, like the kind Brandyce worked at. When I picture Chapter walking through the cast-iron doors, I have to remind myself he was an entirely different person. A young boy named Roman. However he looked.

I feel the strange need to keep up conversation. "I always went right home after school."

"Did you like your home?"

"When my mother was there."

"Most days I avoided going home until it was absolutely necessary," Chapter says.

I want to ask why, and what they did, but I know I shouldn't. I wouldn't want him to ask me the gory details about what Westin used to do.

Westin. Trulivent. Clarus Creek. I don't know if I'd ever be able to go back to all that, much less give someone a tour. Just knowing that the Fishbowl is sometimes set up so close to us—close enough for me to walk right to it from my old house—strikes an absurd fear in me. Chapter must share a similar fear walking around Colburn right now. The lightness in his curiosity back in the hotel is all gone now.

The breeze gets wilder as we go. It's something about the way the air moves through these narrow buildings. I must visibly shiver, because Chapter moves closer to me. He's so warm, it's overwhelming.

"Are we almost there?" I ask.

"We're here."

We stop walking in front of a thin, gray apartment complex made of pure concrete. Like my house, but the stacked kind—towering high beside others just like it. Nothing about the place beckons coziness, and I can understand on a basic, visual level why he might want to avoid it. I'm not sure which of the many windows looks into his place, but there's no light poking through any of them. Either everyone is asleep, or there's no one home.

"It's nice," I say.

"You don't have to compliment it," Chapter says. "I don't miss it."

I try to imagine Norax walking up to a place like this to find Chapter. "And Bree lived here too?"

"Our bedrooms shared a wall."

Bree Arch and Chapter Stones. I'm not sure anyone in the entirety of Delicatum would be able to guess that they both came from here.

"It's weird to look at it like this," he reflects. "I mean, the worst things about my life happened right here, but it's not my life anymore." He steps away from the building, like the proximity is all too much for him. "I'm not that person now."

"What was that person like?" I dare asking.

It might be overstepping. I grit my teeth, ready to backtrack, but Chapter just shrugs. "As insufferable as I am now, I suppose."

"That's not what I meant," I say.

"I know," he says. "I was just wrong. All wrong." He glances down at himself—his Fissarex-perfected figure, his expensive coat. "Now, apparently, I'm right."

"You sound bitter," I say.

"Sometimes."

He's looking at the stained concrete ahead of us, now wracked with some memory. I get the urge to distract him, like he's done for me. Maybe it's why I reach over and grab his hand.

"She looked like me," I say, suddenly.

"Who did?" Chapter asks.

"That girl you brought out from the crowd at Race's art show," I say. "Lex. I was similar to her. Before the Fissarex."

Chapter's eyes meet mine. At once I feel an odd, desperate hope that those have always been his eyes—that nothing has ever had to change their color. And when he next speaks, I hope his voice isn't a bottled-up concoction Zoya picked out special for him. I hope he's always had it. I want every single part of him to be real.

"Then you were lovely," he tells me. "I wish I could've met you."

I wish I could've met him.

"Thank you," I say. "You don't have to be so nice to me, and yet you are."

"What makes you say that?"

"I don't know. I feel like I've caused more trouble for you than anything else."

Chapter touches my cheek. My mind wipes. "You have to stop believing you're some kind of burden. You're not. At all, Sticks."

Someplace in the world, an avalanche is triggered. A mountain caves in. Maybe that place is my ribs; maybe my heart. *Sticks.* All Sticks has ever been is a burden. To my mother. To Brandyce. To everyone.

Not him.

"You're staring at me again," he says.

"So I am," I say.

He smiles so brilliantly, I could burst just looking at him. Are his lips his own, or from the Fissarex? The thought makes me flush. He looks away for a moment, maybe over his shoulder to make sure no one's watching. "I know we made a big point of saying it wasn't, but I wish it had been one, you know."

"What?" I ask.

"The night at Ace," Chapter says. "I wish it could've been a date."

I don't know where my next bit of bravery comes from. Emilee Laurence was not one to ever be bold, and as far as *young, naive* little Emeray Essence goes, no one's expecting much boldness from her either. But in spite of all this, something compels me to grab hold of the back of Chapter's neck. All I can think about is how I don't care if his lips are made from the Fissarex. I don't care. I pull him toward me, and I kiss them anyway.

Every feeling tangibly possible in the world seems to gush through my entire body like a cataract. And then, in an instant, his face is inches from mine, looking at me. I look at him. We look at each other.

The second thought that runs through my head in this moment is, *What have I just done*? If anyone is lurking in the shadows with a camera, they'll have a story for the tabloids to last them weeks, and I would plummet to the bottom of the Volx without a doubt—with only a week left until the Darkening, no less.

But it's not the first thought on my mind. No, my first thought is how I don't care. I don't care at all.

When we pull back, Chapter's voice is lofty and wondrous like silver, like smoke. "Why'd you do that?"

Because I was concerned about him. His definition of that word comes back to me now, holding a new weight to it. I glance over at the complex, at this place he used to call home. There are still no lights on in the window. His family might not even live there anymore.

"So it's no longer a bad memory," I say.

# PART THREE

# DARKENING

# CHAPTER SEVENTEEN

There is a certain strangeness to keeping a secret within the Famoux. We have some that everyone is privy to, like Kaytee and Race being a couple behind the veil of a dating contract. Other secrets, Norax and Lennix didn't know, like DEFED and the Volx's looming threat. The only reason these secrets remain so is because the members are united in keeping quiet. We work *together* to uphold them.

Walking through side streets back to the hotel, the concrete ground beneath my feet feels softer, as if pillows cushion each step. The cold air of our old lives feels full of new beginnings. These are beginnings that need to stay secret, else they'll meet their end.

I know I am in so much trouble. Lennix and Norax have worked tirelessly to prove to the world that Chapter and I have nothing to do with each other. All the outings, the interviews. Chapter's fans have accepted me now. We'd swept the whole issue under the rug.

And now, this.

Yet, I don't know what *this* is. Is it love? It seems ridiculous to consider because I wouldn't know. I am feeling something tedious, yet imaginative. Something slow and burning a hole in my chest. And I'm worried—no, *concerned*—that someone will take it away.

"So," I say, cutting the silence. "What are we going to do?"

But I already know the answer before he replies. Concealing this is the only way. If his fans knew what happened tonight, my Volx ranking would plummet. Staying apart gives me my only chance of surviving the upcoming Darkening. And if we both get through the blackout maybe then we could find a way to be together in the future.

I know it is an impossible dream, but I can't help but think about it all night.

× × ×

The next morning, I am determined to be the actress everyone already assumes I am. Pretend it's nothing—that Chapter is just another person, like Race, like the others. But the way my heart is like a raucous siren, a step away from jumping out of my chest when I sit down beside him for breakfast, I don't know if I'll be able to. Perhaps acting is not going to be my strong suit.

"We have a light schedule today," Lennix informs us through a mouthful of porridge. He's half eating, half addressing an itinerary on his tablet device. But even if he was looking over at us, he wouldn't be able to see beneath the table, as Chapter's hand searches for my hand, as his fingers lace into mine. "Just a couple of meetings about the script, and then we're back in the air."

I barely even hear him over my heartbeat, ringing loud and thunderous into every part of my body. I can feel Chapter's DEFED scar—the curved *E* he decided to keep instead of erase— when I brush it with my fingertips.

When Race, who had gotten up to refill his coffee, comes to our side of the table, our hands separate. Maybe the whole Famoux knows about Foster and Finley and keeps it from Norax, but Finley is a separate entity from this world. They couldn't hold it against him without revealing him as Scott, from Eldae. But this thing between Chapter and me is internal. It's *ammo*. If Race were to find out and tell Kaytee, she could use it against me. Any one of them could, if they wanted to drop my ranking.

"I'm glad we're going home today," says Race. He looks around at the waiters milling about, all identifiable by their generations. "I don't like it here."

"I think it's kind of nice, all this order," says Lennix. He nods toward one of them, Gen 2. "That guy's eighteen, isn't he? The purple eyes?"

His guess is correct. The young adult wordlessly picks up the rest of our dishes, piling them high on his arm, as Lennix hums to himself, looking around the room at the others and their various attributes.

"Man, I just love what they're doing over here," he muses. "It's genius."

"It's a genetic mutation," says Race. "What's so genius about that?"

Lennix leans back in his chair, examining the room a second time. "You know they're saying it'll be hair colors too next year?"

"They always say that."

"Now this one has to be Gen 1. Nineteen?"

He's right. Her golden yellow eyes give her away. They remind me of Brandyce, although she has red hair, not brown. She asks us if we want anything to go. Lennix asks for a peppermint tea, two tea bags.

We drive past the rubble of an old-world building, its rusting sign informing us that it used to be a church. Several other ruins with signs like this dot our journey to the studio, and I am reminded just how deep the destruction of Eldae's area was. After all, the radiation in Eldae is stronger here than anywhere else in Delicatum.

When we stop at a light, a young kid waits to cross the street to her school. She's Gen 12, standing in front of a column from an old-world establishment. Two products of the destruction. It's eerie.

"She's eight, right?" asks Lennix.

Yes, but Chapter messes with him, "No. She's nine."

"I thought eight had the big ears?"

"You must be mistaken."

Our meetings at the studio go by quickly. Maly has us look at locations and give our input. Chapter informs Race and me that this is not at all a job for actors, but it's common for directors and producers to want Famoux members to feel instrumentally involved in the process. They have us pick out props next. In all our activities today, Chapter and I are careful not to stand next to one another. In my head it feels like everything we do could be cause for suspicion. I barely look him in the eye in some rooms, too scared my face will reveal it all. Chapter is so much better at this than I am. He's got all his usual verve, joking with Race and the crew while I'm too petrified to move. I already feel like a terrible actor.

After props, we are given a rewrite of the script, which our director, Maly, worked on all night before today's table read. The circles under her eyes are nearly violet, but she acts energetic all the same.

"We are *so* pleased to have you all on board for this," she tells us. She looks more than pleased, though. A film with more Famoux members than any other before it, with a song by Kaytee, Cartney, and me on the soundtrack—it's a winning combination.

During the table reading, my acting skills are truly put to the test. It's here where Lennix learns about a kiss scene that's supposed to happen between Alondra and Algus, Chapter's character.

"Oh, *certainly* not," Lennix interrupts. "No. We should definitely cut that."

"We can't," Maly says. "The film is called *Algus & Alondra.* I thought you knew there would be a love story."

Lennix rubs his eyes. "We *just* pull her from the gutter, only to throw her back in."

"She kisses me too in this," points out Race.

I look only at Race, suddenly far too flustered. I'm afraid of what I'd do if I looked at Chapter—laugh uncontrollably, completely unravel, and blurt out our secret? Lennix notices my agitation and exhales, exhausted. "Emeray, what are we going to *do* with you?"

But it's just a movie, and Lennix is smart enough to know that. In Bree and Chapter's case with *Key,* actual photos of their kiss scene leaked, and even that wasn't enough for the fans to assume they were dating. No, they only do that when Chapter is seen *off* set with costars. Then, all bets are off.

Lennix doesn't interrupt for the rest of the table read. The movie ends in tragedy, with Algus killing Race's character Peter—but not before Algus also kills Alondra. This makes Chapter's character the last man standing. As cast and crew applaud when we've read the final line, Race makes stern eye contact, and I know what he's trying to say. We're both always at the bottom of the Volx, and Chapter is almost always at the top. This ending feels eerie.

When the car picks us up it already holds our bags. Race and Chapter discuss the movie plot as we drive to the airport. I stare out the window, trying to focus on anything other than Chapter's knee touching mine. With Race and Lennix up in the row ahead of us, we'd be able to touch, but he hasn't tried to grab my hand yet and I don't feel as bold as I did when I kissed him last night. I decide we can't take sitting like this and I turn my body toward the window.

"Everything okay, Sticks?" he asks me. His eyes are asking me to calm down, to play it cool. I can't. When he finally grabs my hand and it makes everything better and worse at the same time.

"What's that nickname, anyway?" asks Race. "I've heard you use it a few times."

Chapter picks up the question with ease, masking the flush that's taken over my face. "It's just what I call her. I honestly don't remember why. But it stuck."

In the front seat, Lennix rattles off stories about the first era of the Famoux, and I can barely look out the window without him accusing me of being uninterested—even though I am.

At a stop sign, my eyes drift away to the sidewalk beside us. Chapter led me right through here last night. It was empty then, but in the light of day it's packed. Generations of all ages, and plenty of those older than nineteen, too, who don't fall in line, crowd through. I'm so busy counting how many of those people I almost glaze right over a sign pasted to a lamppost. It's only the two photos in the middle of it that captures my attention.

The first photo is me. My old self. Emilee. The world suddenly gets fuzzy and I have to look away, to the second picture.

Big, green eyes. Gen 3.

My brother Dalton.

And then I see the words, scribbled in hasty capital letters, Brandyce's handwriting, and everything comes together.

## MISSING PEOPLE: DALTON AND EMILEE LAURENCE
## EMILEE LAST SEEN On DECEMBER 2
## DALTON LAST SEEN On DECEMBER 5

× × ×

"I don't know, lumerpa. I don't know."

We're in my bedroom, back in the mansion. Norax is perched uncomfortably on a piece of furniture, watching me pace the floor in distress. Between us sits a carafe of lemon tea meant to calm me. Today, it isn't working.

The whole flight back to Betnedoor, I had to keep silent about what I'd seen. Lennix would likely be of no help here, since he abhors the idea of checking up on my family, so I had to hold my tears the whole way back. Chapter and Race sensed something was wrong, but they must've understood I couldn't discuss it in the open. They kept their queries to themselves.

Norax hands me another tissue, and I blow my nose grotesquely. Seeing Dalton's photo after months of slowly forgetting his face is more than enough to send me in a spiral. Seeing that he's *missing* is something else entirely.

"How is it possible?" I wail. The poster said he went missing on December 5. That's only a few days after Norax had picked me up. It's almost January now. "You said the guards saw him and my family."

"They could've mistaken him for another Gen 3 kid," she says, voice guilt laden. "That's very possible, lumerpa. I'm so sorry."

My head spins. "He's missing. He's *been* missing."

Maybe he could've run away. However, it doesn't seem like something Dalton would do, especially since a job in Betnedoor was basically a guarantee for him. I clench a fist, trying not to explode and say something I shouldn't in front of Norax. DEFED has made it *very* clear that they know who we used to be. Certainly they could've walked right into my house and seized him at some point?

But then again, if they *had* taken him—and long before the *Riot!* premiere too—they probably would've sent me this *Missing* sign, like the bone cufflinks or Finley's locket. They would've taken credit if they'd done it. Right?

Whatever the reason, he's gone. I can't even begin to imagine what Brandyce might be thinking right now, all alone in the house with our father.

That is, if *she's* not gone too.

"Lumerpa," Norax says. "Please, sit."

The cups on the table billow hoary steam that fogs up my view of Norax's face. I force myself to sit and stay still, lifting mine from the saucer and bringing the rim to my lips. Hot tea. The roof of my mouth gets the brunt of the burn.

"We will solve this. Where was he seen last?" Norax asks.

"The sign didn't say."

"Where is that?"

She frowns. "And your town, Trulivent. It's so overpopulated as it is. So many Gen 3 kids too. It's not going to be easy to find him."

"Norax," I plead. "*Please*."

"You do know that if we were to find your brother, you would be prohibited from seeing him, correct?"

I wince but nod regardless. I just need to know he's safe.

Norax makes a note in her clipboard. She takes me to the Analytix, but I still can't focus. Just sitting still for longer than a minute is a challenge. It's hard to listen to anyone, even as they squeal over the photos of Chapter, Race, and me or buzz about what our new movie could entail.

"*. . . seen leaving a disclosed warehouse in none other than here, in Eldae! As you can see from the photos, they were definitely in Colburn! We here at the* Colburn Times *are* thrilled!"

But how can the *Colburn Times* be thrilled? How can they even take space in their newscasts to show grainy paparazzi shots of us in costumes when there are people in their country who are missing?

By the time Norax tells me to step out of the Analytix, I'm fuming.

I'm doing fine after the trip to Eldae, still in a good fourth place—which guarantees that no one saw Chapter and me together in Colburn—but even so, I feel little relief. I look down at my curved scar with fury. If I had gone to Eldae with the others, when they were getting their scars taken away, would I have seen the sign then? Could we have found him already?

With the Darkening looming, there is little room to breathe

nowadays. Everyone is zipping about in clubs and on sidewalks, hoping to remind the world why they love them enough to keep them alive. I barely see the other members at all besides Kaytee, who begrudgingly has to take photos with Cartney and me for our single's cover art. Later that day my spread for *The X* is finally complete and released, and Abby parades me around all the shops in Betnedoor to sign copies of it.

Fans with wide eyes gush about how pretty the pictures look, and quote the nice things that the other Famoux members have said about me, but I don't even know what they're talking about—I haven't been given a free moment to myself to actually read it. Even so, I'm almost positive the members' articles were written by some staff member from *The X* and slipped in last minute. Abby said back in the beginning that they would write all the things they *loved* about me, but why ever would my fellow Famoux members take the time to do that now when they know any kind of praise for me might mean their name dropping on the Volx?

"The world is *loving* you, lumerpa," Norax gushes to me in the car. She holds up the magazine, beaming. The cover image is a close-up of my face—my lips red, my eyes a piercing centerpiece. "I don't think you could be doing any better if you tried!"

And she's right. When we check the Analytix later, I find I've never done better in my life. Third on the Volx. Sustainably too. This should be something to be over the moon about, but I can't get Dalton out of my head. I can't think of anything else.

The next day, as we return to the mansion from another meet and greet, I find Chapter in the foyer, prepped to leave for another interview for *Key*. The premiere has been moved up to happen in tandem with Bree's gala, both scheduled to happen four days from now, on one magnificent memorial night that will mark the beginning of the Darkening. Which means that, directly after these eulogizing events conclude, the members and I will enter the Fishbowl, and the world will fall into its regularly scheduled darkness.

All in a single evening.

The morbidity of it is not lost on anyone.

Just the sight of Chapter in his maroon suit makes me dizzy. I step toward him with every intention to give him a hug, give him a kiss, but I know I can't. I step back, instinctively, and Norax leads me past him, the distance between us feeling larger than it actually is. We have both been so busy, I haven't spoken to him at all since Eldae. I haven't even been able to tell him about Dalton.

The smile he offers as we go is the one shred of lightness in me right now. "Sticks," he says.

On our way down the hall, music wafts softly from the audio room. I've only been in this room once, during my tour of the mansion with Norax. Peeking through the doors now, Kaytee is playing the guitar for Till and Race. Serenading them. It pains me to know that if I was to walk into the audio room, high on the Volx as I currently am, they would all walk out and the music would cease.

I don't need to check the Analytix to know I'm still doing well, but it's a daily thing. While readers sing their praises over *The X*, I zone out, their cries of approval blending together into one. It isn't until a voice cuts in that isn't as boisterous that makes me snap back to reality.

*"Emeray? We know you're listening."*

Through my faint reflection in the glass, I can see that all the color has drained from my face. I raise my hands in the air to get

Norax's attention, but she's engrossed in her device, smiling down at tabloid headlines as my likability soars.

"*Listen closely, Emeray,*" the voice continues. "*Well. Emilee. Em?*" It chuckles. "*How confusing it gets for us to tell the difference. Anyway, Em, we have what you're looking for. And* you *have the power to keep us from killing him.*"

*Dalton.* They're talking about Dalton. Without thinking, I rise up from the chair, and the voice cuts out. I slam myself back down as it continues.

"*. . . been a little secret your group has been sitting on for some-time, which we think the world deserves to know about. Could you do us a favor, Em, and tell the world this secret? I think Dalton would appreciate it.*"

What secret? I can barely focus as the voice laughs again.

"*We can't wait to see the headlines. Much love, as always. DEFED.*"

*Much love.* The words that bothered the other members so much when we got our golden gifts. I can only imagine the kind of satisfaction Kaytee might feel if she knew it's been twisted into something sinister.

I don't feel much love from DEFED at all.

"*Oh,*" the voice cuts in again. "*We almost forgot.*"

Right before my eyes, the Volx suddenly dissipates, its copper flecks dissolving right into the air around me. As a newscaster from Notness launches into an overview on my magazine tour, I'm left gaping at the window separating Norax and me. The Volx is gone. I don't remember what it looked like before it disappeared.

As Norax shows me a slideshow of nice comments, it takes everything in me not to scream, to burst into tears, to tell her everything. But I know I can't.

What news did they want me to leak? What am I supposed to share with the world? They never told me. Dalton's life is on the line, and I don't even know how they want me to save it.

When I return to my room, there's a golden box on my nightstand. There is no note attached, but I know it's from them. It's got the same glow from the boxes they sent before the *Riot!* premiere.

My mind jumps to the worst. Bones. What if they've sent me Dalton's like they sent Bree's to Chapter? But they told me I could keep him *alive* if I did as they ordered. It's the only thing that keeps me steady as I pull the lid off.

I don't know what to make of what I find inside. Not bones. Not anything from my past. Nothing that once belonged to Dalton.

Just a picture, and not even one of me.

It's from the red carpet of the *Riot!* premiere. Kaytee stands beside Cartney in her blue dress and headband from home. He's smoldering for the cameras, but Kaytee is looking off toward someone at the edge of the frame.

Race. And he's looking right at her.

It's suddenly very apparent. Kaytee and Race. They want me to tell Cartney about them. They want me to tell the *world* about them.

There's a knock on my door.

"Emeray?"

I whirl around. It's only Gerald.

"Yes?" I ask.

"I'm sorry if it's a bad time," he says. "I've been told you have a visitor."

The hairs on the back of my neck stand up. "Who is it?" I ask.

"Cartney Kirk."

So DEFED doesn't want to give me any time to mull this over. They want me to do this.

Tonight.

× × ×

One of the hardest things I ever had to do was tell my father that my mother had left. It had been easier with Dalton and Brandyce. But with him, it was different. Something in me knew that telling him would sting more, sting longer.

It's never been in me to be a bearer of bad news. I would so much rather toss DEFED's photo on the floor by Cartney's feet and let him draw his own conclusions than ever speak it out loud to him. Perhaps it all goes back to my flight instincts. Why be the messenger, when the messenger usually gets shot?

As I walk into the foyer, Cartney is sitting on one of the armchairs, aimlessly flipping through my spread for *The X*. Since his back is to me, I think for a faltering moment that I might be able to slip away, pretend I didn't get the message. But of course, Cartney seems to sense everything.

"Ray." He turns toward me, holding up a full-page photo of me twirling in a pastel dress. "This color looks great on you."

"Who sent you here?" I ask.

Cartney gives me a look. "You did?"

"I didn't," I say.

"So you *don't* have something to show me in the audio room?"

The audio room. Kaytee is no doubt still in there, playing songs for Race.

How do they have it all planned?

"Well?" Cartney asks.

I shake myself, willing some composure. I don't know if I have it in me to do this to Kaytee and Race. This will ruin them.

The *Missing* sign flashes before my eyes.

"Maybe," I decide. "We can check."

Cartney follows my lead as I take us up the stairs. With a concentrated sense of purpose, he makes a big scene of mimicking all my steps. *Left foot, right foot, left foot.* Out of pure vexation, I shorten a step, elongate another, just to try to throw him off—get through to him the message to stop. Of course, this only makes him chuckle and try even harder.

"Do you have a song or something?" he asks. "Want my *expert* opinion?"

"No," I say. "It's . . . I don't know."

"The suspense is killing me."

I've never wanted to succumb to the takedown culture that's come with the Volx. The other members have undermined one another, sure, but no one has *ever* done anything this purposefully cruel. I can't do this.

I blink, and there's the sign again. Dalton's face. DEFED's warning.

Despite all my efforts to prolong this journey, we reach the powder blue doors of the audio room quicker than I'd like to. The soft strumming of guitar fills the pit of my stomach with dread.

"Is Kaytee in there?" Cartney asks.

"I don't know," I lie.

We hover by the entrance, peering in carefully. My heart rattles in my chest. There she is, sitting cross-legged on a navy suede couch, a guitar in her lap. There Race is, sitting right across from her, gazing.

And here we are, on the other side of the door.

Raking in a deep breath, I go to take a step forward, but

Cartney pulls me back. "You can't!" he exclaims. "She's in the middle of playing!"

"What?" I ask.

"Come on, Ray." He shakes his head. "Don't you know *anything* about performance etiquette? We can wait until she's done."

Great. Like I need more waiting time to grapple with this.

Standing maladroit at the doors, Cartney and I watch Kaytee sing an acoustic song to Till and Race. I've never heard it before, but Cartney has, because he whispers, "I love this one."

"Did you help write it?"

"No," he says. "But it's still brilliant."

Somehow, these words coming from Cartney Kirk don't sound even a wink pretentious. My head aches. *Nothing* about this moment seems real anymore.

How am I supposed to do this, anyway? I can't imagine DEFED expects me to burst through the doors and start pointing fingers. Although they very well could. Maybe it'd be better if I explained it to him in private. Or leaked the photo and let them all find out then. But the photo isn't even incriminating. And I don't know how to leak something either.

Meanwhile, Kaytee sings on. With only her guitar, she sounds as angelic as she did in the recording studio. The lyrics paint a picture of an intricate relationship—one with odds stacked against it. Not to my surprise, this happens to be a recurring theme in most of her albums. I wonder how Cartney can hear songs like this and not see any red flags. But even as I listen, the flags get pinker and pinker the sweeter she sings.

The whole time we've watched her play, Kaytee has been looking down at the fretboard and her fingers, but for the final line, she looks up. At Race. They share the sort of smile only those in love would. I'm not sure if Cartney catches it beside me, since his demeanor doesn't change for a second.

"Absolutely beautiful," Race says.

When Kaytee speaks next, I realize, DEFED has done me a service bringing Cartney around tonight. I don't have to do or say anything to save my brother. Kaytee and Race do it for me.

"And absolutely for you," she says.

Beside me, Cartney goes rigid. Even more so when Kaytee leans over her guitar, toward Race, to kiss him.

It's all over now.

"*What?*"

Cartney's foot clamors down onto the hardwood, drawing all eyes to the entrance. And there come the looks of horror, from Till to Race to Kaytee. They look at him with horror.

And then they look at me.

Kaytee stands up, the acoustic guitar sliding off her lap and onto the floor. The sharp *clank!* fills the room like gunfire.

"Cartney—" she starts.

"Don't. Just don't."

"I can explain this. Look—"

Cartney looks to Kaytee, then to Race. Somehow his eyes are full of tears and venom at once. "I've always liked you the least. I guess I know why."

"Cartney," Race says. "We can—"

They don't see Cartney leave like I do. To them, he's running out of the room. To me, he's stumbling, his legs giving out, his balance faltering even on his knees. This reaction is a surprise to me. He doesn't love Kaytee, does he? Maybe he's embarrassed. Cartney Kirk doesn't appear to be someone who likes to be made a fool of, contract or no contract.

He's already out of the hallway when Kaytee rushes to the door, tears streaming down her face as she looks around and sees he's gone. I don't know what she's crying about. Guilt that Cartney didn't know? Or is she fearful of what will happen now that he does?

When her eyes fall on me, they darken immediately. "What did you *do*?"

I don't know what to do, so I play dumb. "Kaytee, I didn't know—"

"You *knew*," she spits. "You did."

"I swear I didn't—"

"How *could you*?" She darts back into the audio room, resisting a sob, but failing.

"Kaytee," I cry out. "Kaytee, please—"

"I don't want to hear *anything* from you right now," she snaps. "You got what you wanted. Go away!"

I watch, helpless, as she runs to the window. I go to the next room over to see for myself. From the way the cameras are going off by the front gates, it's safe to say Cartney is exiting. In a second, he appears in our view, back to us. Instead of running straight to the car, he stops, whirls around. For the whole crowd to see, he puts a hand to his head, runs his fingers through his hair, and *screams*.

Without regret, without thought, without sense. Through gritted teeth and clenching fists and camera flashes. Again and again and again and again, so loud that we hear it from the second floor, he yells their two names a thousand times over. "*Kaytee and Calsifer!*"

He saves my brother.

# CHAPTER EIGHTEEN

The next morning, Cartney sends Kaytee ruby red roses and a note of withdrawal.

Withdrawal from the album.

Withdrawal from the contract renewal.

Withdrawal from everything.

As far as the general public goes, they seem to share this sense of departure. Turns out cheating on Cartney Kirk, and thus tearing apart one of the most beloved musical couples ever, is *not* a good move for someone to make if they want to be in the public's good graces.

They make that very clear.

Every tabloid cover in the world is coated in close-ups of Cartney's distressed face, of Kaytee looking angry, or Race looking happy—all plucked out of obscurity and used in a new context. Reading the headlines, I am reminded of the ones they made of me when I was seen at Ace with Chapter. Much like those ones, Cartney always plays the victim, and Kaytee always plays the villain.

Never have crowds this massive gathered outside the mansion's gates, vested in vengeance, refusing to leave. Overnight, after Cartney's announcement outside, the volume only multiplies, and the bigger it gets, the better their voices are heard from inside the apartment. We don't need an Analytix to know what the world is thinking; no, the whole mansion becomes one.

I brush my teeth and check myself in the mirror to the resounding chorus of "*Traitor!*"

I pick out clothes from my closet as the people screech, "*Cheater!*"

I lace up my shoes and leave my room while they begin the chant, "*Liar!*"

Even when I check the actual Analytix, there's spillover; people can't help but bring the whole debacle into conversations about me. They specifically talk about the song Kaytee, Cartney, and I all made together for the movie with Race in it. How ironic that seems now. But is it still going to be released, they wonder, now that we all know the truth under the surface? I wonder the same thing.

There's no new sign from DEFED about Dalton. I sit in the Analytix for longer than usual, just waiting to hear anything about him, but every new voice is a gossip column for me to tune out. They won't tell me if he's safe or whether or not they kept their end of the bargain. That sinister voice refuses to show. But their radio silence isn't the only thing making me tense, perched on the Analytix stool. No matter how many times I close my eyes and open them again, the Volx never shows. No copper-flaked scale bearing our names. No new ranking updates.

When it dissipated after DEFED's message to me, it appears that it had left for good. And so now, in the wake of everything that has just been recalled to life, and only a few days left until the Darkening, I realize we have absolutely no way of knowing where we stand anymore.

In an effort to brief us on the damage control that will need to be done, Norax has called us all into the Control Room. Since all of us will no doubt be pummeled with questions about this situation at the *Key* premiere and Bree's gala coming up in two days, we need to know how to proceed as a unit.

If we could ever be a unit again. There is a thousand times more tension in this Control Room than there was during my first tea party. And I thought it couldn't get worse. As a maid pours me a cup of chamomile tea—something Norax has picked for us in hopes of calming us down—I try earnestly to make eye contact with Kaytee. She refuses to so much as glance over to my end of the table. She sits as far from me as possible, next to Till.

Today, it's Foster and Chapter who sit beside me. Even in the swirling hostility of the room, I am achingly aware that this is the closest I've been to Chapter since Eldae. I want to grab his hand in secret, but the table is made of glass. They'd see.

My fingers fidget on the detailing of my dress, restless. I wish Kaytee would look at me. I want to explain. I want her to know DEFED was breathing down my back, holding my brother against me. I need her to know I did what I did for Dalton. To save his life. But then again, I also know what she'd ask me. What about *her* life? What about Race's life? But they don't matter as much to me as my brother. It's a catch-22. No matter what, it seems, my decision was going to end with a death.

Cartney's letter in the roses is short—aching and angry. We each read from it one by one as it's passed down the table, like the cream and sugar:

*Kaytee,*

*Our album is canceled. Our relationship is over. You didn't want our dating contract to be renewed in the first place, and now, I suppose, you've gotten your wish. (And now, I suppose, I understand your hesitation.)*

*I was never your first choice, my darling, but I always believed you were mine. When you were distant, I loved you from that distance. When that Calcium whatever-his-name-is got strangely possessive over you, I never once assumed you loved him behind my back.*

*What a mistake it was to put my belief in you.*

*Enjoy the roses.*

Kaytee lets out a quivering breath, breaking the silence. "He doesn't have to be like this."

"He doesn't," Race says, solemn. "He wants to. Because he can."

It's been only one night, but already Cartney has done the rounds of morning television. It appears that his label, Buchan, has pulled out all the stops in making him a victor. He's been on every newscast I've ever heard of, sharing *his exclusive side* of the story.

In other words, he has been weaving a brilliant web of deception that puts him entirely in the right. According to Cartney, he has been but a diligent and dedicated boyfriend to Kaytee. He was receptive to her every need. He gave her space when she asked. And then, with tears glossy enough to make him an actor himself, he tells whichever host it is, "*She didn't need to do this to me. She didn't need to lie. If I'd known that she didn't love me anymore, I would've let her go.*"

As if they weren't arguing about contract renewals a week ago.

"How do we fix this?" Kaytee asks Norax. "Should I do interviews? Tell my side?"

From the head of the table, I have never seen Norax look as defeated as she does today. Her eyes, rimmed with dark circles, tell me she hasn't slept all night. Her voice, usually brimming with pep, is a hoarse whisper. "What would you even tell them?" she asks.

Lennix, on the other end of the table, is beside himself—too shocked by all this information to say a word yet. He's been focused only on me, so he doesn't know the half of the secrets we've been hiding. And as he's mentioned before, all of *his* members were under dating contracts. No such scandal ever befell them.

"He's not an innocent victim here," Kaytee insists. "People need to know that—"

"That what?" Lennix pipes up. "That you've been under a contract this whole time? Fooling them into thinking it was real? Do you expect to get sympathy from people by making them feel stupid?"

Kaytee tears up instantly, just like I have with Lennix so many times before. She once expressed jealousy that I got extra mentoring from Lennix. I'm sure she takes it back now. She looks to Norax and Norax alone. "Please. We have to do something. There has to be *something.*"

But our manager shakes her head. Kaytee deflates, crying harder.

Before anybody can say another word, Race rises from the table and seizes the vase of Cartney's roses. With the most brute force I've ever seen him use, he hurls them right at the wall across the room with a scream.

Carefully curved glass comes in contact with an abstract painting inches away from a window, and the shatter rings through the room as loud as the crowds outside. The canvas hits the floor like an aftershock with a hailstorm of petals.

A perfectly choleric destruction of a perfectly choleric gift.

"He doesn't have to completely annihilate our lives because his feelings got hurt!" he shouts. "We could've just dealt with this!"

"Whoa," says Till. I'm surprised she's the one to speak up. Usually she glowers in the corner. "Race, you don't have to—"

But she's cut off by Race's steel gaze. "*What!*"

"Nothing," she insists.

Race is always the collected one out of the six of us. He's ice that doesn't melt when put in hot water. He's *always* calm, even when he found himself constantly on the bottom of the Volx. Race doesn't panic. Watching him rake in breaths, hold back sobs, I'm struck with the guilt. I did this. For an instant, I'm back in Eldae, the old Em, who could disappear when she needed to—who could put up with the bullying, the endless teasing—because at home Dalton was always there. I had no choice, I remind myself, I *had* to save my brother.

"It's going to be all right," Foster tells him. "Race, he didn't—"

"People are threatening to *murder* Kaytee and me!" He points toward the window, but all any of us can focus on now is the wall beside it, which is stained in water, glass shards, and blood red petals. "I know murder threats aren't so damn unusual anymore, but it's my fans, *her* fans who want us dead too."

"Race," Chapter cuts in, drawing the attention away from DEFED. "This doesn't need to be a big deal. You can still manage—"

"*She* did this to us!" Kaytee yells, pointing at me with truculent might. "She did this to Race and me—on purpose! She wants us dead!"

"I had no choice!" I exclaim. I know my words make no sense to anyone except the members, but I say it again, hoping it sinks in. "I had no choice, Kaytee. I swear, I wouldn't have done it."

But she doesn't believe me. How could she? I have no proof. I was the one who got new ruby earrings when everyone else got tokens from their past lives. To Kaytee, DEFED has nothing to hang over my head. To Kaytee, they like me.

"No," she says. "You are *not* going to get away with this."

Away from the table, Race is stomping on the broken glass. He's in pain. He turns toward Norax. "I want out. Just let me out."

Out of the Famoux, I realize.

Norax frowns. "Calsifer, we've been through this. Somehow you still persist in finding a way to complain about the occupational hazards—"

"Occupational hazards?" he spits. "If I had known *half* the shit you have to put up with as a Famoux member, believe me, I wouldn't have joined. This is all a fraud. A shiny, stupid fraud, and I'm *done* with it."

"Calsifer!"

"You choose *everything* I do!" he shouts. "I don't want to act, but I'm in a movie now! I didn't want to date Kaytee in secret, but you made her sign a contract! I don't want to paint half the things you make me paint because it's for some dumb thing, but those are the only things you send to the galleries! You said this was going to be freedom, but it doesn't feel like it!"

"Do you *really* let your members talk to you like this?" Lennix asks Norax. He clicks his tongue. "Do you have any control over them at all?"

"Father, I want you to leave," Norax says sharply.

"Oh, I'm not going—"

Her voice reaches a fever pitch I've never heard before. It roars through every corner of the room, a dormant bomb left to sleep too long. "*Leave!* This is *my* Famoux! You think you know what's best for them, but you don't know anything!"

By the looks on our shocked faces, I don't think any of us have heard Norax yell like this before. Much like Race, she is always calm. Collected. Not today.

Norax nods to Gerald and another guard in the corner. "I want him out of here," she says.

"Absolutely not," says Lennix.

The guards hesitate. Who is the higher power?

"Get him out!" Norax yells.

Norax is, they decide. They advance to Lennix's end of the table, grabbing hold of his arms. "You've got to be kidding me," says Lennix. "Are you a child? Can't take a little criticism?"

"I know what I'm doing!" Norax says.

Lennix stares at his daughter for a moment before bursting again into laughter. "Choosing you for this job was just as much a mistake as you choosing the girl."

He lets the guards escort him out of the room peacefully after this, Norax glaring as he goes.

For a moment, no one speaks. Norax, a bit calmer, but still heated, turns the fire over to Race. "How *dare* you talk about this organization the way you have? Do you even realize how much better your life is now? How blessed you are to have *these* be your complaints?"

Race pales. He doesn't know what to say. "They want me dead. It's not—"

"Calsifer, *you* decided to date Kaytee in secret. I have never once endorsed that. I implored you both to stop, but I am not my father. I didn't use half the force I could've. That I *should've*." She purses her lips, takes a deep breath. "You claim that I choose everything you do, but this was *your* choice. This mess is *yours*. The fact that they hate you now is on you."

"So let me *go*, then," Race pleads. "If I've really messed it all up, let me go."

"I won't," she says.

Norax falters. Sympathetic.

"Race, this is my fault," Kaytee says.

She stands up and reaches out for him. He nearly recoils but stops himself. Softening in slight, he lets her fasten her fingers around his arm. "It isn't," he says.

"I've ruined everything. I was dating him."

"Then I wrecked it," he says. "They hate me more. You know that."

"It could be me still," she says.

"It'll be one of us."

The mood dims, if there is even a darker setting. Even though Norax is in the room, there is no panic—no care for what she might ask of these words. There is only Kaytee and Race, forehead to forehead, speaking to one another in front of what might be the smallest audience they'll ever have again.

From outside, the jeers of hundreds waft up to the window. Somewhere in the midst of chanting, a mixture of Cartney's songs are blaring—all now weapons used to prove he loved her, and she was cruel.

Kaytee takes a deep breath, feigning strength. "Let's see what happens. We could get lucky."

He stares at her. Perhaps he sees all the pain they've caused in being together. Perhaps he realizes that giving up now would be useless, so close to the end. Whatever reason, he glances over to the rest of us.

"Fine," he finally says. "But I'm doing you all a service here. You just have to watch me die."

× × ×

Once the meeting is drawn to its somber conclusion, I am whisked away toward a far-off wing I've never seen. Everything is dark and robotic, like the walls and the floors are the inside of the Fissarex. I don't like it.

I'm brought to a room where there are no windows, just artificial light pouring onto stone floor. There are two doors in here—the one from which I'd just entered, and another right next to it that leads somewhere I haven't explored yet either. Both doors are white.

Atop a cold metal seat, I fidget with my perfect nails, ruining the skin around them, waiting for Norax. She brought me here on vague orders that she must *have a word with me.* No elaboration.

A part of me fears she's going to punish me for what I've done. Norax has always been able to excuse the small undercutting the members have done on the principle that it keeps the Famoux in the news and makes for greatly dramatic *Fishbowl* broadcasts. But *this* is betrayal on a different level. I've ruined them. Surely, that sort of duplicity is off-limits.

Luckily, Gerald is here, standing watch in the corner, keeping me company. He asks me how I'm doing, his voice small and cautious. As usual this scenario is just as confusing and off-putting for him as it is for me. Sharing in the unknown is at least comforting.

"I'm okay," I say.

"Rough day for the Famoux, huh?"

He has no idea. The number of things Kaytee and Race can do to redeem themselves in the short time we have left is abysmally small. The chances of me making it right with them in that time, even smaller. We're going to go into that Fishbowl as enemies, and there's nothing I can do about it.

My finger grazes past the curved mark on my wrist. I wish Norax would hurry up, so I could check the Analytix again. Maybe I missed DEFED. Maybe they'll be coming back to let me know Dalton is safe.

I need to know what I did was worth it.

The sound of the door creaking calms me slightly. Norax clacks toward me in her high heels, a massive collection of papers in her arms.

"Get here all right?" she asks.

"Is Lennix coming?" I ask.

She frowns. "He won't."

"Oh," I say.

Norax holds out a stack of the papers. I brace for the worst, but then she says, "Here. I have some things you need to sign for *Algus & Alondra*."

"Oh," I say, relieved. "That's all?"

"Were you expecting something else?"

"I didn't know if . . ."

Norax senses what I'm getting at. "You didn't *actually* leak Kaytee and Race's relationship, right? Cartney just walked in on his own?"

Is she giving me an out, or is she seeing the best in me? Probably the latter. She doesn't know my motivations. And how would I explain if I tell her yes? There's no way to see what I've done as anything other than conniving when you remove the DEFED of it all.

"Of course," I say, taking the papers.

The pen is too lovely to rush with—smooth and glossy against the thick contract paper. I take my time, but there are only a few. Once I'm done, I hand the papers back to Norax.

"Is that everything?" I ask.

She takes another heap of papers into her hands and pushes them toward me. "A couple more."

Squinting my eyes, I examine their confusing titles. More movie stuff. The name *Alondra* all over the page. I start signing again, and as I do, Norax makes stiflingly awkward conversation.

"How have you been since the issue of *The X* came out?" she asks. "Good?"

"Okay," I say.

"The other members said some pretty nice things about you," she says. When I admit that I haven't gotten to read any of it yet, she's surprised. "You didn't get a copy?"

"I've just been signing them," I say.

"I'll arrange to get you one."

My signature is gleaming and extraloopy on the last page. Even with Race and Kaytee plummeting in the ratings, I can't help but get a flutter of nerves when I think about how there is a chance I might not make it to any of these promotions. Everything happens so fast these days that it's hard to tell where any of us are going to be tomorrow.

I hand the papers back. "Is that everything?"

"Do you have somewhere to be?"

Norax seems off. Uneasy. "I was just thinking about checking the Analytix," I say. "If we were all done."

"You don't need to," Norax asserts. "You're doing amazing." After a pause, she adds, in a voice much firmer, "A very good development for you."

"Is something wrong?"

"It's just . . ." Norax taps her pen against the table. She closes her eyes, rubbing the bridge of her nose. "We actually need to discuss something, lumerpa."

"What is it?"

"Race and Kaytee are . . . Well, they're properly going through the wringer right now," she says, "as I'm sure you may have noticed. I don't know if I'm going to be able to completely mend this."

She knows it's my fault. She *has* to. I brace myself for the scolding, but then she says, "All I know is that I have to make sure something like this *never* happens again."

"What do you mean?" I ask.

Norax examines her nails. They're all coated in a gleaming green polish that reminds me of Dalton's eyes.

"Look," she starts. "I know I'm right, but I have to make sure. You don't have anything like Kaytee and Race's scenario happening right now, right? Nothing happening in secret?"

I feel dread coursing through me now. I manage a nod.

"That's what I thought," she says, tapping her fingers together. "I knew I must've seen the wrong thing in the cameras."

"Cameras?" I ask.

"The security ones in the hotel. In Eldae. They showed you and Chapter leaving late at night. But now I know, those had to be other people."

I flinch. "Norax, we didn't—"

Her face contorts into anger in an instant. "What were you *doing* out with Chapter that late? Can you tell me, honestly, what was so important?"

There's no way to spin visiting Chapter's home before the Famoux into something she can digest. My hesitation lasts too long. Whatever she's assumed, I may as well have just confirmed it.

"There," she says. "I should've known."

"Norax, it's not—"

"If someone saw you two out there, *you* would've been in a mess like Kaytee and Race! But it would be only you. Not Chapter. Do you get that? Do you understand his fans? This mess would have been a *million* times worse!"

"No, you don't understand," I stammer. "It's not—"

"You're out of the film."

"What?"

"I can't have you two on the same set," she says. "I can't afford that risk."

"But what about the contracts I just signed?"

"Those were for your withdrawal," Norax says. She touches the small stack. "Now, you are legally no longer involved with the film."

"*How* could you not tell me that before I signed them?" I shout. "I wouldn't have if I knew!"

"Lumerpa, don't be upset." Norax reaches out to grab my hand. I swat the gesture away, and she looks pained. "You already saw what happened when you gave the world an inch. You just *stood* next to Chapter for a few minutes, and they hated you. Don't give them a mile. I don't want you to end up like Kaytee and Race."

"But it's not even the same!" I exclaim. "There isn't a Cartney or anything!"

But then, a deep and destructive voice swirls into the room, lacing the air with its own poison.

"It's the same now."

From behind me, the second white door closes with a soft click. We were so busy yelling, I didn't hear it open. Now, the footfall of expensive shoes makes its way toward us, and something inside of me is collapsing. My chest feels so tight, it's hard to take a breath. I keep my eyes trained on Norax's, keen on the way she can see everything collapse in my gaze—on the way she reacts with apathy.

My voice is a whisper. "You didn't."

"I need you to understand, lumerpa, that I'm not trying to be cruel," Norax says. "I'm only trying to be practical."

The seat beside me fills with a man in a dark blue suit. A slender hand comes down on my own, fixed and fatal. When he speaks, his voice lacks the kind of swagger I've grown so used to hearing from him. I turn, and his eyes meet mine. They're red; he's been crying.

"Surprise," Cartney Kirk says dryly.

"You said it wouldn't come to this," I say desperately. "You told Lennix you wouldn't make me."

Norax rubs her forehead. "Look, lumerpa. I'm not a miracle worker. I'm a problem solver."

"*How* does this solve the problem?" I ask. "How is this a good idea at all?"

She clears her throat, the way she does before speeches. She's prepared. "Buchan and I ran the various scenarios last night, and we are certain you are already a couple people will root for."

"*How?*"

"You are the only person whom Cartney has been seen with other than Kaytee for months. As far as the world is concerned, he has been your friend since the beginning. He took you to coffee."

"*With* Kaytee," I say.

"Which means there are plenty of instances where you could have seen their rifts. You became an instrumental force in showing him how much better he deserved. You even carried him, drunk, out of a club when his girlfriend was absent. You took care of him."

My jaw drops. *I don't believe this.* "But people see me as Kaytee's friend," I point out. "They'll think I'm terrible, won't they?"

"Quite unlikely," says Cartney, amused. What is a horror to me, I realize, is a wicked revenge plot to him. "Right now, you're my guardian angel. My shoulder to cry on! They'll hate them even *more* when they see the way you love me!"

Norax nods along. "Suppose everybody caught word that you sent Cartney flowers," she says. "Suppose the note attached to those flowers got leaked, and it had implications that you denounce Kaytee's actions and are on his side, fully."

"I don't want to do that," I say.

"Well tell that to this," Cartney unpins the yellow rose corsage off his suit, waving it at my face. "The crowd outside just *loved* seeing it on me when I walked in."

My mouth falls open at Norax. "You sent flowers in my name? *Already?*"

"You know how you signed your note too?" asks Cartney. "*Love, Ray.* Everybody is freaking out! The public jumped onto this boat immediately, babe!"

He holds out his palm for a high five, but I ignore it. I can't even look at him without wanting to throw up. I keep my eyes trained on Norax, who barely even fidgets.

"It was a lovely note," she says. "Convincing."

My body feels like something is slowly pushing down on it, compressing me until I'm completely gone. Why is she doing all of this to me? I'd understand more if it was Lennix, but *Norax*? She was the one who defended me when Lennix insisted I sign a contract with Marlon York. She was the one who insisted I have a say in my life—the one who *promised* I would.

"But . . . Kaytee," I say again. That look on her face when she saw me by the door with Cartney is burned into my mind. And now, *this*? "What would she think?"

"Who cares what she thinks!" says Cartney. "She's never cared what I thought!"

"How can you do this?"

"She will never love me like I loved her," he says. "Now it's time to spend the next two years throwing that in her face."

*Two years.*

"I won't sign a contract for that long," I say. "I won't. You can't do that to me."

Norax's fingers twitch, tapping decisively against the large stack of papers in front of her.

And then, so suddenly, it's clear, before she says another word.

"Lumerpa, you already signed it."

× × ×

Moving quickly, as if I could break out into a run at any given moment, I walk down the hallway. My breathing is shallow and choppy—at least, as much as a Famoux member's perfect breath can get. My heeled boots clack against the hardwood floors, and I wince with every thud. Commotion is no option. I don't know who could be lurking around, and I don't want any attention. I need to go unnoticed.

The hideaway is still such a mystery to me, so it takes a while to find the wing with the dark red doors. I pass through a few turns of the hall in search of the right painting. There—the two blue eyes at the end of the hall. But which door?

"Sticks?"

I whirl around, and Chapter's there, like the first time I saw him. Hair bronze, eyes oceanic. I'm about to run right at him, perhaps even topple him over, but somehow, I can't. I can't even speak. For a second we are like two crumpled ruins in Eldae, broken and unable to move, staring at one another.

And then I come to my senses. I rush toward him, drawing him into a hug he's unprepared for. I wrap my arms around him tightly, like he might blow away with the draft down the hall if I don't.

"Is everything okay?" he asks.

I can't tell him yet. Before he can note my hesitation, I grab the sides of his face and pull him toward me instead. When his lips meet mine, everything gets sharp, keen—like my senses have been thrown into overdrive. I can recognize my own heart against his, beating fast. With his there's the flutter of something new. With mine, of something ending. I'll lose him. This thing between us has only just begun, and I've already lost everything in a game I didn't even know I was playing. I wish I could pause this moment and live within it, but I can't. I can't. The moment is already over as he pulls back to face me.

Chapter takes the tears sprouting in my eyes to be about something else. "What happened with Kaytee?" he asks. "You said you didn't have a choice? Was it DEFED?"

"They had my brother," I say.

"Is he safe now?"

"I don't know."

His expression turns pained, and I'm reminded of a time when I thought his face was unreadable. "I guess the best thing you can do now is stay as far from Kaytee, Race, and Cartney as possible," he says. "Until this all clears up."

Before I can stop myself, I grimace.

"What is it?" he asks.

No. I'm still not ready to tell him. I try to center my gaze down at the patterned carpet, but he lifts my chin so that we're making eye contact.

"Sticks," Chapter says. "Really. What is it?"

*Sticks.* Like kindling, now, for what I'm about to say. The words begin to feel like fire coming out of me. Everything I've tried to hold close lights up into flames.

"Norax made me sign a contract," I say. "She tricked me into thinking I was signing something else—"

"What kind of contract?" he interrupts, his face darkening.

"It's with Cartney."

We're so close that my lungs fill with Chapter's jagged exhale. "How is that possible?"

"She didn't give me a choice," I say. "She heard about us in Eldae. She knows about us. She just . . ."

He is the one who hesitates now, unsure of what to say. He pulls me closer. My forehead comes in contact with his chin. His breath comes in contact with my hair. As we stay there, I realize just how potently we can hear the shouting at Kaytee coming from outside. It leaks through the walls, perhaps magnified in my mind. *How could you! How could you do this to Cartney?!*

They could shout the same to me someday, if they found out about this.

"Miss Essence?"

We turn toward the voice. Gerald stands at the end of the hall, posture exact and rigid. Unnerving.

"Yes?" I ask.

His lips fidget, like he doesn't want to speak. The words read off like a definition he was told to memorize. "I regret to inform you that I am now in charge of keeping track and recording all your whereabouts. As of today, as per your contract's orders, you are no longer permitted to visit this section of the mansion."

"What?" I cry out.

"You are also not permitted to be anywhere with Mr. Stones alone, both inside and outside the mansion. I am to ensure at any events that you are standing at least two Famoux members away from one another at all times, so as not to arouse any suspicion from your fans."

"That's absolutely ridiculous," Chapter says. "Norax can't just—"

"This has already been agreed upon in the fine print, sir," says Gerald. "Miss Essence has signed the contract. I am merely in charge of relaying its terms."

"Gerald," I beg. "You don't have to do this."

He strains. "I was supposed to be watching your room in Eldae. They will fire me if I fail my job again."

My heart feels like it could explode. If I follow the rules, I lose all contact with Chapter. If I disobey them, Gerald is punished. And after Kaytee and Race, I believe I've already done enough life ruining to last me forever.

My gaze flickers to Chapter, and it does nothing to give me gravity like I hoped. He's looking at me now like one would look at a painting behind a barrier, or an animal locked up for viewers at a park—admiration, with the slightest hint of forlorn. Close, but unable to be reached.

"There's no getting around this, is there?" he asks.

"We could fight it," I say, frantic. "Tell the world right now, before they can even know about Cartney and me. We could stop it before it starts."

"We can't," Chapter says. "With or without him, you know what would happen, what people would say. We're too close to the Darkening . . ."

"I don't care."

"I do," Chapter says.

"But maybe it wouldn't be so bad. Maybe I could—"

My words are cut off by his hand tracing the side of my face. "I'm far too concerned about your life to let you ruin it on my behalf," he says.

Concern. The word he theorized to mean more than just love. I expect a confession like this to fill me with a warm sensation, but I get ice instead. Because it's too late for it.

Chapter kisses me one last time, as Gerald looks at the painting on the wall and pretends not to see. I'm led back to my room to get rest. Apparently, it's going to be a big day for Cartney and me tomorrow. We'll be making our public debut.

Like my first night in the mansion, I rush straight to the bathroom, turning the dial on the crystal faucet until it's piping hot. I bring my hands under the water, hoping to get some feeling, some clarity, *anything*. I scrutinize my reflection—my blue eyes a tired red, my blond hair wild and unkempt. I don't think I have ever looked worse as Emeray Essence than I do right now. But curiously enough, even *this* sight is beautiful. Impossibly beautiful.

And just like that first night again, the sight of this person scares me. I can't see my face from before—her hair, the shapes of her. The closest I can get is picturing Lex from Race's art show, but I know it's not enough. She was different. *Emilee* was different.

I step away from the mirror, feeling sick. Norax took all of that away. She told me how beautiful I was when she first saw me, how she wanted the world to see that beauty too, then changed every last bit. She told me I could do whatever I wanted with this new life, then forced my hand into this contract—sealed my fate for the next two years.

A part of Race's outburst from earlier enters my mind. *You said this was going to be freedom, but it doesn't feel like it.*

He's right.

It doesn't.

# CHAPTER NINETEEN

As we close in on the Darkening, there are enough particles gathered in the air now to make the sky look as though it's stained with soot. In Betnedoor, a state without even a fraction of the daily smog coverage the other two states endure, these last few days of the month are such anomalies, they have a nickname for them: the Gray Days. When I watch the sunrise in the morning, this one is the closest it's ever been to the ones back in Eldae. The vivid pinks I've grown so used to now appear muted and orange, even a little brown. Just like old times. It almost gives me the urge to sneak out of my room and find a place like my mother's favorite house.

But this would be impossible. There are no ruins like that in Betnedoor. Plus, I would never be able to sneak out of this hideaway without someone noticing. Not anymore.

Gerald enters my room after dawn breaks to ask if I want him to fetch me coffee. Chapter is in the kitchen, he explains, which means *I* can't be there—not until he leaves. I tell him I'm fine, but after a few minutes a large carafe is brought in anyway. There's no use wasting it, so I sip a cup or two, watch the rest of the grayish sunrise, and think about getting ready. Should I try doing my makeup now to pass the time, or will Norax have everything planned for today, down to the direction my hair will curl?

Sure enough, a few minutes later, she's at my door with a team of ten employees in tow who bathe me, dry me, and style me like a little doll. I don't even move a muscle past the occasional reluctant nod at whatever Norax says.

"These Gray Days are going to be *full* of sunshine, thanks to you two," she happily insists. "I think you're going to find yourself having a lot of fun!"

She has to be messing with me. Daring me to snap at her so she can scold me, just like she did Race when he tried to complain about his quality of life. Either that, or Norax genuinely thinks she can convince me that this contract is anything other than a two-year sentence. As she outlines my schedule for the next three days, she phrases everything like it's *my* call, not hers.

"You're only going to create intrigue today by going to Cartney's place. He'll walk you out. You don't want anything huge, yet!" she exclaims. "Just enough intrigue to get people talking! *Tomorrow*, of course, you'll go to Wes Tegg's for an actual date and confirm suspicions. Then, I think you'll decide to take a separate jet from the other members on the flight over to Eldae. You'd rather just be with Cartney, right?"

At this point, one of the makeup artists is painting a rouge cream on my lips, so I can't even let my jaw drop without compromising her work. The artist tells me right then to smile, so I do, and Norax takes this as confirmation.

"Perfect," she says. "Then you'll attend Bree's gala and the *Key* premiere together, as a couple. Then it's off to the Fishbowl!"

Oh, the Fishbowl. Of course, all eyes were going to be on me anyway, by principle of this being my first Darkening and all, but *now* it's going to be even worse. I might not be a part of any films anymore, but my role as an actress, it appears, is just beginning. While Norax pulls several bright sweaters from the rack of them in my closet, she takes me through a few talking points to bring up when I'll inevitably have to defend Cartney's honor in front of Kaytee and Race, and it occurs to me that I'm going to have to fight and argue and cry and cause big, big trouble like I've seen the members do so many times before on my screen back home. And the act can never let up either. Not even when I'm alone in my room. Everyone will still be watching and scrutinizing the way I toss and turn in my sleep, wondering what I'm dreaming about. Back when I used to wake early to watch them, this was exactly what I did—imagined what was going on in their heads.

But the thing that bothers me the most about this Darkening isn't even the acting; it's knowing that this fake spat will fill my final moments with Kaytee or Race. The Volx might be gone now, but it's ridiculous to assume anyone other than the two of them is at the bottom of it. DEFED cruelly wants us to not know which one. Now, in one moment I'll be spewing these lies about how *Cartney is more sensitive than you realize*, and the next moment one of them will be gone, and I'll never have had the chance to explain that I had no choice but to seal their fate like I did. Also, even if DEFED stages the death to be an accident like Bree's, the world will definitely at least muse about me playing a part in it somehow. After all, some people believed I killed *Bree*, and I wasn't even in the Fishbowl to do it.

It is important to Norax that we get this first walk done as quickly as possible, so as to allow for a whole day's worth of gossip to spread. We're in the car on the way toward the city barely two hours after the sunrise, and most of the storefronts are closed and sidewalks empty. Just as I was wondering how anyone would see us, Norax answered the unasked question.

"They know you're coming," Norax tells me. "I tipped off a few friends."

*A few* is an understatement. When we turn onto the street where Cartney's apartment building is, there is a horde of paparazzi gathered on the sidewalk that's so big, it rivals the number of flashbulbs of the red carpets I've been on.

"Cartney's waiting upstairs," she tells me. "Room fifteen. You're going to go in there, stay a while, then he'll walk you out. We'll be waiting down the street so our friends can snap a few pictures. How does that sound?"

"Fine," I say, and I realize it's the first thing I've actually said to Norax all day. She's been so easily filling the silence, I'm not sure if she's noticed.

Crossing the barely two yards of distance between the car and the building door is an absurdly hard task. The photographers are so tenacious about capturing this moment, I guess, that they've forgotten I'm a human being. It's a struggle to keep the bashful, lovesick smile Norax drilled me on over the drive. Every time they shove themselves toward me, I get the strange urge to shove back. Say, *you know what, forget this*, and run back to the car. But obviously, that's not an option. Gerald does a good job keeping their hands off me as best as he can, and at some point, we make it through.

Cartney's apartment is in the penthouse of his building. With each floor the elevator passes on the way up, I feel my heart sink an inch lower.

I've been here before, when Kaytee and I recorded our song, but Cartney seems to have redecorated since then. The records on the walls had been framed in black, but now they're powder blue. When I get to the living room, I see most of the furniture is now that color too. Except, of course, for the massive bouquet of red roses on the coffee table.

"Do you like them, Ray?"

I jump at his voice, which makes Cartney laugh. He's standing in the corner by the kitchen, making breakfast. Still in pajamas, too, from the looks of it. Either that, or he's going for a strikingly casual look for our walk.

"I didn't think you did that yourself," I say, nodding to the stove, where a pot of what could be oatmeal is cooking.

"Believe me, I wish I didn't have to," says Cartney. "But we can't all have maids living in our quarters like you Famoux members."

He asks me if I want a bowl, and I decline. I half expect him to make me one anyway, since it's what always seems to happen when I turn things down, but Cartney doesn't. When he crosses over to the sitting area, he has only one bowl in his hands. Something about this soothes me, strangely, just for a second.

"So," Cartney says through a mouthful. "I guess you're my girlfriend."

"You guess?"

"Fine. I *know* you're my girlfriend. What do you want to talk about?"

"Nothing," I say.

Cartney considers this, then shrugs. "That's cool."

Silence stretches over us as he eats. It's unexpected, given how

I've seen him fill plenty of silences before this. Back when I went to Wes Tegg's with him and Kaytee, he never stopped talking once. I decide not to question it, and instead look around. *Everything* is blue. The pillows, the rug, the stain of the wood coffee table. If it weren't the Gray Days, the view of the skyline from his window would be the very same color.

I budge and ask about it. He offers only another shrug. "Thought it might be nice to really lean into my sadness, you know?"

His sadness. He'd been so energetic about getting revenge yesterday, but I remember now how he *had* looked like he'd been crying.

"Listen, I don't want to do this any more than you do," he tells me. "I know you don't want to be with me. You're beautiful and all, but I'm not interested in you. Why don't we just agree to share our misery until it's over?"

"Why would you even agree to this?" I ask. "Why are you always signing contracts with Famoux members?"

Cartney pauses, as if he's not sure why himself. "It was a part of my record deal," he says. "Five albums, dating contract with a Famoux member, renewal every year. Felt like a pretty great deal to me, you know?"

"Does it feel like a great deal now?"

He chuckles. "Everyone knows who I am. That's what I wanted. I just . . . I guess I didn't expect to actually like Kaytee as much as I did. Dating contracts are supposed to be fake, sure, but it didn't feel fake to me." He stares into his bowl, then chuckles again. "But I guess I won't make the same mistake with you, huh?"

Cartney finishes his oatmeal, and we figure it's been an appropriately long amount of time to let the paparazzi wait. He changes into day clothes, plucks a single rose from the bouquet and puts it in my hair, and before I know it, I'm facing the crowds outside again, this time with Cartney's hand in mine.

If I thought they were unbearable with just me, I was sorely mistaken. Shouts build into screams so loud I can barely hear if they're happy, or mad, or *anything*. Cameras are shoved into my face so fast that one actually strikes my chin. It doesn't hurt, but it startles everyone all the same. As Gerald shoves the photographers back, barking orders about giving us space, Cartney takes this opportunity to be tender, cupping my face in his hands. Naturally, all this does is make the paparazzi go even more berserk.

It's here when I realize he is tall, *so* tall—my head barely reaches his nose, even in the sky-high heels that were picked out for me. It occurs to me that he's so much older too. I'm only sixteen—he's twenty.

"How wild would it be if I just kissed you right now?" Cartney asks, some of his usual verve returning. Attention from the crowds seems to have resparked it.

I fight the urge to recoil from his grip. Can't have the cameras catching anything negative like that. "Norax told me we can't confirm anything until tomorrow."

"Fine. You're right," he says. He drops his hands, grabbing a pair of headphones from his jacket pocket and offering one to me. "Take it. They'll think it's a new song or something."

With a path to the car cleared out for us, we officially begin our photoshoot of a walk. This won't take more than thirty seconds at most, but Cartney starts a song anyway. One of Kaytee's, interestingly enough. As her voice floods through the headphone in my right ear, he swings our hands in the space between us to the beat. All the while, my left gets a whole array of questions from the paparazzi.

"*What are you listening to?*"

"*What does this mean?*"

"*Are you two in love?*"

All questions go ignored, met instead with shy, carefully practiced smiles. *Are* we in love? Maybe. They can decide for themselves.

Before we can even reach the chorus, the car door is being opened and Norax beckons me inside. Cartney takes his headphones and shoves them in his pocket, then we wave at an awkward distance before I turn away. The paparazzi clamor for a kiss, but they'll have to wait for it. I'll hold that off as long as I can.

"You did *amazing*!" Norax implores. The device in her hand is whirring, photos taken just seconds ago already popping up in articles with our names in the titles. The ones with Cartney holding my face seem to be especially prevalent. "Everyone is so excited. Perfect reactions. I can't wait for you to check the Analytix."

When I do, she's right. Everyone *is* so excited. The words *epic love* and *soul mates* are thrown around frequently and fervently. There's only a small number of skeptics who are unsure, still mourning the loss of Kaytee and Cartney's relationship and wondering if this might be happening too fast.

It's sort of funny. It seems I'm always replacing something that's died, and I'm always replacing it far too soon.

Gerald is waiting outside the door when I surface from the Analytix, ready to follow my every step. I test this out, taking him wing by wing to the studio, to the gym, and he follows persistently. When we start reaching the wing with crimson doors, he tells me with pained reluctance to turn around. He feels bad, but he doesn't bend.

So I really *can't* see Chapter. I take a turn to the library, feeling gutted.

At first, I think we're alone, but when I turn into a row near the back, I find Foster at a desk, spinning around on an office chair. When he loops and catches my eye, he stops, spreading his arms out. "Well, there she is!" he declares. "Talk of the town!"

His arms aren't exactly an open invitation, but when I reach him, I initiate a hug anyway. Luckily, Foster accepts it, squeezing me tight. Fans always used to talk about how Foster's hugs were the best—how he'd never be the first to pull away from them, just in case they needed more. And as it appears, I need a lot. The end result is a hug that lasts almost an entire minute and breaks when he begins laughing.

"I'm sorry," he says, wiping an eye. "I know none of this is particularly funny for you right now. Chapter told me you had to sign a *contract*?"

It's difficult to hear his name and not react. I frown. "He did?"

"He seemed a little more upset about it than I would've expected," Foster says. "Which leads me to believe . . ." It fades off. He concludes, "I guess I have to commend you both for hiding it so well."

"What am I supposed to do?" I ask.

"What *can* you do? Even if there wasn't a contract, you would've had to keep this secret. Chapter is just . . . off-limits." He pats my arm consolingly, then makes an attempt at levity. "You really chose the wrong Famoux member to start something with, didn't you? You should've chosen me. Or Till."

"You have Finley," I point out. "And Till ignores me."

He flicks his wrist at this. "She would come around to you."

For a while we browse the selection of books, and Foster points out the ones that are Finley's favorites. Somewhere along the line I realize how similar our situations are. Foster could never go near Finley, not even in secret. It would be too reckless. All they can do now is talk through their letters. I try to imagine myself writing a letter to Chapter, but it overwhelms me. I wouldn't know where to begin.

Later that night, Cartney drops a new song, confirming all the wondering over what we might've been listening to in the headphones. It's just a simple guitar track and his vocals. Basically a demo. The lyrics mention someone who's been there the whole time, who he never knew was the one for him, but now is sure of. Just to make it obvious, he calls her his *ray* of sun, calling back to the way I so apparently signed my letter to him that Norax forged yesterday.

Without the Volx, there's no way of knowing if any of this is helping me or hurting me. For all we know, this could backfire and the world could side with Kaytee, berating me for my actions. But the way I can't sit on the Analytix stool without hearing shrill screeches about me over the lyrics seems like a pretty good sign.

In the morning, Norax and the same team of maids parade in before Gerald does to inquire about coffee. "It's no matter," Norax tells him. "She's on her way to get some anyway!"

The date Cartney and I are going on will be at Wes Tegg's. An ode to our first meeting as well as a firm cementation of Kaytee's absence. It's honestly a little cruel, when I think about it for too long. Luckily, the maids don't let me. As they do my makeup, they occupy me with all the many rumors they've heard so far about the relationship. Cartney's apparently shopping for rings already, and we're planning our wedding for the spring.

"It seems fast," one of them says, "but *everything* about this has been so fast! That's what makes it so cute!"

Norax can't hide her delight at this. She nudges my arm. "And Lennix thought I didn't know how to run my Famoux, huh?"

Does she expect me to laugh along? No, that much I refuse. I stare her down until she frowns, relents, and retreats to the closet to grab me a pair of shoes. The triumph I feel is brief, but something.

On the drive over to Wes Tegg's, she primes me on the trip to Eldae tomorrow. Separate jet from the Famoux, separate floor in the hotel to get ready for the events. "Even though it's going to be Chapter's movie premiere," she warns, "you still *can't* break your contract. And in the Fishbowl, I don't want you speaking to him. Okay?"

"If I ignore Chapter, people will think I hate him," I point out.

"Better that than the opposite," she insists.

Cartney is waiting outside the doors when we pull up, surrounded by a crowd five times the size of yesterday's. He wears a gray suit and a smile, a bouquet of red roses in his hand, which he gets down on one knee to present to me. He's clearly heard the marriage rumors too.

"Good morning, beautiful." Cartney has to shout it, just to make sure everyone hears. He gets back to his feet, then gestures to the door. "Shall we?"

Inside, Cartney makes a big show of ordering two vanilla lattes, loudly calling the drink *our* favorite. Before we've even sat down at the table, a chalkboard at the front already proclaims it to be their drink of the month.

"Very nice callback with the hat," he says, nodding to the one I take off my head. "You wore that when we first met. Fitting, for today."

It's also Chapter's hat, which neither he nor Norax knows. I clutch it, protectively, as if he might find out and throw it in the trash. "Thanks," I tell him.

"This is going pretty well, no?"

"I guess," I say. I'd usually say more, maybe something terse, but I hold my tongue. The area around us is suddenly packed now, and people are blatantly staring. Anything we say from now on will be quoted back to me in the Analytix, I'm sure of it.

Like in his apartment, a silence stretches like an umbrella over us—Cartney and me, a gloomy, rain-cloud couple disguised as a sunny day.

"Did you like the song?" Cartney asks. For the sake of those who might be listening, he adds, "You're a great muse, you know."

"It's a lovely song."

What really makes me sick is the fact that if I was still Emilee Laurence, craning my neck to hear bits of it from nearby lockers, my heart would swell at the words, and I might've wished someone would sing them about me. I would've wished for a love that strong. And it's all just a farce. My shoulders slump for a moment before picking back up. Perish the thought that the people see me sad today.

I push my vanilla latte away and stand. "I'll be right back," I say.

Something challenging flickers in Cartney's gaze before dissolving into something coy. "Don't escape out the back!" he jokes for the other patrons.

The lights are dim inside the restroom. I don't really need to use the facilities, I just needed a break, so I stare at myself in the mirror. *This isn't so bad*, I rationalize. As Cartney said, we are sharing this misery. Perhaps I could manage for two years . . .

*Two years*, who am I kidding? That's an empty promise. How many times has Kaytee had no choice but to renew her contract? If this relationship gets as big as it promises to be, even bigger than theirs was, this is something that could keep renewing again and again and again until Norax finally kicks this era of the Famoux out. All that time, and I may never get to talk to Chapter again. The misery will never end.

The door slams open and I jump back as a woman rushes in like she's being chased. At first I think she's a zealous fan trying to snag a private moment with me, the way her eyes are so wide and alert as she advances toward me. Then I realize I know these eyes. They're the same as mine.

The exact same.

"*Mom*?"

She could be a ghost, for all I know. Her coat is long and gray, as gray as her hair, which was brown the last time I saw her. In fact, she looks as though she's aged several years, but it's only been two since she left. Her wrinkles are more set-in. Her figure is weary. I've never seen her like this before.

Except perhaps at Ace. That gray-haired woman who looked like her . . .

She pulls me into a hug. There, she's tangible. Not a ghost. "Emilee," she murmurs into my hair. "We don't have a lot of time. I—we tried to reach you earlier, at that party. We've been trying for weeks now."

"*We*?" I ask.

"I can explain it all later," she tells me. "Right now, we need you to—"

But a threshold has been broken. Holding my tongue is impossible. Not with this. "Wait, where have you been? Why did—" Then

I spot my reflection again in the mirror over her shoulder and I stagger back, hitting the wall. This isn't the same weak body my mother used to cradle after school. "How do you know it's *me*?"

My mother reaches a hand up to my remade face. I'm even taller too. She used to be my height, and now she seems so small. "Emilee, please, I can explain everything to you when we get you out—"

"Get me out?"

"—but first we need your help. They have Dalton."

"You know about DEFED?" I ask.

My mother's face twists up into confusion. Now it's her turn to stagger back, parroting my question back to me. "*You* know about DEFED?"

"Well, yes," I say, wary. "They—they have Dalton. Like you said."

"What are you talking about?"

I try to explain, but my head hasn't even wrapped around the fact that my mother is here, so I stammer on every word. I do my best to take her through it—how they've killed Bree, how they're threatening the Famoux members now. It comes out in fragments. *Branded us . . . bone cufflinks . . .* I presume the horror on her face to be one of pity, for how we've had to deal with so much fear and uncertainty, but then she says, "No, no, that's all *wrong*."

"What?"

My mother puts a hand to her forehead, pacing away from me toward the faucets. "We haven't written any notes or sent any packages. We . . . We haven't even made our *debut* yet. We wanted to get you with us first." Her hands clench up into fists. "All the code names to avoid being heard in the Analytix . . . We were so *careful . . .*"

"Wait," I say, wobbly. "What are you talking about? What do you mean *we?*"

"I created DEFED to *help* you, Emilee," she says. "Not to hurt you."

The room is spinning. No, maybe it's melting. Maybe *I'm* melting, right into the floor. The only thing that tethers me back to the present is a brusque knock on the door, then Cartney's voice on the other end.

"Um, Ray?"

"Just a second," I call out, surprised my voice even works.

"I'm ready to leave," he says. "Could you hurry?"

My mother strains for composure. She grips me tightly. "Em, please listen to me. I know this is all happening fast, and that you're going to have a lot of questions, but I need you to trust me, okay? I have no idea how Norax knows about us, but if she is telling you that *DEFED* is responsible for these sinister things, she is lying to you."

"Norax isn't telling us anything, I say. She doesn't know—"

Another knock. *"Come on!"*

"She knows. Believe me," my mother says. "I understand that you have no reason to trust me, and every reason to trust that she doesn't, but she is not your mother. She is not your friend. Everything she does, she does only to serve herself. *She* is the one who has Dalton. I know how to get him out, but we're going to need your help at Bree Arch's gala to make it happen. Can we count on you?"

"I . . . I don't . . ."

The words fade away while my mind tries to process everything. Over the last two years, I have imagined reuniting with my mother a million times, in a million ways. Most of these ways were incredibly unrealistic. I'd picture her swooping in before Westin could hurt me, like a guardian angel. I'd imagine her walking into class and pulling me out so we could spend the day exploring ruins. At the store downtown, I'd dream of her putting a hand on my shoulder and saying, "*There you are, I've been looking for you!*" and me realizing all the days of pain and wondering had only been a nightmare in the grocery aisle.

But in all my wildest daydreams, I never pictured this. I never saw us standing in the bathroom of a café in Betnedoor, with me as a member of the Famoux, and her as a member of horrible, terrible, menacing DEFED. I never saw *this* being our first conversation, after years and years of nothing.

"Please, Emilee, think about it," she says. "We will see you at the gala."

Then she slips out the door, scurrying right past Cartney. As I surface behind her, my face white, Cartney furrows his brows.

"Who was that?" he asks.

"A fan," I manage.

He hesitates, then feigns annoyance. "I'm not sure why a fan would walk *right* past me, but *okay.*"

Keeping the fake, giddy smile on my face as Cartney and I walk back to the car is a feat. If only Gerald hadn't been so brusque with the photographers yesterday when one of them accidentally hit me, I could use an excuse to grimace, to maybe even cry. Beside me, Cartney is rattling off plans about how to maximize our likability as a couple at the gala, but I can barely hear him. And when he pulls me into our first kiss, and the whole world around us goes totally wild, it barely holds a candle to the chaos in my brain.

"*Showstopping!*" gushes Norax when I get in the car. She's got one hand to her heart, the other holding the same device from yesterday, where photos of the kiss from about a thousand angles are popping up. "Lumerpa, that was *beautiful!*"

Those scathing statements from my real mom run through my head. *She is not your mother. She is not your friend.*

When we get back, Norax wants me to check the Analytix, but I don't think I can take any more voices in my head right now. I already know people are excited too. The kiss worked for them. It's all roses. So when she sends me off to that part of the mansion and promises to meet me there in a moment, I pass right by the doors and head to my room instead. Thankfully, Gerald doesn't protest.

My room has really become a place for breakdowns as of late. Like so many times before, I stand over the sink and try to center myself with my old tricks. State all the facts. If I do that, maybe I can make sense of it.

*My mother is still alive.*

*She knows I'm a Famoux member.*

*She's a part of DEFED.*

Just this should be enough to send me reeling for weeks, but the list is even longer. I close my eyes, concentrating hard.

*She claims that DEFED is not what I think they are.*

*She claims they don't have Dalton—that Norax does.*

*She claims that Norax is lying to us.*

But why would *Norax* do any of this? Why would she create the Volx? Kill Bree? Send Chapter cufflinks of Bree's bones? Force me to expose Kaytee and Race by leveraging Dalton's life? And why would she try to pass it off as the work of a group my mother has made? What is the real DEFED even *about*? What does it even stand for?

So many questions. It's easier to keep asking them, to keep talking myself into the idea that nothing makes sense. But the longer I go, the more it does. A horrible thought begins to cross my mind, and I will it away. *No, I can't think it.* My mother always used to say a thought had power, after all, and this is one I can't allow to come true.

For the rest of the day I fight it off with as many distractions as possible—packing my bags for Eldae, leafing through the selection of books Foster picked for me yesterday—but the thought keeps coming back, again and again. It nags at me. I make Gerald follow me around the mansion for a whole hour as I look for a member to talk it out with. Kaytee and Race's doors are shut and locked for me. Till and Foster are out making last-minute appearances. Chapter, of course, was never an option. By the time we loop back to my door, my head is heavy. All I want to do is share my ideas with someone and let *them* speak the thought out loud. Not me. It looks like I'll have to come to the conclusion alone, though. Pacing the floors, I mouth out my thoughts, too scared to even whisper them. Someone could be listening.

Everything we've done, we've done because of the Volx. Every reeling reveal, every twisting turn. We wouldn't have done half these things so quickly, so ardently, if we didn't feel our lives were on the line—as if ultimate popularity wasn't the only means of survival. But DEFED made us believe it was necessary, because that's what they want. They *want* a constant stream of excitement and drama and backstabbing. They have no interest in watching a group of celebrities living in perfect harmony, coexisting nicely, like Lennix's eras of the Famoux. They agree with Norax's sentiments almost too much.

Again my mother's words about Norax come to mind.

*She is not your mother. She is not your friend.*

*Everything she does, she does only to serve herself.*

A few days ago, I wouldn't have believed this. *Norax is a benevolent, wonderful woman*, I would tell her. *She's not the one who ran off on me. You were.* But the Gray Days have shown me a new side of Norax. A calculated one. A conniving one. One that forces my hand to sign a contract and justifies it only with the notion that this will boost my likability. As if being all alone at the top is the only thing that matters to me. Not being friends with the Famoux members. Not loving who I choose to love. Just a sidewalk full of photographers, screaming my name.

Norax Geddes has done more than enough to prove to me that our happiness and ease are low on her list of priorities. Suddenly it no longer seems unreasonable that she would create an omnipresent death threat to serve her interests. Killing off members, after all, is killer television. Even my siblings, who usually couldn't care less, wanted to tune into *The Fishbowl* broadcast last month. Norax's success in keeping the world's eyes unfailingly on us has been directly contingent upon DEFED forcing our hand.

And now it seems so obvious that it was her hand all along.

She's been DEFED. Or at least, the fake DEFED. She's been the one sending us messages. She's the one who created the Volx. She's the one who branded us . . .

Zoya had said branding was an old-world technique to show ownership of something. It had seemed at the time that DEFED, this sinister group of our biggest fans, was just getting overzealous when they'd done it. But it was Norax all along, I see now she was sending a clear message:

She owns us. She controls us.

It's *her*.

# CHAPTER TWENTY

It is only Cartney and me on our private jet to Eldae. Well, us and a whole slew of bodyguards, but they have their own vestibule blocked off by sliding metal doors. In this front area, it is just the two of us. No managers from Buchan.

No Norax.

She's taken the other plane with the rest of the Famoux, and I won't be seeing her until tonight at the gala. She'll be busy running the show too. Any chance I might've had at confronting her in private is as good as gone.

Not like I'd even know *how* to confront her in the first place. There is too much I'd want to ask. I still don't know what the real DEFED is, and why my mother made it. I don't know why Norax would name this threat after them and make us so firmly believe they are something rotten. All I know is there is something deeper at work here, and my certainty of her malice is but a freckle on a much larger face I've yet to fully make out.

I've never been one to conceal my emotions well, so Cartney

can certainly tell something is off. Either he doesn't want to pry, or he doesn't care, because he ignores me, choosing instead to spend his flight time flipping through tabloids and pressing an *Emergency Only* button to make Gerald come in, so he can read him the headlines.

"You can't keep doing this," Gerald tells him, rubbing his eyes. He's got both the day shift *and* the night shift when it comes to me, stationed ceaselessly outside my door, so I'm sure he wanted to use this plane ride to rest. "This isn't an emergency."

"Oh, but this *is*," Cartney insists. "The word in Notness is that you've stolen my girl! Care to explain yourself?"

I've been ignoring them up until now, but this gets my attention. Cartney shows us both the magazine, pointing at the headline that reads *Famoux Guard Steals Emeray's Heart. How is Cartney Coping?* Beside a hefty block of text featuring quotes from apparent "inside sources" is a blown-up image of Gerald holding my hand to lead me through the crowds.

"Well, that's not at all troubling," says Gerald, sardonic.

"You're really on the chopping block now," Cartney tells him. "I think Kaytee cycled through ten different guards when we were together."

This makes Gerald shift his weight, nervous, and I get a twinge of guilt. "I didn't know bodyguards had such a short shelf life," he says.

"Yeah, your boss is sort of . . . strange about controlling situations."

So even Cartney knew this of Norax. To me, she'd always been enthusiastic and positive, willing to spin bad situations into something good. But firing bodyguards after a measly rumor? That sounds like something Lennix would've done, not her. At least, it used to.

I make Cartney apologize to Gerald, to explain he's only joking, and that nothing's going to happen to him. There's no way of knowing it's true, but it eases him. He retreats back into the guards' quarters with a little more pep.

Now that I've budged and given Cartney attention, he takes a break from pressing the emergency button and reads the headlines out for me instead. Luckily, the one with Gerald is an outlier. Only the one magazine mentions anything of the sort. Everyone else is buzzing over the song, the kiss outside the café, what it all means. I stare at a full-page photo of our kiss, observing our body language. I'm gripping him tightly, so tightly, which surprises me. In the moment I didn't know what my body was doing, I was so lost in thought. I half expected my arms to be at my sides, stiff as a board, frozen in place. Good to know my overwhelm comes off as earnest and yearning; the photos on the next page, where my gaze is brooding, almost liquid, actually make my heart stir. I have to hand it to myself, I'm a better actress than I think.

The next magazine in the stack does not bear any gossip. Blown up to fit the whole cover is that first photo Abby took of me in her office. Below it, the headline:

EMERAY ESSENCE: THE WORLD'S GIRL

My spread for *The X*.

"Boring," Cartney decides, placing it in the stack of tabloids we've already gone through. "I want *gossip*."

"I haven't read this yet," I say.

"It's obsolete," he insists. "There's nothing about me in it."

But I pull it out of the pile and turn away from him. If there was ever going to be enough time for me to read this, it's now.

Most of it is just photos. Full pages of paparazzi shots with me looking as young and innocent as ever. Until seeing all of my outings right in front of me, I've never noticed how I'm always wearing bright colors. Vibrant ones. Looking at myself now, I'm surprised by the hot pink of my sweater.

Next is a chunk of pages dedicated to my backstory. As I read through, some parts surprise me; I'd already forgotten the finer details. Nearing the end, I'm correct in assuming somebody else wrote the "handwritten letters" from the members. There's something about the way they double down on how *cute* and *a breath of fresh air* I am that's ridiculous. The members don't talk like this. I only skim them. I'm about to close the magazine entirely when a word in Chapter's letter catches my eye.

I sit up straighter, taking it line by line. The note has the same automated, made-in-an-office feel to it as any of the rest, except for a final few bits.

> *All this to say, you're great, Emeray. So great, it's concerning. You concern me.*
>
> *But I'm sure you already knew that.*

Maybe he asked the writer to put it in at the last moment. I'm sure they wouldn't so easily decline a request from Chapter Stones. But it doesn't really matter how it was added. All I can focus on is the word. *Concern.* It might've felt hopeless when he said it two days ago, the last time I saw him, but *this*. When did he write it? After we visited his house in Colburn?

"You've been staring at that page for forever," Cartney says over my shoulder. He squints his eyes, then recognizes the scrawled signature. "Ray, try to forget about him, okay? You're only going to torture yourself if you don't."

He tries to take the magazine from me, but I hold it out of his reach. A little childish, but I don't care. "We listened to Kaytee's music," I say. I point to the headphones in his lap. "You've probably been listening to her on the flight."

"That's not the same thing."

Then I remember something else. "And your furniture. The blue. She always wears that shade. I think it's the color of her bedroom door."

"You're being ridiculous."

"Am I?"

Cartney purses his lips into a fine line. "Well, we can't *both* be this lovesick. At least one of us needs to have a head on our shoulders to make this thing work," he says, a little terse. "And if you don't mind, I think my multiple years with her outweighs your . . . couple of weeks with him."

If I were really mad at him, I'd bring up how most of those years were marred by Kaytee's secret relationship, and the love he thought was real had been anything but. There's no use in riling him up. His point frustrates me in the way it trivializes my feelings, but he's right. The time between the first and last time I saw Chapter in his wing of the mansion is, in fact, small. To call it love would be even more trivial. But *concern* . . .

We don't talk much after that. I sink into my seat and try to ignore the braying sort of siren going off in my head the more ocean we cross toward Eldae. I've done this worried song and dance about going back before, but last time, we were only in Colburn, which was doable. But now, for the second time in a row, the Fishbowl will be set up in *Trulivent's* square.

Which means it will be within walking distance of my old house.

The Famoux *never* sets up camp in the same space twice. We were supposed to have cycled through various towns in the other states before coming back. It's Norax's call, though, and I guess she wanted my first-ever Darkening to be *here*, where it all started. Through the Gray Day particles and the usual smog, I can't make any structures out from the window as we begin our descent. Nevertheless, the view feels familiar in a way that makes me shake.

In spite of all my trepidation, the plane lands. There's no going back now. At the door, Cartney holds an earbud out to me.

"People think it's cute," he says. "Let's give them what they want."

Sighing, I take it. As suspected, Kaytee's music plays on a faint volume. So . . . this is going to be a pattern for the next two years.

The paparazzi keep hidden well. If I didn't know better, I would think no one was around at all. But there's a distinct and distant sound of shuttering, and I know that wherever she is, Norax's device must be going off with a hundred new photos of our descent from the jet. They're far less discreet outside the hotel. A huge group crowds the doors, and Cartney blows them kisses while I keep my head down. It must appear rude of me, but I can't look at them. This is *Trulivent*. Any face I meet could very well be a face that once looked at me with disgust.

I'm finally separated from Cartney inside. Gerald whisks me to my room, muttering to me about how rough it was to have to deal with him on the flight. "Don't know how you're dating that man," he says.

"I don't know how either," I say.

"I commend you for your patience."

One thing I can guarantee nowadays is that I'm never alone. I barely get a second in the hotel room before there's a soft knock on the door. I anticipate Norax, but find my seamstress Swanson standing there, garment bag in hand. I haven't actually seen her in person since my first measuring, since long before the Volx. She feels as much a part of my old life as Brandyce or Dalton.

"Are you ready to shine, dear?" she asks.

I expect the dress to be something that reflects the gravity of tonight. Something long and demure. But it is short, shimmery, *golden*. When I pull it out of the bag, it glints so brightly, I have to close my eyes.

The dress slips on easily. There are no buttons to this one—no fasteners, no elastic, just endless glistening sequins. When I look at my arms, I can't tell when the sleeves actually stop. The sparkles turn smaller until they swallow up my skin, almost fusing into me at the wrists. I try scratching it, and the material won't ride up. The same goes for my neck, the grooved sides of my thighs where the dress touches. Baffled by this, I race out to the mirror to see what it looks like.

I am a walking medal—a lissome drop of gold. My face, sunken before from my sleepless night, now appears cool and collected. Confident. I couldn't look anything less than that in this dress, even if I tried.

"Now *that's* the bright-eyed girl I've been waiting for," Swanson says, pleased. "And Cartney has a gold tie to match."

"How did you do this?" I ask, touching the sleeves.

"With help from the Fissarex. I've finally perfected the fabric. It's just like your makeup. You see, this dress responds directly to your skin," she explains. "For others, it would sag or look unfit. You are the only person in the world who can wear it properly."

"That's amazing," I say.

"I'm making a whole line of them for you," she says.

For accessories, Swanson insists we keep the jewelry to a minimum, since the dress is already a jewel in itself. She presents me a small box. When I open it, I don't know what to say. It's the ruby earrings—the ones DEFED sent.

The ones *Norax* sent.

"But I've already worn them," I say.

"It's a memorial gala," Swanson says, "and you first wore these at a memorial art show. I always styled Bree in red, too . . . I think they're a fitting tribute."

The earrings will no doubt set Kaytee off when she sees them. They angered her the first time I wore them, since it seemed like DEFED was playing favorites—giving me a new gift when they gave everyone else threatening reminders of their past. And to think, that was all Norax, making us distrust each other . . .

A dress of this grandeur makes my fresh face look egregiously out of place. Swanson leaves me to do my makeup, and for the first time ever I wish they were real products, so I could actually concentrate on getting my eyeliner to be a straight line instead of thinking about Norax and DEFED and everything. But the eyeliner pen glides, as always, and my mind wanders to more questions of *why*. Why she would do this, what it all means. There has to be so much I don't know.

Collected as I may appear in this dress, I'm anything but. My fingers won't steady as I fasten the buttons on my coat. It crosses my mind that if my mother was here, she would do this for me, like she used to before school. I wouldn't swat her hands away now.

*My mother.* It's like I'm a child again, the way the thought of her makes my shoulders relax. She must've taken a flight today, too, if she's really going to meet me at the gala tonight. It's unclear how she'll even get in—the tabloids claimed the guest list was *very* exclusive—much less how I'll even be useful in helping her get Dalton out. But she told me to trust her throughout the confusion, and I plan on it.

In the hallway, Cartney heckles me over the length of my dress, his voice echoing against the emptiness around us. Like always, it is just us. The members got to prepare for tonight on another floor, making the most of what will be our last private moments. If she really is the one pulling the strings with our death threat, Norax knows this too. And she's keeping me here. It makes my blood boil.

Outside, the camera flashes bling, blinding like always, but it's brighter tonight against the dark gray sky. It should be time for sunset, but there's no room for it—the particles have almost completely blocked it out. As we go, the camera clicks make me shudder. Less a *click*, more a *bang*.

The red carpet tonight is three times wider and twice as long as that of Till's *Riot!* premiere. Between the attendees and the fans blocked off by barricades, it's as if we've entered a stadium. There might be thousands gathered tonight. Maybe more.

As the car pulls up, Cartney focuses on something through the window immediately. "Oh, look, we're late," he says. "Your friends are all here."

Norax probably gave them all stations where they would each begin, because they are perfectly scattered about, either posing or meeting fans or being interviewed. Chapter is the closest to us, no doubt charming a reporter with ease. This is the first I've seen of him since the day I signed the contract, and suddenly, I ache. It hurts to focus on him for too long, so I move onto Till, who is walking toward the barricade for fans where Foster is already stationed, laughing alongside his friend Marilyn as they sign an absurdly large photo of their faces. They are the most joyous looking of the Famoux couples, for sure; beyond them, Kaytee and Race stand still for photos. They are as far from the fan section as they can get, but plenty of the ones nearest to them ring out their disapproval, booing openly. I have to commend them for keeping such straight faces through it.

"I'm sure the dress is just a coincidence," Cartney mutters.

Unlike me in my gold, the other members opted for more respectful, memorial gala–appropriate frocks. Kaytee's is made of a thick brocade fabric, almost entirely black save for a single thin stripe of color around her waist. Powder blue.

When we step out, all the attention goes to us. Even the person who was interviewing Chapter is among the troop of reporters who rush toward us, microphones out.

Doing interviews with Cartney is an exercise in patience. Just like he was at Wes Tegg's when I met him, he takes over every conversation he's in. Even worse, he commandeers them with *very* little truth to his words. When a popular reporter named Elliana in a taffeta gown asks if we're planning on recording anything together, he claims we've already done an entire album, somehow.

"Already?!" She brings her microphone toward me. "Emeray, can you tell us anything we can expect?"

Cartney leans in toward the mic himself, perhaps purposely getting his lips close to mine. "You can expect *excellence*, Elliana."

"Great job," I complain once we've left her. "Now we have to record that."

He rubs his hands together, like a cartoon villain. "All part of my grand plan."

Most of the reporters were likely advised not to ask about Kaytee, the way they dance around the topic, but some can't help it and mention her and Race blatantly. That's when Cartney freezes up and I have to say something about how we are all where we're supposed to be now, as fate intended. *If it wasn't for this mess, I wouldn't have found him*! A chorus of cooing follows us out of every interview.

Soon enough, we're onto the fans. They all greet us warmly, thrilled to see we're the real deal. They're so frenzied, I barely hear a word they say. I just smile, tell them something nice, and take the photo.

"Your eyes are amazing," I say to a girl who's strung herself up in holiday lights.

She's exhilarated, holding a magazine with Kaytee's face on it for me to sign. I hesitate a moment before deciding, why not?

When we're done with the fans, we pose for the paparazzi. As they shout for us to do something cute, maybe give each other a kiss, Cartney leans in close to my ear. "It's nice that you did that," he says.

"What?"

"Complimented them on things they can't change." I'm still confused, so he adds, "Well, you could've told her you liked her makeup or something like that. But you mentioned her eyes. She can't change those."

With the Fissarex, she could. Although he doesn't know about that. Anyway, it's so jarring to hear a kind observation from Cartney, laced with entirely no malice, that I forget to thank him before we step a few feet away from one another for a few solo photographs—which, apparently, are still a thing people want.

No one can quite leave me alone, though, so the photos don't stay solo for long. Just like he did at the *Riot!* premiere, Marlon York is bold enough to stride right up to me and ask, "Do you mind if I stand here?"

"I don't think that's a good idea," I say.

He plants his feet firmly down next to me anyway. Like Cartney just did, he leans in closely and whispers, which no one around us knows what to make of.

"Alexandra told us she spoke to you," he says. "Finally."

I turn toward his face when I hear my mother's name. He's grinning.

"You're . . ." I start.

"You have no idea how frustrating it's been for you to ignore all my requests that we *play music sometime*," Marlon says, exasperated. "We would've had this all fixed so much sooner. Now I've got barely a minute before your boyfriend breaks this up."

Another piece in this dizzying puzzle gets placed in my head. Marlon York is a member of DEFED. His tenacity to be around me always came off as status seeking, but now it makes a lot more sense. While also making no sense at all.

"What *is* this group?" I ask. "Why are you . . ."

Marlon ignores the questions. No time for them. He speaks through his grin. "We're betting they have your brother in one of their buildings on the edge of the state," he says. "I believe you've been to one before?"

The reformation one, where the Fissarex was. I nod.

"So you're aware of how heavily guarded those places are. We're going to need something to distract them. Which is where you come in."

"What will I do?" I ask.

"Disappear."

"What?"

"Slip out of the banquet hall through a side door. We'll hide you," he explains. "By the time it comes for you guys to enter the Fishbowl, and they realize you're not there . . ." He splays out his hands. "Chaos. Your manager is going to be so frantic about making sure they get you back for the broadcast that they'll send most of their fleets from any nearby Famoux buildings."

I see what he's getting at. "Like the place where Dalton's being held."

"Finding you will be a bigger priority than guarding a building no outside person knows about. We'll never have a better chance than this."

The plan would seem easy enough if I wasn't, well, *me*. If being alone for even a second wasn't a cherished rarity nowadays. Cartney finally approaches us, and his grip around my wrist is iron. "What's this . . . meeting all about, over here?" he asks.

Marlon's as good a faker as any of us. Nonchalance trickles from his mouth. "I was giving Emeray advice on the music business," Marlon tells him. "Since she's going to be so involved in it, so much, with you."

Cartney's performative ego bubbles up to the surface. "She'd be pretty foolish to take advice from anyone whose last album did as poorly as yours."

Marlon's eyebrows raise at me. He puts his hands up and backs away.

"You didn't have to be so mean," I say as we walk into the venue.

"I'm just trying to help the man's career," he says. "Doesn't he realize standing anywhere near you is basically a death sentence?

Buchan could have him out on the streets by tomorrow, like your little bodyguard."

The first area we're corralled into is the banquet hall. Completely onyx. The floors glimmer, the chandeliers cast dim shadows. Every instrument, every glass, every slight trimming is the same shade of black.

"Morbid," mutters Cartney.

My eyes scan for any doorways or exits besides the main one. There are the massive doors to the screening room, then a single small one in the corner by the live band. For all I know it could be a closet. I'll have to hope it isn't. It's my only option. The pressure is on now that I know this entire escape plan for Dalton is *completely* contingent upon my actions. If I can't get out undetected, this is all a bust.

As we wait to enter the screening, Cartney and I pick up small talk with the first couple we see, two actors named Melissa and Hannah. Their voices are high-pitched and breathless as they talk about their love story—how they met on the set of a movie, how the end of this month will be their two-year anniversary.

"Two years?" Cartney whistles. "Why, I'm planning on keeping this one for that long. You know what? Even longer. I think this one's forever."

He has his head tilted down now—close enough for me to reach. I know what he wants me to do. Begrudgingly, I lean forward, meeting him in a kiss. When we pull away, I notice Kaytee standing on the other side of the room, gaping.

If only I could talk to her. Or any of them. Explain what I know so far. About DEFED. About the truth. Even if I had the chance to before we enter the Fishbowl, they probably wouldn't listen—or believe me. I have no proof. I have no rebuttal for what

DEFED really is, if not the menacing, faceless threat who pushed their friend down the stairs and plans to do the same tonight. All I have is this arrogant conviction that my mother, who I've had trouble trusting since our reunion, is telling the truth.

The violins finish their piece and are replaced by a voice through hidden speakers. "If I could have everyone gather around the stage," says Norax. "I have a few words to say before we begin."

The guests shuffle toward the stage, where Norax is standing half hidden behind a crystal podium. There she is. Her disposition now harkens back to that speech she made the week before the last Darkening, the way she balances composed and crumbling so well. She clears her throat.

"Welcome to our humble little celebration," she starts. "Tonight, we remember a beautiful young woman the world loved dearly. Our beloved Bree Arch was an irreplaceable asset in our Famoux family."

The crowd murmurs, solemn. My blood boils. What an odd word choice to describe Bree. Norax could've mentioned how she was a television host. A philanthropist. A friend, even. But she chose *asset*.

And it isn't even true. Of all the talk at school, the least of it was being done about Bree Arch. Her talk show was interesting, but not always. She spent so much time asking her guests questions, redirecting the spotlight away from herself, that viewers left never having learned something new about *her*. Chapter said it to me once: Bree was hard to get to know. That translated over. She certainly had to be at the bottom of the Volx during her Darkening.

If Norax has been "DEFED" this whole time, manipulating the Volx, pitting us against one another, then getting rid of Bree was like getting rid of deadwood, to make space for something new. It makes sense that she would kill her first, to make way for me.

*Which one of* us *is the least valuable asset tonight,* I think, trying to get in Norax's head, think in the overrational, callous way she might. Killing Kaytee could give her too much sympathy. Cartney would have to mourn publicly; their relationship lasted too long for him to simply spit on her grave and move on. People might reminisce on the good old days when they'd been together. It wouldn't work in my favor—in the favor Norax has crafted for me. No, Kaytee is far more useful alive, as a constant adversary in the romance between Cartney and me. How many Darkenings could we spin over fights between us?

But Race. Race is the most like Bree. As I've seen before, he's uncomfortable with being treated like a celebrity. He's the most reclusive, too, keeping to himself at events and really reappearing to the public eye only when he's made a new painting. And apparently he's begged Norax more than once to kick him out of all this. He has a foot out the door. Sure, he brings in fans of fine art, but a large chunk of those people cross over into Foster's sector with fashion already. Killing Race would be dramatic, but it wouldn't necessarily disrupt. If anything, leaving Kaytee stranded would make for tragic irony.

Norax is having everyone raise their glasses to toast now, and somewhere during her speech Cartney has corralled a glass for me, which he holds out. I find Race in the shuffle of extended arms, somehow still stoic despite every reason to be a mess. But he's wearing that same look he gave me after the table read of *Algus & Alondra*, when his character was killed off. Deep down I think he knows, too, that he's going to be the one to go.

"I hope you enjoy the screening of *Key*," Norax says. "To Bree Arch."

Everybody repeats it like a prayer. We collectively take a sip, the liquid as bubbly and golden as I look in this dress.

As quickly as the somber moment comes, it goes. Guests are light and excited as they make their way toward the theater. We are seated in the front row with the rest of the Famoux, placed noticeably as far from Kaytee, Race, and Chapter as we can get. The only member who makes an effort to speak with us is Foster, although Cartney's presence makes him squirm.

*Key* is filmed simply, for a story so complex. Bree's character can't tell if Chapter is real or not. She goes mad figuring it out. It's mystifying to see Bree Arch in motion. Speaking like she's still alive. Kissing Chapter with fear, with fervor. I have to look down for most of the movie, hoping onlookers think I'm just scared of the plot. "I hated that," marvels Cartney when it's over. "Why can't they make films that make sense?"

When the theater lets out for the after-party, Cartney makes a beeline to the bar, insisting the film might make more sense when he's got a drink in him. He tells me to wait here, and I realize this could be my best chance to make an escape. I'm halfway toward that door in the corner when I feel a hand on my shoulder, pulling me away.

Lennix.

"Why, you've been pretty busy since I last saw you, right?" he asks in his usual wryness.

"Where did you *go*?" I ask.

He's got a drink in his hands that he fiddles with, which reminds me of our meetings in the Control Room. This isn't peppermint tea, though. That much, I can smell on his breath. "I got booted, remember?"

"And you didn't fight it?"

Lennix shrugs, defeated. "She only kept me around to make herself look good, anyway. And you weren't ever taking my advice. Why stay?"

I wonder if he knows about DEFED. Probably not, since he fought with Norax so often on her choices. He never wanted the group to be so tumultuous. All he could ever talk about was how the drama messed with his chances of being taken seriously on his campaign to become sovereign next year. In that respect, maybe Norax's actions lean a little toward revenge against him too.

"You always impressed me, you know," Lennix says.

"You're kidding."

"I still don't think you're worth all the trouble, sure," he admits. "But you've certainly found a way to make your mark. *The World's Girl*, isn't that what they call you now?"

"You came up with that," I say. "Back in the beginning."

"Oh right." He sips his drink, humming a laugh. "I guess I impress myself."

I try to slip away here, but he presses on, changing course.

"Have you met my grandson yet? Norax's boy?"

"Her *what*?"

"Has she never mentioned him?" Upon my blank face, Lennix nods. "Well, she does like to keep her private life private. Unlike some of your fellow members . . ."

My chances of escaping right now have completely disappeared. Lennix beckons me toward the front of the banquet hall, where a young man in a red suit stands. The other members are already gathered there, waiting one by one to shake his hand. They're all fidgeting, scratching their heads. None of us knew she had a son. We had no reason to believe *we* weren't simply her children.

With Norax nowhere to be seen, Chapter takes this chance to stand next to me. I let my shoulder brush against his, wishing I could transfer everything I know onto him with the touch. He's going to be so confused when the diversion happens and I'm missing from the banquet hall. I wish I could warn him.

"Sticks," he says.

It takes everything in me not to be reckless like I was outside of his old home, and kiss him right now, in front of everyone. Being separated only for these Gray Days has been difficult enough, but at least there was no temptation for such actions. By the look on Chapter's face, he feels the frustration too. And it's going to be like this for every outing now. Small conversations and terrible yearning.

I'm so flustered, I don't realize Lennix is still breathing over my neck. "Ah, *Chapter,*" he says. "If it isn't the cause of all my headaches over the past month, managing Emeray."

"It's always a pleasure to see you, Lennix," Chapter says unconvincingly. To me, he asks, "Did you know she had a son?"

I shake my head. Norax's son has his back to us now, talking to Kaytee. From the shape of his broad shoulders, the thinness of his stature, he could've probably been a Famoux member. Except for his height—as he's a good five inches shorter than Chapter and the rest of them, reminding me of Dalton.

No more time to waste; once this is over, I have to make my escape and try the corner door. I dare to move even closer to Chapter, letting our sides touch again. He radiates warmth.

But that warmth is short-lived.

The young man twists around toward us, and suddenly I barrel back into Chapter, senses going haywire.

"What's the matter, Sticks?" Chapter asks.

My faintness takes another swoop. I put my finger to his lips, barely registering how people must be watching this. "Don't say that."

"Don't say what?"

"Sticks. It's . . . *He* called me that."

Chapter follows my gaze, then comprehends it. In my entirety of knowing him, I have never seen Chapter Stones go as stone cold as he does in this moment. His surname is at once solidified, personified. "No," he says. "No way."

Such nightmares as this seemed impossible, but there he is, standing before me.

His eyes are the stale, boring pewter gray. Eldae's Gen 4. My age. He also has light brown hair, and a splay of freckles across his nose. I am certain I could draw on every one of them if I had to. I know their placement.

I know this face.

Beyond us, Foster is introducing himself and telling him a joke, and his lips are parted in a choleric smile. I know that smile.

I've known it all my life.

"It is so nice to finally meet you," I hear him tell Foster, pleasant. "My name is Westin."

# CHAPTER TWENTY-ONE

When Westin van Horne and his friends first pushed me into Clarus Creek, I thought for sure I would drown. It wasn't because I didn't know how to swim; I could tread water fine. But there was something about breaking through the icy surface that sent my body into paralysis—a terrible, overpowering numbness that pulled me down like an anchor. I had to fight through the numbness to swim to the surface.

That's sort of how I feel now. Numb, and sinking. Only this time, I can't see or find the surface.

All I see is Westin.

There's no time to yell, to jump back, to run away as far as I can. Not when his meeting with Foster ends, and he turns toward me.

"Emeray Essence," Westin says. There's nothing villainous in his voice. There's nothing foreboding. For the first time in my entire life, he's looking at me with actual admiration.

I gawk at Westin's extended hand like it's a weapon. A million things I've wanted to scream at his face fill my lungs, but none of them surface. I'm still frozen—as frozen as little Emilee Laurence always used to be.

Lennix pushes me forward, curt. "Where are your manners, Emeray?" he asks. "Did all those etiquette lessons teach you nothing?"

This has to be a joke. A ruse. But then I think about the lessons—how Lennix pushed my buttons and reminded me so much of Westin. How Norax played with my hair and consoled me like my mother used to . . .

She had walked *right* up to Westin to pull him and the Greyhounds off me. She regarded him like a stranger. A stranger she *hated*, no less. She was the one who asked if he hurt me often, and if he targeted me for being different. I'd felt embarrassed that she kept bringing him up. Then she asked if she could take me away from it. From him.

From her *son?*

This has to be a joke. Some twisted coincidence. It has to be.

I don't know what to make of it, if it's anything other than that.

"I—I'm sorry," I manage.

"It's no problem," says Westin. He directs his attention over to Chapter instead. "Chapter Stones. Pleasure to meet you."

Chapter smiles, and it's bitter. As menacing as I saw it be as a villain in *Key*. "You too."

Right before my eyes, my past comes in contact with my present. The only two people who call me *Sticks*, together in one room, shaking hands. This handshake is prolonged—perhaps intentionally slowed in my sight. When their hands pull away I notice Westin's eyes drop down to a spot on Chapter's wrist. His scar from the branding incident is visible—the *E*.

"So, *you're* Norax's son," says Chapter.

"That is so," says Westin.

Chapter cocks his head to one side, a newly smug look on his face. It makes Westin wince, uneasy.

"Is everything all right?" Westin asks.

"I'm just thinking," Chapter says.

Then he says nothing else, just holds that smug face. Westin tenses up, perhaps filling in the blanks for him, assuming the worst of whatever he may be thinking. Watching this scene play out makes me feel a bit lighter, even for a moment. In all my years of knowing him, I have *never* seen Westin van Horne squirm like this. He has always been one to carry himself with the assumption that he's the most important person in the room. The leader of the pack. The guy everyone is desperate to please. But tonight, he isn't. He doesn't have Felix or any of the Greyhounds with him. In spite of all my Emilee Laurence flight instincts flooding back, I can register he's out of his element.

The silence has created an unwelcoming air between the three of us, thick and humid. I can feel the tension, the competitiveness, like an overcoat. It takes a few seconds of letting it hang in the air before Chapter finally speaks.

"She never mentioned you, you know," he says.

Westin attempts a laugh, which doesn't land. He's not a good actor like the renowned one he's speaking to. "Well, I guess I'm not surprised."

"You're not?"

"My mother has only just recently gotten back in touch with her family in Eldae," Westin says. "My father and I . . . it was always just us."

As they make small talk, I try to recall as much as I know

about Westin having a mother. He spoke only of his father, and even then, it was sparingly. All I knew about his family was that they were wealthy. Extremely wealthy. The other kids were always jealous of the things he had. Westin van Horne got everything he wanted, always.

I guess it makes sense. Who else could give a child everything, if not Norax Geddes?

*Geddes.* Not van Horne. Hers is a well-known, powerful surname. But he never once flaunted this. By the sound of his conversation with Chapter, he and his mother weren't close. I try to make sense of it. If she's only *just* recently reached out to him, too, maybe he *doesn't* know the reality of who it is standing before him. Norax might not have divulged all the many Famoux secrets to him yet. He's a sixteen-year-old boy. Would she really want to trust him with something so big as the Fissarex and our past lives?

But he was there when she plucked me away from him. He was the one who insisted the Greyhounds take me somewhere private. I can't help but think that Westin was in on all of this, leading me to her that night. Still, I don't know why.

All of a sudden Norax is here, right by her son's side. Without giving me so much as a second's glance, she grabs Chapter's wrist.

"Chapter, dear," she says. "I have a few directors who'd love to speak with you."

"Can it wait?" Chapter asks, noticing my panic. "I'm actually having a *very* enriching conversation with your son."

He makes the mistake of brushing against my arm as he speaks, which makes Norax frown. This kind of proximity is off-limits. "Come on, now," she tells him, dragging him away by the suit sleeve before he can protest any more.

And then it's just us. Me and Westin.

My head is pounding so hard that everything sounds like a shout from far away, from underwater. It takes me a while to notice he's saying something to me, that I'm regarding him with a blank, ghastly expression that makes him squirm again.

Westin scratches his nose. "I have to say, you're stunning in person."

Words I never imagined coming out of him. My throat closes up. *Stay quiet,* my mind beckons. *If you stay quiet, he'll hurt you less.*

"Um, thank you," I say finally. I rub my eyes, just to make sure he's there, that I'm not dreaming. No makeup has picked up on my fist when I pull it away—a feat unfeasible to anybody in the world but me and the rest of the Famoux. I scream it a million times in my head, how I'm *not* who I used to be. I am not the girl he used to hurt.

"Do you want some eyedrops?" Westin asks. "I think I've got some—" He fishes through his suit pocket, but I hold out my hand for him to halt.

"No," I insist. It's more of a snap, really. "My eyes are fine."

"Oh, all right." Westin lets his hands rest in his pockets, maladroit. "Well, for the record, your eyes are very interesting. The photos don't do them justice. I've never seen a color quite like them."

My white-blue eyes that never fit in.

"*Never?*" I blurt.

"I live in Eldae, you see," he continues. "None of our mutations have a shade like that. You're my age, right? You would have this gray."

It takes a great deal of strength to suppress my jaw drop. Is he messing with me? I wait to see the flicker of evil in his face, but it never comes. Still cordial. It could be possible, I rationalize, that Westin never *really* examined my eyes much past the initial look and subsequent hatred. He had the Greyhounds do most of his up-close bidding, anyway, opting to watch from a safe distance. It's possible. But this thought unravels itself quickly, and I'm reminded of a time when the Greyhounds held me down and glimpsed them through a magnifying glass just to describe them in grotesque detail and laugh. He knows these irises well.

My silence comes off like Chapter's. He shifts his weight. "I understand why you're all a bit apprehensive about me," he says.

"What?"

"She keeps a lot of secrets. I mean, I had to learn from my father who she was. She didn't want him to tell me." He scratches his nose again. Nervous tick. "I guess she thought I'd tell people about her. Anyway, I get it. It's weird. But I guess I'm here now."

He would've told people. That, I'm certain. He would've called himself Westin Geddes, and everyone at school would've loved him even more. I can't imagine the number of Greyhounds who would've been carrying me to the creek in that case.

Westin has intended this to be a bonding moment, but I don't offer any encouragement. It comes off as a little cruel, but I'm still trying to process the fact that he's in front of me at all.

"Well. Strange happenings for you, huh?" he asks. "I hear you're with Cartney Kirk now?"

I nod.

"Lots of rumors going around." He gestures with his glass, connecting the air between me and Kaytee a few feet away. "How do you guys cope with all the talk?"

I have to stop, blink slowly. Westin is asking how I'm coping with mean comments. Because they aren't just coming from him anymore.

"I ignore it." My next words come as a surprise—I don't notice them until they're *here*, hanging in the air between us. A single shred of the reckless fight instinct I've cultivated as Emeray Essence comes back to me, delayed but welcome. "You know what they say. Sticks and stones."

Westin lets out a laugh, raising his glass. Whether or not his thoughts go back to the girl he threw in the creek, I can't tell. "I'll drink to that."

By the time Westin has finished his sip, I am halfway across the room, darting toward the corner door. People are staring, but it doesn't matter. This dress suddenly feels too tight. Not perfect for my skin. *Suffocating*. I need to get out, now.

Thankfully, the door lets out to a narrow hallway. I barely get a few steps in before I crumple to the floor.

I can't catch my breath. It's like I've just surfaced from Clarus Creek after holding it for ages. As I force myself to breathe in and out, I survey my surroundings. Black walls, red carpet. No doors. In the stark lights above me, my hands have never looked so white.

*Relax*, I tell myself. *It's over*.

I will myself to get up and keep moving, putting distance between me and the room I've come from. The halls are wide and empty, almost ghostlike. There are no doors down these halls, just the same onyx black wallpaper. Black walls, red carpet. The same at every turn. It feels like a maze, like every twist could house some horror. Maybe I'll go left and run into Felix and the rest of the Greyhounds. Maybe they'll drag me out by my golden dress and throw me back into the Clarus one more time. It wouldn't surprise me. Not tonight.

When I turn the next corner, I *do* encounter a piece of my past, but not a bad one. It's my mother, down the hall. I race toward her.

"Emilee." She wraps her arms around me, letting me burrow my head in her shoulder and cry. It's like returning from school after another bad day. "What happened?"

"Westin," I say.

"*Westin*?"

"He's her son."

My mother stiffens. She breaks our embrace, examining me carefully. "I didn't know Norax had a son."

"None of us did."

"So that means . . . if he's been in Trulivent this whole time . . ." She touches one of my ruby earrings, her face going white. "This has been going on for much longer than I realized."

"What has?"

"Emilee, I'm so sorry. I thought we were safe. It's my fault."

From the corner of my eye, Marlon staggers toward us. "What's the holdup?" he asks. "We're running out of time. They'll be leaving for the Fishbowl any moment."

"Does Sloane have the car ready?" my mother asks.

"She's been out there for hours. Let's go."

A voice from beyond the turn of the hall cuts in. "Ray? Are you out here?"

"Who is that?" asks my mother.

"Oh great. He'll alert Norax soon," Marlon murmurs. "Let's *go*."

Marlon leads my mother and me down the hall toward the exit at a brisk pace. Once we break through the exit doors and move toward an old-looking car, I explain to my mother that the voice came from Cartney, and that I'll explain it to him later.

"No you won't," says Marlon.

"The Darkening's only two days," I remind him. "Cartney won't be in the Fishbowl, but he's—" I stop when Marlon's nose crinkles up like I'm saying something wrong. "What?"

"You're with us now," he says.

"Yes, but the Darkening is—"

"What part of *escape plan* did you miss?"

We've already lost so much time, there's no room for us to stop running. My mother can only match her pace to mine so she can touch my shoulder, cautious. "I thought you knew it, when you decided to help us," she says. "You're not going into the Fishbowl tonight, Emilee. You're not going back to the Famoux."

✕ ✕ ✕

*Escape plan.* That's the word echoing in my head as Marlon, my mother, and I duck into the red, rusted car. It's perhaps an old-world one, or at least a replica.

*Escape plan.*

Of course. Why would my mother be pulling out all the stops to free Dalton from Norax's clutches, just to leave me behind under her management? It's common sense that I missed, clear subtext I was too frantic to read into. My cheeks burn in an odd sort of embarrassment, and I'm glad the car has no interior lights for anyone to notice.

"Are you doing all right back there?" asks a Gen 3 girl named Sloane, who's driving. She has to be one of Dalton's friends—I recognize her vaguely from being at our house sometimes. "I know this is no Famoux chariot . . ."

It certainly isn't. Famoux vehicles are high tech, top of the line. This one has a kickback that makes the whole thing rattle if Sloane accelerates too fast. For the first time in my life I feel shamefully Betnedoorian. The kind that Brandyce and Dalton used to mock the Famoux for being on *The Fishbowl* broadcasts. A dozen pieces of silverware. A new coat with every outing. Cars with partitions and leather seats and coolers of sparkling water. I actually find myself turning up my nose at first and have to physically resist. *No.* That was my life for only a month. And if I'm really not going back, this is what my life is now. I'll have to adapt again.

I know I needed to go. Even when I signed the contract three days ago, before I knew the truth about DEFED and Westin and this whole mess, I knew I couldn't stay. What was starting as two years of discomfort was no doubt going to turn into a decade or more of being told where to go, who to see, what to do. Like Race I would grow callous and cynical. I'd hate Norax. I'd hate Cartney. I'd hate myself, for making what seemed to be a golden choice in the spur of a moment, without really thinking it through.

But it's one thing to know you have to go—it's a whole other thing to do it. When I left Eldae to join the Famoux, I was certain that my family's lives would all benefit from my absence. That I was a burden at best, and they would be far better off without me. But I don't know if I feel the same way about my new family in the Famoux, disconnected and despairing as we've become. And what about Chapter? It was going to be hard enough standing in the same room as him and not being able to speak, but it was something. Now, there won't even be those. I never got to say anything to him either. Explain everything We didn't even say good-bye when Norax pulled him away . . .

"Are you doing okay?" Marlon asks. "You look sick."

The bumpy drive takes the blame. He tells me to look out the window, that it helps, but somehow it makes me even more overwhelmed. We're going down a main road, weaving past eager pedestrians. I'm covered in blankets and a hat large enough to disguise me, but no one even looks into our windows—they're too trained on a far-off light, like bugs. The Fishbowl. A report I heard in the Analytix before I left the mansion mentioned something about fans from all over Delicatum flying out to Trulivent for tonight. The first Darkening for the *World's Girl* . . . who they don't know yet has gotten cold feet and fled.

Talk of Dalton from the others brings me back to the moment. They take me through the breakout plan, which seems simple enough once the guards are out of the question. My mother knows the route to where they're keeping him, and we have the magic key to get him out: me. Apparently, I have more uses than just being a distraction—all important figures in the Famoux institution have total clearance on the touchpad locking systems equipped in their buildings. This obviously includes members.

"They're going to know you were there, though," my mother says. "The locks have a history of their handprints. They'll be alerted the second you scan in. We need to work fast."

"Either that, or it's a race back to headquarters!" exclaims Sloane, like this is all going to be a fun adventure.

Soon the streets become empty, quiet. We're pushing toward the edge of town, where the old factories are. The last time I went this way, Norax was leading me to the one with the Fissarex. Odd, now, to think of how she drove me all the way out there before even asking if I wanted to join. And by the time she did, she'd already revealed too many secrets for me to back out, even if said no. But none of that seemed so wrong at the time, not at all.

That reformation building must be somewhere nearby, amongst all these identical brick structures. For all I know, it could very well be the one Sloane pulls up to. She parks behind a wild, unkempt bush along the perimeter, then we watch and wait. Just as I'm about to ask what we're waiting for, the sound of a siren blares, and three big black cars peel out onto the street toward the city.

"I think they might've realized you're gone," says Marlon.

My mother has us wait a long while behind the bush to put distance between the guard cars and the reformation building. "The second you scan your hand," she tells me, "they'll know someone's there, and they'll turn right around."

After a few minutes, we decide it's time to move. Winter wind hits my gold-coated skin as we rush toward the front doors. Sure enough, there's a touchpad. I place my hand on the sensor, and it glows for me, green with my name.

Somewhere, someone has been tipped off about the scan. The clock is ticking now. My mother leads the way down a labyrinth of corridors. There are sitting rooms like the one in which Norax invited me to be a member, and rooms with nothing in them at all, only several different-colored doorways from which my mother chooses with ease. There are no hallways either. Just doors that lead to new rooms that lead to even newer ones. Once we're over ten doors in, I gather the layout of this building must be confusing on purpose; after all, in one of them, they are hiding things they don't want to be found—things they don't want to get out.

This room is three times larger than the others we've been through. The first thing it reminds me of is the library, with rows and rows that stretch down the expanse. However, these rows aren't made of rosewood and filled with literature. They are tall shelves of glass, like boxes lined up next to each other, each with their own touchpad lock. Almost all of them are empty, except two in the back corner. Even from this distance, and with him curled up on the floor with his back to me, I know the closest one is him. My brother.

I was already so sure my mother wasn't lying, and that Norax did have him, but the visual confirmation is almost too much to bear. He sits straight up when he hears my high-heeled foot-falls, whirling around to look at me with the widest, wildest eyes I've ever seen. His hair is dirty and disheveled. The white shirt he wears is in tatters. And he looks so thin, so sunken in, so petri-fied, so *different*, for a moment I'm not even sure it's him.

"Dalton," I breathe out. "Dalton, you're safe now."

He's cowered away from me now, wincing. He tries to grip the glass, the ground beneath him, bracing himself for something. "Don't hurt me! Please!"

Tears prick up in my eyes. Seeing the way his collarbone juts out the top of his shirt makes my skin crawl. Have they fed him? How long have they had him?

"You're safe now," I repeat. "Dalton, hey, you're okay."

My brother's voice is a quivering arrow, unsure of its aim. It's nothing like that lively, joking tone I used to hear from him every day. It's broken to pieces.

"Who are you?" he asks.

"It's me," I say. But then I catch the glint of my dress in the lights. Right. "I mean . . . it's Emeray Essence. You're okay, though, you're—"

"Who?"

"You don't know me?"

Dalton pushes himself as far into the corner as he can get. Again he says, "Please, *please*, don't hurt me."

The others have caught up now. "We're losing time, come on," says Marlon. I quickly scan for Dalton's cage, then the one beside him, where a young man lies unconscious. As Marlon props him up, I get a glimpse of his eyes as they open, glaze over, then close again. Plum purple. Based on these, he's Gen 2. Eighteen. No one I recognize, but my mother insists we take him with us. If Norax thinks he's important enough to lock up here, that means he's worth saving.

Marlon and Sloane hold onto either side of the boy. Dalton is dazed, but coherent enough to recognize my mother, and he wraps himself around her for dear life, murmuring that he must certainly be dead now. I feel a little useless not helping out, but I'm instructed to lead the way, unlocking the doors as we go.

By the time we make it back outside, Marlon spots headlights in the distance, coming toward the building. I have to help hold up the Gen 2 boy to get him in the backseat of the car as quickly as possible, and we manage to get on the road and make several turns through factory alleyways before they can get too close and try to follow us. The guards are probably storming the building instead of checking the streets, going through every door in that maze in search of me. Then they'll find that Dalton and this boy are gone, and they'll alert Norax.

A strange, triumphant feeling kicks in, like delayed adrenaline. She took my brother from me, and now she will know that I have taken him back. She will know I'm gaining on her, and whatever secrets she's been trying to keep.

Just like Chapter managed to make Westin van Horne squirm earlier tonight with his silence, I intend to do the same with Norax. There is power in my silence. Defiance. I am away from the contract, and the Fissarex, and everything else that tried to change who I really was but couldn't. I am away from *her*, with no warning or explanation.

The car is really roaring now. Even with Sloane putting her full force on the gas, we barely get to a fraction of the speeds I know Famoux cars are capable of. It's good that we're not being chased, else we would've already been caught.

"It's going to be a long drive," Sloane tells us. "Sleep if you can."

I have every intention not to, and to instead ask my mother about DEFED, about what it all means, about what happens next. But the adrenaline leaves me as swiftly as it arrived, and the steady trembling of the old-world car lulls me into the first sound sleep I've had in what feels like a lifetime.

# CHAPTER TWENTY-TWO

It's dark when I wake. At first, I think it's still night, and I've only dozed for a minute or two, but then I remember it's the first day of the Darkening, so it could be any hour. When Marlon, illuminated by a small flashlight in his hand, sees I'm awake, he informs me I actually slept for a long time. It's nearly the afternoon.

If the particles weren't blocking it, I would've missed the sunrise today, for the first time in two years.

We're somewhere in Notness. Much like the building from which we retrieved Dalton, DEFED's headquarters is hidden in an empty factory—one of thousands that cover this land. This way the group is a needle in a haystack. It would take months for Famoux guards to raid every warehouse, and by then the group would be tipped off to that fact and would move accordingly.

"We try to think of everything," Sloane says.

*Everything* is more than I even realize. I barely begin to mention Norax's name, and Sloane, Marlon, and my mother hush me in unison. They are aware of the Analytix's existence, it appears.

They know that mentioning a name outright means the potential to be heard from that person within the hideaway. For this reason, they've developed code names for the Famoux. The Famoux itself is the Golden Group. Norax is the Leader. Lennix is the Founder. When they were planning ways to get me on board, I was the Daughter.

The Daughter. The World's Girl. Sticks. Ray. Lumerpa. Emeray. Emilee. I have so many names, I can't keep up.

"How do you know about the Analytix?" I ask. Come to think of it, DEFED knows a lot about the inner workings of the Famoux. Things we've kept well under wraps. The layout of that prison building, for one. My mother led us through it like she knew it well—like she could lead us with her eyes closed. There were so many different entrances and exits, instances where she could've messed up, but she didn't. The entire escape mission went off without a hitch. "Or . . . everything?"

Glances are exchanged. Beside me my mother adjusts her posture to face away from me, tentative. "I was hoping to wait until your brother woke up," she says, "so I could explain it all to you both."

But she can't say something like that and expect me to wait patiently. Now is the time for explanations—for the veil of confusion to finally come up.

"Please," I say. "You asked me to trust you, and I did. You said you'd explain when we got out."

In the back, Dalton is in a deep slumber, even with the bumpy roads. Marlon brings the flashlight over to them, and while the Gen 2 boy's face scrunches up and he turns to face the window, Dalton remains stationary. Peaceful, even. After the emotional toll of last night, it's dubious he'll wake any time soon. My mother decides she will give the explanation to him once we get to DEFED's headquarters—once he's had time to eat and bathe and register his safety. It might be better for him to take things slowly.

For me, however, the time is now.

"This is a long story," my mother prefaces. "You see, your ties to the Famoux began far, far earlier than when the Leader asked you to join. She has been tied to your life before you were even born." She hesitates. "Those earrings you're wearing are mine, Emilee," she says.

I put a hand to one of the rubies. "They are?"

"Norax stole them from me years ago. When we were kids."

"How is that possible?" I ask.

My mother takes a deep breath. Marlon's flashlight is trained at the front, where he and Sloane are already focused on some new topic, but the glow is strong enough that I can see her conflicting expression, her struggle to find the words.

"She is your aunt."

The words don't fully absorb at first. It's only when my mother is halfway through her next point that I fully register their meaning.

"We have never been on good terms, even when we were younger. Our father, the Founder . . . Well, *I* was the oldest. He favored me. Compared her to me. And she was so bitter, and bent on making me pay for the praise I never asked of our father. But she never got mad at him for it. Only me."

Now I'm catching up. My aunt. My *aunt.* My mind must be trying to latch itself onto something different, else it could freefall, because I connect the sentiment to Brandyce. She blamed me, never our mom, for leaving. It was this very argument of it being my fault that got me out of the house that early morning and over to the Fishbowl. Blame is a thing with many faces. I can understand that, at least, within my swirling turmoil.

Everything else whirs and twists if I think about it for too long.

"I was never suited for life in Betnedoor," my mother continues. "It's all too new, too fast, too impersonal. We traveled with our father every month for *The Fishbowl*, and I took a liking to the ruins in Eldae. The world seemed to move slower. Even the cities were considerably calmer and less crowded. By the time I became a teenager, my father was already speaking to me loftily of how I'd inherit the Group when he'd retire. But I was already sure, even then, that I'd decline when the time came. I wanted a simpler life.

"My family didn't agree with. They liked the new things. The advancements. In fact, my father had become heavily involved in Betnedoor labs. He helped create many inventions, including the Analytix, which he took for himself and the Group. It was in the Analytix where my father caught his name being mentioned by the sovereign at the time, Sovereign Vance. Vance was musing about getting his help for a scientific feat, since my father so impressively distinguished himself in the tech world. When the phone rang days later, my father told them it was about time. He'd been waiting."

She stops here for a second to laugh, lightly, at this memory of her father. This memory, somehow, of Lennix Geddes. Then the joy dissolves, and she presses on with a frown.

"That scientific feat was the genetic mutations," she says.

My eyes widen. For the first time in the last few minutes, I feel able to articulate myself. "The ones in *Eldae*?"

From the front seat, Sloane says, "The reason I have these eyes."

"But the mutations happen from radiation," I say. "From the End."

"That is the cover-up," my mother says. "The genetics are administered through an injection given to mothers just before they give birth."

"What?" I ask.

"A few years before the Generations began, Sovereign Vance made all births hospital mandated. As you know, few sovereigns ever help improve conditions for Notness and Eldae, so this was a very big deal. He even had Betnedoor's best scientists come up with a vitamin booster to be administered right before the procedure, so as to protect the newborn from exposure to toxic air, since the radiation can be so bad in some areas. He insisted the booster had a shelf life of one year, so annually, a new shipment of this booster would be sent to all hospitals and would be replenished as needed," she explains. "The new shipments come in January. Changing Month. This assures the genetic makeups would stay within their designated year."

My mind struggles to process this. "How does the injection work?"

"Fissarex technology," she says. "The same kind they used to recreate you. The booster includes the necessary genetic codes for the year."

"But if Notness gets the booster too," I say, "wouldn't they be affected?"

"They just tamper with Eldae's shot," she says. "They're testing it out and making sure it's perfect before making it widespread. This has been years in the making. Sovereigns have been passing on the information to their successors, adding to it . . . My father was the first to really aid Vance in the research and execution.

That's when they figured out how to mutate at least the makeup of the eyes. Everything else is an imperfect practice, but they're working on it to this day. The goal is to someday make every feature the same each year—so every age group is easily identifiable."

"Why would they even want to do that?"

"Why are we one nation, instead of many? Half the troubles of the world before us came from differences, from disarray. It's order."

The conversation at breakfast in Colburn comes back to me. Lennix, looking around the room, guessing all the ages of the waiters and patrons. *I think it's kind of nice, all this order*, he said. *I just love what they're doing over here.* He'd been so coy about it, too, when Race pointed out they were random mutations.

My mother shifts in her seat. "Before I left, the plan had been to test in Notness. That wouldn't be until many years, though. They wanted to perfect the mutation and have it all sorted out before testing. But . . . then I left.

"When my father shared his work on the mutations with my sister and me, neither of them understood my outrage. They thought this to be a reasonable thing—an exciting one, even." My mother shakes her head. "We had so many arguments about the ethics of it. I started to realize how little we agreed on things, especially where it counted. I was old enough then to leave, so I did. I told them I wanted no part of the family anymore, and I went to Trulivent. They never reached out. No Famoux guards ever came to my door. I thought I'd escaped. I met your father, and we bought our house, and we started a family.

"Then Brandyce was born with golden eyes, and I knew. They were punishing me. It wasn't until after Dalton that I realized it was the mandatory shot. So I decided to forego it. It wasn't easy. I spent a year over here in Notness for you, hiding out."

"You did?"

"Your siblings were too young to remember it. I told your father there was a family emergency. I had you in secret. It was dangerous, but that is why you weren't born with the Gen 4 eyes." My mother bites her lip. "I thought they didn't know what I had done. Or if they did, that it was too late to do anything. But it seems I was wrong."

Revenge. It perks up everywhere like weeds. The image of Westin's face at the gala last night enters my head. He was the one who'd led the pack of Greyhounds. The first to throw a stone, out of everyone in the whole school. The one with such staunch beliefs that the mutations were good, and I was bad . . .

She takes my hands in hers. "I had no idea Westin was Norax's son," she says. "I should've moved us away the moment you came home crying. I knew people would have their judgments, but I never thought . . . I never meant to—"

"It's okay," I say.

But more words tumble out of her. New thoughts, old guilt. "I don't want you to think I ever gave up on you. I didn't. I never would've left you, Emilee. It was the first thing she did when he gave her the reins. She took me from you."

Something shifts in me. A core piece of understanding. When my mother ran away two years ago, the latest generation of the Famoux sprung up: Norax's. I had grown to think the timing had been perfect, because of how they filled a void she left. Now, it contorts into something much more sinister: they had taken my mother and replaced her with fairy tale lives to keep me occupied. The Famoux was all I had then. Westin's torments were only getting worse, and my family blamed me for their unhappiness.

Early Darkening mornings, sitting in front of the television set, were the only things that kept me going. Otherwise, I was miserable, vulnerable, and desperate for the love that had left me.

What a perfect state to place someone in, if you want them to join.

Norax had been planning everything, all along. She made my old life a nightmare, took my mother from me, then pulled me into her perfect world. And then she controlled my every move—made me think some faceless thread was going to kill me. She pitted all of the Famoux members against each other with DEFED . . .

I'm reminded again of her branding us. The message of control.

And if only I'd known then how she'd *always* been controlling me—from the moment I was born.

My mother explains how she escaped Norax's captivity. She'd been in the same building Dalton had been kept in, which explains how she knew where to go. But she didn't do it alone the first time. A benevolent guard she befriended over time, named Jenson, helped her. It had been a year and a half in captivity, with no one to talk to but him. She told him stories. Soothed him in the way she'd done me and my family for years. One Darkening, Jenson helped her escape, then escaped right with her. He's at headquarters now, watching over the whole operation. Still a guard, now for DEFED.

Which brings my mother to her final point.

"The Disorder Evolution Federation. DEFED for short."

"Federation?" I ask.

"It's an old-world term for a group," she explains. "Jenson and I created it when we got out. We knew the world needed to know about what's going on behind closed doors. The next Changing Month will mark the third decade of mutations, and every decade they've gotten more elaborate. They could have an *entire* genetic makeup down this time. We can't be sure. So we need as many people against it as possible. Before it gets worse. Before it spreads past Eldae."

"So Nor . . . *the Leader* using DEFED as a threat to us . . ." I start.

"We think it means she wants to invalidate our case," she says. "If she can convince the world that we've done bad things, no one will take our side."

I lean back in my chair to absorb all this. Marlon might've joked earlier that DEFED thinks of everything, but Norax might *still* be ahead of them.

The car makes a quick turn onto a dirt road, the headlights homing in on something large and concrete and ugly. Like my old house, but bigger. I have just pieced together what they are, and now we are here. DEFED's headquarters. Industrial garage doors open up for us, then swallow us whole.

The space is wide, fashioned like a campsite. On one end, a sleeping area and a kitchenette. The other end is for working, with tables and boards with photos pinned to cork. In the center is a small, ancient-looking television set with a few chairs in front of it. Sloane parks in the corner, and a man with dark hair and gentle eyes helps us get Dalton and the Gen 2 boy out of the back. This man must be Jenson, since he is the only new person who I don't recognize.

The other people are the rest of my family—Brandyce and my father.

They're perched on their cots, surveying the scene from a

distance. Dalton is brought to the cot beside Brandyce's, and she rushes to his side, murmuring how malnourished he looks, how relieved she is to have him back. We make eye contact for only a second before she averts her gaze quickly, then walks away. The difference in these sibling reunions sends a stinging feeling right through me.

My father ignores me too, lying in his cot as though it was his bed at home. Considering the way my mother goes out of her way not to walk near him, I gather they might not have reconciled yet. He carried so much guilt about why she left that it ruined his life, lost him his job, and tore our family up. All because of secrets she'd kept from him. And even before she left, they'd had rifts.

I want to approach him, but the others need help checking Dalton and the Gen 2 boy for any wounds that need addressing. They're both fine, we confirm, just underfed. My mother tells us that they don't use violence often in Famoux captivity—at least, they didn't on her. But I remember the way Dalton had begged me not to hurt him.

As they retreat to the kitchen to make dinner, my mother says, "You should go see your sister. We can take care of this."

Brandyce is standing on the other end of the room, in front of the corkboard. I approach her carefully, so as not to intrude, but I meet a narrowed eye gaze when I pluck up the courage to face her.

"You can't really sneak up in a dress like that," she says.

Right. In the overhead lights, the sequins make me a golden mirrorball. The exact same color as her eyes. "Sorry," I say.

"Here," she says, holding out a jacket. Blue. My corduroy one. "You left it behind."

When I take it, I notice her hands are shaking. I've never seen her look at me like this. Awed, but not like when she'd gape at my shortcomings. It's different. She's starstruck, I realize. This is a Famoux member standing in front of her.

"It's really . . . *you*," she says, almost like a question. "Emilee."

"It's me," I confirm.

"Doesn't seem real," she says.

"No. I guess not."

This conversation is so careful, so maladroit. Our last was chaos. Her outburst. Me sneaking out to get a break from it all. This set everything in motion. But now that I know what I do about Norax and Westin and my mother, I also know I can't place any blame on her. Getting me in the Famoux was Norax's goal. Revenge on the sister she hates. I don't want Brandyce and me to be sisters like that. When she finally breaks down and starts making an apology, I pull her right into a hug.

"It's okay," I tell her.

"I didn't know anything," Brandyce says.

"None of us did."

When we pull apart, Brandyce wipes tears from her eyes. I'm surprised I'm not crying too. The weight of everything I learned in the car has certainly hit me, but not enough. And after so many etiquette lessons from Lennix, I guess I've learned to control the urge.

From the center of the room, Marlon calls us over. "Did you see this?" he asks me, nodding to the television set.

"They've been playing it all day," says Brandyce. "Since last night."

The *X* in the corner of the screen tells me we're on the Famoux's broadcast channel. In place of what should be *The Fishbowl* is a black screen with white text.

DUE TO UNFORESEEN DIFFICULTIES,
THIS DARKENING'S FISHBOWL BROADCAST HAS
BEEN CANCELLED. WE APOLOGIZE FOR
ANY INCONVENIENCE.

"*Unforeseen difficulties,*" Marlon chuckles. "Em, I think that means you."

I read the words over and over again, to make sure they stick. Relief briefly passes through me, then is replaced with that adrenaline from back in the car. My diversion at the gala has done more than just save Dalton—it has saved the members, at least for another month. No one will die tonight or tomorrow in the broadcast. The broadcast isn't happening. Norax tried all she could to make me seem selfish and desperate when she had me ruin Kaytee and Race's lives, but this is a selfless act she didn't call for.

Shame on her for calling me a lumerpa, a bird so bright it absorbs its own shadow when all along she was keeping me in the dark.

The rest of the day is spent attending to Dalton and the Gen 2 boy. They finally stir at around dinnertime, and while the boy is still too overwhelmed by what's happened to him to talk it out yet, Dalton adapts to his new surroundings with considerable aplomb. The initial shock from the escape last night wears away with a few bites of the soup Jenson has prepared. Talk is light, and Dalton manages to crack a smile when Brandyce jokes about his resilience. When he notices Sloane, his old friend, he even blushes.

All the while I sit off at the edge of the group, contributing little. We haven't explained to him who I am yet. According to Brandyce, he went missing just a day or so after I did, before Emeray Essence was even leaked to the public. He will have to process so much about what happened to him and why before he can even begin to tackle the fact that his sister has transformed into a Famoux member. I understand and resist the urge to speak of memories.

It isn't until we're putting plates away in the kitchenette area, bowls in a line by the sink, that I realize we have just had our first dinner as a complete family in two years.

× × ×

The second Darkening day feels like an eternity without a *Fishbowl* broadcast. It never occurred to me that in these times, the Famoux acts as the sun for Delicatum: when they wake, the sun rises. When they retreat to their quarters to write songs, paint, and so on, we know it's at its peak, noontime. And when they gather around the table for dinner, the sun sets in the orange silks and pinks taffetas of their evening wear.

Without them, the darkness has little rhyme or reason. The clocks still work fine, but there is no real cue for anything. It isn't until the afternoon that I remember I should eat, maybe shower in DEFED's facilities. I hadn't the energy to take off my Fissarex-magnet makeup from the gala last night, and after an entire extra day with it on, the mascara should surely be crusted up, and the liner smudged from so much crying and chaos. But the mirror in the bathroom tells a different story. The blush is still bright and rosy on my cheeks, as if newly applied. Every lash of mine is straight and long and defined. I am still perfect, even after all of this.

It takes several tissues under water to scrub it all off.

Brandyce has lent me some of her clothes, since I have none. A worn-in burgundy sweater, a pair of dark denim pants. Nothing Norax would've styled me in, or Swanson would've picked for me. My glittery golden dress lies in a bundle on the floor next to my cot, looking egregiously out of place. The way everyone's eyes keep flickering over to me, I wonder if that's how *I* look too.

The Gen 2 boy has regained his strength enough to speak. His name is Lee. He doesn't know why any of this has happened to him. "One moment I was walking to work, just taking the same route I always do, and the next I'm in the back of this car . . ."

"You don't know the Institution?" my mother asks, using their code name for the Famoux.

The idea makes him cackle. "Do you think *I* know a *celebrity*? I work at a grocery store!"

"In Gateswood?" I ask, remembering something.

His eyes widen. "How do you know that?"

"You're Finley."

My assumption during the escape plan was correct. Norax had to have been saving him for next month, and the next round of DEFED threats that would've followed this Darkening. I can't imagine what Foster would've done had he gotten a message about him. This also means Norax has definitely known about their letter writing, even though Foster thought he'd been so careful with his deal with the mail person.

I can't say Foster's name, since they could be listening for us in the Analytix, but I do my best to explain to Finley that Scott, who he has been writing to, is in fact a member of the *Institution* now. The model, I tell him. The one on all the billboards. Finley gathers who I'm referring to and goes through a whole spectrum of reactions that ends with melancholy. "Everyone always made fun of him, but he never changed. Never tried to hide. But I guess in the end, he did."

We fill the rest of the day with stories. Finley tells us about him and Scott. The notes they'd pass at school. The day Scott made him a yellow scarf that he wore well into spring. The times they snuck out of their houses late at night to go see each other. It's this last story that makes my heart sting when I think about Colburn, being led down side streets by Chapter, his hand in mine. I tell that story, however lightly uncomfortable it makes me feel to tell it in front of family, and Finley and I share in the melancholy of it all together.

"The papers say you were with that musician," says Sloane.

"Had to be a dating contract, right?" asks Marlon.

"It was," I say. I reveal to Marlon how Lennix once tried to get me in a contract with him in the beginning, which makes him laugh.

"We would've had you in DEFED sooner, then," he says.

Marlon York is the only other celebrity here; Jenson was the one to approach him. If you aren't a Famoux member's personal bodyguard, like Gerald, you work in shifts. Some of Jenson's duties required going to parties and premieres. When forming DEFED, he and my mother agreed they needed celebrity endorsements to help spread their message. Jenson reached out to those who seemed kind, approachable. Marlon might be a Buchan artist, but he isn't quite like Cartney in ego and entitlement. He heard about the cause and agreed immediately.

"The plan has been to get a few more celebrities on board before making any public announcements," says Jenson, a little bitter. "But it seems the Leader found out anyway. Maybe we should change our code names . . ."

Since he's still a working musician, Marlon goes back and forth between Betnedoor during the month in his jet. When the sun comes up tomorrow, he'll be leaving for a video shoot. "Although I think it's futile to release a single right now," he teases me, "after that little number from your fake boyfriend."

Other stories include those from childhood—Marlon's, Jenson's. Brandyce and Dalton's. The memories I recall of theirs usually have a blue tint for me, especially the ones involving school. But most of them are new. Things they did with friends. Sloane adds onto these, telling embarrassing tales of things Dalton did on weekends. I realized how little I knew either of my siblings. And the thing that has omitted me from these memories, that left me in my room at night staring at the ceiling instead of living, is also the thing that has gathered all of us into this warehouse tonight: the mutation.

The next morning, I watch the sky turn from black to a shade similar to Gen 4 gray, like Westin's eyes. Beyond us, actual functioning factories come back to life, buzzing and sending smoke up through concrete chimneys. Back to work. The Darkening is over.

As I make cheap coffee at the kitchenette, I notice that the television screen bears a new message. There will be a statement from Norax coming briefly. I wake everyone up, and we gather around to watch. There are only a few chairs, so I opt to stand. Though, the moment the screen switches to a view of the hideaway, I wish I was sitting.

Norax wears a long black dress and the face of a woman who has seen too much hardship in the last few months. Lennix and Westin are standing just beyond her, painting a grave portrait. A family unit. *My* family. My aunt, my grandfather, and my *cousin*. It doesn't seem real.

Just beyond them are the Famoux. Tears weren't coming easy for me yesterday with Brandyce, but they spring up instantly once I see them.

Their expressions range from confused, fraught, devastated, and numb. Till and Kaytee wear tea-length black dresses, and Foster, Race, and Chapter wear all-black suits. Mourning clothes, just like the ones they wore for Bree.

And today, for me.

They must think I'm dead.

About a hundred or more reporters flank this scene. The camera doesn't catch them all because of the way the spotlights dim out, but I'm sure the number of fans gathered just behind the gates is even greater. Their murmuring is all I hear at first before Norax clears her throat. And when she speaks, her voice is as clear as water. Her words ring out with purpose, with perfect calculation. I am mesmerized in a distorted, unsettling way. Like she always has, even before I joined, she grips me from the moment she opens her mouth.

"There are no words to describe the agony we are all experiencing at this time," Norax begins. "It pains me to have to make a speech so soon, but I know I need to address what has happened."

A pause. Camera shutters, taking her photo.

"Having a monthly *Fishbowl* broadcast is not a chore, but a blessing for us at the Famoux institution. Bringing you entertainment during this time, and all the time leading up to it, is quite literally our purpose. So being unable to provide for you a broadcast over these past two days was something we never wanted to have to do. However, after an event transpired at our memorial gala for Miss Bree Arch, new information was brought to light, and we ultimately found it too risky to put our Famoux members into the Fishbowl. It was much safer to have them in our private care, watched carefully by our security team."

Norax closes her eyes now, as if enveloped in pain. When I was Emilee Laurence, I really believed this. When Brandyce and Dalton called her out for her deceit, I judged them. I saw the best in her. Even then, she was fooling me.

"There have been rumors, but I am here to dispel them. On the night of Bree Arch's memorial gala, our newest member, our beloved Emeray Essence, was kidnapped." The crowd erupts into questions and concerns, but Norax talks over them, raising her voice. "We have yet to identify her location, although we *have* identified her captors."

This gets them quiet again.

"Emeray Essence's kidnapping is at the hands of a hostile organization that goes by the name of the Disorder Evolution Federation. DEFED for short."

The TV crowd might still be silent, patiently listening, but the warehouse isn't. Anyone who's sitting stands, gasps, although what Norax says is technically true. They *did* kidnap me, in a way. But not the way Norax will make the world think.

On-screen, Norax scoffs. "They are no federation. They are merely a fringe group of citizens—no, *cowards*—in Eldae who have been attempting to spread lies and misinformation through our members. They saw this organization's wide, global influence, its massive reach, and they sought to exploit it for their own sinister gain." Norax's voice has modulated now, growing louder in tandem with her anger. It's a slow rise—a perfect walk between inflamed and in control. I know it's not true, but I'm believing it. "My members informed me that DEFED has been threatening their lives for a long time now. Right under my nose they sent each member a ransom note, demanding that the members share their false beliefs with their audience in exchange for their lives. DEFED wanted to manipulate you."

Now she's softer. A break for tenderness. "But our members respect you. They refused to do this. DEFED thought they could scare them into it by staging the power outage in the Darkening that killed Bree Arch, but again, faced with danger a second time, they refused to budge. Your Famoux are so brave. They would rather lay down their lives than feed you lies."

"She isn't doing this," says Jenson in disbelief. "Not already . . ."

"The lies they wanted our members to spread are so baseless, we don't find it important to even tell you about them. For that would be to amplify their message. But are meaningless *rumors* really what Bree Arch had to die over? What *Emeray Essence* might die over?"

Beyond the reporters, whatever number of fans gathered are booing at the thought.

"I say, no!" Norax shouts. "This sinister game will go on for no longer!"

Now they are cheering. Here, Jenson has walked away and begun pacing the perimeter of the warehouse. Everyone else has their head in their hands.

"We are not going to stop until we find Emeray Essence!" Norax says resolutely. To the camera once more, "DEFED, you might only work in the shadows of the Darkening, but believe me, we are in the *light* now. You are a shadow we are going to swallow up whole. We will bring you to justice!"

The crowds are really encouraging now, crying and cheering her on. Norax might be saying something more, but my attention is on the other Famoux members. Their faces. They have no reason not to believe that everything Norax has said is true. She is their manager, after all. It is her job to have their best interests in mind.

The broadcast is over. Norax steps back from the podium, and they slowly retreat into the mansion, one by one. When Chapter passes her, she stops him to give a consoling pat on the shoulder. For some reason this bothers me so much, I have to walk away.

The patio area outside the warehouse, I have been told, is off-limits for me. Nearby factory workers could spot me, tell their friends, and the whole circus of fans, paparazzi, and Famoux guards could follow in a matter of minutes. With Norax's speech, the danger has only increased. My only compromise to get some air is to linger in the doorway with my corduroy jacket collar popped up to hide the bottom half of my face. The view is nothing special—just a flat expanse of gray sky and barren land. There's a sign stuck in the middle of the dirt. A construction notice. Soon this view will be another factory, which somehow makes me sad.

"You should get back inside," my mother says from behind me.

"I am inside," I point out, a bit more sardonic than intended.

I can hear the smile in her tone. "You've always been more stubborn than I think. I never understood why you didn't stand up for yourself. With Westin."

"You told me thoughts had power," I say. "So, I thought about it."

"What are you thinking about now?"

The first Betnedoor sunrise I ever saw—on this day, a month ago. Everyone's eyes on me when I arrived at Bree Arch's memorial service. Chapter's arm extending out as he gave me a cup of coffee my first morning in the hideaway, then the look on his face after I plucked up the courage to kiss him. Foster drinking too much at the nightclub, and Gerald escorting him out. Kaytee smiling at me before she had any reason not to. I am thinking of everything and nothing. Nothing of importance to this moment, anyway. Nothing of the backstabbing, or the contract, or the looming glow of the Volx. Nothing of Norax. My memories of home had been a blue tint, but these memories of the Famoux are all a shade of gentle, rosy pink.

I can't let the other members stay in that mansion if they don't know everything I do. I can't let Norax feed them lies to share with their fans. I have more than just concern for Chapter; I have concern for all of them. I tell this to my mother, and she nods. "We're already planning an escape for the others too," she assures me.

Norax won't stand for that. She'll tell the world DEFED struck again, *that horrible group*. I picture her warning the world not to believe a word that comes out of our mouths. That we're being held hostage and forced to support the cause. No, we can't take them. It'll make things worse.

Any bravado from last night about me wanting to make her squirm is gone now. I'm the one squirming. Norax has created a scenario where she will always come out on top. But then I think of something that I'm sure she hasn't considered.

"I should go back," I say.

Marlon is near enough to catch this. "Are you kidding?"

I turn from the view outside. "You're going back to Betnedoor today, right?" I ask. "I need to come with you."

"That defeats the whole purpose of everything we've done!"

"I know you miss your friends, but this will not help our cause," my mother says. "The Leader will make you publicly go against us."

"They already are, with my silence," I point out. "The longer I'm gone, and everyone is searching, the crueler you become." The distressed faces of the Famoux come to mind. Norax putting her hand on Chapter's shoulder must've sent his fans over the edge. Anything that upsets him, they'll denounce. "We're already lucky she didn't make the others take turns at the mic telling their fans outright that our group is evil. But that will come next if I don't explain it to them."

Marlon offers that same concern I had earlier. "What are you going to do? Tell them we *didn't* kidnap you? She'll say you were brainwashed."

An idea unwinds out from the back of my head. Lennix's idea, weeks ago.

"Not if I claim DEFED didn't take me. Not if I come back with you."

"*What?*"

"We can say we ran away together," I say.

The red-carpet photos of us conversing earlier that night can look like we were planning our escape. Cartney's terseness when he approached will only play the feud up more. This kind of reveal will make me just like Kaytee, no doubt, but I've been following her path since the beginning, anyway. It could be fitting.

And I know Norax. Would she be able to resist the irony of it all? The attention that Cartney getting cheated on, *again*, would give us?

I outline those things, and Marlon is perplexed. "Oh, this is ridiculous," he says. "No one's going to believe it."

"They will. They already think I'm young and naive—running away with someone, changing my mind, and coming back . . . This is something I could do. And no one will think DEFED kidnapped me anymore."

"They'll still think we killed Bree!"

"I'm not sure they'll even remember those details," I say. "Not immediately. When they find out about *this*, it's going to be all they'll talk about for weeks."

This conversation has brought most of the others over toward the door. They're at a safe distance, offering no input except bewildered expressions.

"This is the best option," I state, louder so they know I'm talking to them too. "We have to make this story more twisted than it is, so everyone forgets the threat. At least for a while. It'll buy us time to figure out what happens next."

My mother bites her lip. She has a readable face like mine, so I know she agrees with me. She goes to say this, but she's cut off by Jenson, a few steps beyond her.

"You really are her niece, aren't you?"

A month under Norax's care, under my aunt's care, has rewired my brain. Or maybe it hasn't. Maybe I have always had the propensity to think this way—exploring every option, bending every meaning, twisting every narrative—and have never been given the chance to really do so until now.

That settles it. There's no need to pack my bags, and Marlon's flight will be leaving soon, so the good-byes begin the second I step fully back into the warehouse. Both Brandyce and Sloane hug me. Dalton, who still doesn't know who I am, but I'm sure will get the explanation soon, bids me good luck. Finley tells me to say hello to Scott for him. My father finally speaks directly to me for the first time since I've arrived, to say he loves me, and the guilt he wears on his face tells me why it took him so long to say anything. He knew what my mother had done for me from the beginning.

Outside the car door, my mother buttons up my corduroy jacket for me, and it all feels strange. Like I'm on my way to school again, where I'll duck through hallways and hope the Greyhounds won't find me. Except school is not a building at the edge of Clarus Creek anymore, and the hallways all have different-colored doors, and the Greyhounds searching through classrooms aren't sixteen like me.

This is a new world. My old one is over, diminished to ruins. A house I can visit in memories, but I can't live in. Not anymore.

The many names I've collected circle through my head again as Jenson drives us to Marlon's private jet. *The Daughter. The World's Girl. Sticks. Ray. Lumerpa. Emeray. Emilee.* It's like I am always being thrown into the Fissarex and coming out someone new. I imagine the names they'll call me next: Traitor? Liar?

This would be a very stupid thing to do if I was hoping to remain at the top of the Volx. Cartney and I had a good thing going. I could've lived comfortably for years. No sticks thrown my way. No stones thrown my way.

But if my old world has taught me anything, it is that I can endure insurmountable pain and keep living. I can be thrown headfirst into icy water, and I will surface. And this time around, I know I won't let myself be so easily pushed in.

No. This time I'm in charge. This time I'll take them all down with me.

# ACKNOWLEDGMENTS

Oh, wow. How do I begin? I feel like I'm at the Oscars and the theme music is playing already and I've forgotten every single person I've ever known. Okay, all right, let's think:

First off, I want to thank everyone who helped edit this story down from the actual quarter-of-a-million words it used to be. (Which often felt like chipping away at a massive slab of marble and thinking, *Oh, I am certainly not a sculptor!*) First, the wonderful Deanna McFadden, whose expertise, kindness, and patience, pass after pass, guided me through many months of work. I am so thankful for your very existence. Next, the incredible Jen Rees, who I cannot believe even looked at this book, thank you endlessly for helping me realize so much about my dystopian world. I can't thank Crissy Calhoun enough for going through the very first draft of this and helping me figure out what concepts and characters could be cut. Without you, this book would still be 800 pages! Thank you *immensely* to Jen Hale, the most magnificent copy editor there ever was, for finding all the little things

I missed. Thank you to the proofreaders and anyone who even vaguely glanced over this book. I appreciate it all so very much.

Thank you to I-Yana Tucker, an exquisite talent manager and even more exquisite human, as well as the whole team at Wattpad HQ. I feel so lucky to have stumbled upon this website when I was in high school, and I feel even luckier to have gotten to know all of you. Thank you especially to the wonderful team who designed this pink, purple, blue, neon cover that I'm so obsessed with, and to everyone involved in the marketing of this book. You're amazing.

I am so thankful for my entire family. It would take half a page to list out everyone, so I'll do my best to be concise here:

My mother, for finding all those dystopian books back in middle school that sparked this idea. I know this isn't the romance book you wanted, but I'll write that one next. Maybe.

My father, for reading the Little House books to Kalina and me growing up and making trips to the bookstore the most exciting thing in the world.

Kelsey, for making reading seem *so* cool when we were younger. I honestly think the main reason I wanted to write in the first place was so I could write a book that impressed you as much as *Ella Enchanted*. And also Maekel, of course, for being my brother.

Kaili, for talking through every idea with me, even the super ridiculous ones where every major character is killed off for no reason.

Kalina, for reading every iteration of this book and making it effortlessly better with your suggestions. Also, for telling me to post on Wattpad in the first place. And also for coming up with the name Emeray. And Kaytee. And Till . . .

Thank you to my friends who are writers, for always understanding. To my friends who aren't writers, for constantly astounding me with your talents. To all my professors and teachers who bettered my writing, especially Katy Beykirch, Hanina Osborn, and William Stanzel, from middle school, who believed thirteen-year-old me when I said I'd publish this one day. I promised to put your names in the acknowledgments, and it's surreal to fulfill that promise.

Finally, to my readers from Wattpad: I don't know where I'd be without you. You held me accountable to posting a new chapter every Friday (Famoux Friday!!) even when I had no idea where the story was going. Your support through commenting long paragraphs or funny jokes, making photo edits, writing fanfics, or even naming your *pets* after my characters have meant more to me than you know. Writing is often a solitary act, and my first draft process was anything but that, thanks to you. And so, as if we were ending a chapter, I'm going to leave you with these parting words: *Sticks and stones may break your bones, but haters make you Famoux.* Ahhhh!

# ABOUT THE AUTHOR

Kassandra Tate has been writing stories for as long as she can remember. Her work on Wattpad has accumulated over five million reads and a Watty Award for Science Fiction. She was featured in the anthology *Imagines: Celebrity Encounters Starring You* (Simon and Schuster), and worked alongside Lin-Manuel Miranda and Jonny Sun as curator for their *New York Times* best-selling novel *Gmorning, Gnight!* (Penguin Random House). She graduated from Chapman University in 2020 with a BFA in screenwriting and currently lives in Los Angeles with her sisters and—most importantly—her cats, Purrsephone and [Good] Will Hunting. *The Famoux* is her debut novel.

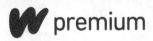